Broken Seals

NO SAFE PLACE

Broken Seals

NO SAFE PLACE

Larry Simmons
Former Commander of SEAL Team Five

Penmarin Books
Granite Bay, California

Editorial Offices:
Penmarin Books
2011 Ashridge Way
Granite Bay, CA 95746

Sales and Customer Service Offices:
Midpoint Trade Books
27 W. 20th Street, Suite 1102
New York, NY 10011
(212) 727-0190

Penmarin Books are available at special discounts for bulk purchases for premiums, sales promotions, or education. For details, contact the Publisher. On your letterhead, include information concerning the intended use of the books and how many you wish to purchase.

Visit our Website at **www.penmarin.com** for more information about this and other exciting titles.

Printed in Canada
1 2 3 4 5 6 7 8 9 10   05 04 03 02 01

Library of Congress Cataloging-in-Publication Data
Simmons, Larry (Larry W.)
 Broken seals : no safe place / Larry Simmons.
   p. cm.
 ISBN 1-883955-20-3
   1. United States. Navy. SEALS—Fiction. 2. Terrorism—
 Prevention—Fiction. 3. Retirees—Fiction.   I. Title.
 PS3619.156 B7 2001
 813'.6—dc21   2001036322

This book is a work of fiction. Neither the events nor the characters described in this book reflect any actual incidents or portray any real persons. The names of some public figures have been used in passing, but they are not characters in the story.

For all those injured in the line of duty.

About the Author

LARRY SIMMONS entered the naval service in 1966 and rose through the ranks of the U.S. Navy SEALs from seaman to commander. He retired as Commanding Officer, SEAL Team Five, after more than twenty-seven years in special operations. A graduate of Ohio State University, he has a master of science in operations research from the Naval Postgraduate School in Monterey, California, and a master of science in education from National University in San Diego. In 1998 he authored *Silent Option*. In addition to writing action adventure novels, he has also written several screenplays. Commander Simmons is still teaching men to move, shoot, and communicate and is employed as the manager of special warfare strategic operations and training in a Middle Eastern country.

The father has eaten sour grapes,
and the children's teeth are set on edge.
—Jeremiah 31: 29–30

Prologue

Cameroon, Africa
May 1995

DR. CALVIN POLAND brushed a hungry mosquito off his cheek and whispered to his guide, "Omgali, are you sure this is the right village? It's abandoned."

"I sure, Doctor, sir," insisted Omgali-Ninggali. "That Nguru's house," he said, pointing with a broad smile to one of the mud-and-grass huts on the far side of the compound.

Smoke was seeping through the roof, keeping the thatch dry and water-repellent. Inside the conical structure Poland saw the light of a fire flickering, warding off a swarm of bloodthirsty insects. The other huts were dark and lifeless. He glanced at Omgali. The whiteness of the black man's teeth was all he could see against the darkening jungle.

"Okay. Let's check it out. But this is the last one." Poland swung wildly at the cloud of mosquitoes that had gathered around his body and trudged along behind Omgali. The huts that surrounded them marked the outpost of civilization.

Poland's colleague, Dr. Nicholas Fawcett, was less confident of Omgali's navigation. He sat alone in the Land Rover, running his hands pensively through his gray-streaked black hair and watching the two dark figures moving about inside the abandoned compound. Exhausted from the search, his thoughts were jumbled and distressing. His assignment to Africa had delayed his plans to change the map of the world.

I have to get back to the CDC, he thought. *The future of my people depends on me. I've got to find a way to terminate this assignment without arousing suspicion.*

As Fawcett pondered his situation, Poland hiked toward the only hut in the compound with signs of life. He was looking for the powerful spiritual leader of the Bamileke, the only native likely to take them to the scene of the disaster they had been sent to investigate. They had visited several villages searching for the old witch doctor and had received conflicting directions in several dialects. Frustrated, Fawcett had given up hours ago. But not Poland. He kept insisting on searching one more village, and then another, and another, until Fawcett had refused to get out of the truck.

The scientists were searching for invisible killers, and their mission had taken them to the racial crossroads of Africa where more than one hundred ethnic groups competed for survival. Death was a way of life. In Cameroon, tribal conflict and disease had plagued humanity since the beginning of time, producing the ethnic diversity that guaranteed continued existence in spite of massacres and pandemics.

Twenty paces from the hut, Poland stepped on something that went squishy under his boot heel; the smell of rotten flesh assailed his nostrils.

"Oh, sweet Jesus," he gasped, straining his eyes to see.

Thinking he had stumbled onto a human corpse, he flipped on a small penlight and illuminated instead a pile of chicken remains decomposing in the tropical heat. Relieved, he swallowed hard and pressed on to where Omgali was standing. As he neared the entrance to the hut, his boot steps alerted a dog, which snarled and barked. Omgali shrieked something unintelligible and received a harsh reply from the man inside. The guide let loose with a barrage of friendly salutations until the man appeared in the doorway: an old man dressed in the finery of a witch doctor. The firelight dancing off his obsidian form gave him the appearance of a shimmering spirit. He eyed them suspiciously.

Omgali's tone of voice changed from solicitous to low and respectful.

Still eyeing the men warily, Nguru growled at his dog and reluctantly beckoned them closer with a feathered stick.

"Hey, Nick!" Poland shouted over his shoulder.

The sound of his voice spooked a coop of chickens that began squawking in the dark.

"Yeah, Cal?" Fawcett answered from the safety of the Land Rover.

"I think we've found him!"

"Great," Fawcett replied under his breath. "Just great."

He got out of the truck and walked toward the hut.

When Fawcett caught up with Poland and Omgali, they were seated around Nguru's fire. Dead chickens hung from the walls of the smoke-filled hut. Some, still dripping blood, were suspended from strings tied to the ceiling poles. The dog growled as Fawcett entered, causing him to flinch and step away. He bumped into a chicken carcass hanging from the ceiling, then stepped in a pool of congealed blood that had accumulated beneath another bird.

"Oooh, my God!" he groaned in a low voice. He looked at Poland with disgust written on his face.

Fawcett eased his way to where Poland was seated on a straw mat and sat down beside him Buddha-style. The witch doctor glared at him with coal-black eyes set in a countenance carved out of ebony.

"So this is Nguru?" Fawcett whispered, eyeing the old man like a museum piece.

"Yep," Poland replied.

It took several minutes for Omgali to explain to the old man that his white visitors had come to Bamileke territory to seek his help in investigating the death of Pygmies. The scientists were part of a program funded by the World Health Organization to identify and control contagious diseases before they reached epidemic stage. Recently, the Centers for Disease Control in Atlanta, Georgia, had received reports from Yaoundé, the capital of Cameroon, that an unknown disease had killed hundreds of Pygmies. In fear, many Bamileke had abandoned their villages that bordered the jungle where the Pygmies lived.

Nguru sat motionless as he listened to Omgali, unblinking, like an ancient statue. As the fire crackled and hissed, the guide rambled on. Finally, the old man nodded his head, grunted, spat out a few rapid-fire syllables, then resumed his stone face.

Smoke rising from the fire filled the hut, causing the doctors' eyes to water. From time to time an insect, overcome by the fumes, would drop down on them from the thickly thatched roof. They ignored the bugs and the dog, which snarled with each shift in body position, as Omgali continued his loquacious explanation. Fawcett was the first to run out of patience.

"Enough!" he interrupted. "Will he help us?"

With a blank face Omgali shook his head no.

"Does he know any Pygmies who have died from evil spirits?" asked Poland.

Omgali nodded. "He know. All in village die."

"What?" Poland croaked. "Has he seen dead people or just heard others talking about them?"

"He see. All die."

"Where? How far is this village?" asked Poland anxiously.

After several minutes of jabbering with the old man, Omgali pointed out the doorway. "He say village that way. Three hours' walk."

"Will he show us the way?" Fawcett asked.

"He say no. He say evil spirits live in jungle," answered Omgali.

Poland noted the fear in Omgali's eyes. "Ask him if he will take us near the village and point the way so we can find it."

After several more minutes of this give-and-take, which seemed to go on and on without pause, Omgali answered, "He say no."

Fawcett took a deep breath and coughed from the smoke. He pulled off his fanny pack and opened it slowly, showing Nguru the contents. Inside were the treasures of modern life. Nguru eyed a pocketknife, a razor, a compass, and other useful items. After five minutes of negotiation, the old man conceded. "He say he take you to jungle. But he not go to village. He say evil spirits there."

"What kind of evil spirits?" asked Poland.

Omgali asked a question and Nguru replied in Bamileke with what sounded like a series of barks or cracking concrete. The guide listened intently, then translated the medicine man's reply.

"He say bad wind."

"Like the wind that came from the volcanic lake?" asked Fawcett.

"He say no. No bad smell. Bad spirit."

"What does that mean?" Poland pressed.

"He say evil spirit in jungle. It kill peoples who sleep there," answered Omgali in a trembling voice. The scientists knew that to Nguru and Omgali evil spirits of all temperaments roamed the countryside, so Poland and Fawcett dropped their line of inquiry, satisfied that the old man would take them near enough to the village that they could find it themselves.

Nguru shook his feathered stick, signifying agreement with those conditions, and invited them to sleep in his hut until morning. Fawcett looked at the dripping chickens, then down at the blood on the dirt floor, and whispered to Poland, "Cal, I'm not sleeping in here. No way. I don't care if it's a hundred and twenty degrees in that truck; that's where I'm going."

"I hope you don't snore, Nick, 'cause I got dibs on the backseat."

As the two scientists crept through the darkness toward the Land Rover, they heard the medicine man chanting melodically in the strange language of the Bamileke. He was warding off the evil spirits that lurked in the rain forest of the Pygmies.

The next morning Omgali, looking refreshed from a good night's sleep in the old man's hut, woke the exhausted scientists with tea and bush bread. They got out of the truck and relieved themselves on the tires, grumbling about the insects.

"The national bird of Cameroon should be the mosquito," said Fawcett. He had a nasty bite on the back of his neck.

"Yeah. The proboscides on the suckers that attacked last night were so big they penetrated the roof of the Land Rover," said Poland. "If we'd bent them over with a hammer we could've turned the truck into a helicopter and flown back to Yaoundé."

Fawcett zipped up his pants and gave Poland a hard look. "Cal, when we get back to Johannesburg I'm putting in for an early transfer to Atlanta."

"But your tour is up in six months, Nick," said Poland, puzzled.

"Yes. I know. But I'm anxious to get back to more serious work." *Your heart would stop if you knew how serious,* Fawcett thought.

"You want serious, Nick? Something has scared the bejesus out of these people. We could be on the verge of discovering a new disease."

"Maybe. Or an old one. And perhaps they're just killing each other off again. I'm tired of chasing phantoms, Cal. I've wasted six months of my life here. I want to get back to serious research in a proper laboratory."

"I can identify with that." Poland studied Fawcett's face for a few seconds. "When we get back to base I'll give Reinhardt a call and ask him to expedite your replacement."

"And what if this does turn out to be an epidemic?" Fawcett shot back. "He'll want me to stay on for another six months, and then another, and another."

"Then I'll, uh, I'll have you assigned to take the samples back to the lab. Someone's got to brief Lubeck and Dorn."

"Thanks, Cal. I appreciate your understanding and support."

"Don't mention it."

After breakfast, Nguru gathered up two live chickens and trudged off into the rain forest with the three younger men in tow. Once in the jungle the air was cooler, but the old man's pace was relentless. He walked nonstop for three hours. Both Poland and Fawcett were dripping with sweat and about to drop from exhaustion when Nguru suddenly stopped in a small clearing. Noisy birds and frogs sang their jungle songs to the accompaniment of water dropping from the canopy as he drew a wide circle in the dirt. With one violent twist, he pulled the head off one of the chickens and showered the spraying blood along the line he had traced in the earth. Then he stuck his feathered stick in the ground and sat down inside the circle. From there, Omgali explained, Nguru would go no further. He told them the Pygmy village was up the trail, and with that he sat down inside the circle with the old man.

"Evil spirits there, bwana. I no go. I wait with Nguru," he insisted. His eyes darted around the jungle, searching for evil spirits.

"Very well, coward," Fawcett replied with a look of enmity. "We'll find it without your help."

"Yes, bwana. You find. You find."

Nguru offered the doctors his other chicken. They declined politely.

"Let's go," Fawcett muttered. "Let's get this over with."

As they hiked down the trail, he carped about their mission.

"You know, Cal, we're probably investigating a mass murder. For ten thousand years the Bamileke have been killing Pygmies for sport."

Deep jungle was the last refuge for the little people. They rarely came out to trade, and when they did, they were wary of ambush. In the constant bickering over land, women and resources, the little Pygmies always lost in physical confrontations.

"If this is a mass murder, why have the Bamileke abandoned their villages?" asked Poland.

"Superstition," opined Fawcett. "They're just two steps away from the Stone Age."

"Something spooked them. Old Nguru is warding off evil spirits with chicken blood."

"Proves my point," said Fawcett.

The two sweaty scientists hiked for ten minutes along the trail Nguru had set them on. They were about to give up when Poland got a whiff of the odor of death. He grabbed Fawcett by the arm and stopped in the middle of the trail.

"Nick. You smell that?"

"Yeah. Could be a dead elephant, or a hippo, but I'll give you two to one it's mutilated bodies."

"I'm not taking that bet."

"Why not?" challenged Fawcett.

"'Cause you're probably right."

They continued up the trail for fifty more yards. Then the jungle opened into a clearing large enough to contain about twenty huts constructed of tree branches and sticks. From the edge of the clearing they could see decomposing figures of human form inside.

"Cal? You notice something?" said Fawcett in a hushed voice.

"What?" Poland snapped, unnerved by the gruesome sight.

"No animals. No lizards. No frogs. No birds pecking at the bodies. Nothing."

"Oh, God," Poland groaned. "The smell is making me sick."

"Let's work a little closer to that corpse," said Fawcett, pointing with his walking stick to the entrance of the nearest hut.

"Okay."

Fawcett pulled a surgical mask and gloves from his pocket. He eyed them and looked at Poland with one raised eyebrow.

While taking out his own mask and gloves, Poland mumbled, "A body condom might be more appropriate."

They put on their protective gear and crept closer to the nearest corpse. When they were a few yards away, they saw that it was little more than a gelatinous mass in the general shape of a person. The body was so badly decomposed it was barely recognizable as human.

"Nick," Poland whispered, with icy fear in his voice, "the cellular structure has completely dissolved."

"Only the hair and bone are unaffected," Fawcett said loudly.

The sound of his voice spooked a rat. It scurried from the hut and ran between his feet.

"Aaaah!" he shrieked. "Rats scare the shit out of me!"

The sound of his voice caused a mob of rats to scamper about the village.

"Whatever caused this doesn't affect rats," Poland remarked.

"Cal, this is not normal decay," observed Fawcett as he stared at the rotting form. "What do you make of it?"

"I don't know. No flies." Poland gently poked the corpse with his walking stick. "No sign of maggots."

"No visible signs of attack on the village or trauma to the bod-ies," added Fawcett grimly. "They all seem to be curled up in fetal positions."

"As if they suffered from chest and abdominal pain," Poland postulated.

"Ebola?"

"No. A filavirus wouldn't account for the cellular disintegra-tion," Poland replied as if thinking out loud. "There's no evidence of scavenging."

"Perhaps the scavengers are smarter than we are. I suggest we return to base as soon as possible. We need a complete quarantine of this area," said Fawcett.

He tossed down his walking stick, pulled Poland by the arm, and briskly took to the trail.

"I concur," said Poland, following him into the jungle. "We'll need to capture some of those rats. They could be the reservoir," he said, half-jogging to keep up.

"Most likely. Or their parasites," Fawcett agreed, in full stride.

"We'd better contact Lubeck and Dorn and alert them . . . that we may have . . . a new biological monster on our hands," Poland panted. "Still want that transfer, Nick?"

"I most certainly do. The only way to study infectious disease is in a proper laboratory."

Chapter 1

"GOOD MORNING, GENTLEMEN. I'm Dr. Susan Dorn. I'll be your es-cort this morning."

The group of distinguished men standing in the lobby of Build-ing 15 turned to see an attractive woman dressed in a white lab coat. Her bright eyes hinted of Asia, but her accent was pure Southern molasses. Derek Evans studied her lovely face appreciatively as she spoke.

"Before we begin the tour of our Atlanta facility, I have a few administrative announcements to make." She glanced nervously at her clipboard. "First, here at the Centers for Disease Control, we take security matters very s-s-seriously," she stuttered. She took a deep breath and abandoned the clipboard on the reception counter. Here she was, a senior virologist, assigned the most unpopular duty that could possibly befall a scientist: tour guide for a group of fact-finding congressmen. She was worried about her lab experiments and uncomfortable with leading nosy politicians around the facility. The CDC staff had gotten wind of a budget cut, and she didn't want to hurt the facility's image with a faux pas.

"By nature, our work here in Atlanta is potentially very dangerous," she continued in a soft Southern voice as sweet as a Georgia peach. "Accordingly, we are required to follow military standards of security to maintain accreditation. If you would, please, verify your identity with Chief Johnson as you pick up your security badges. For your personal safety, I ask that you wear your badges at all times during the tour, and please, please, don't stray from the group. We are studying some very nasty diseases here at the CDC."

"Dr. Dorn, you know who we are, and you know why we're here. I don't see the need for an identity check," grumbled a weathered old senator.

His eyes focused menacingly on the uneasy scientist. But his attack backfired. She smiled for the first time, showing perfect teeth.

"Senator Rawlings, sir, our security personnel will instantly recognize you because of your long and distinguished career on Capitol Hill. However, others in your group are not so familiar."

Rawlings, somewhat mollified, nodded in agreement.

"We are simply following the security measures used at USAMRID," she continued, referring to the military's biological warfare facility outside Washington. "I believe it was your office, Senator, that insisted we follow military protocol." Her words had the effect of a boxer's jab on the senator. She gestured toward a portly man seated behind the security desk. "Chief Johnson's job depends upon thorough compliance."

The security chief raised one eyebrow in acknowledgment.

Rawlings shook his head disagreeably and reached for his wallet with a sour expression on his face.

Chief Johnson scrutinized each man as he double-checked photo against face and marked each name off his access list. He recognized several of the legislators from TV, but most of them were just faces to be compared to ID cards. He glanced at Derek Evans three times before checking him off the list. Evans was different. He wasn't a congressman or a staffer, and he looked too young to be retired, as his ID card indicated. Then Johnson noticed the body type. Fit, trim, athletic. He winked at the ex-SEAL commander as he handed him his ID card and a security badge.

Johnson also noted the annoyance on the face of the petulant old senator when he looked at his badge, clearly marked VISITOR ES-CORT REQUIRED. He decided it was imprudent to mention to the visitors that they were required by law to return their badges upon completion of the tour. When he was satisfied with the accounting, Johnson pushed a red button located behind the reception counter, and allowed the guests to enter Building 15.

Inside the thick concrete walls of the CDC, doctors like Susan Dorn studied the pathogens that threatened the existence of mankind. Unconsciously, Chief Johnson touched the handle of his .38-caliber wheel gun and reflected on his awesome responsibility: keeping quarantined an array of creatures he couldn't see, smell, taste, or feel—vanishingly small little monsters that killed simply to survive. He was understaffed and outgunned, and no matter how much he protested, they kept cutting his budget. He knew all too well that security at the CDC was only a facade.

As he followed her, Derek Evans couldn't help imagining the shapely curves under Susan Dorn's lab coat as she proceeded down a sterile hall, giving her carefully prepared briefing. Along the way, he studied the facility like a thief casing a bank. The building was antiseptic, like a hospital, but there were no patients. Surveillance cameras dotted the exterior of the building and the passageways as in a prison, but there were no inmates. Unlike the others in the group, Evans had done his homework. He understood the reason for such expensive equipment. He half-listened to Susan Dorn while simultaneously studying her considerable feminine assets.

"Gentlemen, there are four levels of protection here in Building 15," she said, stopping so they could peer through a window. "Our labs are rated by the level of danger they contain. This is Level One. The only personal protection required is good hygiene."

As she turned and led the group up a stairway, Evans noted the security camera outside the window. It commanded the atrium that separated the wings of the huge, multistory complex. From each corner, cameras fed additional images back to Chief Johnson's desk in the reception area.

"This is Level Two," Dorn announced, pausing in front of a set of double doors. "It is a minimum-security laboratory. Lab coats and gloves are all that are required in this environment."

Through the windows, Evans saw several scientists busy with microscopes and other scientific instruments. Secure inside the lab, they were unaware of the visitors in the hall outside. From the breezeway he noted the ease of access for an intruder entering the building through the atrium. He followed Dorn up to the next level, wondering if she was married to a man who dreamed in equations or of germs in a petri dish. When they reached the third-floor landing he forced his mind from her anatomy to the angle of the security camera. It was in a poor location, limiting its view.

"This is Level Three, gentlemen, our medium-security facility," she said, pointing to a set of stainless steel doors marked AUTHORIZED PERSONNEL ONLY. "Protective masks are required to work in this environment. In addition, the atmosphere is maintained at a negative pressure and is continuously filtered to ensure no infectious agent escapes the lab."

"Dr. Dorn? Derek Evans, Senator Carson's office. Is this where you study the AIDS virus?"

"Yes, Mr. Evans. We understand the epidemiology of HIV quite well. Level Three management is sufficient."

"I see," Evans replied.

"Well, I don't," blurted Senator Rawlings. "I thought AIDS was deadly."

"Senator, while it is true that HIV has a high mortality rate, we clearly understand its method of transmission. Level Three security is sufficient to protect the scientists who study this class of retrovirus," Dorn explained. "Our Level Four facility is reserved for pathogens whose epidemiology is unknown."

"Then what the hell are you people studying up there, the Andromeda Strain?" Rawlings demanded. The old man scowled as he asked the question.

"Senator Rawlings, Level Four is reserved for pathogens of unknown origin, uncertain means of transmission, and extremely high mortality rates."

Disappointment crossed her face. Dr. Susan Dorn had expected more from the nation's elected representatives, and it showed. She turned abruptly, marched up the stairs before the senator could press the issue, and led the group down the fourth-floor breezeway to a corridor secured by heavy stainless steel doors polished like mirrors. Using a key card she wore on a chain around her neck, she unlocked the entrance with a loud click.

Evans noted the sign: RESTRICTED AREA. AUTHORIZED PERSONNEL ONLY. He followed her closely down a long passageway to another set of security doors and watched out of the corner of his eye as she punched a code into the keypad, mentally noting the numerical sequence. As they entered the control room, he looked for a wedding ring. She wasn't wearing one, and there was no tan line on her finger.

The control room overlooked the laboratory through large viewing ports in the bulkheads, and it was separated from the lab by airlocks. Evans eased up next to the man seated at the control panel.

He's not armed, he thought, making another mental note.

The panel was filled with gauges and instruments monitoring the activity of the scientists inside the lab, but it didn't contain a screen for monitoring the passageway leading to the lab.

He can't see who's in the hall. The window is too small.

At a glance, Evans could tell that serious thought had been given to hermetically sealing the laboratory from the outside world. It had been designed to keep germs from escaping. Little if any thought had been given to the possibility of forced entry, however.

Chief Johnson's .38 and a few doors are the only things between this lab and the street, thought Evans. *Nothing in here is secure.*

Through the viewing ports, Evans observed two scientists dressed in blue space suits. Inside one plastic helmet, he could see the face of a middle-aged female as she shuffled across the lab to a freezer marked in large red letters BIOHAZARD LEVEL FOUR. She was breathing air supplied by a hose that slid across the floor behind her like a long pigtail. When she opened the freezer, a cloud of nitrogen gas spilled out, covering her boots in white smoke.

"Gentlemen, this is our Level Four laboratory," said Dorn. "Here, our Special Pathogens Branch studies contagious diseases of unknown classification. We maintain an epidemiologist, a toxicologist, a virologist, and a pathologist on call twenty-four hours a day as a task force to investigate contagious outbreaks anywhere in the world."

"Dr. Dorn, I understand the need to maintain a small staff of experts to investigate dangerous incidents such as domestic flare-ups of Legionnaires' disease, but we simply must rein in the cost of supporting this army of expensive scientists. Congress cannot go on payin' you people to run all over the world chasin' bugs. I, for one, intend to see that appropriate measures are enacted to prevent the frivolous use of . . ."

Screech! The intercom interrupted the senator. The squelch control was turned up too high.

"Extracting Ebola Zaire, sample one-five-nine," said the scientist inside the lab. The communication system distorted her voice. "Thomas, make that sample one-three-nine."

Her voice was accompanied by a metallic sound as she scraped the frost off a stainless steel bottle the size of a large thermos.

"Roger, Dr. Lubeck, I log, extracting Ebola Zaire sample one-three-niner," the technician replied while writing in a dog-eared logbook.

The sound of the woman's breathing was labored, like that of a diver working under pressure. She carefully cradled the frosted thermos and walked through the cloud of gas toward a lab bench. Dorn continued her briefing before Senator Rawlings could begin his tirade again.

"Our Level Four facility is a space capsule separated from the earth's atmosphere. The air inside the chamber is continuously filtered to destroy any biotic matter, and all materials that leave the facility are thoroughly decontaminated with disinfectant at 260 degrees Fahrenheit for twenty minutes. This is where we study the most dangerous diseases known to mankind."

"Why don't you destroy the damned things before they escape this confounded contraption?" asked the cantankerous old senator.

"Senator, we are locked in an evolutionary war with these pathogens," Dorn replied in a condescending tone. Surely you are aware of this."

"I don't know what you're talking about, Dr. Dorn," snapped Rawlings. "Please clarify your statement."

Susan Dorn chose her words carefully.

"Senator, living organisms are constantly undergoing genetic mutations, which can be either beneficial or harmful in dealing with the environment in which they live. Tuberculosis, for example, a deadly and widespread disease at the turn of the century, was almost eradicated after the advent of antibiotics. Today many strains of the bacteria have become drug resistant, and it is flourishing again. We are currently losing the battle against tuberculosis because the disease has evolved defenses against our arsenal of antibiotics."

"Bugs versus drugs? So as we develop chemical weapons to kill our pathogens, they develop chemical defense mechanisms to protect themselves?" Evans interjected. Evans was hoping to parry some of the vitriol that Rawlings was directing toward Dorn.

"Precisely, Mr. Evans," said Dorn. "Our pathogens mutate and adapt. To protect ourselves, we must understand how they replicate, how they mutate, how they are transmitted from person to person, and from animal to person, and how we can defeat them."

"Are all of the viruses in this lab a mystery to science?" asked Evans.

"Yes, Mr. Evans. In one aspect or another."

"So we don't know where these things come from, how they infect people, or how to get rid of them?" the senator pressed.

"That is correct, Senator. That's why we are studying them. We are locked in an escalating evolutionary contest with our pathogens, with natural selection playing the role of umpire. The price of defeat is death."

"Dr. Dorn, I resent hyperbole in any form," Rawlings barked. "I just want the facts. Do I make myself clear?"

"Yes, Senator, you do. Marburg, Lassa, dengue, Hanta, and Ebola viruses are not fantasy. They are facts," she stated, with a degree of annoyance. "The Ebola-Zaire virus Dr. Lubeck is studying is named after three epidemics of hemorrhagic fever in the Ebola River valley in the 1970s. Eighty-eight percent of those infected died—quickly, horribly. Before the victims died, blood oozed from every orifice in their bodies, and the blood that didn't exsanguinate clotted like cottage cheese."

"Could such a virus be deliberately spread?" Evans asked. He was thinking of terrorists, criminals, fanatics, and how easy it would be to raid the lab.

"Yes, given the knowledge required to culture and dispense the agent," replied Dorn.

"Then what you fear the most is a killer virus with delayed symptoms, one that spreads like the flu before people realize they are sick?" It was more of a statement than a question.

"Absolutely, Mr. Evans. Precisely our greatest fear. Are you in the medical field?"

"No. Far from it." He smiled. Then his facial expression turned serious. "Do you have such a virus in your lab, Dr. Dorn?"

The question disturbed her, and her face showed it. She paused several heartbeats before answering the question.

"Possibly, Mr. Evans."

"With modern air travel, a person could leave Africa, where people are dying in droves, and twenty-four hours later be in central Atlanta, just coming down with symptoms. That's a frightening thought," suggested a staffer.

"Yes, it is," Dorn replied. "No one can be certain whether Hanta, Ebola, or some new emerging virus will become the next global scourge. Explosive outbreaks of infectious diseases have occurred regularly since antiquity. There is no reason to believe the future won't look like the past. That's why it is so imperative that we study such diseases."

"Doctor, how easy is it to develop vaccines against killer viruses?" asked Evans.

The loudspeaker interrupted the conversation.

"Thomas, I'm through for the day. Preparing to store Ebola sample one-three-nine."

"Roger, Dr. Lubeck. I log storing Ebola-Zaire sample one-three-niner," replied the technician, making an entry in his log-book.

The group watched as Lubeck shuffled across the room toward the nitrogen freezer. To their horror, she tripped on her air supply hose and disappeared, face first, into the nitrogen fog.

"Are you okay, Dr. Lubeck?" Thomas shrieked. "Dr. Lubeck? Dr. Lubeck?" he pleaded.

There was no response. Inside the lab, Lubeck's assistant rushed to her aid.

"Thomas, code red!" he bellowed. "We have a spill!"

Thomas pushed a button on his console and the room erupted with a noise that sounded like a submarine preparing to dive.

"Redline! Redline! ERT to Level Four! ERT to Level Four!" he shouted on the public address system. Noise and motion filled the control room as Lubeck's assistant pulled her across the floor and into the decontamination lock. As soon as they were both inside, he started the disinfectant shower.

The visitors stood aghast, staring through the portholes as emergency technicians rushed into the control room and hurriedly suited up. The first two men entered through an airlock and began cleaning up the spill. Two other men entered the decontamination shower and began scrubbing Lubeck's and her assistant's protective plastic suits. Several minutes passed in a cloud of steam and disinfectant spray. No one spoke over the deafening sound of the alarm. When the emergency response team emerged from the disinfectant spray, they loaded a naked Dr. Lubeck into a special airlock designed to contain and treat an infected person.

The congressmen looked on with concern as an elderly man with wispy silver hair and a white beard appeared from behind a throng of technicians. He looked through the porthole at the stricken scientist and then at Thomas at the control panel. Pointing to the alarm light, he shaped his hands into a T, like a coach calling time out. The technician immediately turned off the alarm and the room went dead silent, with the exception of a voice coming from inside the chamber. To Evans's amazement, Dr. Lubeck was singing "Amazing Grace." The silver-haired man peered inside the laboratory, and the ERT personnel gave him a thumbs-up.

"That will be sufficient, Thomas. That was an excellent drill. Excellent. Get Dr. Lubeck out of the isolation chamber. Everyone meet in the conference room at thirteen hundred for a debriefing," he ordered as he turned to leave.

"That was a goddamn drill?" Rawlings yelled.

"Yes, Senator, we . . ."

"Your theatrics, Dr. Reinhardt, I assure you, have not won any points on the Hill!" he shouted. "Escort me out of here. Immediately!" he growled at Dorn. Rawlings stormed out of the control room and walked briskly down the hall.

As they walked back toward the lobby, Evans fell in step beside Susan Dorn.

"Very impressive facility, Dr. Dorn."

"Thank you, Mr. Evans," she replied, "but I wonder how long it will remain so?"

"I wouldn't worry too much about Senator Rawlings, Doctor. He's only one vote, and he doesn't control Capitol Hill."

"Oh," she said, slowing her pace at the lobby.

Rawlings stormed out of the building, still wearing his security badge.

"Yes. I believe the others got the message. I work for Senator Carson. How can he help you?"

"Two things, Mr. Evans. Protect our budget, at least at the current level. We need adequate funding to continue the fight against these deadly microorganisms," she pleaded.

"I understand. You said two things?"

"Yes. We need to improve the physical security of this facility."

Evans had just seen for himself some very serious security breaches. What surprised him was to hear a scientist voicing such concerns. He focused his eyes on her pupils like laser beams.

"Why?" he asked. "From what I've seen, you could quarantine and study the Andromeda Strain."

"That's not what I mean, Mr. Evans. I mean a threat from outside," she said.

"Have you said anything to the local authorities?" Evans asked.

An FBI agent had recently alerted Senator Carson to some incidents Susan Dorn had reported. As the head of the subcommittee on international terrorism, the senator was often briefed on potential domestic problems. The report had struck a nerve with Carson, so he had asked Evans to investigate the CDC as well as several other facilities in the state of Georgia.

"Yes, I have, Mr. Evans. I'm afraid they think I'm an alarmist."

She looked at Evans, searching his eyes for clues to his thoughts.

"Well, I don't," he said, holding out his hand. "Derek," he said as they shook.

"Susan," she replied.

"Susan it is."

Evans smiled, not wanting to release his grip. Her touch communicated as much as her eyes. There was fear and unease in her soul. Evans sensed it. He stared at her, wondering what or who was upsetting her.

In preparation for the mission, Evans had read all of her published work. He had expected to meet an unattractive prude. She acted proper and stiff, hiding her beauty by apparel and mannerism, but behind the facade was real beauty. Dressed in a white lab coat with her hair tied up in a bun, she looked like the quintessential scientist. Yet as he stared deep into her green eyes, he saw the woman within. Beautiful, frightened, alone and very vulnerable.

I wonder if she'll level with me, he thought.

"Senator Carson chairs the subcommittee on international terrorism," he said, holding his gaze until she grew uncomfortable.

It was a habit he found hard to break. The eyes revealed so much. He was trying to read her reaction to the word *terrorism*. He quickly glanced at the security desk and then back at her before continuing.

"He asked me to evaluate the security of the CDC and assess its vulnerability to terrorist attack."

Susan's pupils constricted as she focused in on him like radar.

"He understands how easily a small group of fanatics could do great harm to our nation," Evans continued.

"In this case, Mr. Evans, to the world," she corrected.

"Yes. I can see that."

Evans studied her face for a few seconds. Her Asian ancestry had long since been dominated by Caucasian genes, but just enough of the Far East expressed itself in her face to fascinate him. He had spent many years in Southeast Asia while on active duty with the Navy SEALs. With her delicate features and hypnotic eyes, Susan Dorn was an irresistible Americanized version of the Oriental goddess Evans had fallen in love with at age twenty-four.

"The senator often uses my consulting firm to evaluate special situations. Here," he said, handing her his business card. "Feel free to call me, any time, day or night."

"Then you're not part of Senator Carson's staff?" she asked, puzzled.

"Oh, no. I'm with a private concern. Special Operations Consultants, Incorporated. It's an organization of retired military and law enforcement professionals. I don't mean to be forward, but are you free for dinner? I'd like to discuss your feelings and observations in greater detail."

She examined him like a patient, carefully studying his face, his square jaw. Evans was brutally handsome and athletically built. Slight scars here and there about his eyes hinted of a violent past, but his touch was comforting, and his deep voice was sincere. Something about the man told her she could trust him, at least in a business sense. A failed marriage had taught her to be wary of men in the other sense.

"Ahhhh, Mr. Evans. I don't think so. It might be better if you made an appointment to visit me in my office."

"No, it wouldn't be better, Dr. Dorn. I would like to discuss a range of subjects, uninterrupted by daily business."

"Such as?" she shot back.

"Such as the possibility of creating a biological weapon of terror using one of the monsters you have in your lab."

"Huh," she gushed, then she looked at him and said, "That, Mr. Evans, is a nightmare beyond Stephen King's twisted mind." She took a deep breath and exhaled. "Okay. If you think it will help your analysis, I'll meet you on neutral ground."

"Great. Where shall I pick you up?"

"Here in the lobby. Eight o'clock," she answered curtly.

"Eight it is, then," Evans said with a pleasant smile.

She pretended to be busy at the reception counter so she could watch Evans out of the corner of her eye. From a distance, he looked like a tall version of Robert Conrad. Though dressed in a suit, he moved like a cat, with careful steps, seemingly aware of everything around him. At the lobby exit he instinctively scanned the street in all directions before heading up the sidewalk toward the parking lot. She was intrigued, fascinated, attracted. Then she thought of her ex-husband. It had been more than a year since her divorce, and in that time she had scarcely glanced at a man with interest.

Don't even think about it, Susan, she told herself. *They're all the same.*

Chapter 2

AMAN ABRUZZI AYYAD lit a cigarette and inhaled deeply. The pungent smoke of hashish and black tobacco filled his nostrils and enveloped his brain like a dense fog.

Allah chose me, he thought. He coughed, expelling a lungful of narcotic fumes. *He commanded me to let loose the plague.*

"O Lord! I will do as you command," he mumbled.

They are just infidels, he silently cursed, and he envisioned all the nonbelievers of the world dying like insects. Such thoughts gave him comfort.

As he stared out over war-ravaged Beirut, a smoky bus down in the city momentarily seized his attention. Visions of his recent mission inside Israel detonated inside his skull in an explosion of light and sound. The evil of terrorism came to him in a kaleidoscope of raw images. In his mind's eye, he saw an Israeli bus begin a slow climb up a twisting mountain road that led to the Sea of Galilee. Birds chirped in the crisp air of first light, welcoming a new day to the Promised Land. Inside his head he could hear the laughter of children—Jewish children. From his ambush site high up on the mountainside he could see his ancestral village. He could see his family home, now reduced to a pile of stones. It had been the house of his father and his father's father and for generations back in time. The ghosts of his ancestors roamed the valley. They were all there. They spoke to him in his dreams and gave approval to his mission. Hate exuded from his pores as he envisioned the Jews bulldozing their family home.

"Remember Deir Yassin," he mumbled.

The sound of schoolchildren singing echoed off the wadi walls as the bus approached the kill zone. The song drifted in and out of his mind, at times drowned out by the rumbling of a diesel engine. Reliving the adrenaline rush of the moment, he visually checked the position of his men with a sharp, hawklike glance, giving each machine-gunner a signal with a nod of his head and a quiver of his chiseled cheek.

Ayyad took a deep drag on his cigarette and held his breath as long as he could, but still the bus rumbled on inside his head.

As it rounded the curve he screamed, "*Allah akbar!*" and opened fire. Four AK assault rifles cut loose simultaneously, spraying the front of the bus with a lethal fusillade of hot lead. The driver swerved to avoid the bullets, but it was too late. He was dead before the vehicle crashed into the guard rail. The deep-throated chugging of machine guns drowned out the children's screams. But Ayyad heard them and it pleased him. He heard them as the bus careened over the cliff. Like a CD skipping track and repeating over and over again, he watched the vehicle bounce off the sheer stone wall of the wadi and break into pieces like an egg, scattering its cargo on the rocks five hundred feet below. Thoughts of shattered and bleeding Jewish bodies smashed on the rocks of the Promised Land energized him. Thirty Jews had died. The fact that they were children had no impact on him.

And He will spare his chosen people. My people! He will spare the Palestinian people. This I believe.

For ten days after the attack, he and his band of terrorists had hidden in a cave in the mountains near Har Meron. There they had fasted and prayed until it was safe to make their way down to the Mediterranean in the back of a produce truck. They slept in the bilge of a fishing boat for two days before slipping out of Israel. In Lebanon they had returned to a hero's welcome in the Shatila refugee camp. But his strike against the Jews had angered his powerful leader, Ibrahim Nasrallah, because it had not been planned and coordinated by the Palestinian Freedom Council. Two weeks after Har Meron, Aman Abruzzi Ayyad found himself back in Beirut, staring out over the sea in a drug-induced trance like the one in which he had first conceived the mission. As he waited for his reprimand, he fortified his nerves with hashish.

The safehouse belonged to Nasrallah, a wealthy Lebanese merchant of Palestinian extraction. It was a luxurious villa with a commanding view of the bay from the foothills above the bombed-out city. Built on several levels, it was a remnant of the days when Lebanon was the playground of the Middle East, before warring factions shelled and mortared the city to ruins. The villa had escaped damage, and it was a secure location to plan terrorist missions. It even had a swimming pool, with a terrace above.

Ayyad studied the sea and the city as he waited for his meeting with Nasrallah. He finished his smoke and swallowed the butt just as his superior arrived.

"*As-salam alaykum*—Peace be upon you," said Nasrallah as he walked out on the terrace to greet the young fanatic.

Ayyad replied with a traditional greeting. "*Alaykum as-salam*— And upon you peace. Ibrahim, my uncle, what news is there from Prokaryotes?" he asked, taking the initiative.

The heavy-set, middle-aged man eyed him. He saw the hashish haze and sniffed the air. "He is concerned that someone may be watching the merchandise," Nasrallah replied.

"Someone *is* watching the merchandise, Uncle. Me," Ayyad smiled.

"What?" The big man's eyes grew fierce.

"A figure of speech, Uncle," said Ayyad cautiously, with a wave of his hand. "The babbling of an anxious warrior."

Ayyad did indeed have men watching the Centers for Disease Control in Atlanta and the U.S. Naval Base at Kings Bay, Georgia, but he wasn't about to inform Nasrallah of the unauthorized surveillance. He was in enough trouble because of Har Meron.

Nasrallah nodded. "Prokaryotes wants to delay Desert Decree."

"No, Uncle. No!" Ayyad pleaded. "Our people are starving like dogs in the refugee camps. Jews stomp on their hands in Palestine. The Kuwaitis beat them. The Saudis spit on them. The Egyptians piss on their graves. For fifty years there has been sand in the eyes of Allah. He has lost sight of us because we have not had the courage to strike boldly, without mercy. We must act, Uncle. We cannot wait. I beg you. I have seen this place with my own eyes. Compared to the submarine, the CDC mission is a job for women," Ayyad argued.

"Aman, nothing is ever as easy as it looks," Nasrallah scolded. "Weapons, communications equipment, vehicles, safehouses. All of these things must be arranged."

"I can buy everything we need from greedy Jewish merchants right there in Atlanta," argued Ayyad.

Nasrallah frowned. "Aman, listen to me. We do not want American agents snooping into our affairs. Thus we must bring everything together at the very last moment. To avoid exposure, we will import the weapons and the communications equipment."

"Uncle, I can buy weapons in Chicago or New York and bypass Al Fucra if you are worried," Ayyad said, referring to the radical Black Muslim sect that had communal farms widely scattered about the United States which were perfect for staging terrorist operations. "Weapons are everywhere in the United States, Uncle," he continued. "Even schoolchildren have them." He bowed deferentially to the older man.

"I know this," Nasrallah growled, annoyed by Ayyad's naiveté. "Listen to me!" he bellowed. "Operation Desert Decree will change the course of history. The council will not revise the plan without good reason. We will carefully consider Prokaryotes' request, and yours. I will personally make your objections known. In the meantime, you must not let impetuosity get you killed. No more raids into Israel. We cannot afford to lose you to a Jewish bullet dipped in the fat of a swine."

"As you wish, Uncle."

Nasrallah shook his finger in Ayyad's face. "I will say this to you only once. Operation Desert Decree is too important for camel jockey tricks. No rogue operations! In the past I have allowed your unsanctioned missions because they have been good for morale. But if you stray from the war plan by one centimeter, I will have you replaced. Understand?"

Ayyad stared at Nasrallah, then quickly looked down at the ground. He could be replaced. His second-in-command, Omar Azed, was a competent and dedicated leader who had proven himself in numerous battles. Azed was already assigned the most difficult mission in Operation Desert Decree: the seizure of an American nuclear submarine.

"There is another matter we must discuss, Aman. Prokaryotes is a man of science. He abhors violence. He is not a warrior like you or

Omar." Nasrallah stared deep into Ayyad's eyes. "He asked me to lodge a formal request on his behalf to stop all acts of violence against those not directly involved in the conflict."

Fire flamed in Ayyad's eyes. "Americans," he growled. "He's spent too many years living as an American, listening to Jewish propaganda. He does not know that the ground he stands on is not a real place. For Palestinians, reality ceased to exist in 1948." Ayyad pointed down the coast. "Reality lies to the south, beyond those hazy mountains, where Jews live real lives on our land. We are just ghosts, living ghost lives, denied the right to return to our tombs. Uncle, we do not need Prokaryotes to conduct this mission. I can do it," bragged Ayyad, high on hashish.

"Yes, we do!" Nasrallah boomed. "Now you are talking like a damned camel keeper. We cannot afford to lose you on some minor operation, and we cannot afford to lose Prokaryotes. He is the only man we have who knows how to construct a biological weapon and how to make the vaccine we need to protect our people."

"Allah will protect our people, Uncle."

Nasrallah's eyes narrowed. "You are talking like a keeper of camels again. Don't you understand? Aman, only Prokaryotes knows how to turn germs into a weapon to use against our enemies. You must protect him at all costs. If necessary, with your life."

"*Tayyib*—Fine! *Al-hamdu li-llah*—Praise be to God! The few must be sacrificed for the many," Ayyad intoned, agreeing to sacrifice himself. His thoughts were filled with lovely golden-haired houris. They had fat breasts and bellies and large buttocks.

"Prokaryotes is a child of Deir Yassin, a genius, and a true patriot. It is your duty to see him through this mission," Nasrallah preached. "And you. You are the last of the venerable family of Ayyad. There will be no martyrdom except in the cause of Operation Desert Decree. Is that clear?"

"Yes. As you wish, Uncle," replied Ayyad subserviently.

Nasrallah studied the younger man's face. "One more thing. Listen to me carefully," he said, shaking his finger. "Prokaryotes is concerned about communications, particularly telephone communications. We will no longer use the telephone for coordination."

"Why?"

"He believes the Americans are listening in on all calls."

"That is impossible. There are too many," Ayyad insisted, but with a look of concern written on his face. While conducting unauthorized surveillance operations on the CDC and Kings Bay, he had made numerous telephone calls to coordinate his agents' activities.

"If Prokaryotes says it is so," Nasrallah snapped, "it is so. The Great Satan has computers that select and translate conversations from words they are programmed to listen for."

Nasrallah's lecture was completely over Ayyad's head. Nasrallah had contacts all over the world. With his business as a cover, he moved in circles beyond the reach of Aman Ayyad. The younger man, raised in a filthy refugee camp, could not conceive of a machine listening to a telephone conversation. Lost in a hashish haze, he tuned out the older man.

"Uncle, if it pleases you, I will not use the telephone."

"It would please me greatly if you would follow my orders in exact detail. No telephone calls and no unencrypted correspondence. I will arrange for the necessary equipment to be available when you need it. Use the relationship we have with Al Fucra and buy nothing in the United States! Concentrate on training your men and on arranging for their infiltration. I will see that the equipment is delivered to you when you need it."

"Very well, Uncle." Ayyad stared at the sea, his mind on the other side of the world, where he was committing a brutal act of retribution for the injustice he had endured as a child.

Ibrahim Nasrallah wasn't his blood uncle. The title was used as a term of endearment for his rich and powerful superior. Aman Abruzzi Ayyad was alone in the world. He had grown up in a refugee camp in southern Lebanon, the seventh child of Aman bin Abruzzi Al-Ayyad. There he had helped his mother bury his father and then his four older brothers, who had all martyred themselves in the *jihad,* the holy war against the Jews. He suffered with her as she threw dirt on the graves, not really understanding the nature of the conflict. He survived the rocket attack that killed her and his two sisters and, alone, threw dirt on their graves. Six months after his mother's death he entered Israel through Jordan to stay with a distant relative. There, in Samaria, at the age of thirteen, he experienced the defining moment of his young life. He personally encountered the demon that haunted the Promised Land. It found him alone, and it consumed his soul.

On a dusty back street in the Promised Land, a group of Israeli soldiers called him over for an identity check. They had been watching the village for weeks and had recorded him telling stories of life in the refugee camps of Lebanon and Jordan, stories he had embellished with the lively imagination of youth. The Jews used such recordings to divide and conquer the Palestinian population by turning Arab against Arab. Under interrogation, and using just the right words, the occupying authority could convince a man that a brother, an uncle, a father, or a cousin had turned informant.

When the soldiers called him over, Ayyad was petrified with fear. He was mature for thirteen, but the sight of so much blood and brutality had scarred him. All his life he had heard stories of Jewish monsters torturing Arab children to death in Deir Yassin. The look in the eyes of the Israeli soldiers froze him with fear.

"Arabi Kalb!" a young soldier bellowed.

Ayyad stopped, paralyzed with fear, not knowing whether to run or comply.

"Arab dog!" he commanded. "Come here!"

When Ayyad failed to jump at his command, all the soldiers began screaming, which frightened him even more.

"Come here, you filthy little Arab shit, or I'll beat your fucking brains out!" screamed one of the soldiers at the top of his lungs.

Although Ayyad was too afraid to move, his paralysis was interpreted as resistance. Shouting with anger, the soldiers surrounded him. One of them knocked him to the ground with a rifle butt to the back of the head. Before Ayyad regained his senses, another planted a jackboot on his neck and held him down with such force that grains of sand and little stones were pressed into the flesh of his cheek.

One of the soldiers grabbed his wrists and trussed him up like a convict. Blindfolded, with his hands bound behind his back, he was led away to a dark, dirty prison cell. The smell of piss and shit overwhelmed his senses. Ayyad had heard of such places. Terror gripped his whole body when the blindfold was removed. The bare light bulb hanging from the ceiling illuminated the filth left from the torture of scores of human beings. With eyes wide with fear and knees trembling, he stared at the filthy floor, avoiding eye contact with the soldiers who now controlled his life.

"You little bastard, we know you threw rocks at us yesterday," roared a huge man dressed in olive-drab fatigues.

He grabbed Ayyad by his face and with one huge paw squeezed the jawbone until he cried out in pain. The man's hot breath was fetid, and the look in his eye was pure hatred.

"You will tell me what I want to know, boy," he growled like a madman. "When I return, you will tell me everything."

But when the interrogator returned, Ayyad didn't talk. For days they worked on him. They spat on him, threw insects on him, dripped water down his nose, and interrupted his sleep—anything to break him psychologically—all the while demanding information about the men he had told his cousins he had met in the refugee camps. They took turns beating him, one always playing up to him in a friendly sort of way, pretending to stop the other from killing him. To Ayyad's amazement, they recounted conversations that he had had with his adoptive family verbatim. Eventually, they convinced him his cousins were informers for the state.

Unable to get any useful information from him, mainly because he didn't have any, one soldier accidentally beat him unconscious. Thinking they had killed him, they hid the incident from their superiors and hauled the body into the Negev Desert. Under cover of darkness they hastily buried the evidence in a shallow grave. But Ayyad wasn't dead. When he regained consciousness he was underground, buried under two feet of dry desert sand. Like a zombie, he clawed his way to the surface and thanked Allah for his rebirth. There in the desert he committed his life to the struggle against the Jews. The soldiers thought they had killed him, and they were correct in a sense. They had killed the most important part: his humanity. Aman Abruzzi Ayyad had arisen from the desert sands of the Promised Land as an animal. His first act of vengeance was to kill his cousins. He burned them alive in their beds.

Alone, he fed on the militant Islam of the refugee camps. When a man has lost his parents, his house, his land, his freedom, his dignity, and his sense of humanity, he has nothing else to lose. Hate was the demon that roamed the Promised Land, and it stripped human beings of their humanity. Brutality, oppression, and injustice twisted developing minds, creating explosive rage, the kind of rage that knows no limit, that knows no bounds. That rage consumed Aman Ayyad. He had no way of knowing that the soldier who had beaten him to near death had lost his family to an Arab car bomb. It wouldn't have mattered. It was an eye-for-an-eye, a tooth-for-a-tooth world, a brutal world where violence begat violence, and hate begat hate. Ayyad was locked in an ever-escalating battle, one that had gone on for seven thousand years. Hate ran so deep in the Middle East. It overflowed the Promised Land.

Ayyad turned and looked Nasrallah directly in the eye. "All will be as you wish, Uncle. We will destroy the infidels."

With his right hand, he made the traditional gesture, touching his forehead, his lips, and finally his heart.

"Inshallah—God willing," replied Nasrallah. "Next week we will talk more about Operation Desert Decree. Until then, I have a small job for you. Here," he said, handing Ayyad a fistful of money and a slip of paper with a name written on it.

Ayyad read the name out loud. "Kamal Samir?"

"While you were away, a serious intelligence leak came to my attention. Fawaz and Hamid have been following this man. Go to Old Town and deal with the problem. Be creative. Make an example of Samir so this doesn't happen again. Then you and your men can take a break." He smiled. "Go to Bikfaya. Show them a good time. *Ma 'as-salama*—Good-bye."

"*Ma 'as-salama*," replied Ayyad.

Nasrallah wheeled and returned to the main house. Ayyad waited until he entered the building before lighting another cigarette. The pungent scent of hashish filled his nostrils and soothed his emotions. He breathed the harsh smoke deep into his lungs, and soon visions of beautiful golden-haired houris filled his mind and the sound of a kanoon and drums beat inside his head. Belly dancers whirled about, trailing diaphanous silken scarves.

Camel keeper? he thought. *Me? A camel keeper? In the name of the Prophet, all the infidels will die. Allah has chosen me to unleash His vengeance. This I will do. It is Allah's will. But don't worry, Uncle. His chosen people will survive. The Palestinian people will survive the plague. Inshallah.*

Chapter 3

As DEREK EVANS walked down the darkening streets of Atlanta on his way back to the CDC, he questioned whether his senses were playing tricks on him. He was seeing Arabs all over the place. Intelligence reports indicated that a radical Middle Eastern terrorist group was planning to strike somewhere in the state. Prime targets included military bases that stored nuclear and chemical weapons and the petrochemical and nuclear power plants that dotted the rolling red clay hills. Even the CDC, with its nasty residents of the Level Four lab, was a potential target. Because it was the top microbiology facility in the world, training more than eleven thousand health workers a year, students came from all over the planet. As he walked by a group of graduate students, some of Middle Eastern heritage, he eyed them carefully, looking for faces he had memorized during the day. Seeing none, he pressed on down the sidewalk toward Building 15.

I'm seeing a terrorist on every street corner, he thought. *Nonsense. They're only students.* Then he thought, *What a great cover.*

Several times earlier that day, he'd had cause to wonder whether someone might be following him. Senator Carson had secretly hired SOC Inc., and he was using personal funds to pay the bills, a fact that told Evans something of enormous consequence was at stake. On two occasions he noticed dark, swarthy individuals sauntering along the sidewalk behind him. But each time they had passed him by without a glance when he stopped to peer into store windows, using them like mirrors to watch his back. And each time he reminded himself that his presence would mean nothing to any terrorists who might also be in town. He wasn't a target, not even a potential target.

Evans arrived at Building 15 promptly and took a seat in the lobby. While he waited for Susan Dorn, he made use of the time by studying the building's access control system. From behind a newspaper he watched people come and go, sometimes in large numbers. The single guard on duty was often overwhelmed. The man simply didn't have time to carefully check ID cards if he was to watch the bank of closed-circuit TV monitors and answer the telephones as well. People frequently held up their ID cards from a distance. When busy with a visitor or on the phone, the guard would push the red button on his desk that unlocked the steel doors and waved them through without a check. Sometimes individuals leaving work would hold the door open for those coming on duty.

Spotting a doctor of Middle Eastern descent, Evans surreptitiously watched from behind his newspaper. By dress and manner, the man was CDC staff. He walked directly to the security doors and waited for them to open from inside.

Huh, thought Evans, as he watched the guard who was busy at the desk. *He never saw the guy.*

Evans's thoughts drifted back to Senator Carson's briefing and the FBI file he had read in the senator's office. It contained an incident report signed by Dr. Susan Dorn in which she stated that she thought a young Arab male was stalking her.

Maybe she has a secret admirer. She is a gorgeous woman. Perhaps one of the students has taken a shine to her and is just looking for an opportunity to make her acquaintance on a personal level. But then, terrorists generally surveil their targets for months before striking. The question is, why would a tango be watching her? And why the CDC?

He knew the answer to the latter question. The nasty bugs on the fourth floor. In his mind's eye he hypothesized ways of using the biological monsters in Dorn's lab. Each scenario devolved to the same limitation: a vaccine. Terrorists would need a vaccine to save their own people from a man-made plague. The thought occurred to him that a fanatical group might be planning to hit the Level Four lab and kidnap Susan Dorn. Once in possession of the germ and a capable scientist, they could create a vaccine as well as a biological weapon.

One thing is for sure, he reflected, watching the security guard wave a dozen people by without an ID check. *This place is a revolving door. He hasn't looked at the monitors for at least ten minutes.*

Evans, as a retired Navy SEAL, saw the world through a commando's eyes. Years of training had honed his mind and his reflexes to razor sharpness. He was a martial artist, an excellent parachutist, a superb diver, and an outstanding marksman. Moreover, as a master of assault operations, he was an expert at penetrating the most sensitive government facilities ever constructed—strategic U.S. and Soviet military installations. Upon leaving the service, he had turned his talents to the inverse of assault operations, reasoning that if he could get around the security of a top-secret nuclear weapons facility, he could evaluate and improve any civilian system. His objective at the CDC was to examine every door, every lock, every procedure, and everyone remotely related to the Level Four lab and Susan Dorn. But first he had to gain the woman's confidence.

Forty-five minutes late, Susan Dorn finally appeared in the lobby.

"I'm so sorry to have kept you waiting, Mr. Evans, but the tour put me so far behind I never caught up. Perhaps we could have our meeting some other time," she suggested.

Evans studied the weariness on her face.

"How about a quick sandwich and a cup of coffee at the little place across the street? You must be hungry," he persisted.

Her eyes brightened, but she didn't smile.

"Yes, I am. But I can't stay long. What I really need, Mr. Evans, is rest, not coffee. I have a lot of work to do in the morning."

"Tomorrow is Sunday."

"The experiment I'm conducting cannot wait."

"I understand," said Evans.

Her formality and tone of voice told him she was uneasy in his presence, so he filled the walk across the boulevard with small talk. When she didn't respond, he realized she wasn't going to loosen up. She was simply too tired or too preoccupied. He waited until after they had ordered before probing further.

"Susan, today you said you're concerned about two things. Specifically, I'm interested in your concerns about physical security— outside threats, inside threats—of a human kind."

"As you have seen, Mr. Evans."

Evans interrupted her. "Derek, remember?"

"Yes, of course. As you have no doubt observed, Derek," she said stiffly, "the CDC is a very large facility with numerous buildings. Thousands of people come and go at all hours. I am concerned that we lack adequate physical safeguards around the potentially dangerous biological material in our possession."

Evans placed his elbows on the table and formed his fingers into a triangle under his chin. He looked deep into her eyes.

"That is a most unusual statement for a scientist." He paused before continuing. "While I waited for you, I watched the security guard in the lobby. By the book," he lied, hoping to elicit her thoughts on the matter. "He checked everyone who entered the building. When he wasn't checking badges, he was watching security monitors."

"Security Chief Johnson is a very thorough and responsible man, Mr. Evans. But his resources are limited."

"Derek."

"Sorry." She smiled, slightly embarrassed by his second correction.

"So what's the problem, Susan?"

"I have a feeling."

Evans cut her off. "Feeling? What specifically is driving your concerns, Susan?" Looking directly in her eyes, he asked, "Is it something you've seen?" She looked away quickly. Evans knew he had touched a nerve.

Then she met his eyes with a glare. "I hardly know you, Mr. Evans. I can't confide in you until . . ."

"Give me something to work with, Susan." *Tell me about the man you reported to the FBI,* he thought.

"Recently I read an article about a man who set up a phony lab and placed an order for botulism. It was delivered to his address by UPS," she said.

"Dr. Larry Harris. I'm aware of the incident, Susan. But I fail to make the connection. What's that got to do with the CDC?"

"The pathogens inside my lab make botulism look like the common cold. There are people in this world who, if they possessed those agents, might use them for evil purposes."

"On that we agree, Doctor," said Evans. "That's why I'm here. The question is, how could an outsider gain access and spirit away those germs? How could an insider pull off a heist without leaving a clue that something was missing? What would they do with such hazardous material? If it's so dangerous, how could they possibly use it and survive?"

"Do you think it's possible to steal viral material from my lab, Mr. Evans? Without us realizing it?" she added. She carefully studied his face.

"Yes, I do," Evans answered. "But that's not what's troubling me."

"What is troubling you, Mr. Evans?"

"The consequences of releasing such a killer. But then if I were a terrorist, I'd steal both a virus and you, and make you create a weapon and a vaccine at the same time. Then I'd change the population distribution in this world."

"No. No, you wouldn't, Mr. Evans."

"And why not?"

"Because no virologist in this world would knowingly do such a thing," said Dorn emphatically.

"I beg to differ, Susan. Criminals, crazies, and fanatics don't hesitate to use torture to get what they want. They would just twist your arms and pull out your fingernails until you complied."

"My father was a virologist, Mr. Evans. Ten years ago, before the development of Level Four procedures, he was accidentally exposed to an agent similar to the one I am currently studying. Rather than risk the lives of countless human beings, he destroyed his lab and himself. By fire." Her face twisted with grief. "No virologist would create such a weapon."

"I'm sorry about your father, Susan." Evans took a deep breath, then asked, "Have you ever heard of Vector?"

Vector was an old germ warfare lab hidden deep in Siberia. There, the Soviets had created secret weapons so horrendous that even the most fanatical communists were frightened by their destructive potential.

She glared at him. "Point taken, Mr. Evans. I am aware of what went on at Vector during the Cold War. I was referring to the scientists I work with here at the CDC."

"Susan, sometimes people wake up and discover that they don't even know the person they're married to."

She stared at him as the face of her ex flashed inside her brain. "Yeah," she nodded. "You got that right."

"What is it exactly that has you worried?" Evans persisted. "Have you seen something I should know about? Are you missing anything?"

"No," she answered emphatically.

"Physical security is not the kind of thing a scientist anguishes over."

"And just how would you know that, Mr. Evans?"

"Simple logic, Doctor. Killer viruses are enough to worry about without fretting over security matters."

She liked his straightforward manner and his penetrating eyes, but she couldn't confide in him without first speaking with the CDC security chief. Evans sensed the impasse.

When she met his eyes, she looked away quickly because he was studying her face like a map. Just then, the waiter delivered their sandwiches. Evans used the break to back off from his interrogation, turning again to small talk and pleasantries. A couple of times he got her to smile stiffly. But he couldn't get her to open up. He decided to press the issue at a later date. When she finished her sandwich, he offered to escort her to her car. She agreed with a yawn.

As they strolled down the sidewalk, he thought, *I need another man for surveillance. Ray Keith would be perfect for this job.*

"Susan," he said, "it's going to take me several weeks to finish my audit of the CDC. Do me a favor. Call me if you think of anything that will help my investigation." Then he spoke the words that told her he knew everything she had reported to the FBI. "Be sure to call me if you spot a young Arab male following you. Okay?"

She looked at him in shock, then down at the sidewalk.

"Okay. I will," she agreed, "but only after I speak with Chief Johnson, of course."

Evans wanted to know whether her antennae were working over-time, whether she was so edgy that she was imagining things, the way he had been earlier during that day. It was test time. One of his SEALs would watch her closely, so closely that she could spot him if she was savvy enough. And he didn't look Arabic like the man she had reported to the FBI. Evans still wasn't convinced that she needed protection, but he was certain that the CDC was in dire need of professional help.

At her car door she shook his hand politely and apologized for making him wait so long in the lobby. He almost chuckled at the formal way she ended the evening.

As she drove away he thought, *That woman is not only fright-ened, she's lonely. I'll bet work is the only thing in her life, work with deadly diseases.*

He was assailed by the memory of the day six years before when, returning home after more than twelve months of back-to-back de-ployments overseas, he had been handed divorce papers. She needed more from a man, she had explained; she needed a man who stayed at home. Later, when he found out she had taken up with a Navy doctor while he was overseas, intense rage had flooded his body. As a warrior, he knew a thousand ways to kill nonattributably. But he didn't lash out. Burying the hurt in his work, he simply turned his back on that part of his life and walked away. Four years later, after another terrible disappointment, which changed the course of his life, he turned his back on Uncle Sam and retired from the Navy.

He waited until Susan Dorn pulled away from the light, then hurried to his car and followed her home. From a distance he watched as she unlocked her door and went inside, apparently unaware he had followed her. He picked up his cell phone and dialed a local number.

A sleepy voice answered, "Hoo yah."

"Fred?" Evans said.

"Yeah, Boss."

"Meet me in the morning. I want to talk to you about hiring another man."

"Who?"

"Mañana."

"Roger, Boss. Luego."

Evans terminated the connection and drove back to his hotel.

Chapter 4

THE BAZAAR IN the old city center was full of shuffling people and raucous sounds. The smell of spices and breads mixed with the dry, hacking chatter of Arab entrepreneurs barking their wares. Like a rat with a serpent on its trail, the young Palestinian made his way through a maze of narrow, twisting streets. No more than eighteen, he had a brooding look about him and a wisp of a mustache that served only to accent his youth and immaturity. He glanced behind him, then ducked through several shoulderwide alleyways, each stinking of a different odor: first rotting coffee, then stale urine, then dogshit. He had made the trip across the so-called Green Line—the invisible border that separated Phalangist East Beirut from Palestinian-dominated West Beirut—many times. With peace, demarcation was not well defined but real nonetheless.

Near the edge of Old Town he stopped at a filthy cafe frequented by the truck drivers who hauled produce to market. Inside he could see several men drinking Turkish coffee and smoking hookahs of tobacco and hashish. He eyed them suspiciously before stepping through the doorway. The smell of roasting meat filled his nostrils. An old woman in a faded gray djellaba standing over a charcoal brazier looked at him for just an instant, then at her daughter, who was busy serving a customer.

"Psst! Psst!" she hissed at the girl.

The young woman looked at her mother and then at their visitor. Without smiling, she went about her work. She had large, dark, Persian eyes, sensuous, almost pouty lips, and a charade of demureness, an art form perfected in the Middle East.

The teen ignored the men and the women as if he had entered the wrong establishment. He backed out the door and scurried down the cobbled street into the shadows. In a narrow alley, he waited for her to pass, then from a distance followed her home to a squalid apartment located next to a lot filled with produce trucks. In the darkness he came to her, and they kissed softly, then passionately. With practiced swiftness, he slipped his hand beneath her clothing.

"Not now," she whispered in a husky exhalation. She pushed him away.

"Why not?" he pleaded.

"My mother might come home."

"She's busy at the restaurant," he whispered in her ear.

She felt his hot breath and hungry lips on her neck and his throb-
bing penis pressing against her thigh. Kissing her passionately on the
neck, he again slipped his hand under her dress and up her leg until
his fingers reached her panties. Deftly pushing it aside, he teased her
warm, moist clitoris with soft, circular movements. For a few seconds she tolerated his caresses.

"No," she insisted, pushing him away. "Not now."

Their eyes met in the dim light filtering in from the street. She
glared at him with an obsidian stare.

"I won't live like this, Kamal," she said. "I don't want to live in
a land of hate and death and war, a land where Muslims kill Christians, and Christians kill Muslims, and Jews laugh at the sport. If we
are to have a life together, I want it to be in a safe place. Not here."

She ran her fingers through his hair.

"You understand, don't you? I want so much for us, Kamal,"
she said softly. "So much. Children. A home. We have to find a way
to leave this wretched place," she begged in a tiny voice tinged with
despair.

"We will," he promised, putting his arms around her waist. "I'll
find a way."

She pushed him back a few inches.

"What have you found out about Desert Decree?" she asked
impatiently. "Do you know what it is? Hassan will give us all the
money we need to move to Italy, if only we can find out what it is."

"It's a big operation against the Great Satan," Kamal mumbled.

"How do you know that?"

"A lot of fighters will be going to America soon," he whispered.

"Kamal, that is not enough. Hassan will want to know what the
PFC is going to do in America."

"I will find out, Haroun. Just give me time. I promise," the
youth pleaded.

She pulled him close and kissed him passionately. With one hand
he began massaging the nipple of her breast; the other he slid up her
dress. As they kissed, he caressed her, played her. She tried to hold
herself back—business was business—but he had taken her too far.
Her hips began to push forward, matching the rhythm of his fingers.
Then she began to make soft cooing sounds in his ear.

"Oh, Kamal, I love you."

She was completely lost in the magic of the moment when she
heard a dull thud and felt Kamal's body go limp in her arms. He

slumped at her feet, unconscious. The rough hands that grabbed her
smothered her scream.

"You fuckin', Jew-lovin', Phalangist bitch," growled the voice
in the dark. The man's breath smelled of stale coffee and garlic.
"Fawaz," he shouted.

A few seconds later, a skinny man appeared in the doorway. The
light outside the hovel illuminated his silhouette.

"The truck. Quickly."

The scrawny man scurried off, and seconds later a heavy truck
appeared at the curb, smoking and belching diesel fumes. Two men
jumped out, rushed in, and carried Kamal outside. Through the open
doorway Haroun watched as they threw his limp body up into the
cab like a sack of rice. Shivering with terror, she struggled to get free.
But the man's iron grip tightened, and he spun her around. With one
vicious punch, he smashed her in the face so hard she lost consciousness.
When she regained her senses he was dragging her, rolling her
to the curb, holding her down with his foot in front of the tandem
rear wheels of the rumbling truck. She heard him yell, but the sound
of his voice was detached, surreal. Then she felt the vehicle lurch
forward, climbing up her legs, crushing her bones, her life. At the
top of her lungs, with her very last breath, she let out a bloodcur-
dling scream that rang through the narrow, twisting streets of Old
Town and penetrated the filthy cafe where her mother was working.
There was a throng of onlookers. When the old woman found her
daughter's crushed body, she too shrieked in a shrill, piercing voice.

"Yiiiiii! Yiiiiii! My God, help me! All my sons are dead," she
cried, beating her breast. "My husband is gone. What am I going to
do? Oh, Allah. Oh, God, oh, God. Who will take care of me?"

The girl's death didn't make the news. Lebanon was a simmering
pressure cooker of ethnic stew. Death by unnatural cause was com-
monplace. Druse, Sunnis, Maronite Christians, and Shiites eyed each
other suspiciously from mob-protected villages and neighborhoods
throughout the country. The ancient feud between the Arabs and the
Jews had overcome the Promised Land, and it had precipitated civil
and religious wars. Palestinians fleeing Israel congregated in squalid
refugee camps of grinding poverty, armed to the teeth, unwelcome
by their warring hosts, pursued by their enemies, and ignored by the
United Nations. Fed on militant Islam and violence, camps like Sabra
and Shatila were breeding grounds for the most fanatical terrorists.

Discontent bred faster in filth, and more virulent. It was Aman Ayyad's world.

Ibrahim Nasrallah, wealthy even before war engulfed Lebanon, grew more prosperous by providing arms, food, and medical supplies to any group that could pay his price. Palestinian by ancestry, he was Lebanese by manner and comportment. He was Christian when necessary, Muslim by faith, and a friend to numerous Jewish merchants in scattered lands. His extensive holdings both in the region and overseas were perfect cover for the Palestinian Freedom Council, an organization of hardcore Palestinian nationalists dedicated to establishing a homeland in the Middle East. As a senior member of the council, he was an important player in all decisions. Moreover, his overseas business enterprises provided a network of bases and safehouses for military operations. It was in one of Nasrallah's cover businesses in Bikfaya that Aman Ayyad had Kamal Samir interrogated.

The tiny village of Bikfaya in the mountains above Beirut existed solely for one purpose: pleasure. Both sides of the narrow main street were lined with restaurants and cafes that had once featured the best Oriental dancers and singers in the Middle East. That was in the town's heyday, before the war. The clientele—those who still came to visit—were strictly the rich and powerful, the businessmen and sheiks who could afford to travel there to escape the rigid moral code and the boredom of the Muslim world. In Bikfaya men were anonymous. There they could indulge in all the things that were forbidden at home. They could drink liquor and taste the foods and delights that Muslim law forbade. And no matter how well one man knew another, he would not recognize him on the street or speak to him unless invited to do so.

In defiance of his superior's directive not to use the telephone, Aman Abruzzi Ayyad had called his most trusted lieutenants and ordered them to meet him in Bikfaya. He arrived late, after eight o'clock, to find the village streets empty. Israeli jets and artillery had put a significant damper on the pleasure business. But the welcoming sound of the kanoon and drums greeted him as he entered the cafe. On the small stage at the side of the great room a dancer whirled, her multicolored scarves floating around her, the silver bangles of her brassiere sparkling with light. Seated around a horseshoe-shaped table at the foot of the stage, four of his men watched intently, eyes riveted on her exposed flesh. Ayyad followed the receptionist through the great room and up the staircase at the rear of the establishment.

The apartments on the second floor were reserved for special clients who, after a night of amusement, might be too tired to make the long journey back into Beirut or might wish to stay and partake of further pleasures provided by the management. As Ayyad followed the receptionist down the hall, he passed a young boy clothed in silken shirt and trousers. His eyes were heavily made up, his cheeks rouged, his fingernails long and painted. The boy smiled salaciously and waved his fingers daintily at Ayyad in a feminine manner. The battle-hardened terrorist ignored the greeting, so the boy blew him a kiss.

At the rear of the building, the host unlocked a door and held it for Ayyad. Once inside, he closed it behind them, then opened the closet. He pushed on the back wall, a wooden panel that opened onto a hidden staircase down to the basement.

"Ensure that that faggot doesn't enter my room or I'll feed you and him to a Jewish dog," Ayyad ordered.

"Yes, your excellency," replied the servant, wide-eyed. "Will there be anything else?"

"I would like company tonight. Your best."

"Your wish is our command, excellency. The honorable Ibrahim Nasrallah has given us explicit orders to provide for all your needs."

The servant pressed his praying hands to his forehead, lips, and heart, then withdrew.

Ayyad locked the door, closed the closet door behind him, and descended the stairs to a cave carved into the rock beneath the building. It was dark and ancient and secret, a place to hide from the world above, a place where rats and terrorists felt secure. He stepped around huge amphoras and kegs of food and drink to make his way deeper into the mountain. At the back of the cavern he opened a heavy wooden door and entered a smaller chamber. Two of his lieutenants stood over a naked Arab teenager strapped to an *al-abd al-aswad,* a Black Slave. It was a Syrian contraption used to encourage confessions. When switched on, a hot metal skewer forced its way into the victim's anus, burning the intestines. There were also Russian tools for ripping out fingernails and Iraqi pincers and scissors for plucking and cutting flesh.

The boy had been beaten badly. His eyes were swollen shut, and he was bleeding from the nose and mouth. His head rolled about on his shoulders with blood and saliva drooling from his mouth.

"What miracles have you performed, Hamid?" Ayyad asked.

Hamid had a vulturelike appearance. Only two gray irises, like galvanized steel washers, moved about in the broad expanse of Hamid's face, flicking methodically back and forth.

"He is a fucking traitor," Hamid answered.

"Are you sure?" Ayyad asked.

"Yes," Hamid answered confidently.

"Fawaz?" Ayyad inquired, glancing down at their victim.

Fawaz was a skinny rail of a man with the face of a ferret and a gnarled tree stump for a nose. He spat out a few harsh syllables that sounded like concrete cracking. "He's a traitor. We caught him with his Maronite, Phalangist, Jew-loving bitch girlfriend."

"What did he tell her?" asked Ayyad.

"Everything he knew."

The boy moaned. Blood bubbled out of one nostril.

"And what was that?"

"That we are planning a big operation in America," Hamid answered. "He told her the name of the operation and that a number of fighters were going to leave soon. He didn't tell her anything else because the little shit doesn't know anything."

"May a thousand fleas infest his mother's crotch," Fawaz cursed. He spat on the boy and backhanded him with his fist. "Filthy traitor."

A gush of saliva and blood issued from Kamal Samir's mouth as his head wobbled. He was already beyond feeling a little swat in the face.

"And the girl?"

"She had a most unfortunate accident," Fawaz grinned. "Got run over by a truck."

"Good. Make an example of this camel dung, too," Ayyad ordered, turning to leave. "Then join us upstairs. We have many things to discuss."

"How would you like us to do it, Aman?" asked Hamid.

Ayyad paused at the door, then turned to face his men. "Cut off his arms and legs and head. Stuff them in orange crates and have them delivered to his mother."

"But she is Palestinian," Fawaz protested. "The old woman has done nothing wrong."

"Draw a Star of David on the box containing the head."

Both men stared at their commander.

"They'll blame it on the Jews," Fawaz blurted.

"You catch on quickly, Fawaz. Now be done with it."

Hamid switched on the Black Slave. The noise of the motor and a turning screw reverberated off the stone walls of the chamber. Kamal's eyes opened when the hot metal rod entered his anus. As it burned its way deeper into his colon, he sucked in air with a horrible groan of pain. He screamed in agony and passed out again.

"Fucking traitor," Fawaz cursed.

To minimize the mess, the two henchmen unstrapped the boy and severed a jugular to bleed the corpse into an amphora. But Hamid cut too deeply and severed his windpipe. A horrible hissing-gurgling sound filled the chamber.

Ayyad waited until nine o'clock before going downstairs and taking his place at the foot of the stage. Behind his six men, young boys, all wearing the same elaborate makeup as the youth who had greeted Ayyad in the hallway, were seated on small stools. Standing behind them were waiters and other members of the staff. There were bottles of champagne in buckets near each man, and their glasses were constantly filled. The horseshoe table at the foot of the stage was covered with more than twenty-five varieties of hors d'oeuvres and delicacies. The men ate with their fingers. After each mouthful, servants delicately wiped their hands with fresh, warm, damp cloths. They shared hashish from a hubbly-bubbly, a communal waterpipe, and continued to eat, drink, and chat for several hours. Finally Ayyad gave the signal for the entertainment to begin.

At the first note of music, the lights dimmed, and gradually the room went dark, with the exception of a pale orange light that illuminated the stage. Seven dancing girls appeared, dressed in flowing, multicolored scarves that floated around their bodies. At first they belly danced to the music with slow rhythmic movements. But as the music grew louder and more intense, their abdomens began shaking in more exotic and seductive ways. They shimmied around the stage, bewitching the men with their sensuous bodies. The loveliest of the dancers positioned herself in front of Ayyad, captivating him with her beauty. Light reflected off a diamond ring as a delicate hand drew his attention to the apex of her thighs. With the light behind her, Ayyad could see through her diaphanous costume to the chasm of delights, dark, alluring, inviting. The dance lasted more than fifteen minutes, building to a climax in which the girls seemed to reach a frenzy of sexual excitement. Then, on a beat of the drum, they collapsed on the dance floor, motionless.

For the longest time after the music stopped there was silence, until Ayyad began to applaud enthusiastically. His men, their brains numbed by hashish, joined in, and slowly the lights came up to reveal the dancers more clearly. Still prostrate on the floor, they began to rise to their feet. To Ayyad's amazement, the dancers on the stage were not the girls who had begun the dance but the boys who had been seated behind them. He stopped clapping and threw a fistful of crumpled notes on the dance floor.

It was two in the morning when Ayyad adjourned the meeting and went to his room, reeling from the champagne and hashish. As he entered, a faint scent of musk came to his nostrils. Pausing just inside the door, he stood still in the darkness, his eyes trying to make out the form in front of him. Was it a woman or a boy? He had to know, but he could see nothing until a match scratched and an orange glow illuminated the face of a female dancer.

"Your excellency," she said with a faint Egyptian accent.

Heavy-lashed eyes smiled at him as she turned to light a candle. Ayyad recognized her as the prettiest of the dancers who had performed for him, the one who had invited him with her eyes and hands. The only portion of her costume she had changed was her brassiere. Her breasts were covered by a silken scarf, through which he saw the dark areola of her nipples.

"I have a warm bath prepared for you, excellency," she said.

She clapped her hands and two more women came from the corners of the room, where they had been standing in the shadows. They wore thin, see-through veils that covered their breasts and fell from their hips around their legs. As they moved, they crossed in front of the candle. Ayyad could see the shape of their bodies and the carefully depilated mounds between their slim legs. Only their eyes were visible behind their traditional Muslim veils.

The first woman turned on soft music and began gently swaying to the rhythm. Another took his hand and led him to his bath. All three undressed him, their touch light and gentle on his body. They helped him into the warm water and bathed him with soft sponges until every inch of his skin was alive with sensation.

"What is your name?" he asked the dancer.

"Soad, excellency."

She lit a cigarette and gave it to him. He took a drag, and the sweet, pungent odor of hashish and tobacco floated into the air. A warmth flowed through his body that descended to his loins. He took another puff and gave it back to her. At her touch he felt a surge of excitement course through his entire body. Standing up, he looked down at his unit, long and lean and hard. Then he looked at Soad.

"Tonight I want all three of you."

She bowed her head and made a gesture of obeisance. They toweled him off and led him to the bed, where he stretched out like a lion with his pride. Soad kissed him softly on the lips, and the girls began licking him. They licked his nipples, his belly, his scrotum, his anus, his penis, his entire body, until he was so knotted with sexual tension he exploded. In his hashish-induced trance, all he would remember was a tangle of bodies and warmth and exquisite sensations that caused the juice to burst from him in one huge, exhausting geyser and then sliding into a deep sleep.

At four in the morning he was blasted awake by an explosion that hurled his bed into the air. He felt himself falling as the room pancaked down onto the lower floor. Then there was silence and a ringing in his ears. The sounds of pain began rising around him. Moans and screams pierced the darkness, and cries for help. Slowly he got up, naked, and made his way out of the debris.

At first light it was clear what had happened. A car bomb had gone off beside the cafe, decimating the lower wall. The building had been blown in half. The part still standing was cut open as though it were a life-size dollhouse, with jagged pieces of concrete dangling from the second floor. The half that had been blown down by the explosion collapsed into a ten-foot-high stack of smoldering concrete. Dazed servants staggered through the rubble like zombies, looking for survivors. It was a metaphor for the war, for his people—the Palestinian people—wandering around foreign lands searching for a home.

Miraculously, four of Ayyad's men had survived. With the first light of morning they began searching for their missing comrades. Ayyad found Hamid first, or part of him. He no longer had a vulturelike appearance. Only his two steel-gray irises were recognizable as they stared vacantly from his severed head. Nearby he found Fawaz. Blood bubbled from his gnarled stump of a nose as he struggled for breath. His chest was crushed beneath a section of concrete wall. He was only half-alive and in great pain.

"Fawaz, Fawaz," cried Ayyad.

But there was no reply. With his men standing around, Ayyad stared into the eyes of his suffering comrade. "Fawaz, Fawaz. We'll make the Great Satan pay for this. I promise. *Allah akbar!*" he shouted.

"Allah akbar!" cried his men in unison.

"Idbah al-adu! Slaughter the enemy."

"Idbah al-adu!"

Ayyad touched his forehead, lips, and heart in the traditional gesture and placed his hand over Fawaz's bloody nose and mouth. There was no resistance, just a faint glint of Praise-Be-to-God in Fawaz's tortured pupils. Ayyad held tight until he saw the life force leave the body, until Fawaz's eyes stared at something beyond. Then he turned away and walked, a sick man, stumbling through the rubble. As he made his way through the debris he came across a severed arm, partially charred at the elbow. Soad's diamond ring sparkled on one delicate, undamaged finger.

We have more than one leak, Uncle Nasrallah, he thought. *The Jews are everywhere. They are in the water and the air that I breathe. I am a bug on a twig in a flood, surrounded by freeze-dried Zionists who spring to life with every drop of their slimy blood that I spill.*

"Allah akbar. God is most great!" he screamed. *"An-nasr!* Victory," he shouted over and over until his men joined in the chant.

When his emotions were spent, despair descended upon him like a noxious gas, and he collapsed on the rubble near Soad's severed hand. Aman Abruzzi Ayyad, ignorant child of a Palestinian refugee camp, could not have imagined that he had brought on the attack simply by using the telephone to order his men to Bikfaya. Israeli intelligence capabilities were far beyond his ability to comprehend.

Chapter 5

DEREK EVANS WIPED the sweat off his brow. While he was having lunch in the small town of El Indio, the interior of his rented gray Oldsmobile had heated up to over 130 degrees. On maximum, the air conditioner was barely staying even with the California sun. Seeking a breath of fresh air, he stopped the car on the side of the road and got out. A blast of sauna-hot air from a passing truck hit him in the face. As he looked out over the vast depression, waves of baking heat shimmered off the desert floor.

How the hell can human beings live out here? he wondered, knowing at the same time that it was the solitude, the peace, and the escape from metropolitan insanity that drove them.

He tossed his suit coat onto the passenger seat and looked south-east over the Salton Sea. It was so vast it was difficult to believe it had been created by a man-made disaster in the late 1800s. On the other side, near the base of the Chocolate Mountain range, the SEALs had a training camp. It was covered in creosote bushes. He smiled, fondly remembering the men he had taught to move, shoot, and communicate among the creosote bushes of Niland. Ray Keith had been one of those men.

Too bad about the accident, he thought. *Keith was one of the finest chiefs in SEAL Team Five.*

Evans had trouble visualizing Ray Keith with one leg. He kept seeing him running down the Silver Strand, leading a group of trainees on a six-mile beach run.

The snowbirds are gone, he observed, ridding his mind of the accident for the moment.

The only recreational vehicles left in the desert heat belonged to permanent residents. They were a hardy breed of lizards and coyotes who shot first and asked questions later. The snowbirds were migrants from Minnesota, Wisconsin, and other frostbitten states who wintered in the area. Every year they established a huge RV camp on the eastern side of the Salton Sea. The SEALs called it Slab City. But they left before the inferno of summer arrived.

Since his forced medical retirement, Ray Keith had been scratching out a living doing odd jobs for snowbirds. The more permanent residents—solitary people who kept to themselves—occupied the ramshackle beach houses and trailers on the western shore. They made a meager living off the seasonal snowbirds and their government pensions.

Fred Swan had told Evans where to find Keith, and he had warned him about his eccentric behavior. "Ray don't see nobody no more, Boss. He won't even come out of his trailer for a Team guy. Nobody 'cept me."

Like Keith, Fred Swan was disabled. He had lost one eye in the line of duty, and Ray Keith identified with the disability.

"I'll have him in Atlanta in a week," Evans had replied. "Until then, dog Dr. Dorn and make it obvious she's being followed."

"You got it," Swan had replied.

Ray Keith lived alone in a thirty-four-foot Airstream on a street with no name and no addresses. With Swan's warning echoing inside his head, Evans climbed back into the car and turned on the air conditioner full blast. He breathed in the coolness directly from the vent.

Something big is going down, he thought. *I saw it in Carson's eyes. If I can get Keith to cover the CDC for a few weeks, the rest of us can finish up the power plants. He's perfect for the job, if I can get him to lay off the booze.*

In his mind's eye he saw Keith competing on a pistol range, running from target to target like a machine.

He was a hell of a man, big enough to get over the loss of a leg by now. He's drinkin' heavy because he misses the Teams. So I'll give him a team. If I can find him.

Evans slipped the car in gear and eased onto the road, still picturing Ray Keith in action. Exactly 25.3 miles south of Mecca, California, on Highway 86, he turned onto a dirt road that led down to the Sea. He counted the trailers for half a mile, then stopped.

"Bingo," he said when he spotted the one that fitted Keith's personality.

It was parked on a quarter acre, just as Fred Swan had described. The lot was surrounded by a six-foot chain-link fence with a run of barbed wire at the top. Among the weeds in the yard was a battered pickup truck, and in the back, a mangled Harley mounted on a steel pole like a sculpture. The migrant responsible for the damage to the motorcycle had also taken Ray Keith's right leg.

Evans stopped the car and stepped out into the hot desert sun. A homemade sign on the gate read

TRESSPASSOURS WILL BE SHOT.

Scrawled in grease pencil below the block letters was a handwritten message:

No Solisoters! i will shoot your ass!

Ray Keith was one of the most talented men with a pistol Evans had ever known. He could shoot the eyes out of a snake on the move at fifty yards. But he couldn't spell. Evans smiled and shook his head as he surveyed his comrade's refuge.

The air conditioner at the back of the trailer clamored away in the dry desert air, a lonely sound in the vast expanse of sand and rocks and creosote bushes. The windows on the trailer were covered with aluminum foil to reflect the sun's heat. The gates in the chain-link fence were padlocked, so Evans couldn't knock on the door.

Opening the car door, he tooted the horn several times and watched for a response. He saw the foil on the front window move slightly, but there were no other signs of life.

Sweat was pouring down his body in rivulets, so he got back into the car again and relished the cool air for a few minutes, waiting for Keith to give in and open the door. When he didn't, Evans honked the horn several more times. He waited for about ten minutes, then decided to visit a small bar he had passed up near Highway 86.

The interior of the Pastime was dark and cool like a cave after the bright light of the summer sun. The smell of stale beer and cigarettes accosted Evans's nose as he eased inside. He stood behind the door for a few seconds while his eyes adjusted to the dim interior. An old man and an old woman seated at the bar gawked at him as if he was an alien. Evans sauntered up and took a stool.

"What'll you have?" asked the barkeeper. He was elderly as well, and his manner was rough.

"Coors Light," replied Evans. "Cold. Ice cold."

As the bartender served the drink he examined Evans curiously.

"Do you know Ray Keith?" Evans asked.

"Yep. And I know you, too. Remember me, Commander? Dusty Rhodes. I was with the base fire department at NAB," he said, holding out his hand.

"Yeah, Dusty," said Evans, searching the old geezer's face as he shook hands. It was worn by the sun but looked vaguely familiar.

"How are you, Dusty?" he asked out of politeness, not really remembering the old coot.

"Great, Commander. Just great. Judgin' by the long hair, you're a retired man like myself, or are you one of them secret agent men now?" he asked, giving Evans a wild-eyed look.

"Got it right the first time, Dusty. I retired a few years ago."

"I'm mighty sorry to hear that, Commander. That'd be a big loss to the country." He waved to the couple seated at the other end of the bar. "Hey, Albert, Martha, come meet Commander Evans. He was the commandin' officer of SEAL Team Five over in San Diego when I was the base fire marshal."

The fire department on the Naval Amphibious Base was a one-truck operation. It rarely left the hangar, and when it did it was for a parade. The old couple came over and greeted Evans warmly.

The woman spoke first. "What you doin' in these parts, Commander?"

"Please call me Derek."

"If you don't mind, I'll just call you Handsome," she replied with a husky cigarette smoker's giggle.

"Do you know Ray Keith?" Evans persisted.

"Yep. 'Course we do. He lives a couple of blocks down on the right. One of those Airstreams," said Dusty with a desert twang.

"The one with the tin foil all over the winders," Martha added.

"Chain-link fence? Old truck in the yard?" Evans asked.

"That'd be the one," Albert affirmed. "He don't much come out this time of day. Too hot." The old man leaned over close to Evans as if to prevent someone from overhearing him. "Drunk beaner run into him, you know. Took off his leg just above the knee," he said with a gravely serious expression. "Had a sculpture made out of the motorcycle. It's in his backyard."

"Some of the fellers from the base come around to see him now and again, but he won't come to the door. Best bet is to catch him here Friday evenings just after sundown. He swills down a few with us old folks. Sometimes Albert and Martha have to help him home. Gets too drunk to use his artificial leg," Dusty reported.

"Is he there now?" asked Evans.

"Yep, he's there," said Martha. "He'd be listenin' to Rush Limbaugh 'bout now," she observed, looking at the clock behind the bar.

"Gate's locked from the outside," said Evans.

"He's there, Commander. I seen him last night crutchin' hisself down to the lake. He likes to sit and look at the water and have a snort or two," said Albert, raising one eyebrow for emphasis.

"You think maybe he went to Indio or Brawley?"

"Nope. His truck's broke," gossiped Dusty.

"Well, thanks for the info. I think I'll mosey down there and try to get his attention," said Evans. He gulped down the rest of his beer and set the glass on the bar with a thunk.

"He won't come out fer ya, Handsome," the old woman insisted.

"We'll see. Nice meetin' you folks. You take care now."

"Hey, Commander, you remember that time you guys had that party for the undersecretary of the defense, and you got the base XO so mad she was spittin' fire?"

"Yeah, Dusty. I remember," said Evans, trying to break away.

Rhodes continued his story. "Those rascals hired this dancin' girl to rub her boobs in this feller's face. But that ain't what got 'em

in trouble. They shot the chef with a magazine full of blank ammunition. That man shit all over hisself." He chuckled. "He set the kitchen
on fire trying to escape out the back."

Evans interrupted. "I'm sorry, Dusty, but I got to get goin'.
Take care."

Dusty continued his story without pause. "We had this female
XO, you see, and she didn't have much of a sense of humor."

Dusty was still spinning his yarn as Evans walked out the door.

Evans stopped the car in front of Ray Keith's drive and blew the horn
several times. When there was no response, he opened the car door,
got out, and checked the padlock on the gate. It was locked, so he
got back in the car and laid on the horn nonstop for a couple of
minutes. The aluminum foil on one of the windows moved just a
little, so he laid on the horn again. When Keith failed to appear, he
sat motionless in the car for a couple of minutes with the air conditioner blowing full blast in his face. Finally, he jammed the car in
reverse and hit the accelerator. He came to a screeching halt on the
opposite side of the dirt road and slammed the car into drive. Throwing gravel and dirt and with the horn blaring, he knocked down the
gate and drove the car up to the front door of the trailer. For three
minutes he blew the horn until the door opened. An angry Ray Keith
appeared, brandishing a 1911 Colt .45. He looked like Charles
Manson, although he had blond hair instead of brown. It was tied
back in a ponytail. His fiery eyes stared out from behind a scraggly
reddish-blond beard stained by tobacco juice. As he was dressed only
in a pair of undershorts, his stump of a leg was painfully obvious.
Evans let off the horn and got out.

"You were always a stubborn son of a bitch. You know that?"
Keith yelled, with a sour expression on his face.

He spat a big gob of tobacco juice on the fender of the car. Evans
brazenly walked up and held out his hand. Keith just stared at it. He
spat another gob of juice that landed with a splat at Evans's feet.

"Is this the way you treat old friends?" Evans asked.

"Who says you're an old friend?" Keith growled, pistol in hand,
eyeballing Evans with disdain.

Evans gave Keith the once-over. "So how the hell are you, Ray
Keith?"

"Fine. I was doin' just fine until some mule-assed commander
knocked down my gate and interrupted my Rush Limbaugh."

"Ray, you've got to have better things to do than listen to a fat man with an inferiority complex."

"Maybe I do and maybe I don't!" Keith snapped. He glared sourly at Evans, but then his expression gradually softened. "Well, I am sort of gettin' tired of his self-aggrandizement. I wish he would just stick to the damn issues."

Keith continued to study Evans with a twisted, suspicious look on his face. He spat another gob of tobacco juice out the door and wiped his beard with the back of his hand.

"You want a beer?" he asked, a sudden shot in the dark.

"Thought you'd never ask."

"Wait here. I ain't invitin' you in. The place stinks."

Keith hobbled away on his crutches. The sun outside was so bright that the interior of the trailer was pitch black, like the mouth of a cave. A few seconds after Keith disappeared, a can of beer flew out the door as if it had wings. Evans was lucky to catch it.

"I see your reflexes are still good," Keith commented from the dark void. "But can you still shoot?"

"Bet your ass I can."

Evans found shade under the trailer's awning and took a deep pull on the cold beer. Leveling his eyes on Keith, he gave the veteran SEAL warrior a hard look of disapproval.

"You look like shit, Charlie Manson," he said, wiping the sweat off his forehead.

"Case you didn't know it, Commander Asshole, Charlie Manson's got two fuckin' legs. I don't owe you shit. You know that? I don't have to call you sir no more, and I don't have to get no fuckin' haircut. Not for nobody. And I don't like the way you look in that fancy zoot suit either."

"Well, thanks for being honest about my five-hundred-dollar threads. And thanks for the beer, asshole," Evans growled.

"Well, that's all you're gonna get," Keith replied bitterly. A few seconds later he completely changed. He said, "Outspokenness and honesty are basic parts of my character, sir. Now what the hell do you want?"

"You don't have to call me sir."

"I said that, didn't I?" Keith snapped.

There was an awkward moment of silence broken by the air conditioner kicking on. The door was wide open.

"Well, you always treated me square for a cake-eater," Keith finally said. "Suppose it was your ELQ. If it wasn't for you, I'd be missin' some mighty fine memories."

Evans had come up through the ranks from enlisted to officer. The enlisted men of SEAL Team Five had accused him of having ELQ, "enlisted-like qualities." It had been a compliment.

"You don't owe me anything, Ray."

"I said that too, didn't I?"

"That you did," Evans shot back.

"What do you want? You come bargin' into my yard, knock down my fence like some crazy son of a bitch. How'd you know I wouldn't shoot your sorry ass?"

Evans took another pull on the beer then said, "I got a job for you."

"What? You ain't noticed I only got one leg? Hardheaded as a mule and now you're blind."

"I noticed," Evans said with a scowl.

"I don't want no damn job. I'm gettin' ready to go up to Montana to do some huntin'."

"How you gonna get there? Your truck's broke," Evans stated.

Keith gave him a dirty look. "I see the patrons down at the old folks home have been gossipin' 'bout my business," he scowled.

"What's wrong with it?"

"With what?"

"The truck, dumbass!" sassed Evans.

"Transmission's busted. I think."

"Why don't you fix it?" Evans inquired.

"Just in case you haven't noticed, Commander Asshole, I only got one fuckin' leg. I can't fix it!"

"Bullshit! Quit whimpering, you puss! You're gonna make me cry!" Evans shouted.

"No. I'm going to shoot your pigheaded ass if you don't get the fuck out of my life."

In a flash Evans produced a 9-millimeter pistol and racked out a round. The bullet landed in the hot sand at his feet.

Keith didn't move an inch and he didn't blink.

"Did you notice this?" Evans asked.

"Course I did. Damn peashooter," Keith snarled, without taking his eyes off Evans's gun hand.

"Mexican standoff."

"Don't say Mexican around me, sir!" Keith shouted. "I ain't too fond of beaners. 'Sides, I could always outshoot your officer-ass."

"You were taught by the best, and you had more time to practice than I did."

"Who said you were the best? I don't like self-aggrandizement, remember?"

"Ray, that's a mighty big word for a desert rat. You're wearin' it out."

Keith hobbled back into the trailer. Evans was watching for the barrel of the .45 when another beer flew out the open door. It was an easy catch. He popped the top and took a big swallow, then walked over to the truck. When Keith hobbled outside wearing his artificial leg, Evans was down underneath the truck without his shirt and tie.

"You are the hardheadedest son of a bitch I have ever had the displeasure of knowing."

Shaking his head, Keith mumbled, "I suppose there is no way of stoppin' ya. I'll get some overalls and wrenches."

Together they took the transmission out of the truck, accompanied by nonstop verbal jousting. Covered in grease and sand, Evans dragged the transmission to the rear of his car. He was just picking it up to put it in the trunk when his cell phone rang.

"Get that, would you, Ray?"

Keith gave him a dirty look, then hobbled over and picked up the phone.

"Mr. Evans's office. May I help you?" he said pleasantly. "Yes he is. Just a minute please."

He hopped around to the rear of the car and handed Evans the phone.

"A Ms. Dorn for you, sir," he said, with a curtsy and a smug expression. He held up his head so he could hear the one-sided conversation better.

"Hi, Susan. What's up? . . . Uh-huh. Different guy? Does he have a black patch over the right eye?"

Ray Keith's interest was piqued.

"That's my guy, Susan," Evans continued. "Whenever he's around, you rest at ease."

When he hung up, he wiped the phone on his overalls, threw it onto the backseat of the car, and waited for Keith's interrogation. It was not long in coming.

"You got Popeye down there doggin' that gal?" he asked.

"Yep."

"Why?"

"Can't tell you or I'd have to kill you. You're not on the payroll yet," Evans shot back.

"Ask the man a simple, straightforward question and get a smartass answer. I just want to know why Popeye's follerin' that woman, sir. Her husband tryin' to kill her or somethin'?"

"She's a very important lady scientist who's studying some very nasty germs," said Evans.

"So?"

"So, they're not the kind of bugs you'd want to fall into the wrong hands."

"And why not? And why do you want me to help Popeye dog this bug-studyin' broad?" he asked, watching Evans's face for clues.

"First, the bugs are bad news. In the wrong hands they could do more damage than a thousand nukes. Second, I don't want you to help Swan. I want you to do the job by yourself. Third, she's definitely not a broad."

Keith raised his chin and looked at Evans as though sighting down the barrel of a gun with one eye. "What's in it for me?" he asked.

"Two hundred a day and expenses."

"How much you payin' Popeye and the boys?"

"Same thing," said Evans, incensed by the question.

"Then why ain't you payin' me five or six hundred, seein' as how I'll be relievin' more than one man?"

"'Cause you ain't worth it, dumbass!" Evans snapped.

"The expenses part includes my beer?"

"One a day. No more."

"Sixpack. No less!" Keith insisted.

"Two cans. Tops! The rest is on you."

"Four, on you, Commander."

"Three. Not a drop more," Evans growled, running out of patience.

"Well, I guess I could get a haircut for three tall-boy cans of beer a day." Keith drew the adjective out in a desert twang.

"No, no, no. I want you just like you are, buck-o. I want you to make up a sign and sit outside this fancy building and panhandle. You know, 'homeless vet, will work for food or money.'"

"What?" Keith was shocked. "My pride won't let me do no such thing."

"Your cover is a homeless Joe, jackass. What do you want me to do? Write a job description for you?"

"Now wait a minute, Commander."

"You're already in character, Pegleg. You look like shit. Like death warmed over. That's perfect cover for this job."

"I might be persuaded to do it, seein' as how the beggin' part is all cover and such." Keith spat out a mouthful of tobacco juice. "But it's gonna cost you four beers a day if you want me to beg for money. And I get to keep the proceeds of my panhandling."

"Done deal."

"And as for you alludin' to my appearance, this ain't one of my better days, I'll have you know."

Keith studied Evans with a menacing expression. He bit off a fresh chunk of tobacco and handed the plug to Evans with a greasy paw. Evans declined with a contorted expression.

"You know, if I'm goin' to Atlanter, I don't need to fix this truck." He gave Evans a hard look. "I'll tell you what. Let's bust some caps. I don't wanna work for no man who's lost his touch."

"Back on you, Pegleg! But if we're gonna do some serious shootin', I need a real gun. Got a .45 I can borrow?"

"No problema, Hoss," Keith grinned. "I got an arsenal the BATF don't know about."

"My puppy is good for packin', but it's poor competition for the range."

"It's a piece of shit, that's what it is," said Keith with scorn. "Say, who's payin' the bills for this job anyhow? The navy kicked me out 'cause I'm deficient in the leg department. So I ain't too fond of Uncle Sam right now."

"Senator Carson."

"Well, I'll be a jackass mule. How many broke-dick SEALs you hangin' around with? Swan's only got one eye. Carson is missin' a leg. I'm beginning to think that ax you took down your chest has affected your brain."

Keith was referring to a war wound Evans got while on a mission in Indonesia. A Russian Spetznaz had nearly killed him with a razor-sharp spade.

"Well, there's Sam Decker," Evans continued.

"He's got a friggin' pacemaker stuck in his ticker, Boss," Keith gasped. "Are you nuts?"

"And then there's J. R. Jennings. But don't count him. Mr. Perot's fancy doctors have just about fixed his bum foot. Free."

"Holy shit, sir. Why don't you hire some talent?"

Jennings had been one of the most highly skilled young men in SEAL Team Five. When he incurred a permanent foot injury while on a mission in Southeast Asia, Navy doctors had botched the surgery, leaving him with a permanent disability. Jennings's brother had also been a SEAL, one of the men killed in Panama during Operation Just Cause. Ross Perot had helped his family then, and he had come to Jennings's aid again, providing the best doctors in the country to repair the damage.

"I'd say I've overloaded the boat now that I've added the finest pistolero in the world to my stable," Evans grinned.

"I hope your stable ain't full of horseshit. It sticks to my metal appendage, you know." He eyed Evans sternly. "And I'm mighty glad to hear you finally be a man about it and admit you're second best. I just wish I had it on tape so I could play it fer Popeye." He grinned.

Keith missed the Teams, and he was excited about his new prospects. His old commander had just given him a new lease on life, a new team of SEALs that was just his style.

Evans studied the maimed warrior. For a few seconds he questioned his decision to hire Keith. He was missing a leg and was heavy into alcohol. He didn't look like he was up to a counterterrorist mission.

Suddenly Evans felt as if he was walking into an ambush. A little voice inside his head was urging caution. During the last year of his tour of duty as commanding officer, SEAL Team Five, he had lost half a dozen men on a covert mission in Southeast Asia. Deceived by a female case officer and the U.S. military, a green platoon from Team Five had taken on a dozen battle-hardened Spetznaz in the jungles of Cambodia. Evans succeeded in recovering two nuclear weapons from the renegade Russians, but the human cost had been high. When his killed-in-action were reported as training accidents, he retired from the service a bitter man. Emotionally Derek Evans wasn't prepared to lose another team member in a secret battle against terrorism.

"What's wrong?" asked Keith, reading the vacant expression on Evans's face. "Scared?"

"I wouldn't say second best just yet, Pegleg," Evans warned.

"Wait till I get your ass on my private shootin' range," Keith bragged. "I've had a lot of time to practice." He grinned and patted his stump with his gun hand.

"Let's go do it," Evans barked.

Chapter 6

"VERDUCHI, PLAY THAT tape again," Rice ordered, then exhaled a cloud of cigarette smoke.

"Which one?"

"The one where young Mrs. Aguilar is screaming for more," Rice leered, showing a rack of yellow-gray teeth. His thin, dull hair was combed sideways to cover a bald spot. His ferretlike eyes were set wide above a bony nose, pinched cheeks, and a small Vandyke.

"Rice, you perverted son of a bitch. How many times are you going to watch that whore get laid?" groused the equally pale and seedy-looking Verduchi.

Both men had oyster-white complexions. Verduchi had long, curly hair combed almost like an Afro.

"As many times as I want," Rice said threateningly. "Three weeks in this buggy with the likes of you is driving me bat-shit."

"What is your problem, Rice? Are you some kind of voyeur?"

"Any way you cut it, what we do is voyeurism," Rice retorted, getting angrier by the second.

"Hey, man, it's one thing to surveil dopers and quite another to get off watchin' 'em get laid."

"So you think I'm a pervert, huh, asshole?"

Verduchi read the look on Rice's face and kept his mouth shut.

"Just remember who's in charge of this fuckin' operation," Rice shouted, coming unglued. "I got you this high-dollar job, Bobby-boy. Don't you forget it!"

He glared at Verduchi with unblinking eyes. The anger in his voice gave Verduchi pause.

"Hey, Ralph. I don't have a problem with that. I know you're in charge. I'm just tired of the same old shit, man," Verduchi simpered, trying to defuse the spat.

"All right then. Me too," Rice conceded. "While we wait for the DEA to bust these assholes, let's see what's happening in the condo."

The equipment inside the motor home provided audio and video surveillance over a distance of two miles, day or night, rain or shine, without the need to plant bugs or touch a telephone wire. Rooftop antennas intercepted atmospheric microwaves that were processed by onboard computers. Microphones picked up sounds inside buildings and used radio, telephone, and television speakers as receivers. Thermal and magnetic imagers penetrated the windows and walls of some buildings like X rays. They even had telescopic video capability.

Satellite communications allowed operators of similar equipment all over the world to relay information to headquarters in Texas and North Carolina, where it was processed and fed to the Drug Enforcement Agency, the FBI, and the CIA. It had taken Rice and Verduchi only two weeks to gather the necessary intelligence to bust the Aguilar cartel, a mission that would have taken the DEA years to accomplish.

During their spare time, the voyeurs had gotten to know the neighborhood intimately. Their equipment literally allowed them to become flies on the wall. The tape Rice was so fond of watching was of the Aguilars in the privacy of their bedroom. Their hot bodies showed up on video as reddish-orange figures. The computer filled in details, giving them an alien appearance. On each viewing, Rice would roar with laughter when the drug lord's erect penis began glowing like a candle in the night.

"Look at that donkey-dick son of a bitch, man! He's going to choke her to death with that thing!"

But it was Mrs. Aguilar's moaning and cooing that excited Rice and compelled him to visit the motor home's bathroom. That disgusted Verduchi.

Surveillance operations were by nature boring. They consisted mainly of watching people do ordinary things like eat breakfast, cook dinner, or wash the car. As they waited for the crucial conversation that would allow the DEA to arrest the narcotics traffickers in the act, Rice and Verduchi had amused themselves with the marvels of the electronic age. It was easy. Too easy. And no one knew they were there. Not even the DEA knew they were involved in the operation. The real-time intelligence they provided passed through a filter.

Verduchi focused the microphone on the wall of a condo and twisted the control knob. As he tuned in the signal, a woman's voice crackled over the speaker.

"Joan, you're not going to believe this," the woman said. "Donna told me Cindy is having a fling with Chuck."

Verduchi punched a button on his console that linked the microwave signal of the call.

"Mary," warned the lady on the other end of the line, "the way Donna gossips, you can't believe a word she says."

"Well, where there's smoke, there's fire, and I've seen the smoke with my own eyes. Someone's got to tell her," Mary continued.

Verduchi terminated the signal and shook his head. He focused the microphone on the next apartment. The sound of a shower running caught his attention. He raised one eyebrow as he looked at Rice.

"I hope it's an outside wall," Rice muttered.

The surveillance equipment worked better if it only had to penetrate one wall. Rice directed the powerful imager at the apartment. It took several seconds for him to adjust the signal. When the computer finally locked on target, a heavyset woman with pendulous breasts came into focus. She was rubbing soap under her armpits.

"Yuck!" exclaimed Verduchi. "I guess we'll have to wait for Judy-Judy to come home to see some nice T and A." He hit a button and the recording of the Aguilars in action filled the monitor.

"You know, Bobby, I think I'm gonna ask for a female partner for my next op," Rice announced. "You're beginning to get on my nerves," he continued, rubbing his beard. "You think Nancy would like to play? Does this kind of shit turn her on, man?"

"How the hell should I know, Rice?" The question pissed him off.

"I just have a hunch you know what trips her trigger, good buddy," Rice snickered.

"If you request a new partner, I'll tell your wife what you do for a living."

"And just what would you tell her, Bobby-boy? You blow the cover on S-Systems and the Company will terminate your ass. Permanently."

"Oh, I'd tell her you keep a library of videotapes—special ones, ones documenting the sexual exploits of the rich and famous. Then I'd send her a copy of the one of you giving a blow-by-blow commentary on the Aguilars' sexual performance."

Mrs. Aguilar's heavy breathing and moaning filled the motor home as she reached orgasm.

"I wouldn't do that if I were you, Verduchi," Rice growled.

"And why not?"

"Because I'd send Cheryl a copy of that little rendezvous you had with Fancy-Nancy in the backseat of your Chevy."

"Rice, you son of a bitch!" Verduchi yelled. "Have you been doggin' my ass?"

"That's the price you pay for working in this business." Rice grinned. "I was just doin' my job, Bobby-boy, makin' sure you're not a Commie."

"You didn't?" Verduchi pleaded.

"Don't piss me off," Rice threatened, "or you'll find out the hard way."

"Works two ways, Ralph," Verduchi warned.

"I've been at this a lot longer than you, Bobby-boy. You'll be playing catch-up for the next ten years," Rice taunted.

Verduchi looked at his partner long and hard, wondering where Rice kept his private stash of videotapes.

"I'm tired of this shit hole, and I'm tired of watching other people get laid," Verduchi exploded.

"Calm down, Bobby-boy. As soon as this bust goes down, we're out of here."

"What next?" asked Verduchi in a subservient tone.

"Atlanta."

"Atlanta? What are we gonna do there?"

"To keep tabs on some lady scientist."

"What kind of scientist?" asked Verduchi, with a dubious expression on his face.

"Some ditsy virologist," Rice answered. "The FBI had a tail on the bitch, but they're too short of agents to follow up."

"Espionage?"

"No."

"The Feds don't follow people around without a damn good reason. So why are we puttin' the dog on her?"

"A favor," Rice replied. He was watching the Aguilars so intently he lost track of the conversation.

"For who?"

"Oh, somebody very, very important," Rice babbled.

"Who?" Verduchi demanded.

"Senator Carson."

"Carson, as in antiterrorist task force Carson?"

"Yep. One and the same," Rice replied.

"Doesn't figure. Why would terrorists hit on a scientist?" Verduchi argued.

"According to Bullethead, it's just a loose end," Rice replied.

Bullethead was the nickname they had given their bald boss, David Shipler.

"I thought something big was supposed to be going down. Why's Shipler wasting our time in Atlanta?" asked Verduchi.

"Who knows."

"What are we supposed to do after Atlanta?" Verduchi pressed.

"I don't know," Rice moaned. "We get paid to run surveillance, asshole. It doesn't matter who the target is. You'll get home to Fancy-Nancy in a few weeks." He grinned.

Verduchi ignored the comment. "Whatever keeps the suit happy," he said, referring to David Shipler. "You know, she's probably uglier than sin," he continued.

"Who?"

"The lady scientist. We'd better get you some new porn before we head for Atlanta," said Verduchi.

"Yeah, maybe a couple of kids doing it in the backseat of an ol' Chevy." Rice grinned. "A big old chunky-butt girl who squeals like Fancy-Nancy. 'Ohhhh, Bobby, Bobby. Ohhhh, Bobby. It feels so gooood!'" He burst out laughing.

"Rice, you son of a bitch!" Verduchi shouted. "Remember, paybacks are hell."

"You can't win at this game, Bobby-boy. Don't even think about it."

Chapter 7

DR. SUSAN DORN stared at Dr. Doris Lubeck as she entered the small office they shared on the fourth floor of Building 15. Lubeck artfully dodged her way around a stack of books, threw her purse on the desk, and slumped into the chair opposite Susan. The room was barely large enough for one person. With two scientists sharing the space, it was cluttered to the ceiling with books and papers.

Lubeck read her colleague's face and said, "What's wrong, Susie? You look like you've seen a ghost."

"Worse. Mussorgski's dead," she said, referring to one of two cynomolgus monkeys they were using in a Level Four experiment.

"What?" Lubeck gasped, sitting bolt upright in her chair. "When? How?"

"About two hours ago. A few minutes after you left the lab he began coughing and wheezing with typical influenza symptomatology."

Lubeck's face turned ashen. The virus they were studying was cultured from samples taken from the victims of a deadly epidemic in Cameroon. It was unusual for a virus to be lethal to both man and monkey. For months they had worked on classifying agents in the tissue samples taken from human and rat corpses Fawcett and Poland had found in the Pygmy villages. Finally Dorn had a breakthrough. She succeeded in isolating a new filavirus that turned out to be similar in structure to Ebola Zaire. But it was significantly different, and difficult to culture. For weeks thereafter they had labored to grow the new virus under laboratory conditions. After exhaustive effort, Lubeck had discovered a culture process. With sufficient quantities of viral material on hand, they proceeded to animal studies. They had named their test animals Beethoven and Mussorgski after their favorite composers.

"Did he drown?" asked Lubeck.

"I don't know. We'll have to wait for the necropsy."

The words that most disturbed Doris Lubeck were *typical influenza symptomatology*. She, like Dorn, feared a virus that was transmitted like the flu but was lethal like Ebola Zaire. All of the scientists at the CDC feared such a biological monster, and they knew with a degree of certainty that one would eventually emerge from the rain forest to cause a raging pandemic. They also knew that mankind wasn't prepared for a biological disaster of that magnitude. Lubeck studied Dorn's face, reading her emotions like a book.

"What else is troubling you, Susan?" she asked, already knowing the answer.

"Delay in the onset of symptoms, but quick cellular disintegration once symptoms appear."

"Susan," Lubeck cautioned, "let's take this one step at a time."

"Two weeks ago we isolated Mussorgski and Beethoven in the lab. Four days ago we injected Mussorgski with the virus. There was no reaction for three days, Doris. Three days. But within an hour of the onset of symptoms, he was in terrible condition. His temperature soared. Mucus streamed out of his nose. His stomach distended until I thought it was going to rupture. After an hour of agitated distress, he curled up in a fetal position, wheezing and gasping for breath, and died of massive exsanguination."

"How bad was it, Susie?" Lubeck asked ungently.

"Here's the video," said Dorn, handing her colleague a tape. "Doris, it was horrible. He presented the entire gamut of symptoms, from acute respiratory problems to gastrointestinal distress. During the worst bouts of coughing, the conjunctiva literally exploded. Blood oozed from his eyesockets. Then his nose. Before he expired, blood was seeping from his anus. And then the most bizarre thing happened. The entire cellular structure collapsed. The only thing left is fur surrounding a mass of decomposing protoplasm."

Their eyes met and they exchanged a look of naked terror.

"The question is, how is the disease transmitted?" Dorn continued.

"Is Beethoven showing any symptoms?" Lubeck asked.

"Not when I left the lab two hours ago."

Mussorgski had been deliberately infected by injection. Beethoven was the control animal. The next experimental question to be answered was whether Beethoven would contract the disease from Mussorgski.

They had been careful not to allow the two monkeys to have physical contact of any kind. The only thing they shared was the air they breathed inside the Level Four lab, and it was constantly filtered. If Beethoven contracted the disease, it was logical to assume that the method of transmission was aerosol, through microscopic droplets ejected during Mussorgski's sneezes and coughs.

"When is the necropsy scheduled?" asked Lubeck.

"First thing in the morning. Dr. Reinhardt is going to conduct it himself."

"I'll suit up and run a chem panel on Beethoven," Lubeck said.

"I'll go with you," Dorn offered.

"No. You look exhausted, Susan. Go home. Get some rest. You've been here more than twenty hours."

"Doris?"

"Yeah."

"Have you looked in the mirror lately?"

"No! Do I look that bad?" Lubeck asked.

"Like you haven't slept in days."

"I always look that way," Lubeck snapped. "You don't."

"Neither of us has been getting enough sleep. Let's go check on Beethoven, and then I'll go home for a few hours," Susan insisted.

"Susan Dorn, I'm going to have a sign made up to remind you not to worry so much. How about, 'The viruses that infect mankind have good reason for sparing our lives. They need us to survive'?"

"I know, I know. I've told myself a thousand times that we have evolutionary defense mechanisms against these monsters. But if Beethoven dies, we could have a killer on our hands the likes of which the world has never known."

"I disagree. Mussorgski died less than ten hours after the onset of symptoms. Right?" asked Lubeck.

"Yes."

"And the epidemic hasn't spread beyond that one isolated patch of jungle in Africa. Right?" she continued.

"Correct," Dorn agreed.

"And neither Poland nor Fawcett, nor any of the other field investigators, contracted the disease. The evidence so far indicates that this virus is not easily transmitted, and when it is, it kills so quickly it wipes itself out. It's self-containing by virtue of its own virulence."

"That was true in the age of the horse, Doris. This is the age of the airplane. This disease has the potential to spread like wildfire," Dorn argued.

"One step at a time, Susie. Let's suit up and check on Beethoven. Maybe he'll play us some sweet music on the bars of his cage."

Susan fell in step with her colleague on the way to the lab. "Don't forget, I'm going to that microbiology convention in Rome next week," she said as they walked down the hall.

"How could I forget, you lucky hussy," Lubeck teased. "I wanted to go to that conference. I was hoping a good-looking Italian doctor would pinch my butt." She looked directly at Susan, trying to add humor to their deadly serious lives. "Who are you going with?" she asked, knowing the answer.

"Nick Fawcett."

"Nick, Nick, the handsome prick."

"Doris!"

"Well, he is." Lubeck grinned and shook her head. "He's a brilliant man, Susan. But he's a strange bird." She looked Susan directly in the eyes, knowing she was wondering what motivated the statement. "We are sort of an item, you know."

"What do you mean, 'sort of'?"

"Before he went to Africa, we used to spend a weekend every month at his beach house in Panama City. If you don't mind, I'll skip over the specifics of what went on inside that house and move on to the general relationship. We just drifted apart while he was in Africa. I must have written him two dozen letters. He only sent me a couple, and they weren't very affectionate. Since he's been back, he's been distant, like I have some kind of contagious disease or something."

"Has he asked you out since he's been back?"

"Yep. But things are not like they were before he went to Africa. Now he's as cold as a fish. Something's leaning heavy on the man's conscience. Maybe he's got a little African Princess on the side he doesn't want to tell me about."

"Perhaps it's his work," Dorn suggested.

"Maybe. Heck, what can you say about a guy who's into bizarre prokaryotes? Perhaps one of them has infected his brain . . . or his prick."

"Doris!" Susan protested. "None of us are getting any time to socialize."

"That's for sure," Lubeck agreed.

When they reached the passageway leading to the lab, Lubeck stuck her security card into the reader. The thick stainless steel doors opened with a loud clack.

"So how's *your* love life, Susan?" asked Lubeck as she pushed open the heavy doors.

"I don't have one and you know it."

"None at all? Not even a small distraction on the side? Some milkman or something?"

"No," Susan insisted.

"That's very unhealthy, Virologist of the Year. It's time you got over that jerk of a husband. How long has it been since your divorce? Two years?"

"One year, two months, three weeks, and two days."

"Not that you've been counting."

Dorn had recently received a prestigious award. As her immediate senior, Lubeck had submitted her name and had pressed hard to see that she was selected. The trip to Rome went along with the honor. She also knew Susan didn't have much of a life outside Building 15. There simply wasn't time. Susan worked sixty to eighty hours a week and had done so since her divorce.

"Nick is a bit too moody for you, but I wouldn't be surprised if he fed you a bottle of Italian wine and tried to jump your bones in a drunken stupor."

"Doris! Nick's a colleague and a gentleman. And he is seeing *you*. He wouldn't do such a thing."

"Don't bet on it," Lubeck smiled. "Any man who looks like Omar Sharif is used to plenty of action, and he's certainly not getting any from me anymore. Take it from me, honey, Nick's all man, and men are always true to form."

"How so?"

"Men are walking sacks of testosterone looking for a depository. Poor creatures spend their whole lives on the hunt, just following their penises around. They can't help it. It's hard-wired directly into their brains."

Susan giggled.

Doris continued, "I've often wondered why God didn't attach it to their foreheads. It would be much more useful to us women up there."

Her levity got the normally introspective junior scientist to laugh out loud.

"That would certainly make life a lot easier, wouldn't it?" Susan agreed.

"You bet. Among other things, we'd know at a glance when they were interested. The old flagpole would stand at attention and we'd know."

Both women laughed out loud. They reached the second set of security doors, and Lubeck punched in the security code on a fingerpad.

"Doris, have you ever met anyone you were instantly attracted to? I mean, from the first moment you saw him," asked Susan in a serious tone of voice.

Lubeck paused to look her in the eye. "Yes. Every good-looking guy with an Italian accent."

Unlike Susan, Doris was only average-looking. She took what life had to offer when it came her way. To her, Nick Fawcett was a prize beyond expectation.

"I'm serious," Susan insisted.

"So am I," Lubeck said with a smile. "But add French, Spanish, and German to the list." She stared at Susan, wondering what motivated the question. "Okay, gorgeous. Who is it?"

"Oh, you don't know him. But he knows who you are. In fact, he's seen you naked." Susan smiled.

"What? Now I'm really intrigued. Who is this handsome devil who has examined my anatomy without my permission?"

"One of the men with the congressional delegation we had through here a few weeks ago. I had dinner with him, or more accurately, a sandwich. I made him wait for me in the lobby for forty minutes."

"Good girl. Keep him on his toes," Lubeck said, pushing open the heavy doors.

"I have a date with him tonight. A real date this time."

"You hussy. I turn 'em on and you scoop 'em up."

Susan grabbed Doris by the arm. Panic flashed across her face as she stared at the other side of the room. Mouth open, Doris turned to look. Through one of the portholes she saw Beethoven moving back and forth in his cage in obvious distress. They rushed to the window and gaped at the poor creature. Mucus was pouring out of his nose. Blood was oozing from his eye sockets.

Chapter 8

DEREK EVANS ARRIVED at Building 15 at precisely seven-thirty P.M. to pick up Susan Dorn. On their first date she had seemed so ill at ease in his presence that when he had called to ask her out this time, her warmth and ready acceptance had surprised him. She wasn't in the lobby, so he took a seat and waited.

At eight he glanced at his wristwatch and wondered if she was going to make him wait as long as the last time or maybe stand him up altogether. At half past the hour he walked over to the reception desk and asked the guard on duty whether she was still in the building. She was, so he grabbed a newspaper and pretended to read while studying the people coming and going through the lobby. At nine Chief Johnson stopped to chat with him on his way out of the building as he headed home, informing him that something big was going on in Level Four. Evans decided to wait a little longer. At nine-thirty, nearly two hours after their rendezvous time, he was scribbling a note for her when he saw her pass through the security doors and check out with the guard. Her hair was still tied up in a bun, and she was dressed in a lab coat with white nurse's shoes. She absentmindedly headed out of the lobby without looking up from the notebook she was carrying.

"Dr. Dorn?" he said, catching up to her outside of the building.

"Oh, my God! I'm so sorry," she apologized, quickly taking off her glasses. They were dark-rimmed and schoolmarmish. "I . . . I . . . I completely forgot," she stammered. "Something came up and . . . and I forgot. Please forgive me?"

"Sure, Doc. But now you'll have to make it up to me." He grinned.

"How?"

"You buy?"

"Oh, Mr. Evans, I look a fright. I can't go anywhere looking like this."

"Derek, remember? And why not? You look marvelous to me."

"But I can't," she protested.

"Another man?" he growled, with a fake frown.

"No!"

"Then you can," he insisted, taking her arm. "I waited for you for two hours. The least you can do is have a chat with me." He led her protesting down the sidewalk.

"Too late for dinner, so how about a drink?" he asked, scanning the street in front of them like the point man on a patrol.

"No, I can't," she demurred, walking along beside him. "I have a lot of work to do tomorrow."

As they strolled along, she apologized over and over.

"I am really sorry about making you wait. Something came up that was rather shocking, and I lost all track of time."

"Let's have a glass of wine—on you, of course—and you can tell me all about it. I'm a great listener."

Evans escorted her to a small establishment that catered to many of the grad students at the CDC. He found them a cozy booth where he had the wall to his back and a view of the entrance, and when the waiter appeared, he ordered a carafe of wine and a plate of cheese and bread.

"So tell me about this problem that so intrigued you you forgot all about me," he said with his most engaging smile.

She blushed a little. "Actually, it's not the kind of problem I should discuss outside the building."

When the refreshments arrived, Evans poured her a glass of wine and passed it to her. She accepted it without protest. Even without makeup, Dr. Dorn was strikingly beautiful, Evans observed with pleasure. Her lips parted when she realized he was staring at her. They seemed to invite a kiss, even though her eyes were distant.

"Is something wrong? Are my eyes bloodshot?" she asked, thinking of Beethoven pacing in his cage.

"No. No. I just couldn't help noticing how beautiful you are."

"Why, thank you."

In the dim light of the bistro he locked eyes with her.

"You are an incredibly beautiful woman, inside and out," he said with sincerity.

"You're . . . you're very kind," she faltered, thrown off balance by the compliment. "But I know I look as tired as I feel. I've been working fourteen hours a day."

"Well, I won't keep you out late, and you don't have to tell me what's on your mind. It's written all over your face."

"That's the second time someone has said that to me today," she said testily. "Are my feelings really that transparent?"

"Yes."

"Well, just exactly what is my problem, Mr. Evans?" she demanded sharply. She regretted her tone as soon as she had spoken.

He shook his head in a knowing manner without taking his eyes off her. She looked away out of discomfort, and when she looked back he said, "A biological monster. A really, really, dangerous one. Dangerous enough to cause you to forget a date with a devilishly handsome man."

"You know all this by just looking at my face?" she asked in a tiny voice.

"Give me your hand," he ordered, "so I can confirm my suspicions."

He reached across the table and took her hand in his. His strength and warmth relaxed her and made her nervous at the same time. He examined her palm like a fortune-teller, then stared into her eyes. Still holding her hand, he said, "Something alarming is going on in your lab."

He watched her pupils closely. They constricted slightly and jumped to the right, indicating she was disturbed by the comment.

"That's amazing. You're right," said Susan, surprised by the accuracy of his guess.

She took back her hand and sipped her wine. After a few drinks she opened up. She needed male companionship, despite what her conscious mind told her.

"For several months Doris Lubeck and I have been studying a virus that we suspect killed several hundred people in Africa. One of our primates came down with the disease today."

"By your reaction, I take it the animal died horribly?"

"Yes," she said, studying his face.

"I'd bet a glass of wine that the disease spreads like influenza and kills like Ebola," Evans said.

"Were you a premed student at one time?" she asked.

"No. Just field medicine for combat."

"For a layman you certainly have a firm grasp of the problem."

"I had an excellent teacher."

"Oh?" said Dorn, raising her eyebrows. "Who?"

"You and several good books." He smiled. "I've read all your published works."

A look of pride crossed her face. "You should have studied medicine, you know."

"I don't like shooting at things I can't see, Doc," said Evans, not taking his eyes off hers.

The comment disturbed her. His physical power and presence were commanding. The words he used and his grasp of the situation were right on target, beyond the level of understanding she was accustomed to encountering. And the way he used the word *shoot* indicated he was involved in a world of violence she couldn't comprehend. She stared back at him with a level gaze until he spoke.

"I read an interesting article today. It said that the greatest single epidemic in history killed nearly twenty-one million people during the First World War."

"That is correct. It was Spanish influenza. The flu," she replied.

"This thing you're studying, does it have that kind of potential?" he asked.

"Oh, yes. Much worse. Much, much worse," she said. "But it's so virulent it kills within just a few hours, limiting the spread of the disease. As my colleague Doris puts it, it's so virulent it's self-limiting."

"Susan, I don't know much about medicine or diseases. But I have good instincts for danger. And I sense danger here."

She sipped the wine and stared at him. "Then I'll be your teacher," she announced. She gathered her thoughts for a few seconds before speaking. "The infectious diseases that visit us as epidemics share several common characteristics. First, they spread quickly and efficiently from infected persons to healthy persons, with the result that a whole population gets exposed within a relatively short period of time. Second, they are acute illnesses. People either die or recover in a relatively short period of time. Third, these diseases tend to be restricted to humans or animals. The agents causing them tend not to live in the soil or the air. Fourth, the fortunate ones who survive develop antibodies that leave them immune to a recurrence of the disease."

"So killer viruses need densely packed human populations to

sustain them, don't they, populations large enough for a new crop of victims to be available each generation?" Evans asked.

"You do understand."

"The one that has you so unnerved is different, isn't it?" Evans asked.

"Yes, I believe it is. I'm afraid it spreads long before the onset of symptoms. And therein lies the danger. Many of the emerging viral infections that concern me—for example, the twelve Doris and I are studying right now—are recent additions to our scientific knowledge. But they are not new in the true sense of the word. They've been around for eons. They are either already infecting humans in remote areas of the world, or the reservoir for the virus is some animal that mankind has little contact with."

"What causes these outbreaks?"

"More often than not, some form of human activity, some environmental or social change that promotes the transfer of virus from animal to man and man to man."

Evans peered into her eyes. "Could someone—say, a fanatic— deliberately spread such a disease?"

Her eyes opened wide. "Yes. I had a bad dream about just that sort of disaster. But anyone who deliberately spread such a disease would essentially be committing suicide as well as mass murder."

"But couldn't terrorists develop a vaccine for one of these killer viruses and then use it for extortion?" Evans returned.

"That is possible, given the knowledge and equipment required to develop a vaccine."

He looked deeper into her eyes. "When we first met, you told me you were concerned with physical security. Why?"

"I spoke to Chief Johnson about you. He's very impressed. He said that you're a Navy SEAL commander."

Evans nodded an affirmative. "Retired."

"He said I should tell you everything. I hope you don't think I'm overreacting," she said apologetically.

"Try me."

"Well, one night I was working late. It was two, two-thirty in the morning when I left the lab and walked down the breezeway toward my office. You know the feeling you have when you think someone is watching you?"

"Yes."

"Well, I had a feeling someone was behind me, so I turned around quickly. I saw a face in the window of the door, you know the double doors on the fourth floor that separate the breezeway from the stairwell?"

"Uh-huh."

"Well, I made eye contact, or at least I thought I did. It was just an instant. The light reflecting off the window obscured the image. I went over to the doors, but there was no one there. I was exhausted, so I thought I might have imagined the whole thing. I would have forgotten about it, but a few days later I saw the same man leaving the coffee shop across the street from Building 15. Then I saw him in a car. He followed me for miles."

"Describe him."

"Young, black hair, dark skin, deep-set eyes. A handsome young man with a troubled face."

Evans's thoughts were running wild, but he didn't dare let it show on his face. "And I'm the one who reads faces?" he teased.

She flashed a smile.

"I guess you don't see many Arabic men around here?" he asked, knowing there were hundreds of Middle Eastern students at the CDC.

"On the contrary. Thousands of students pass through this facility. Many of them are from the Middle East."

"Then it was what you saw written on this guy's face that disturbed you?" he probed gently.

"Yes. And my nightmare. I dreamed that terrorists blew up my lab and caused a terrible world pandemic that killed hundreds of millions of people. The nightmare kept recurring until I told Chief Johnson about the man. I haven't seen him since."

"Could it be an admiring student? I couldn't blame any man for becoming infatuated with you, Susan," Evans suggested.

She looked down at her glass coyly. "You think I'm overreacting?"

When she looked back at him he said, "No. No, I don't. Like you, I can read faces, and right now I can see you are in need of rest. I'll walk you to your car," he suggested with finality.

As they left the cafe, Susan gasped and grabbed his arm.

"What is it?" Evans asked.

"There!" she cried out, pointing at a gray sedan. "There he is!"

Evans looked in the direction she was pointing and saw a car peel out from the curb across the street. It melted into a stream of passing cars. He dashed out into the street, trying to get close enough to see the license plate, but the vehicle was moving too fast. Giving up, he rejoined Susan on the sidewalk.

"Are you sure it was the same man?" he asked.

"Yes. I'm sure. He looked straight at me. It's his eyes. His eyes," she insisted.

Evans knew it wasn't one of his men or a lawman. The FBI was too busy to tail a scientist.

"I'll follow you home," he suggested.

"Thank you."

They walked the short distance to the parking lot with Evans scanning the street like radar. When they reached her car she unlocked the door and turned to face him.

"I feel terrible about spoiling your evening. I'd like to invite you to dinner—on me, of course," she said apologetically.

"When, where, and what's the dress code?" asked Evans eagerly.

"I'm going to Rome next week for a medical conference. When I return, I'll arrange something. Perhaps Dr. Reinhardt can attend."

"As long as you're there, I don't care who else attends." Evans smiled.

Dorn blushed slightly. "Thank you for the compliment, Derek," she said in a soft feminine voice. "I . . . I really enjoyed your company tonight."

She held out her hand. He took it and looked into her eyes. As she stared at him, frozen by his gaze, her lips parted again, inviting him. So he pulled her closer.

"The feeling is mutual, Doc," he said, bending down to kiss her lightly on the lips.

Susan stood frozen like a schoolgirl staring at her first beau. She wanted to respond with fervor but couldn't. The wine and exhaustion had numbed her senses.

He smiled at her and said, "For the next few days I'll be out of town, but I'll be within three hours of Atlanta. Call me on my cell phone if you spot that guy again. Okay?"

"All right," she agreed, still stunned by him.

He helped her into the car and shut the door. As she drove out of the parking lot, she felt butterflies. The day, the wine, and the kiss had turned her stomach to quivers and her nerves to jitters. Then images of Beethoven invaded her mind, and the face of a troubled young Arab standing behind a thick glass window on the breezeway of the CDC.

Evans followed her home and watched from his car as she unlocked her front door. When she waved good-bye he sped off down
the street.

What a beautiful man, she thought.

Then she remembered her ex-husband.

Forget it, Susan, she told herself. *You're only seeing the surface.*

Chapter 9

ON THE OUTSKIRTS of Peshawar, Pakistan, Omar Azed watched as
three of his best men and a group of ex-Waziristan Scouts boarded a
beat-up tandem truck. They were all dressed in slate-gray clothes
that hung loosely about their bodies. The baggy clothing hid the
weaponry of close personal combat: pistols and razor-sharp knives.
Some of the men wore traditional Pakistani turbans, others saggy
woolen hats. All had the close-cropped beard and mustache of the
faithful. Azed waited until all of the men were on board before climbing up into the cab. A machine gun mounted over the top of the cab
announced their willingness to fight anyone who challenged them.

Suckled on Islamic fundamentalism in a squalid refugee camp
called Sabra, Omar Azed was the most fanatical terrorist in the Palestinian Freedom Council's ranks. He had taken Jewish blood on every
continent. Trained in Baghdad by Iraqi agents, he had prayed with
all his being for Saddam Hussein's success in the Gulf War. As a
member of Ibrahim Nasrallah's fifth column, which was allied with
Saddam Hussein, he knew that the tiny country of Kuwait was the
first step in Arab domination of the world's oil supply. But the Great
Satan, with his computers and secret aircraft, had won. When it was
over, Azed fell into a state of deep depression. He was preparing to
martyr himself with a suicide bomb when Aman Ayyad filled his life
with hope. Ayyad told him of a plan to strike the heart of the Great
Satan and asked him to join a secret society of *fida'i,* the faithful,
dedicated to the creation of a Palestinian state.

Known as Yassinists, after the village of Deir Yassin that had
been destroyed by Zionists in 1948, the *fida'i* had developed a campaign modeled on an American war plan. Azed wasn't briefed on the
details, but he was told that a brilliant Arab scientist, whose identity

was known only to the inner circle of the Yassinists, had conceived it. He knew only the man's code name: Prokaryotes, a word that had no meaning for him and sounded strange to his ear.

With piercing, hawklike eyes Azed glanced at the driver, then back at the other trucks in the convoy.

"Go," he grunted.

His mission was simple: Acquire the weapons of diversion for Operation Desert Decree. But it was no easy task: he was about to enter one of the most dangerous places on Earth. At thirty-three, he had been hardened by a lifetime of struggle and calloused by the sight of death. The Pathans didn't frighten him, or the Jews or the Americans. Like Ayyad, he was *fida'i*. Dreams of martyrdom and beautiful golden-haired houris anointing his body with oil filled his head. Nothing frightened him. He looked forward to death because he knew in his heart that beautiful houris were waiting for him in heaven.

The driver ground the truck into gear and let out the clutch, and the battered vehicle lurched away in a cloud of diesel fumes. Azed took off his cap and ran his fingers through his jet-black hair. In shape, size, and facial features, he was the spitting image of Aman Ayyad. Both terrorists had close-cropped beards, deep-set, coal-black eyes and dark olive skin. To Western intelligence organizations they appeared to be one man, a fact they often used to great advantage. Azed glanced back at the other trucks to ensure they were rolling, then settled into his worn-out seat for the long trip into the Khyber.

The little convoy rumbled west on an asphalt ribbon that wound through the mountainous tribal area of Pakistan's northwest province. A belt of land 80 miles wide running along the 350-mile border with Afghanistan, it was a no-man's-land of extremes. It was the stronghold of the Pathan, a wily, warlike tribe who, in a thousand skirmishes, had earned the grudging admiration of the British as the best guerrilla fighters in all of Asia. That was in the heyday of the British Empire, before 1947, when independent Pakistan and India were born. The old spirit endured. Guns still decreed justice in the tribal areas, where clansmen prized their weapons more than they did their women.

The Khyber Pass, the stepping-stone between central Asia and India, had served as a corridor for invasion since time immemorial. Those who lived there lived by the gun and the knife, a marginal existence of subsistence farming, arms dealing, and narcotics. In good times, the barren land was barely capable of supporting the Pathan. In bad times, people starved without the proceeds they got from the poppy and cannabis. Through the Khyber Pass flowed the refugees of the Russo-Afghan conflict and the Afghan civil wars, and with them the weaponry of modern warfare.

The Pathan, crafty and ruthless, easily separated their unfortunate guests from their weapons by trade and by force and made them available on the black market, along with hashish and heroin. Azed's mission was to procure four boxes weighing less than fifty pounds each and ship them to Atlanta, Georgia. Pathan sympathies were naturally with the Palestinians, as long as the price was right. Islam bound them together, along with fear and hatred of anything Western or Jewish. The key to Azed's success was money, and the PFC's secret Saudi benefactor had money to burn.

The weapons they sought were special: Stingers. A lightweight, portable, shoulder-fired air defense missle, the Stinger uses an infrared guidance system that allows the operator to acquire, track, and engage a target from any aspect. Once a gunner visually acquires a target, he aligns it in an open sight and interrogates the target with an IFF (identify friend or foe) transponder to confirm it is an enemy. When launched, the missile automatically homes to intercept. It is supersonic in speed, 2.75 inches in diameter, and weighs only 34.5 pounds. The United States had supplied them to the Afghan freedom fighters under a strict agreement regarding their accountability and use. But in war, accountability is impossible.

After Islam, the single most important weapon in defeating the Red Army was the Stinger. Even in the hands of ignorant guerrilla fighters, they were lethal. Stingers changed the course of the war in Afghanistan and sent the Russians back to Moscow licking their wounds like a buckshot bear. To the Afghan freedom fighter, it was Allah's revenge. To the Yassinists, it was pure and perfect terror. With a single Stinger missile they could bring down a fully loaded 747 at several thousand feet, like blasting a sparrow at close range with a shotgun, and they could fire it from almost any location in the approach corridor of an airport. But the Stinger was only a weapon of diversion in Operation Desert Decree. The Yassinists' real plan was to commandeer an American nuclear submarine.

The trucks labored along a dry riverbed and up a gorge, which led through the Khyber Pass. It was a harsh, rocky landscape, almost treeless, with gravelly, dry streambeds below and sun-blistered peaks above, and it bristled with violence. Stone walls and fortresses dotted the mountains. Picket posts capped every dominant crag. And men carried weapons openly. Feuding was a way of life. Some blood feuds had continued for more than a hundred years. The causes were the same: land, water, and women. Revenge was essential, weakness lethal. Ironically, the eye-for-an-eye justice of the Pathan discouraged violence. An armed society is a mannerly society. Disputes in Islamabad or Rawalpindi might lead to the courts. In the Khyber they led to the graveyard.

Twenty miles up the canyon they stopped at a small village clinging to the side of the road. Azed met Sami, the Pathan chief's son, and exchanged greetings. Sami informed him that the exchange would take place at his father's house. Azed had dealt with the Pathan before, but he had never been invited to the chief's house. He reluctantly left his armed escort at the village and with his three men followed the Pakistani on foot. They trudged for half a mile up a narrow wadi before entering a small valley no more than a thousand yards across. Sami led them down the twisting, rocky trail toward a collection of hovels in the valley. Azed expected each step to be his last. There was no defense against a well-planned ambush. So he followed Sami closely enough to cut him in half with his AK if a shot rang out from his flanks. But there was no treachery, although the locals eyed them suspiciously.

They hiked directly to the center of the village to Haji Rehmullah's house, which was larger than most but little more than mud and stone with a sod roof. Inside a walled courtyard outside the main house, Sami invited them to sit at a table prepared for their meeting. The table was laden with raisins, cakes, almonds, and cups for tea. It was a good sign. Azed leaned his rifle against the table and took a seat in the shade to wait for his audience with the Pathan chieftan.

After a few minutes, the grizzled leader walked out in a flowing gray robe, making a show of his appearance. His turban was perfectly tied and his beard groomed like a holy man's. He took his seat at the head of the table and without speaking waved his hand at the open door. As he waited for tea to be served, he stared at the Palestinians with a menacing expression. Without looking at the bowl on the table in front of him, he fished among the almonds, selecting those with soft shells that could be easily cracked. Those he pushed toward Azed.

Another good sign, thought the terrorist.

When the tea arrived, Rehmullah spooned in the sugar and poured the milk himself, taking his time with the preparation. By serving his guests, he demonstrated his humility to Allah and welcomed Azed and his men. Hospitality among equals was as much a tenet in the Khyber as revenge.

Through Sami, they talked of battles won and lost and of the Palestinian war against the Jews. No mention was made of the Stingers Azed had come to procure. Haji Rehmullah recounted the Pathans' battle against the Moguls. He told Azed that his people had slaughtered forty thousand Moguls not two miles from where they were seated. Then he spoke of the British with bitterness in his voice. He sent one of his sons into the house for an old breechloader captured from an English soldier he had killed. Holding the weapon fondly, he made a gift of it to Azed. Then he spoke of a Pathan leader who had been slain by treachery, all the while eyeing the Palestinians with hard, suspicious eyes.

"The British tricked him, killed him, and cut out his heart. They took it to England in a little casket lined with silk. It is in a museum there," he explained. Then he spoke in a booming voice. "No one shall cut out my heart." He slapped himself proudly on the chest with an open palm and searched his guest's eyes for weaknesses. "It is peaceful now," he continued. "The government has convinced me to cooperate."

The Pathan did cooperate with Islamabad as long as the government looked the other way when it came to the poppy and cannabis. What the world called drug smuggling the Pathan simply called trade.

"Besides," said Rehmullah, "it is my government now. The government of Pakistan. I have no cause for fighting my own people."

He waved his hand and two of his sons ran into the house. A few seconds later, they appeared carrying a wooden crate painted U.S. Army olive drab. They placed it on the ground near their father and retrieved three similar crates. Azed bowed his head in respect, not moving to inspect their contents. To do so would have been an insult.

"I do not want to shoot down the planes of my own people. But with these you can shoot down the planes of the Jews." Rehmullah smiled for the first time, nodding his head like a monarch. Taking his cup, he sipped the sweet tea, watching Azed carefully as he reached into his robe.

The terrorist's movements were slow, deliberate, and nonthreatening. To do otherwise invited death. He respectfully handed the old man an envelope containing the numbers to a Swiss bank account established in his name. Rehmullah put down his cup and opened it, expecting to see money; upon seeing only numbers, his eyes grew angry. He slammed the envelope down on the table and glared at Azed. It took several minutes for the Palestinian to explain the advantages of banking through Switzerland. But still Rehmullah was not convinced. He had allowed the Palestinians to train on his land. He had sold them weaponry, explosives, ammunition, and drugs to finance their operations, but always on a cash-and-carry basis. He smelled treachery, and he wasn't about to let a Palestinian put his heart in a little silk-lined casket.

"Malik, I have a gift for you," said Azed, using the Pathan word for chief. He reached slowly into his robe and pulled out a small cloth sack containing a handful of sand.

"This is the sand of Mecca I promised I would bring to you, Malik," he said, handing the old man the bag. "I swear before the Prophet that it is from the ground near the holy Kaaba."

Azed made the traditional gesture, touching forehead, lips, and heart.

"Allah be praised," mumbled the old man.

With great reverence Rehmullah took the bag and marveled at its contents. He had fulfilled four of the five pillars of Islam: belief, prayer, almsgiving, and fasting. He had recited the *shahadah,* confirming his belief in God and His sacred book. Five times a day he prayed directly to Allah, kneeling, prostrating himself in humility and facing toward the Kaaba. He had given more than 2½ percent of his income to the poor of his village, sharing God's blessings with those less fortunate. And during Ramadan, the ninth month of the lunar calendar, he always fasted faithfully. But he couldn't conceive of fulfilling the fifth pillar, the *hajj,* the holy pilgrimage to Mecca, which he considered beyond his reach because of his age and the great expense of travel to Saudi Arabia. Rehmullah had no idea that the Swiss account Azed had funded for him could pay for a hundred trips to Mecca. Reluctantly, he agreed to the transfer of two of the four missiles, more for the sacred sand than for the promise of wealth beyond his dreams.

Azed departed the Khyber with half his merchandise and drove nonstop to Islamabad. There he delivered the weapons to Raji Shah, a professional drug smuggler and business associate of Ibrahim Nasrallah. Shah's job was to smuggle the weapons into the United

States, one concealed within a crate of soccer balls, the other in a shipping container of clothing produced in the sweatshops of Islamabad. The probability that U.S. Customs would open the containers and discover the illicit cargo was nearly zero.

Mission complete, Azed dispatched his men and serviced his dead drop in Islamabad. Only two people in the world knew of the drop's existence, and he was one of them. But still his heart raced with anxiety as he walked into the crowded post office. His tradecraft training in Baghdad had stressed the importance of servicing dead drops professionally. They were the weak point in clandestine communication. Iraqi instructors would watch a drop for weeks for the opportunity of following a pigeon back to its loft in hopes of catching a whole flock. They had always picked him up at his dead drops because they had created them and assigned them to their students. The penalty for allowing an instructor to follow was severe, and Azed had learned his lesson the hard way. But discovery in the real world would bring more than the wrath of an Iraqi instructor. Israeli agents would kill him, given half a chance, and they were hot on his trail.

He unlocked the mailbox and peeked inside. His heart began pounding when he saw the envelope.

A message from Ayyad, he thought.

He stuck the envelope into his pocket and left the building as quickly as he could without drawing attention to himself. Outside on the street, he looked for a bus. His heightened senses told him not to look at the cabdrivers. Israeli informants and agents often took jobs as cabbies. It was excellent cover and put them at the center of activity in many major cities. He kept his gaze downcast or straight ahead as he walked toward the curb. Out of curiosity or stupidity or both, he sneaked a glance at the corner. One of the cabdrivers was turning in his direction just as he did so. A second more either way and he would have been safe. But their eyes met, and although they held the glance for the briefest of flickers, it was enough. In that instant he was made, and he knew it. Azed saw the blandness and the boredom of a cabby's life disappear, replaced by a spark of recognition. As he turned away, he saw the malevolent frown and a hand motioning for assistance.

Azed cursed bitterly through clenched teeth. There wasn't a bus in sight. Grabbing the nearest taxi, he ordered the driver to go to the south side of town, hoping that he wasn't an agent as well. He positioned himself directly behind the driver and watched the rearview mirror. Behind them he spotted a beat-up blue cab turn around and race after them. Two men were in the backseat.

Ordering the driver to hurry in crowded Islamabad was a waste of words, so Azed kept silent. Through luck, they put several blocks between them and the pursuers. Then they got snarled in a traffic jam. Fidgeting, Azed watched every direction like a hawk, expecting the doors to fly open and armed thugs to drag him out for interrogation. Paranoia consumed him. When he saw the back doors of a blue cab swing open halfway down the block behind him and two burly men exit in haste, he bailed out in a flash and ran into the crowd on the sidewalk. With an angry, unpaid cabby shouting curses at him, Azed ducked into a side alley and sprinted half its length. He cut through a restaurant and back through the messy kitchen, knocking down an old woman carrying a large pot of steaming rice. Pans clattered and porcelain crashed as he scrambled to get out of the building. In full stride he ran down a narrow alley full of wicker baskets overflowing with garbage and spilling onto the pavement. Near the intersection with the street he slowed to a walk. Wiping the sweat from his brow, he rounded a dogleg corner and bumped into a man, almost knocking him down. Seeing it was a Sikh, he apologized and hurried up the street. He caught an overloaded bus at the corner and lost himself in the crowd.

Several miles down the line, he jumped off and ran two blocks. With chest heaving and lungs burning, he caught another bus headed in the opposite direction. For hours he rode around the city until he was sure no one was following. Finally, well after dark, he caught a bus that took him to within a mile of his safehouse in a dingy apartment building owned by Ibrahim Nasrallah. On foot, constantly searching the faces on the sidewalk around him, he hurried to a restaurant he frequented. There, using the house telephone, he called his second-in-command and gave orders to rendezvous at nine o'clock. He ate a big meal, then, using the alley behind the restaurant, sneaked up to his apartment building. Before entering, he cased the entire area.

Azed faded into the entrance like a phantom and raced up the stairs to the second floor. Once inside his room, he threw the envelope on the bed and went directly to the window. Standing behind the curtain, he observed the street for several minutes. Israeli agents were everywhere, and they would torture him to death for what he knew. Satisfied that no one had followed him, he took out the envelope and opened it. Inside there were several photos of an Anglo, the size required for a passport, and a message written in code on a single sheet of paper. He recognized the penmanship as Ayyad's.

333-1-14 778-1-17 1279-2-6 1116-1-8
911-1-5 563-2-5 444-2-1 371-2-22 861-2-20
John Albert Robbins 3-19-67
336-1-14 447-1-29
971-2-6 114-2-1 1255-2-4 1337-2-6 297-1-19

Azed checked the street again, then took an old pocket dictionary out of his suitcase. Its spine was broken, and some of its yellow, worn pages had separated loose from the binding. It was the first of twenty editions, and it had been out of print for more than a decade. He opened it to page 333. In the first column he counted down fourteen words and wrote the word "do" under the numbers *333-1-14.* He continued the process until he had decoded the entire message.

do not use sponsor
procure identity for enclosed picture
John Albert Robbins 3-19-67
eliminate forger
rendezvous strike two without delay

Azed looked at the photo again and grimaced. It was the picture of a skinny Caucasian with cropped blond hair. The face was sharp, angular and pallid. To a Palestinian with dark olive skin and black eyes, he looked sickly white and ghostly. There were several photos. Personal information was written on the back of one of them. Azed recognized the numbers 3-19-67 as the birth date Ayyad wanted on the identity papers.

An American, he thought. *Aaaah! . . . The Judas goat.*

The first line, "do not use sponsor," ordered him to conduct the mission without the help of their Iraqi or Saudi patrons, who often provided money and forged identity papers.

Ayyad is worried about leaks, he thought.

Both men were paranoid to the point of delusion. Ayyad didn't completely trust all the members of the Palestinian Freedom Council, and he had made his suspicions known to Azed.

"Jews are experts at infiltrating Arab organizations," he often told him. "We must be careful in everything we do."

I know one Jew bastard we won't have to worry about again, thought Azed, *because tonight I'm going to kill him.*

Strike Two was a prearranged location in the farm country of southern Georgia. Azed retrieved one of several fake passports from a secret compartment in his luggage and made reservations for a flight to Rio de Janeiro with connections to Panama. In Colón he could acquire a passport and a new identity for John Albert Robbins before infiltrating the United States by cruise liner.

At nine o'clock Mohammed reported as ordered, and the two of them took a bus to the outskirts of town. There they collected two more men and four AK assault rifles. Using an old English Ford that had seen its best days, they drove to the center of the city, to the airport, to the train station, and back to the center of town. For an hour they cruised the streets around the post office searching for a beat-up blue cab. Azed was about to give up when he spotted it parked outside a coffeehouse. They waited up the street until the driver appeared.

"That's him," Azed hissed. "Let's kill that Jew bastard and leave this wretched country."

"How do you want to do it, Omar?" asked the driver.

"Follow him!" Azed yelled. "Wait until I tell you, then cut him off."

"Okay."

Mohammed squealed off in pursuit. Speeding through the busy streets of Islamabad, they followed the blue cab until Azed lost patience.

"There! Cut him off!" Azed barked, pointing at the intersection ahead of them. The cabby had stopped for a traffic light at a busy corner.

There were other vehicles at the intersection and people on the street, but Azed didn't care. When the mission was over, he intended to burn the Ford and leave the country. Racing up beside the cab, Mohammed jammed on the brakes and screeched to a stop. When the Ford came to rest, its front bumper was slightly in front of the taxi's. From the backseat, Azed leveled his rifle at the cabdriver. Sheer terror flashed across the man's face as a spark of recognition registered in those dark Jewish orbs. He turned away to jam the car in reverse, but it was too late. Azed cut loose with a thirty-round magazine. The heavy-caliber weapon blasted through the thin metal of the door and tore the body to shreds. A single round struck him in the head, exploding his skull like a ripe melon, spraying the inside of the vehicle with blood and brain matter.

"Muktub, you fuckin' Jewish pig! *Idbah al-adu,* slaughter the enemy!" Azed screamed.

At six hundred rounds per minute, the savage attack took mere seconds to execute. Mohammed peeled off in a cloud of dust and smoke, leaving dumbfounded witnesses in shock, too numb to accurately describe the assassins.

Chapter 10

"THE 1990s HAVE WITNESSED a steady, upward spiral in terrorist activity around the world," Derek Evans announced to the gathering of security personnel from the Savannah River nuclear power plant. They were dressed in uniform, complete with wheel gun, ready to go on watch. The pictures he was showing of the aftermath of terrorist attacks shocked them. Men and women, young and old, had their eyes glued to the screen as he talked of atrocities in faraway places. The images were mostly of bombed buildings such as the Marine barracks in Lebanon and the NATO headquarters in Brussels, but some were of bloody human victims. The carnage of the Lod Airport massacre achieved the results he was looking for.

"Much of the growth in terrorism is due to the virulent virus of religious and ethnic warfare."

He knew the second he'd said it that the metaphor was out of place. Evans had Susan Dorn on his mind.

"Let me rephrase that," he said. "Terrorism is the tool of the oppressed and the fanatic. It is a method of warfare used by those who cannot fight major battles, so they strike at symbolic targets to get attention for their cause. Incidents inspired by ideological agendas continue to increase around the world as faith and flag motivate fanatics and crazies to assault the existing order. Radicals believe that they must destabilize the political environment to achieve their objectives. Both the nature and scope of recent attacks point to a growing willingness to resort to ever more destructive methods. With our borders wide open, we can't hide behind our two giant tank ditches like we did during World Wars I and II. In the day of the airplane, the Atlantic and the Pacific are just too small."

He clicked the slide projector and a picture of a huge collapsed building in Oklahoma City filled the screen. "Bombing is by far the preferred method of the fanatic. Recent targets have included embassies, military bases, bars, hotels, cars, and the World Trade Center. It's just a matter of time until some crazy strikes a nuclear power plant like Savannah River. And you'd better be ready when they do," Evans warned.

He walked out among the guards in the briefing room. They all sported Smith and Wesson .38-caliber revolvers tucked away in hip holsters, and they were range qualified, but they were no match for the firepower of a squad of terrorists armed with assault rifles. They weren't trained warriors, just family men and women with kids at home. Security guard was simply a job they did to feed hungry little mouths.

Evans wanted to impress upon his proud-to-be-redneck charges that the plant was a choice target, without telling them he suspected an attack was imminent somewhere in the state.

"The controversy surrounding nuclear power and the potential for catastrophic accidents makes any nuclear site a highly desirable target for extremists," he continued. "You must be vigilant! In today's climate, with crime and terrorism on the rise, security personnel must be proactive. Planning and exercising are essential. You see, training is like insurance. When you urgently need comprehensive security coverage, it may not be available unless you have trained as a team to provide it."

Evans hit the button on the slide projector, and a picture of Ayatollah Khomeini filled the screen. The religious ruler was standing with a group of American hostages from the U.S. embassy in Tehran. Behind him was a sign in large block letters that read, "Carter is supporting this." The audience could relate to Jimmy Carter, the peanut farmer from Plains, Georgia.

"My analysis shows a clear trend. Attacks on business interests around the world are increasing. Our mission at SOC Inc. is to help you improve your security posture in the most cost-efficient manner. We have been evaluating Savannah River for the last two weeks, and tonight my men will try to penetrate the plant. Your job is to stop them."

He looked around the room from person to person.

"Don't allow yourselves to get into a hostage situation. And if you do, don't overreact. You can't allow terrorists to gain access to this facility under any circumstances."

Evans turned on the lights and turned off the slide projector.

"Now I'll tell you something no terrorist will ever tell his victims: the time and place of the attack. My men will assault this facility between 2200 and 2400 hours."

Reading the faces in the audience, he continued, "For those of you who don't speak military time, that's between ten and twelve tonight." He smiled. "I don't know what method of infiltration they'll use. They may try to climb the fence, run the gate, or even drop in by parachute. There is one thing you can count on. They'll be here during that two-hour window with intentions of causing a nuclear meltdown. They have never been inside this facility, so they are working at a disadvantage. The only information they have concerning the operation of this plant is what they have been able to learn from libraries, city hall, and, well, let's say, from sneaky intelligence-gathering methods like buying liquid refreshments at local watering holes."

Several of the guards looked at one another with serious expressions of concern. Evans picked up on the eye signals.

"I see some of you are worried about things you've said in local bars. You should be! The first thing you have to get through your head is that this plant is a potential target, and your job is to protect it. It's nobody's business what goes on inside this facility. So don't tell curious strangers about your job. Be sensitive to surveillance, and if you suspect someone is watching you or the plant, report it immediately to Chief Townsend. Terrorist attacks are usually well planned. They will watch for days, weeks, months, perhaps years to learn your habits, your patterns, your comings and goings. My men have been studying you for the last two weeks. Has anyone noticed any suspicious-looking characters snooping around?"

The guards looked at one another with worried expressions and shook their heads.

"Okay. All personnel going on watch must physically show me that their pieces are unloaded," Evans said. "So we are not completely vulnerable during the exercise, an emergency response team will be on station in security headquarters. Chief Townsend and I, along with the ERT, will watch the perimeter and the exercise on the monitors. Are there any questions?"

"Are all of your men Americans?" asked a rough-looking country boy with shaggy hair.

"Yep," Evans replied.

"Well, it ain't fair, that you been spyin' on us with Americans," he drawled.

"Terrorists come in all flavors, mister. Make no mistake about that. And they don't all have funny accents like me," said Evans.

With the briefing and safety checks out of the way, Evans and Townsend headed for security headquarters. As they walked outside along a huge cooling tower, Evans marveled at the nuclear power plant. "This is an incredible facility, Chief," he commented. "You must be very proud of it."

"Yes, I am," replied Townsend. "A nuclear power plant is one of man's most sophisticated structures, but would you believe it's just a simple steam engine?"

"No."

"Well, it is. Heated water produces steam, steam drives the turbines, and the turbines drive the generators that produce electricity. It's that simple. The big difference is the heat source."

"In this case uranium-235?" asked Evans.

"Correct. Both Savannah River reactors use U-235. The dangerous part of the system, the business part, is the reactor core. That's why they're housed in huge cement containment buildings. The walls in some places are more than six feet thick. They prevent the release of the hot stuff in case there's a problem inside, like a busted pipe or something, and they keep out bad boys with bad intentions, like your crew," he said with a smile.

"My understanding of the system is rudimentary, Chief," said Evans, "but essentially the core consists of fuel rods separated by control rods, which can be raised and lowered depending on how much energy is needed, correct?"

"Right again," said Townsend, looking up at the containment building.

As they walked toward the security office he explained the physics of nuclear power. "Bundles of fuel rods composed of thousands of uranium pellets about the size of your thumb are separated by neutron-absorbing rods that can be raised or lowered to regulate the rate of fission. Energy from the reaction heats the water that surrounds and infiltrates the core. Actually, thousands of gallons of water circulate through the core all the time, but it's the same water used over and over again. It never leaves the containment buildings. This superheated water is pumped under pressure into tubes in a steam generator inside the containment building, where the heat is transferred to a secondary water system. It's this secondary water that produces steam for the turbines."

"And it's this separate system that transfers the energy out of the containment buildings to the turbines?" Evans asked.

"Yep. It prevents radioactive materials from escaping the containment building in case of an accident. We have redundant safety features like backup cooling and emergency systems to lower the control rods. A meltdown is almost impossible."

"What would happen if there was a meltdown?"

"If hot nuclear materials contact groundwater? Disaster. A radioactive cloud and a shower of poison would fall on the surrounding countryside. Contaminated land would be unusable for thousands of years."

"Chernobyl?" mumbled Evans.

"Uh-huh," Townsend mumbled back.

"But small amounts of explosives in just the right places could destroy the control mechanisms and backup systems, couldn't they?" Evans asked.

"Yep, but first, a terrorist would have to know where to place those explosives." Townsend smiled wryly. "And he'd have to get through my security to place them."

To prevent sabotage, the plant was surrounded by a heavy chain-link fence topped with razor wire. Cameras and guards constantly monitored and patrolled the perimeter. Motion sensors planted in the no-man's-land surrounding the plant were so sensitive that rabbits regularly set them off. Heavy gates with armed guards controlled all access points, and everyone who entered the facility was searched or electronically frisked. The plant appeared to be impenetrable, and Chief Townsend was confident his men were going to give SOC Inc. a black eye.

"Chief, do you know what 'Chernobyl' means?" Evans asked.

"No," answered the older man.

"It's a Ukrainian word for wormwood."

"So?"

"The book of Revelations tells of a poisonous star called Wormwood that will fall to Earth on Judgment Day, infecting the water."

"How about that," Townsend commented. "It fell too damn soon."

Country music blared from a small battery-powered radio in the bottom of the rowboat. Randy Travis was singing a sad song in his distinctive twang as the three men fished. They were dressed in jeans, sneakers, t-shirts and Atlanta Braves baseball caps.

"Ol' Sherry sure do fry a mean catfish," said Swan as he whacked a big cat in the head. He had just landed it, and he had to hit the fish several times before he succeeded in killing it.

"Maybe the commander will let me stick around here for the after-action report. I'm beginning to like that ol' girl's cookin'," he continued.

"Who you tryin' to shit, Popeye? It's the head you're attracted to. Me, I'm sick of fish, man," said Decker. "Greasy hush puppies, farts that smell like onions and women who talk in slow motion. I want a good burrito, man."

"Turn up your pacemaker, Sam, and beat your meat. You're just jealous 'cause me and Popeye have been gettin' laid regular," Jennings taunted. "You missin' your little Mexican tortilla?" he added in a fake Mexican accent.

"Yeah. Both of 'em," Decker snarled. "And if Evans don't start paying me more money, I'm headed for California."

Sam Decker was an awkward-looking man who could fix anything and had premature heart disease. Evans had hired him when the Navy mustered him out on a medical discharge.

"I don't want to hear no more insubordination," Swan growled.

"Insubordination? I'm not in the damn Navy no more," Decker snapped back.

"Look, partner. I don't know where I'd be if the commander hadn't have come along when he did. He's the only suit that'll give us busted-up bastards a chance," Swan declared.

"I'm just grousin', Popeye," replied Decker. "I don't mean nothin' by it. You know that. I like this sneak-and-peek bullshit. Hell, I'd work for room and board on any job the commander ramrods."

"I know what's wrong with Sam, Popeye," Jennings interjected. "He's pissed off 'cause he can't get in the water with us."

"Yeah. You're probably right. Short circuit," agreed Swan, changing the tone of his voice.

He didn't like the troops speaking ill of Evans, even in jest. Fred Swan had lost an eye while serving with the SEALs during Desert Storm. It had cost him his career. He was a good-looking man, well-proportioned and as muscular as an Olympic athlete. Unlike Sam Decker, who always looked like he needed a shave, he was clean-cut and clean-shaven. He had a boyish Dennis Quaid look about him that attracted women like a magnet. Swan grinned at Decker and winked with his good eye.

"I can too get in the damn water," Decker protested. "I just don't like the critters in there."

"You gonna miss all the fun," Jennings goaded.

"Oh, no, I'm not," sang Decker. "You don't know what's up in that pipe at night. Maybe one of them big Florida gators swam up in there, not to mention the giant likes of these slimy mothers." Decker smacked the head of a catfish with the kill-stick to make his point.

"Well, pretty soon they'll be a couple of SEALs up in that pipe, so the gators and the cats had better get out of the way," said Swan. "Saddle up, J. R. Time to go for a little swim. I'm tired of Sam's bitchin' and moanin'."

"Hoo yah!" Jennings answered with the SEAL battle cry.

For several days they had been studying the conduits into and out of the Savannah River plant, and they had discovered a critical weakness: an environmentally friendly fish return system. The main cooling water intakes were buried concrete pipes eighteen feet in diameter. They circulated water to and from the river through the plant's cooling condensers. From plans acquired from an environmental impact study, they had learned that river water flowed into a series of huge holding tanks and through a series of vertical concrete vanes, where fish were shunted off to a removal area long before the water reached the circulating pumps. Twice a day a basket lifted the live fish from a holding tank and flushed them back into the river unharmed. The return line was six feet in diameter and, when not in use, was mostly high and dry. In the reconnaissance phase of the operation, Swan and Jennings had gone into the line expecting to swim the two hundred yards to the fish holding tank. Sixty feet from the riverbank, however, they stood up and walked the rest of the way to the holding tank.

From other plans they conducted a target analysis, called CARVER, an acronym for criticality, accessibility, recoverability, vulnerability, effect, and recognizability. They discovered the critical nodes to the communications and control systems for the reactors, the cooling and backup cooling systems, and the piping that carried water in and out of the containment buildings. Using Play-Doh, they fashioned mock explosive charges just large enough to incapacitate the critical systems.

"Son of a bitch! I got a big one," yelled Decker, pulling up on his cane pole.

It was bent over so far it was about to break. He wrestled with the fish for two minutes before bringing it to the side of the boat. Jennings netted it for him and hauled it in. He shined his flashlight on the fish and tried to whack it with the stick to kill it but thumped the bottom of the boat instead. "Be careful, J. R. You'll knock a hole in this garbage scow," Decker complained.

"I don't care. I got my scuba on," replied Jennings.

"And be quiet, for Christ's sake," Decker barked. "One of them rovin' guards might get suspicious."

"Of what? Country music and rednecks drinkin' beer? We been out here four nights in a row slappin' mosquitoes, and no one's so much as said howdy," Jennings argued.

"Knock off the bitchin'. It's almost ten. Ah, hell. Let's go, J. R.," Swan ordered.

Jennings gave him a thumbs-up and slipped quietly over the side of the boat. Once Jennings and Swan were in the water, Decker handed them the waterproof bags containing their dry clothes and the mock explosive charges.

"Watch out for the snakes, J. R. I saw a big ol' cottonmouth slitherin' along the bank a few minutes ago," goaded Decker.

"Oh shit, man! I hate snakes," Jennings complained.

Without the use of flashlights the men felt around in the water for a few minutes, cursing as they searched for the underwater buoy they had rigged to mark the entrance to the fish return line. Finally Jennings located it and signaled Swan with a hiss.

"I got it," he whispered.

Swan swam over to the buoy. "Okay. Let's go," he said, then put his regulator in his mouth.

It was pitch dark as soon as they put their heads underwater. The two men carefully worked their way down the line by feel until they reached the cavernous opening that ran back into the plant. Once inside the pipe, Jennings turned on a powerful mag light to illuminate the passage. It was clean, dark, and cool inside the huge conduit. His flashlight gave off an eerie glow as it bounced beams off the walls that diminished into empty, watery space. Jennings slowly worked his way along the pipe, wary of cottonmouths, until he broke surface sixty feet inside the perimeter of the plant. He crawled on his knees for several feet before standing up.

When Swan took off his face mask, he commented in a whisper, "Man, I sure am glad this ain't a shit pipe."

Jennings chuckled. "Yeah, then we'd be fightin' off brown, wrinkle-necked trout instead of catfish."

"The kind that float on the surface when flushed?" Swan inquired.

"That be the ones. You ready?"

"Let's go do it."

The men waded and walked for two hundred yards. At the fish holding tank they observed the area for ten minutes before scaling the walls and scurrying to an outbuilding. In a janitor's room they removed their wet clothing and dressed in guards' uniforms, complete with wheel guns and badges. As they walked toward the first target, Swan told a joke in his best Southern drawl.

"Hey, J. R.?"

"Yeah, man."

"You know what catfish and women have in common?"

"No, Boss. What?"

"They're both bottom feeders, man," he said, grabbing his crotch and hitching up his pants with a grin.

Jennings chuckled. "You're bad, dude."

Evans was scanning the bank of security monitors in headquarters when he spotted them. He almost spilled his coffee in disbelief. It was 10:45 and they were already inside, and in the most critical area of the plant. He smiled inwardly as Townsend pointed out the elaborate security system.

"Commander, there's only one way to get into this plant without tripping a sensor, and that's through the gate," he said, pointing to the monitors covering the main entrance.

An older black man and an overweight white woman manned the kiosk.

"In addition to sensors in the fence, there are seismic detectors buried in the ground. When a sensor trips, a red light illuminates on that schematic and a tone alerts the man on watch. Perimeter cameras can be swiveled to the location to see what, if anything, caused the sensor to fire. Mostly we have to contend with rabbits, but occasionally a coon or a possum will light one off."

"What's to keep a helicopter from landing inside the perimeter and a squad of men assaulting the control room?" asked Evans.

"Nothing. We'd just batten down the hatches and wait for help to arrive. Getting into these massive buildings would be a big chore for anyone. Besides, I have several men on each shift who are experts with a long gun. We could pin down a small army until the cavalry arrived."

"I noticed that all the critical buildings have heavy-duty security doors. But I got to tell you, Chief, a little plastique would knock them down very easily. What kind of weapons do your men stand watch with?" Evans asked. The only weapons he had seen were the .38s.

"They have standard-issue pistols. But I have an armory here on site, where I store a few AR-15s and some Remington 700s for issue during emergencies," Townsend answered.

"You know, Chief, an unloaded weapon is like a car with an empty gas tank. Not much use. Your long guns are in a worse position. Keeping with the analogy, your jalopy has an empty gas tank, and it's locked up in the garage."

"I understand what you're saying, but the probability of someone assaulting this plant is so low I keep 'em locked up for safety. Between you and me, Commander Evans, I don't have the money for good training, and I ain't gonna let no unqualified person pack a loaded weapon. As you noticed, everyone has bullets, but not in their guns. Truth of the matter is, with affirmative action and all the other bullshit regulations I have to put up with, I have serious doubts about the weapons-handling ability of a sizable portion of my force. But there's always a few on watch I can count on. And besides, this place is built like a damn fortress. I worry more about one of the engineers going crazy than anything else."

Evans watched Swan and Jennings disappear off one monitor and reappear on another. They were joking and talking like they had worked in the plant all their lives. As he scanned the bank of monitors, his eyes stopped on the one focused on the main gate. The female guard had stopped a Ryder rental truck driven by Ray Keith. Evans knew Keith would get into the act somehow. His immediate thought was, *No one is watching the CDC.* Townsend saw Evans staring at the monitor and smiled. He had SOC Inc. up a tree and he knew it.

"You see that big gal there at the main gate, Commander?"

Evans nodded.

"Well, she's one of the best I got. She can shoot the eyes out of a possum on a dark night, and she's never late for work. Now watch her take your boy down." He smiled complacently and turned up the volume so they could hear the interchange.

"May I help you, sir?" she asked politely over the sound of the truck's engine.

"Nope. But I can help you, seeing as how you like to eat," Keith replied. "I have a delivery for the cafeteria."

"Sir, let me see your bill of lading, please," she said politely, although she was clearly incensed.

Keith fumbled around in the cab for several minutes. All the while, she held one hand on the grip of her pistol and stood just inside the door of the kiosk. Finally Keith handed down a clipboard piled with papers. She scanned them for a moment, confused by the disorder.

"It'll just be a minute, sir, while I confirm with the cafeteria."

She backed further into the kiosk without taking her eyes off Keith and picked up the phone. To her amazement, the cafeteria was expecting an order that corresponded to the bill of lading. She hung up the telephone and waddled back outside with a puzzled expression on her face.

"Excuse me, sir, but I'm not used to seeing a rental truck make deliveries to our cafeteria."

"Our regular truck crapped out," said Keith, spitting a big gob of tobacco out the window of the truck. A streak of juice ran down the side of the cab.

"Sir, I'll have to ask you step down and open up the rear of your vehicle," she insisted.

"Listen, lady. I only got one leg, and it's a long way down. Give me a break," Keith snarled.

She walked back inside the kiosk and called Townsend.

One of the women in the control room came over to the security chief and whispered in his ear. He quietly slipped away, leaving Evans at the monitors. He was gone just a minute. Shortly after he returned, both gate guards exited the kiosk with weapons drawn.

"Sir, get down from the truck!" ordered the big woman.

"What the hell is this all about?" Keith complained, staring down the barrel of her pistol. "Don't point that damn peashooter at me!"

"Sir, get down from the truck!" she yelled again.

"I'm gonna get down, all right, and shove that pissy little wheel gun up your fat ass," he yelled, opening the door of the truck.

He put his good leg down on the running board first, then lowered himself with his arms. The guards stared in disbelief at his peg leg. Keith had chosen an artificial leg with a narrow rod that ended in a circular rubber foot that looked like a toilet plunger.

"Sir! Get on the ground!" the big woman ordered.

"I ain't gonna do no such thing. And if you don't stop pointin' that gun at me, I'm gonna get pissed off, woman. I can see it ain't loaded," Keith snapped.

The older man holstered his pistol and walked quickly toward Keith. "Hands on the truck!" he ordered.

Keith stepped quickly to one side and tripped the old guy with a sweep of his metal appendage. The woman holstered her pistol and attacked like a pitbull, knocking Keith to the ground. She sat down on his chest, butt in his face. In the control room Evans burst out laughing.

"One of your men, I take it?" Townsend chuckled.

"You'd better hope so, Townsend," said Evans, "or you're in for one hell of a lawsuit."

Worry crossed the security chief's face.

With the help of her partner, she cuffed Keith, while he barraged her with obscenities and tobacco juice. With Keith subdued, they searched the back of the truck and found only food for the cafeteria. It took an hour of phone calls to prove that Ray Keith was a legitimate temporary deliveryman who possessed no contraband. During the hour, Big Bertha was treated to the scorn of an extremely angry Ray Keith, complete with curses she had never heard before and would never hear again.

Evans looked for Swan and Jennings on the monitors during the course of the exercise, but he never saw them again. They quietly placed their explosives and retired by means of the same tunnel they had used to gain entry. They ended the evening at their favorite bar on the river. It was a little all-night jukejoint where patrons brought their own bottles and told jokes. Moonshine was also available, and they had a jug ready when Ray Keith showed up. He described his part of the mission in graphic detail. Big Bertha was apparently fond of beans and had nearly gassed him to death during the struggle to cuff him. The story brought tears to their eyes.

The next evening, Evans debriefed the exercise for Chief Townsend, who was in total denial until he touched the mock explosive charges and checked their placement. The look on his face was more than embarrassment. It was shock. In his own video recordings, Evans showed him Swan and Jennings dressed as guards walking around the plant nonchalantly while Keith's diversion at the main gate was taking place.

"We could have engineered any number of diversions, Chief.

And we could have used a number of methods of infiltration, such as hang gliders or parachutes, to get in without tripping your sensors. Never rest on your success. The key to vigilance is training, drilling, and major exercises such as this one. A good exercise once in a while keeps people on their toes and prevents boredom. I recommend you form an exercise branch, a mirror image of your security team, only smaller. Transfer people back and forth from offense to defense to keep them fresh and involved. Challenge the exercise branch with finding new ways of penetrating the plant. And challenge the security branch with stopping them."

A defeated Chief Townsend nodded in agreement. He was the only member of the Savannah River security team who knew that the fake explosives had been planted in the right locations to cause a nuclear meltdown. The others received positive strokes for stopping Ray Keith at the main gate. Townsend quietly made a personal commitment to improve security, unaware that the eyes of terrorists were already focused on his plant.

Chapter 11

SHIMMERING WAVES OF overheated air rose in the darkness, enveloping the silhouette of the 747 parked on the tarmac. It had been there for three days, with a body lying at its nose. Another American would die within the hour if the terrorists' demands were not met. Walead Kasim stood watch with a pair of binoculars and a parachute flare. His mission was to warn his comrades if ground troops assaulted the big bird. From the rooftop of a small house in the hills above the airport, he saw patches of shimmering night air coalesce and float over the tarmac. Like ninjas, silent phantoms scurried rapidly toward the aircraft from all directions. At first Kasim thought he was seeing a heat mirage, but then the phantoms took shape under the belly of the plane. Not believing his eyes, he stood frozen with doubt and indecision.

It is the Great Satan!

When his mind registered the fact that commandos were assaulting the aircraft, he grabbed his parachute flare and with trembling hands ripped off the cap. Reversing it so the firing pin was in place, he struck the bottom of the flare on the rooftop. With a swoosh, it flew up toward the stars. Kasim waited anxiously for the telltale pop, signaling that the parachute had deployed and the flare had ignited. To his horror, a sparkling trail curved back to earth without sending the crucial signal.

Misfire, he thought, watching the rocket's trail fade. His mind was churning with indecision, and his heart was pounding so hard he couldn't think. He only had the one flare, so he grabbed his AK and fired into the night sky, sending up a stream of green tracers.

"An-nasr! Victory!" he cried out.

It was all he could do. But Beirut was a city at war, and shots in the night were the norm, not the exception. No one inside the great silver hulk noticed his signal. He grabbed his binoculars and focused on the 747. Men were scurrying up ladders into the belly of the aircraft. Explosions flashed on each side of the wings, and then the sound of thunder rolled by him. Flashes of light continued to appear like lightning inside the cabin—concussion grenades exploding in the aisles. The sound of voices seemed to float into his semiconscious mind.

Get down! Get down! Everybody down!

Screams of fear and moans of agony filled his head. Death and destruction came in the dark of night like an ill wind. In his mind's eye he saw finely tuned machine guns spitting bullets at the heads of his brothers-in-arms. His job was to warn them and he had failed. Screaming with anger, he pointed his rifle at the airport and fired off an entire thirty-round magazine.

In the name of the Prophet, die!

Green tracers arced out the distance in the darkness and disappeared, falling harmlessly to the ground a quarter mile short of the runway. In thirty seconds it was over. His comrades-in-arms were dead, new martyrs in the fight against Israel. It was the kind of precision work the Americans bragged about; two shots to the head of anyone who resisted; instant death at the hands of professional warriors. The heavy hand of Satan had fallen.

All is the will of Allah. Allah akbar, he mumbled in his sleep as his brain flooded with unconscious fury.

The effervescent images of his dream continued in a funeral cortege, surreal like the shimmering night air off the hot tarmac. Women wailed in high-pitched ululations, their tongues flicking back and forth in their mouths. Children cried, and old men yearned for their villages in Palestine. The black forms swayed back and forth, back and forth, as the cortege meandered toward the top of the mound where the heroes were to be laid to rest. There were no bodies, only photographs of the martyrs.

There is sand in the eyes of Allah. He has lost sight of the Palestinian people, Kasim dreamed. *Man makes his own heaven and his own hell right here on Earth. I only want to free my people.*

From the parapet of a minaret, a muezzin keened a lamentation for the dead.

Then the phantoms struck without warning: American-made F-16s. Like lightning knifing through the night sky, they came out of the south with a thunderous roar. Flashes of light filled the darkness in their wake with images straight from hell. Rockets exploded, sending fragments of steel whirling through the air like buzzsaws. Body parts rained down from the heavens, showering the pictures of the martyrs with flesh and blood and bits of bone. And like some thunderous moment from hell, the night grew silent, hot, and oppressive. Only the moans of the dying broke the silence.

From the disorder of his nightmare, Walead Kasim dreamed that he awoke to find himself in a sweat, seated on an airplane. He stared out the window at the earth below. In a flash, an explosion cast him into space, ripping the breath from his lungs as it blasted him outside the aircraft. He plunged toward the earth still strapped in his seat, still alive, unable to scream.

The bomb must have exploded. This is how she died. Strapped in her seat, holding her baby in her arms.

The wind took his breath as the aircraft seat spun and twisted in the air, plunging toward the surface of the planet at 120 miles per hour. *"Allah akbar!"* he cried, eyes closed in fear. When he opened them, the ground phantasmagorically rushed at him with certain death. He screamed, "Aaaahhhhh!"

"Nicholas! Nicholas! Wake up!" pleaded Susan Dorn, her hands on Fawcett's forehead and arm.

He opened his eyes wide. Mouth agape and pupils dilated, Nick Fawcett focused on Susan's worried face.

"Are you okay, Nick?"

"Yes! Yes!" Fawcett gasped in a quivering voice. "I just had the most horrible dream. I dreamed the airplane exploded and I was falling."

"Heaven forbid." Dorn carefully studied his demeanor. "Would you like a glass of water?"

"Yes. Thank you, Susan," he replied, then swallowed hard.

Dorn pushed the call button and, when the flight attendant appeared, asked her for water.

"I have a Valium in my purse," Dorn offered.

"Please. I could use something to calm my nerves," answered Fawcett, hands covering his face. He was still trembling when the flight attendant returned with the water. Nick Fawcett, given name Walead Kasim, code name Prokaryotes, took the Valium, gulped down the water, and slumped back in his seat. He closed his deep blue eyes and took several breaths. His blue eyes and aquiline nose were his heritage from a French Crusader, long since dead. They had masked his true identity for more than four decades. Fawcett didn't look like an Arab, he didn't talk like an Arab, and for the most part, he didn't think like an Arab. His cry to Allah was insincere. Nick Fawcett wasn't a Muslim or a Christian. He was an atheist. He didn't believe in the god of the Jews or the god of the Arabs. He was a scientist, a mechanist, grounded in facts and cause and effect.

Walead Kasim had been born in the small Palestinian village of Deir Yassin, which Zionist soldiers attacked in the spring of 1948, killing 250 men, women, and children like sheep on an altar, a sacrifice for the creation of the state of Israel. Tales of the atrocity spread like wildfire. Through the years, the infamy grew to embody the justice of the Palestinian cause. The words *Deir Yassin* stirred the blood of Palestinians. Kasim was one of twenty-five who survived the Deir Yassin massacre.

Fawcett was a striking man, immaculately dressed, debonair, and confident in his abilities as a scientist. In his early fifties, the only sign of middle age was the streaks of gray in his wavy black hair. But his pleasant features wore a troubled expression, which Dorn assumed to be the result of his nightmare. It wasn't.

"Do you have nightmares often, Nick? I have a colleague who specializes in . . ."

"No," he cut her off. "No, Susan. I don't. But thank you for your concern. It must have been that news report I saw in Rome. You know the one, where the woman and her child were ejected from the airplane over Greece?"

"Yes, I saw it. Horrible!" Dorn exclaimed.

"She was alive during the fall," he mumbled. "She held on to her baby until impact."

His dream was caused by guilt. Fawcett was in part responsible for several terrorist acts, including the bombing over Greece. The small bomb had blown a hole in the side of the airplane, which otherwise was undamaged. The pilot had managed to land the aircraft safely at Athens. But several passengers and a flight attendant had been sucked out the hole, among them a new mother and her baby.

"No wonder you're trembling," said Dorn. "For the life of me I can't understand how anyone could do such a thing."

Her statement tripped a trigger. He had to make her see. People had to understand . . . to understand the Palestinian cause. Talking about it was the only way to maintain his sanity.

"Rage, Susan. Pure unadulterated rage. That's what motivates them. Brutality, oppression, and injustice motivate them."

"There is no excuse for murdering innocent people. No excuse," Dorn insisted.

"I agree. But it's a matter of cause and effect," he said, breathing deeply. "Oppression is the highest form of terrorism. State-sponsored brutality and injustice practiced by the Israelis rob men of their souls. Do you know anything about Middle Eastern affairs?" he asked.

"No. The violence seems so senseless to me I avoid the subject," Dorn answered.

"There are some interesting similarities between microorganisms and us humans. The analogy leaps right out of a petri dish." He looked at her before continuing. "When I was at Berkeley I attended a course on Middle Eastern affairs. It was quite informative," he lied.

"I see no solution to the problem," Dorn replied, " and I have enough problems of my own without pondering philistine violence." Susan was trying to change the subject but there was that word *philistine,* synonymous with the word *Palestinian.*

Fawcett took a deep breath before taking up the intellectual challenge. In a professorial tone, he said, "Many people see images of deserts and camel caravans when they think of the Middle East. What they should envision is a struggle for survival since the beginning of time. What they should envision are separate species trapped in a big petri dish. It's a land of extremes, a godforsaken place parched by a blazing sun, where water is as precious as gold," he rambled. "The conflict, Susan, is over land and water and gods, and it began before recorded history. In the Middle East the dryness of the sand has blinded the eyes of men. Hate runs so deep it consumes them."

Dorn studied Fawcett's face. Calmer now, he had assumed his normal countenance.

I don't know why he's babbling on about the Middle East, she thought, *but if it makes him feel better, I'll listen.*

"The Middle East is interesting for several reasons. First, it's a microcosm of human nature. Second, the historical picture is fairly clear. It's recorded in the Torah, the Bible, and the Koran and by the Greeks, Egyptians, and Assyrians, and an excellent archeological record is well preserved by the dry climate. The feud between Arab and Jew began around 1200 B.C., when a migrating nomadic tribe settled in Canaan. They killed most of the inhabitants and seized their land. By 700 B.C. these people were known as Hebrews. But did you know that there were less than ten thousand Jews in Palestine in the early 1800s?"

"No," answered Dorn. "I didn't."

"Today there are millions," he continued. "Think about it from an Arab perspective. Here you are, tending your goats and olive groves in the land of your birth and a flood of illegal immigrants seizes your land, taking control of your life."

"But I thought the Jews were there first."

"In the late 1800s there were about ten million Jews scattered throughout the world, but only about ten thousand lived in Palestine. In many of the places where the Jews lived, they were discriminated against and cruelly persecuted as the killers of Christ. In eastern Europe and Russia, for example, where more than half the world's Jews lived, they faced brutal oppression. Afraid of what lay ahead, Jews began to dream of a homeland. Some called themselves Zionists, after a hilltop in Jerusalem. They believed that the only way to overcome oppression was to create a Jewish homeland. The first wave of immigration to Palestine began in 1882."

"I remember reading somewhere that the Arabs and the Jews are both descendants of Abraham. If the Arabs trace their ancestry to Abraham's first son and the Jews to the third son, how can you make a distinction between Arab and Jew?" Susan asked.

"They are cousins in time, and that's what makes the politics of the region so fascinating. The issues are inextricably tied to human nature and heritage. The fight is over the land, as barren and dry as it is. I personally can't tell an Arab from a Jew," he lied. "But they can."

"How can anyone kill innocent children, hijack airplanes, and blow themselves up, especially when their victims may have had the same great-great-grandfather?" asked Susan.

He paused for thought, then said, "In many respects, human warfare is like competition between species of microbes. Each tribe struggles against the other, vying for space and sustenance. It doesn't take much of a difference to produce tribalism. Terrorism, as a form of warfare, is the last gasp of the oppressed, the subjugated. It's a tactic born of utter desperation."

"I don't know why we're having this conversation, Nick," Dorn complained. She'd had enough. She had assumed Nick had Greek ancestry. She began to wonder if his ancestors were Arabic.

"Let me recapitulate," he said, like a math professor. "I had a dream about terrorism, and you said you didn't understand how anyone could do such a thing. I believe I know the answer. Terrorism is the systematic use of fear to incite hysteria in a population other than the victims of the act."

"Surely you don't approve of such barbarity, Nick?" she replied, drawn into the debate against her will.

"Of course not," he gushed with complete sincerity. "But I understand it."

"Understand it?" Susan snapped. "It's beyond comprehension."

"Let me explain it this way. In the course I attended at Berkeley, there were several guest speakers. I remember one old man. He was just an ignorant old Arab farmer displaced by war. He showed pictures of his village before and after it was leveled by the Israelis. With tears in his eyes he said, 'When I see the house in which I was born, the pastures in which I grazed my goats, the well I cleaned as a child, the places where my friends and I played, how can I say that the land is not mine?' Then a young Jewish student stood up and began shouting at the top of his lungs that the land belonged to the Jews. He kept screaming that it was written by the hand of God. The old Palestinian just stared at him with blood in his eyes. Tribalism, Susan. Philistine tribalism."

"Nick, man has been contesting the right to natural resources since time immemorial. Disagreement among civilized people does not justify violence in any form," Susan argued.

"Personally, I concede that point. But for an agrarian people, the ties to the land are strong, and the Palestinians have been completely and utterly displaced by the Zionist immigrants who now claim the land as their own. You have to put yourself in their place to understand their rage."

"What about the Jews? They've been oppressed since the days of the Babylonians. For heaven's sake, the Nazis tried to exterminate them."

"Two wrongs don't make a right, Susan. I'm sure you agree

that persecution of the Jews doesn't justify the displacement of the Palestinians."

"Still, I don't understand how anyone can kill a child," Susan said emphatically. "It's beyond me."

"It is the ability of man to mentally project himself into the body of another that we call humanity. Do you know that if you give a small child, say, three and a half years of age, a stick and tell him to hit one of his playmates, that he will do it. But at age four and half, most children will not comply. If asked why, they usually say, 'because it will hurt him.' At about four most of us develop a sense of empathy with others. State-sponsored brutality, oppression, and injustice shatter human empathy. They steal the soul and turn men into animals."

Susan stared at him, wondering why he continued to press the subject.

"I have a theory, Susan. Family violence begets family violence. The oppressed become oppressors. Did you know that an Israeli official can tell an Arab from a Jew just by the numbers on their identity cards? Arab names are underlined in their passports. New Jewish immigrants are cared for by the state. Within a few weeks of settlement, a new Jewish village will have electricity and running water, while there are Arab villages older than Solomon that don't have either. Everywhere the Arab goes, he hears the words *Arbey molokhb* or *Arbey calev*. Do you know the meanings?" he asked gently.

"No."

"It means "dirty Arab." "Arab dog." Humiliation, discrimination, and fear, combined with hopelessness, create rage. That is the algorithm for creating a suicide bomber. When a man has lost his land, his dignity, and his freedom, he has nothing else to lose."

The lecture was dragging on. Susan looked for a way to change the subject, but she couldn't get a word in edgewise.

"In the Middle East one man's terrorist is another man's hero," he continued. "The most recent attempt at resistance is called the *intifada*. It means the uprising against oppression. It's actually semipassive resistance against prejudice and subjugation."

"You call throwing rocks semipassive?" Dorn protested.

"Did you know that thousands of young Arab hands have been crushed."

"What?"

"Yes. If they catch a youngster throwing rocks, they beat him and crush his hand with a jackboot. That sort of brutality creates deranged people capable of carrying out the most horrific acts."

"The Israeli government doesn't condone such policies, Nick."

"Maybe not. But it happens."

"Tell me something, Nick. Why do they blame the United States for this?"

"Why?" he echoed incredulously. "In the Arab's mind Israel and the United States are one and the same. It was American influence in the United Nations that led to the creation of Israel. It was American dollars that turned Israel into the superpower of the Middle East. It is American dollars, directly or indirectly, that build Jewish settlements on Arab lands today, Susan."

"We didn't create the conflict," she argued.

"But we chose sides, Susan. The targets terrorists choose are symbolic. Their purpose is to produce fear. Think about it. For all we know there is a bomb in the cargo hold of this airplane."

"Oh, my God, Nick! Don't talk like that," Susan gasped.

"I just dreamed it, Susan, and it filled me with fear. In that respect, Palestinian freedom fighters have obtained their objective. They have our attention."

Wanting to change the subject before he could continue his anti-Semitic diatribe, Dorn offered, "Perhaps I shouldn't mention this, but I spoke with the FBI concerning an incident that happened to me at the CDC."

"What incident?" He gaped at her.

"I thought I was being stalked," she explained.

"By whom? Your ex-husband?" he said hoarsely.

"No. An Arab terrorist."

Fawcett's hands began to shake uncontrollably. *I must get word to the Council, he thought.* "Are they still investigating?" he asked.

"No. They think I'm seeing things."

Fawcett breathed a sigh of relief.

"Do you think terrorists would attack the CDC?" Susan asked.

"No," he blurted. "Preposterous! Of course not! Surely it's a secret admirer, Susan."

"That's what Chief Johnson thinks," she admitted. "But if I do, he's Arabic."

Fawcett was stunned by the revelation. *Perhaps the Council doesn't trust me because I haven't been able to develop a vaccine for Ebola. Maybe they've assigned agents to watch me, he thought.*

He studied her profile for a few seconds. All during the conference in Rome he had pumped her for information about her work on the new virus he and Poland had investigated in Africa. Afraid he may have pressed her too hard for information and that his inner turmoil would show on his face, he decided to drop the subject.

"Do you have a significant other, Susan?" he asked.

"I have a new friend, but I wouldn't call him a significant other," she replied.

"May I ask who he is?"

"You don't know him, Nick. He's a private contractor. Doesn't know a thing about medical research."

"Well, I'd like to meet the man who has stolen the heart of my favorite virologist."

"Favorite?"

"Well, would you be offended if I said second favorite?" he said, with a phony smile.

"Not at all."

"Perhaps the four of us could have dinner. You, me, Doris and your new friend. I'm in hopes of rekindling my relationship with Doris and uh . . . well, uh . . ."

Susan smiled. "Sounds like an excellent idea. Now, if you'll excuse me, I need to use the ladies' room."

With gnawing anguish, Fawcett watched her walk up the aisle. He closed his eyes and took several deep breaths.

Desert Decree has to succeed. The future of our people depends on it, he thought. To ease his troubled mind, he recited a hodgepodge of poems he had heard on the streets of Lebanon like a mantra.

Jerusalem's stone is the only stone that can feel pain.
It has a network of nerves.
From time to time Jerusalem crowds into protest,
Like the tower of Babel.
But with huge clubs, gobs of police beat her down.
Houses are raised and walls flattened,
And afterwards the City disperses,
Muttering prayers and complaints,
And sporadic screams from churches and synagogues
And loud moaning minarets,
Each to his own place.
Write down that I am an Arab,

And that the number on my identity card is fifty thousand.
I have eight children and the ninth is due this summer.
Are you angry?
Write down that I am an Arab,
Working with my fellows in the quarry.
I have eight children.
For them I pull the loaf of bread, the clothes
And the exercise books from the rocks
And beg no alms at your door.
I do not lower myself at your doorstep.
Are you angry?
Our land, this green land of ours,
Its flowers as if embroidered on women's gowns,
Is now controlled by an iron fist.
Blue shadows lurk among the olive trees of our valleys,
Where once all our villages stood
But now are gone to the hard plow.
No monument, no flowers,
No memorial, no verse, no curtains,
No blood-soaked rag from a shirt once worn by our faithful.
No stone with their names inscribed on it.
Nothing at all! Such dishonor!
Their ghosts ever wandering dig up their tombs
Among the ruins of Coffercusem!
Deir Yassin! Deir Yassin!
My village! My village!

When Susan returned, Fawcett's eyes were closed. He looked tired and troubled, so she tried not to disturb him as she slipped quietly into her seat. All through the conference in Rome, he had seemed distracted, as if pondering some great experiment that required Level Four containment. She'd assumed it was some vaccine or prophylactic research. It wasn't. It was a weapon of terror.

Chapter 12

LIEUTENANT ALEX GOMEZ looked out over the Bay of Limón and nursed a Cuba libre. It reminded him of his blood oath to kill Castro. Each swallow renewed his commitment. Gomez was Cuban by birth, but like many children of Cuban immigrants, he knew little of his father's homeland. He had grown up in southern Florida and was more American than Cuban.

Throughout his childhood he had heard bitter stories of how Castro had robbed him of his birthright. During his teenage years he had dreamed of reclaiming his native land. He had even joined the U.S. Navy and endured the hardships of SEAL training in hopes of one day storming the beaches of Cuba and putting a bullet in Castro's head. But in his heart he knew there was nothing left of his father's estate, nothing but a run-down plantation inhabited by hungry peasants. His patrimony was no longer worth fighting for. But killing Castro was something else. That was something worth doing, and his present assignment was a step in the right direction.

He took a sip of the rum and Coke and sank deeper into the plush chair, musing over more mellow thoughts of luscious lips and soft thighs. He eyed the waitress and mentally relived their last encounter. The faint scent of her musk seemed to fill his nostrils as she walked close to his table. She was Panamanian, dark-skinned and exotic, brimming with hot Latin juices. As she swayed from table to table serving customers, he mentally undressed her. He saw her breasts, no longer covered by a waitress uniform, bathed in a soft yellow light shining from his open bathroom door. He saw himself kneeling on the bed, looking down at her. He gently turned her over so the half-moons of her firm buttocks were staring at him. In his mind's eye he could almost feel the moment he pushed his unit into her. He could almost hear her moan of pleasure. Then he tried to count the number of times she had climaxed during the night. But he ran out of fingers.

She can't get enough, he thought.

Gomez felt excitement coursing through his body as he anticipated the night to come. Then he felt his erection under the table, hard and pulsing under his pants. He took another sip and tried to clear his mind by visualizing himself killing Castro.

Master Chief Boomer Savarese, a veteran of a thousand battles, had read the vengeful thoughts on the lieutenant's face before he had tuned the channel to passion revisited.

When that look returned, he asked, "What's up, Boss? Another mission?"

"Yeah."

"When?"

"I don't know. We're kind of on standby," replied Gomez.

"Good. I'm bored shitless," Savarese grumbled.

"Don't you ever get tired of the chase, Boomer?" asked Gomez in a weary voice.

"No! Never. What else is there for a man to do? Make love and war. Each improves his performance in the other. It's the chase that makes life worth living, Loco. That's what gets your motor warm and your pecker hard." He grinned.

The lieutenant's nickname was an honorific earned in fierce combat. While serving in Team Six, he had jumped onto the running board of a moving truck and shot an armed terrorist through the temple. Lieutenant Gomez shook his head as he stared at the city lights of Colón across the bay. Ignoring Savarese, he watched a small freighter approaching anchorage, barely moving at half a knot.

"Sir, I never said this before, but thanks for bringing me into the CTS. I know they don't generally take guys like me."

The Counterterrorist Squad was a secret organization composed of hand-picked military men of plausible foreign extraction. Men with surnames like Hernandez, Diaz, and Salinas. Men whose roots could be tied to any country other than the United States. Gomez could pass as Cuban or Central or South American. A handsome man, he sported a neatly trimmed mustache and curly brown hair that hinted of Conquistador ancestry. He was short for a SEAL at five foot ten, but built like an Olympic wrestler with powerful arms, and he had keen eyes. His Latin good looks had all the waitresses drooling for attention.

Savarese was only assigned to the CTS because Gomez had insisted on a partner he could trust with his life. SEALs always work in pairs, as swim buddies, and Gomez was tied to Savarese with a hawser. But constructing a false identity for Boomer Savarese had proven difficult. The master chief had been married five times and had fathered children by each of the women. With child support going all over the country, he was a hard man to make disappear, even for S-Systems, the new entity in the world of special operations. It was completely civilian, with the exception of the warriors at the bitter end of the line, and they were cannon fodder. On the surface, S-Systems was a self-sustaining, legitimate business enterprise, with a profitable line of avionics equipment. Underneath, however, was layer upon layer of shell companies. Gomez and Savarese were just operators looking for action. If not for Savarese's expertise in special boat operations, and Gomez's trust, he would have been cooling his heels behind a desk in Norfolk, Virginia.

"Boomer, you are un-fuckin'-believable. Do you realize you just thanked me for nearly getting your ass killed a half a dozen times?" asked Gomez, incredulous.

"Like I said, L. T., a man's got to fuck and fight, and I'm gettin' my share. We got time for a sperm dump?"

"Yeah. A man's got to have his pleasures," replied Gomez, thinking of the Panamanian waitress. "I think we've got a few days, if that's enough time for you to get off, old man."

"I got my eye on my maid," Savarese specified. He leered. "The chase is on." After a brief reverie, he broke the silence. "Boss?"

"Yeah," answered Gomez, still watching the ship out in the bay. There was something about it that gripped his attention.

"You think they'll kick me out of the service next year?"

"I don't know, Boomer. Probably. With all the cutbacks, they aren't granting waivers for anyone over thirty years. Besides, with the kind of action we've been seeing, I wouldn't count on living to retirement."

"Actually, I wanted to do forty years, until they elected that pot-smoking, draft-dodging, queer-loving, socialistic, liberal-assed razorback as president."

Gomez glanced at him, then back at the ship. "I noticed you left out womanizing."

"Yeah. So? . . . I wouldn't hold that against any man. Would you?"

"Master Chief, I'll remind you that I'm an officer and a gentleman and I swore an oath of allegiance to the president of the United States. Don't ever speak ill of the commander in chief in my presence," Gomez ordered. He looked at Savarese with a deadly serious expression.

"Screw you, sir. You know if he was briefed in on Poison Fruit he would cop out like a yellowbelly rat. Like he did during Nam." Savarese growled more than spoke his words. He studied Gomez's face and asked, "You still planning on getting out at twenty?"

"I don't know. Maybe. Sooner or later I got a date down in Cuba," said the lieutenant.

"Can I go?"

When the lieutenant didn't answer, Savarese glared at him and demanded, "Evans made you the same offer he did me, didn't he?"

Gomez frowned. "The commander only hires men who are seriously handicapped."

"Huh?" Savarese gulped. "Oh, yeah? In about ten months I'll be the first non-gimp in Soc Inc."

"Boomer, you're mentally fuckin' handicapped. You're pussy-struck."

"Screw you, Lieutenant, and the horse you rode in on," Savarese snarled.

"Just the horse, please, Master Chief. I'm still a virgin."

"Now the shit is really getting' deep," Savarese groused. "Since you're not going to level with me, I ain't buyin' the next round."

He slammed down his drink in one gulp and placed his glass on the table. Using his fingers, he combed his hair and retied his pony-tail. Savarese was a big man. His six-two, 225-pound frame declared that he was not a man to lock horns with. He had a Robert Deniro type of face: brutally handsome with keen, intelligent eyes. In his mid-forties, his coal-black hair showed streaks of gray. Sloppy groom-ing was part of his cover and it annoyed him. He twisted the ends of his handlebar mustache.

"Did you know that Ray Keith is working for Soc Inc?" he asked. He held up two fingers, gesturing to the waitress for another round.

"No. Last I heard, he was drinking himself to death in an old trailer out on the Salton Sea."

"Not anymore. Him and a bunch of other gimps are checkin' out the security of nuclear power plants," Savarese continued.

"Sounds boring to me," Gomez sneered.

"Me too." He paused for thought and focused his eyes on Gomez like lasers. "I had a few drinks with Fred Swan when I was back in the U.S. of A. last week. He told me that he, Jennings, Decker, and Keith busted the security of the Savannah River power plant. They got in and out undetected."

"Knowing those guys, it doesn't surprise me. They were damn good men before they got hurt."

"The best," agreed Savarese.

"Did they get to kick the shit out of any rent-a-cops?" asked Gomez. He turned to watch the ship out in the harbor. Something about the old freighter compelled him.

Savarese ignored the question for a few seconds as he studied Gomez's profile. "The rum's gone to your head, Loco. I told you, they got in and out without anyone seein' 'em. Keith created a diver-sion at the main gate, and they snuck up inside a big underground culvert and planted dummy explosives on the shit that keeps the core from meltin' down. They almost had one KIA, though."

"Oh?"

"Yeah. Some big, chunky-butt woman almost took out Keith. She sat on his chest and farted in his face."

"Get serious," Gomez growled.

"I am serious. And to hear Swan tell it, the security chief nearly pissed himself when Evans showed him the IEDs." IED was SEAL slang for improvised explosive device.

"They're wasting their time on AT as long as we're in the CT business," said Gomez. He went back to watching the freighter.

"Damn straight," Savarese agreed.

AT, or antiterrorism, referred to proactive security measures like guards and surveillance cameras. CT was short talk for counter-terrorism. As in football, AT was purely defensive and completely proactive; CT, on the other hand, was all offensive and totally reactive. CT forces trained or sat around most of the time like firemen waiting for the bell to go off. Gomez was waiting for the bell.

When the barmaid delivered their drinks, Savarese pointed at them, then at Gomez, indicating for her to put them on the lieutenant's tab.

"Señor?" she asked. She gave Gomez a provocative smile.

Savarese couldn't see her lick her lips and wink at the lieutenant. While she was occupied, he pressed the inside of her thigh up high near her privates. She ignored his hand but quickly stepped away. Savarese grinned at Gomez and watched her wiggle back to the bar. When he turned to face the lieutenant, he licked his lips lasciviously.

"Nice ass," he muttered.

Gomez nodded agreement. As quick as flipping a light switch, Savarese turned serious again.

"Sir, I mean it. Thanks for pulling me in. It's been a hell of a ride, and I wouldn't have missed it for my left testicle."

"Damn," exclaimed Gomez. "Now you're gettin' all maudlin on me. I'll feel bad if you get greased on the next op."

"Not a chance. Like shootin' ducks on a pond. By the way, what the fuck does *maudlin* mean?" Savarese inquired, frowning. He choked down another swallow of his rum on the rocks.

The CTS was designed to stop terrorism, decisively and without attribution. There were sister programs similar to Poison Fruit for drug interdiction and intelligence collection, but Gomez and Savarese had no knowledge of them. All programs were compartmentalized. Poison Fruit was like the core of an onion in a big bag full of onions. To get the nonattributable kernel you first had to find the right onion and then peel back layer after layer of cover story to get to the non-attributable kernel. At the center of S-Systems Corporation was an intelligence service modeled after Pinkerton Risk Assessment. It employed the most sophisticated electronic surveillance system on the planet. Men like Rice and Verduchi constantly frisked the airwaves for intelligence without anyone being aware of their presence.

"My maid has a good-looking sister," Savarese teased, breaking a long spell of silence. "About eighteen." He grinned. "Okay, sixteen."

"Thanks, but no thanks. I prefer to find my own squeeze."

"Suit yourself. I'll just have 'em both." Savarese downed his drink. "You're not much for conversation tonight, Loco. I'm outta here."

"Mañana. Remember those maintenance checks on the Prancer. We'll be needing her in a few days," the lieutenant said, referring to one of the three vessels they used to chase down infiltrators.

"I got it covered, sir. Luego," Savarese growled with a scowl. The reminder insulted him. Boomer Savarese prided himself on his warrior skills, and taking care of the gear was one of them. As he stood up he said, "Keep your powder dry, Loco, and your dick in your pants." He gestured at the barmaid before turning to leave.

After Boomer left the bar, Gomez watched the lights dance on the water as the old freighter dropped anchor in the middle of the Bay of Limón. Ships came and went in vast numbers, waiting for their turn to pass through the Panama Canal. But the MV *Nicosia* wasn't waiting for passage, and she wasn't waiting to take on a load of narcotics. She was a simple freighter carrying assorted cargo to and from the Mediterranean and the gulf ports of Central and South America. Bananas, nuts and rawhide in exchange for wine, cotton, and dates. She was also carrying a very special crew, men who spoke Arabic and broken English, men bent on changing the world. Among them was Aman Abruzzi Ayyad, the object of intense intelligence interest to S-Systems Risk Assessment. Though Alex Gomez didn't know it, the target of his impending mission was in plain sight.

. The barmaid sashayed over and placed a free drink on the table.

"I'll be off in twenty minutes," she purred.

"I'll be waiting," replied Gomez, gazing at her cleavage.

As she walked back toward the bar he admired her slim brown legs. A surge of excitement passed through his loins. He had seen

Savarese goose her. It was characteristic behavior for his master chief, and it told him Savarese was unaware he was sleeping with the girl. He smiled inwardly. Keeping secrets from fellow SEALs was difficult at best. Keeping a secret from Boomer Savarese was nearly impossible.

Aman Ayyad left sixteen men on board the *Nicosia* and went ashore by skiff. In Colón, he made contact with the Palestinian underground and arranged for the necessary papers and a plane ticket to Mexico City. Forged papers were easy to acquire in the Panamanian underworld, and if he had wanted to, he could have procured the necessary paperwork to move all his men up the spine of Central America. The border between Mexico and the U.S. was easy to penetrate. Hundreds of illegal aliens crossed daily, and even if the U.S. Border Patrol were to catch one of his men, they would almost immediately release him. But not if the man was carrying weapons and explosives, and Ayyad wanted to smuggle in a load of arms and equipment as a backup to Nasrallah's logistical plan. To do so covertly, he intended to slip across the border alone and direct the infiltration from ship to shore as the *Nicosia* sailed north along the coast.

For two days he watched the *Nicosia* standing in the harbor, offloading and loading cargo at anchor. On the third day she put to sea for a ten-day voyage to Tampico, Mexico, a small Gulf port south of Brownsville, Texas. He waited until she cleared the port before leaving Colón for Mexico City and the route north to the States.

The extra equipment he'd loaded on board the ship in Cyprus was similar to the gear Ibrahim Nasrallah promised to provide him in the United States. Ayyad intended to carry out Operation Desert Decree exactly in every detail, and he wanted to be prepared if anything went wrong logistically. So, in violation of orders, he had secretly assembled backup gear. Through connections in Algiers he had procured weaponry and explosives. Through the French he bought his communications equipment. That was his first big mistake. After the ship sailed from Cyprus he discovered frequency incompatibility between types of radios. So when the *Nicosia* put into Naples, Italy, for its last port of call before sailing to Panama, he made his second major mistake. Against Ibrahim Nasrallah's explicit orders, he broke operational security and called a Palestinian sympathizer in Rome to buy more radios. It was the telephone call that turned the eye of the S-Systems' machine upon him.

The telephone key report went unnoticed for several days until David Shipler, an S-Systems analyst, evaluated a machine translation of the conversation. The rush order of unusual electronic equipment procured by a known Palestinian terrorist sympathizer in Rome was traced directly to the port of Naples and the Cypriot ship *Nicosia*. When she sailed into the Bay of Limón she was under satellite surveillance and no more than a mile from S-System's secret base at Fort Sherman, Panama Canal Zone. As Gomez gulped down the last of his Cuba libre, he could not have imagined that in just a few days he would have a date with the young Arabs on board the vessel.

Chapter 13

"Hey, Popeye."

"Yeah?"

"You see that white elephant parked down the street from the Doc's house?" Ray Keith asked.

Upon completion of the Savannah River project, Evans had rented several apartments for surveillance. One was just down the street from Dr. Lubeck's house.

Swan focused his binoculars. He had trouble with his depth perception, and it took him several seconds to bring his eye into sharp focus in the waning light.

"Yeah. A motor home? So what?" asked Swan.

"Well, it's also been hangin' around the germ factory and at Doc Dorn's house."

"There are a thousand buggies like that in the state of Georgia, shit-for-brains."

"Read the license plate, knothead," Keith snarled.

Swan strained his eye to read the plate numbers.

"Look here," said Keith, pointing to the numbers written in pencil on his artificial leg.

"Okay, Tonto. So I see. I didn't know you could read and write," Swan shot back.

"What do you think?" Keith asked. "FBI?"

"Maybe."

"The commander said the FBI had been called off." Keith spat a stream of tobacco juice into an empty beer bottle.

"Yeah, he did."

"So what are they still doin' here?" Keith asked. He made a face like Charlie Manson with a furrowed brow.

"I don't know. Maybe he got his wires crossed," Swan suggested. Keith grinned with a wild-eyed look. "Let's bug 'em."

"What? Bug the Feds? Your brain must be in your ass, Ray, and it's numb from sittin' too long."

"Why not?" Keith demanded.

"Because it's against the law without a court order, knucklehead."

"We can use the directional microphone with a voice-activated tape recorder. No entry, no intrusion, no fuss. No one will ever know 'cept us. And since we're not gonna use the info in a court case, it don't matter."

"What could those fan belt inspectors be up to?" Swan mumbled, thinking out loud.

Ever since the disaster at the Branch Davidian compound in Waco, he had referred to the FBI as "fan belt inspectors" because in his opinion only a bunch of dumb-ass grease monkeys could have let so many children get killed.

He mulled the motor home situation until curiosity overwhelmed him. "Okay, but we'd better not let the commander find out," Swan cautioned. "He'll kick our asses all the way back to San Diego."

"Aw, c'mon," Keith replied, showing his tobacco-stained teeth. "He don't always play by the book."

"It's okay when he breaks the rules, but if we do it, he'll ream us out." Swan exhaled heavily and stared at Keith. "I'll set the ears up," he said, surrendering.

"Let's grab some grub at Clyde's while we're out," Keith suggested. "I'm gonna stick Evans with a thousand-dollar bar tab." He chuckled.

"Not a good idea," Swan cautioned. He thought about warning Keith that Jennings had already made that mistake. Then he thought better of it. "You need any help?" he asked with a wry smile.

"Sure. I started a tab in his name. It's on me, or should I say, it's on Commander Asshole," Keith sniggered.

Swan covered his mouth and coughed to hide his smirk.

"We'll plant the equipment, then head down to Clyde's for a toddy. I've got to work on Johnson some more. You know, he's a pretty good ol' boy. He would have made a good SEAL in his younger days."

"Bullshit. He's too damn fat," Keith growled.

Derek Evans drove up to Susan Dorn's condo and walked briskly to the door. He pressed the bell just as she opened it.

"Come in. I'll just be a minute," said Susan, still fretting with her hair.

"Wow," he exclaimed as he stepped inside the cool apartment and out of the sticky August evening. "You look marvelous."

"Why, thank you," she replied with a luscious smile.

She wore a simple, off-the-shoulder, red silk dress that clung to her slim body. It flowed smoothly down to mid-calf to sheer stockings and summer sandals. In her ears she wore tiny heart-shaped jade studs, and around her throat a single jade pendant suspended from a gold chain. It looked ancient, like a Chinese art treasure. Her jet-black hair was down, and it flowed over her bare shoulders in gentle waves. Without her glasses and lab coat she looked like a different person. Her face was so perfectly proportioned that she could have been a fashion model if she had chosen to.

As she disappeared into the bedroom she spoke over her shoulder in a low, inviting voice. "Help yourself to a glass of wine."

"Thanks. I will."

On the counter near the kitchen was a bottle of Chardonnay, chilled and ready to serve. Evans glanced around the room, looking for pictures and signs of men as he poured two small glasses. There were none. The house was neat and spotless, with an exotic appeal. It was obvious that her ancestry was Chinese to some degree. A small Buddhist figurine sat on the coffee table. Oriental paintings adorned the walls. The ambiance was that of a temple garden, complete with scent. Through an open bedroom door he saw a desk piled with books and papers. The clutter of the makeshift office contrasted sharply with the neatness of the rest of the apartment. The living room was obviously her oasis, her escape from reality. He sipped his wine and took a seat on the sofa.

When she came out of the bedroom he got to his feet and sucked in his breath. "Wow," he whispered.

"You like?" she asked, with a wave of her hand in front of her body.

Evans's eyes were wide with appreciation. He nodded. "Fabulous. You look absolutely fabulous. On the way to the restaurant we'll need to stop by my place to get my gun."

She frowned.

"So I can keep the mob of lecherous men away from you," he explained.

She smiled brightly as he handed her a glass of wine.

"Thank you."

"To the most beautiful scientist in the world," he toasted, holding up his glass.

"Now you've gone too far," she protested modestly.

"Oh, no I haven't."

She sipped the wine and asked, "Ready?"

"I would just as soon stay here and finish this bottle of wine and look at you," he said without taking his eyes off her.

"Flattery will get you in trouble, buster," she said, shaking one delicate finger at him.

"I certainly hope so." He grinned.

She grabbed her purse and headed for the door.

As the couple left the condo Jennings did a double take through his binoculars. "Man. I want the boss's job," he said, passing the glasses to Decker. "Have a look."

Decker studied Susan's anatomy as she got into Evans's car.

"Whoo-ee! Me too," he panted. "Two to one he jumps her bones tonight?" he dared.

"Two to one it's her idea," Jennings returned. "Did you see that get-up? She must have painted it on."

Jennings failed to notice that the motor home parked near the condo had pulled out and followed Evans at a distance.

"Yeah. And it gives me an idea," Decker mumbled. "I'll check the germ factory if you'll dog the captain tonight."

"You're on, Pacemaker. But I know what you're up to. You got your eye on one of those little gals down at the coffee shop, don't ya?"

"Hey, a little latte never hurt any man," Decker grinned.

"You got that right, partner. See if latte has a lady friend?" Jennings ventured.

"You're on," agreed Decker, hauling butt toward the door.

At the restaurant, Susan formally introduced Evans to Doris Lubeck and Nick Fawcett. After greetings and pleasantries, Evans took the offensive.

"I'm afraid I'm out of my element," he said. "I'm the only non-Ph.D. at this table."

"What *is* your line of business, Derek?" asked Fawcett pleasantly, like a big brother evaluating a sister's new suitor.

"I'm the president of a small company," he replied, looking at Susan and then back to Fawcett. "And what sort of bugs do you study, Nick?" he added, purposely directing the spotlight away from himself, a tactic he intended to use all night.

"My specialty is prokaryotes, but I have a passion for all exotic microbes."

"You'll have to break that down for me, Doc." Evans flashed a boyish smile.

"In simple terms, I study unusual bacteria."

"And you, Doris?" Evans asked.

"My specialty is prions," Lubeck answered, not expecting Evans to understand.

"Ahhh. Self-replicating matter. I've read about them." Evans replied. "There's a disease in Borneo called kuru that's caused by prions. It affects the brain, as I recall. And sheep scrapie, and mad cow disease in England are also caused by such primitive forms of matter, aren't they?"

"Actually," Fawcett interjected, "kura is confined to New Guinea."

"You're very well read, Derek," Lubeck said approvingly. "But I wouldn't go so far as to say prions are matter, in the sense of living matter. On the molecular level, they're merely sticky, pleated sheets of protein that don't dissolve in water. They kill healthy cells, perhaps by creating molecular traffic jams."

"And you're studying the link between prions and viruses?" Evans asked.

"Well, not exactly. Like Susan, I make a living studying nasty viruses. But someday I hope to discover something useful about prions to add to our understanding of life. My job is studying viruses. Prions are my passion," she said in a lusty voice.

"Strange passion, Doris," Evans remarked.

Susan joined in the exchange.

"Derek, Doris is considered by many to be the most knowledgeable scientist in the world in that area of research," she said. "It's not a giant leap of evolution from prions to viruses to cellular life."

"I see."

"Doris, Derek was with the congressional tour that observed the Ebola drill a few weeks ago," said Susan. She grinned.

"Oh, yes. Well," Lubeck said, eyeing Evans, "I hope you weren't offended."

"No, not at all. Such drills are necessary for safety."

"Oh, I don't mean the drill," Lubeck leered. "I mean, me. Stark naked like a baby."

"Did I miss something?" Fawcett asked as Lubeck and Dorn giggled.

"Next time, I'll arrange it so Susan takes the fall," Lubeck added.

"I'll be sure to bring my camera," Evans chucked. Dorn blushed.

"I definitely missed something," said Fawcett. "I was about to give Derek my lecture on the differences between eukaryotic and prokaryotic forms of life and you moved from prionic nonlife to real life. I'm intrigued. I want a transfer to Level Four," said Fawcett, staring at Lubeck with desire.

"Nick, you'd better stay down on Level Three," said Evans. "Doris sings a wicked verse of 'Amazing Grace.'"

Dinner arrived and the ensuing conversation was at times over Evans's head. He faked it, and each time Fawcett directed a question to him about his personal life Derek deflected it with a question about his. When Fawcett eventually got around to asking him about his company, he answered in generalities.

"The business world is very competitive, Nick. It's survival of the fittest, just like the world of microbes."

"Tell me, Derek, do you think races of men sometimes act like business enterprises and bacteria, gobbling up their competitors in hostile takeovers?" Fawcett asked.

"Hmm. Interesting question."

"Derek," Susan jumped in, "Nick enlightened me on the politics of the Middle East at some length during our flight back from Rome. It seems he's interested in human nature and has developed a unique theorem that man and microbe engage in internecine warfare in similar perfidious fashion."

For the first time during the evening, Evans and Fawcett locked eyes. It was a knowing look, like the one between a hunter and his prey, like the stare between two boxers before a bout.

"Nick, are you equating the defenses of nation-states to the defenses of bacteria?" asked Evans, with a furrowed brow. The look in Fawcett's deep-set Omar Sharif eyes had disturbed Evans.

"A purely intellectual exercise, I assure you, Derek," Fawcett asserted. "In the face of continuing threat, bacteria have constantly improved their weaponry and defense mechanisms. They attack each other with vigor and develop extraordinary chemical defenses. Penicillin is just one well-known example of thousands of chemical weapons developed by fungi and bacteria to protect themselves from attack. Plants do the same thing. Have you noticed that grass doesn't grow under some types of trees? It's not from a lack of sunlight," he chattered excitedly. "The tree defends itself with chemical warfare. Similarly, microbes attack rival organisms and defend themselves from attack. It's an escalating war that has gone on since the beginning of life on this planet. We are an extension of that life and of that struggle. In the human equation, it's called tribalism."

"It's quite a stretch to equate bacteria behavior to human social behavior," said Evans, studying Fawcett's face for his reaction.

"Yes. But don't you agree that either way it's still mindless warfare?" Fawcett insisted.

"Well, I don't," Susan interjected. "Humans have the capacity to think through issues. Microbes don't. We don't have to slaughter each other in the name of Vishnu or Baal or Allah."

"I'm afraid Nick has a point, Susan," Evans said gently. "There are many places in the world where the combatants don't think about issues. They just do what their leaders tell them to do. They simply fight to survive. From stick to knife to gun to nuclear bomb, we have evolved ever more destructive weapons. But human nature is basically the same as it was when Alexander conquered the world."

"I don't understand it," said Susan flatly.

"It's all about power . . . and land. We're blessed in this country, Susan. We don't often see the dire struggle for survival that goes on in other parts of the world," Evans continued.

"Have you traveled widely, Derek?" asked Fawcett, probing for information.

"Yes, Dr. Fawcett. I have." He was about to comment on the phenomenon of terrorism when Fawcett interrupted his thoughts and changed the subject.

"Well, I propose a toast before Visigothic hordes burst through the door and interrupt this friendly gathering. To friendship and peace on earth."

"Hear, hear!"

Evans locked his eyes on Susan. Her stunning face had an extra glow from the wine. She moved closer to him.

As the two couples left the restaurant and walked through the parking lot, Evans noticed a figure in the shadows. At first he thought it was Jennings or Swan or Decker until the man sneaked past a light. Seeing he was young and black, Evans tried to hurry Susan to the car. But before he could get her inside the vehicle, the thug was upon them, gun in hand.

"Give me your money, you white muddafuckas," he growled, shoving a pistol in Fawcett's face.

"Do what he says, Nick," ordered Evans from five yards away.

"You heard da mon, sucka!" the thief taunted, waving his pistol.

Fawcett nervously reached for his wallet.

"Easy, mon, or I'll gut-shoot you," warned the huge assailant, his face hidden behind the low brim of a Braves baseball cap, "and I'll piss on your grave."

Nick's hands were trembling as he handed the thief his wallet. Doris, supported by the fender of Nick's car, was shaking as well. It was her turn next.

"Give me the purse, bitch. The earrings and necklace too."

Doris complied without protest. When the crook turned toward Susan, she clutched the pendant around her neck. It was an ancient family heirloom.

"Now you, bitch!" he said, moving closer to Evans and Dorn.

Evans took Susan's purse and carefully handed it to the hood.

"You one good-lookin' who'e, foxy mama. Maybe I'll have some of your ass before I go."

"Just take the money, man," Evans urged.

The mugger stared at Evans. Eye to eye. Evans knew he was calculating, trying to decide if he should shoot. His lips quivered and his cheek twitched. Guns make a lot of noise. They draw too much attention.

Sticking the gun in Evans's face, he growled, "Give me da watch, cracker!"

Evans complied.

"Now the wallet, mon," he demanded, shaking the gun too close for comfort.

Evans knew the moment had come. When a man gives you an order at gunpoint, he expects you to obey. And Evans had complied with every command. It is that expectation of obeisance, that split second of indecision it takes for the brain to distinguish compliance from noncompliance that gives the victim of crime an edge. Evans could see the man's mind working in slow motion: *The sucka is reaching for his wallet just like I told 'im. No! He's not reaching for his wallet. He's . . .*

By the time his brain had registered what he was seeing, it was too late. Evans's left hand parried the gun as his right hand seized it. Pulling and spinning violently, he twisted his body into the brute's elbow. The movement caught the thug off guard and dislocated his elbow with a loud snap. His body slammed into the side of the car. Reversing the spin, Evans pulled on the broken arm, controlling the gun with an aikido wristlock that took the thief to the pavement in the opposite direction, howling in pain. Spinning him around on the ground using his broken arm like a rope, Evans stomped down hard on his face, shattering his jaw with the heel of his shoe. The force of the blow knocked the criminal unconscious. Evans then stomped on his right hand and right foot, crushing the bones in two violently brutal moves. The entire encounter was over in four grunts. When Evans looked up, Fawcett was staring at him, mouth agape, eyes frozen in fear.

Evans unlocked the door of the car and pushed Susan inside. Retrieving the valuables, he ushered Lubeck and Fawcett to their car. Not wanting to draw attention to himself, he hurried them out of the parking lot before the police arrived.

He followed Fawcett's silver Cadillac for several blocks to ensure that no one was following, then waved good-bye at a traffic light. All the way to Susan's he watched the rearview mirror for signs of a tail. There were none, so he parked in front of her condo.

"Are you okay?" he asked gently.

She was still trembling. Her hand clutched the jade pendant around her neck as she answered in a shaky voice, "Yes, thanks to you."

Evans walked her to her door and unlocked it for her.

"Would you like me to check the house?" he asked.

"Would you?" she concurred, still quivering.

Inside, he carefully checked every room. His reconnaissance completed, he returned to the living room to find Susan with two glasses of wine. She handed him one and then sat down on the sofa without speaking. For several minutes they sipped the wine in complete silence, during which time he studied her visible emotions. When she finally spoke, the subject of the conversation completely surprised him.

"My marriage was a disaster," she began. "I was impetuous. He was insensitive. It just didn't work out, and it got worse and worse until it became a living nightmare. I don't know what caused it to turn so bad. Jealousy perhaps. Perhaps his resentment of my success as a scientist and his failures as a businessman. We just grew farther and farther apart. I've never told anyone this before, but he used to beat me. Sometimes terribly."

Tears came to her eyes. "Imagine that. A doctor. A renowned virologist. Beaten by her angry husband. I never thought such a thing could happen to me. I was so embarrassed, I hid it from everyone and buried myself even further in my work. But the more I worked, the worse it got."

She paused, gathering her courage. Evans was silent, surprised by the revelation, waiting for her to speak on her own terms.

"Tonight brought it all back. The senseless brutality. The fear," she said, shaking her head.

She buried her face in her hands, but when she looked back at him she put on a brave face, hiding the sadness and shame.

"I believe in defending myself, Susan. Sometimes you have to fight back. But I'm really sorry about tonight. Perhaps I could have handled it differently."

"Oh, I'm not criticizing you. You did what you had to do to protect us. It's just that the horror of it all brought back the memories of my terrible marriage. It's something I've repressed for years."

She stared at him, her green eyes moist with tears.

"I'm afraid I don't know how to act around a man anymore," she said, attempting a smile. "I mean, a man I like . . . a . . . a lot," she stammered. "God, I can't believe I'm saying this. I'm making a complete fool of myself." Staring at the wine in her glass, she swirled it as if to change the subject.

Evans gently placed his arm around her shoulders. He pulled her closer. She stared at him uncertainly, then slowly, cautiously, she encouraged a kiss, which lasted and it soon grew to fiery passion. Susan Dorn gave in to her desire, and like a woman possessed, she kissed him insatiably, deeply, with abandon. Her breath grew hot and her lips blazed and Evans knew what she needed. When he returned the intensity of her emotions with hot kisses, she exhaled in near orgasm, quivering.

Sensing the moment, he softly gathered her in his powerful arms and carried her into the bedroom. Standing beside the bed, he kissed her tenderly while expertly releasing the zipper on her dress and the catch on her brassiere. Willingly, with a little shudder of her shoulders, she let her clothes fall to the floor, exposing her sensuous body.

Evans savored the beauty of her form, bathed in the pale moonlight from a window. Not wanting to forget a moment or the beauty before him, he softly stroked her cheek while peering into the depths of her jade-green eyes, then gently caressed her long black hair, letting his hands descend from her bare shoulders to her waist. Pulling her closer, he kissed her. With her small breasts quivering against his bare chest, she returned the embrace with equal vigor. Warmed by the wine and the heat of desire, she dug her fingernails into the heavy muscles of his back. As passion's fire consumed them, she pulled him to her bed and, with gasps of ecstasy and soft moans of pleasure, guided him into her.

"Ohhhhh!" she exhaled deeply, abandoning herself in a great gush of pleasure. For hours they made unending love, not wanting the dance to end. And for unmeasured time he held her in his arms, cherishing every fleeting moment. All weekend Susan Dorn desperately tried to make up for the years lost inside a sterile laboratory, while Evans savored each beautiful note of the love song she sang him. For the first time in her life, Susan Dorn felt complete, secure and safe, wrapped in the arms of a man she barely knew. But they weren't alone during their hours of ecstasy. Not really, truly alone.

Chapter 14

"WHAT TIME DID the Boss say he'd be here?" Fred Swan asked, over the blare of the jukebox at Clyde's Bar and Grill.

Ray Keith gave him his best wild-eyed Charlie Manson expression and said, "You gettin' forgetful, pretty boy? Five-thirty."

Swan squinted at his watch with his one good eye and then out the window toward the parking lot. "Any time now," he mumbled. "He's never late."

"Maybe we'd better not bring up the tape," said Jennings. "He's going to explode like a haversack of C4."

"Count on it," seconded Decker, "and I don't want to be in the frag zone."

Swan looked undecided. "We got to, guys," he said, picking up his beer bottle. "No way out of it."

Clyde's was a friendly little southern establishment located a few miles from Chief Johnson's house. Swan had chosen it because Johnson frequented the place.

When Evans finally entered the bar, Keith yelled, "Betty, how about a round for the house? Get one of them special drinks for yourself and put it all on Mr. Evans's tab."

"I don't have a tab," Evans protested, taking a seat at the table.

"Oh yes you do, sir," Jennings said, beaming a boyish smile. When the commander met his eyes, he quickly looked down at the table. Evans glared at all of them and waited for the nonsense to settle down. It took five minutes of jokes and laughter for them to get around to the reason for the meeting.

"Chief Johnson will be here in . . ." Swan peered at his Rolex, straining his good eye, "about five minutes sir."

"He's a good ol' boy, Cap'n," said Keith. "Gives me a few bucks every day. When this op is over, maybe I'll give his money back, seeing as how you're payin' us so generously."

"Bullshit!" Jennings protested. "Johnson makes big bucks. A lot better than us," he said, cutting his eyes at Evans. "Give me the damn money. I'll show you what to do with it."

"I ain't givin' you shit, J. R.! 'Cept maybe a hard time," Keith grumbled.

Swan looked at Evans. "Before Johnson arrives, Cap'n, we gotta play a little music for you," he said, cutting a hard look at Decker and then at Jennings.

"You're not going to like this, Skipper," Decker muttered, pulling a small tape recorder out of his pocket. He placed it close to Evans and hit the play button. The sounds were muted and somewhat distorted but distinctive. After a few seconds Evans recognized them as those of a man and a woman making passionate love. Then his eyes sharpened and his face took on a brutal expression as the realization came to him.

"You assholes," he growled, ready to kill.

Decker threw up both hands and shook his head. "Not us, Boss! Not us! Listen," he pleaded.

Evans listened for a few seconds to the moans and sighs and was about to stop the tape recorder when he heard the sound of laughter in the foreground.

"Listen to that bitch, man! That donkey-dick bastard is driving her wild," said an excited male voice that came through more clearly than the sound of the lovemaking. "I'll bet he's got a ten-inch shvantz."

Evans looked at Jennings and then at Decker. They raised their eyebrows quizzically. Keith dropped his gaze down at the table. Swan examined Evans's expression and stopped the tape.

"Boss, Ray spotted this white elephant hanging around the germ factory. When we saw it outside Doc Lubeck's hootch, we had to set up a remote sensor to see what they were up to. We figured it was the FBI. Remember, you told us the feds had been called off. We just wanted to know what they were up to. So we culled through the tapes and found that," Swan explained, gesturing at the small Panasonic on the table.

"Who are they?" Evans demanded.

"We don't know, sir," answered Swan.

"A couple of guys named Rice and Verduchi," Decker answered. "All they do is sit around spyin' on women. Somehow they can see 'em naked, or something, right through the wall of a house. They gotta be major players."

"I ran a check on the plates," Jennings added. "Nada. It doesn't exist. It's gotta be some sort of government rig. FBI, if you ask me. Only a bunch of fan belt inspectors could pull off that kind of shit."

"We thought you might know somethin', Cap'n," said Swan.

"Well, I don't," Evans snarled, grabbing the tape recorder.

He stuck it in his suit pocket and took a hard pull on his beer. They all recognized the look on his face as he stared out the window. Little age lines appeared at the corners of his eyes, and his cheeks twitched with rage.

"But I'm going to find out," he added. "And when I do . . ."

"Someone's gonna die," Jennings finished.

"Cap'n, I hope you ain't pissed at us for buggin' those guys. It was my doin'," Swan volunteered.

"Bullshit, sir. It was my idear," Keith objected. "And to tell you the truth, we had a big laugh when we come to that part about don-key-dick. How'd that guy know your nickname, Commander Donkey-dick?" He snickered.

"Raymond Edward Keith, if you ever call me that again, I'll stick your metal appendage up your ass," Evans declared, with a glare that was all business.

"Okay, Boss. Okay, okay. I got the message," said Keith, with big eyes. "You know, you used to have a sense of humor, when you was young."

Just then Chief Johnson walked into the bar, breaking the death stare Evans had leveled at Keith.

"I'm still young, goddammit," said Evans, too loudly.

"Yes, sir. If you say so, sir," three voices chimed in unison.

Johnson scanned the establishment like a pro and zeroed in on Evans, and upon seeing him with his men, a look of realization crossed his face. He shook his head like a farmer who had just discovered an infestation of boll weevils.

"The usual, Clyde," he said, as he ambled over to the SEALs' table.

"Have a seat, Chief," Swan offered.

"I should've known," he said, shaking his head at Swan, who had filled him full of beer on several occasions. "All these guys work for you, I suppose?" he asked, eyes leveled on Evans.

"Yes. We're here to help you, if you'll let us."

"I feel like a damn fool who's been had by a bunch of con artists. I bared my soul to Swan here, or whatever your name is," he said, glaring at Fred.

"My name *is* Fred Swan. But you can call me Popeye, Chief. You're okay by us."

"I second the motion," added Keith. "Thanks for all the donations, Chief."

Johnson sat down next to Evans. "You already know my problems, Commander. What do you want?" he said. He sucked on his beer and watched Evans's eyes.

"We want to go over your place with a fine-tooth comb. After hours. We want to evaluate every opening in Building 15, every door, every window, every maintenance tunnel," said Evans.

Johnson's eyes brightened.

"We know there's a direct shot from the city sewer system into the basement of the building," added Swan. "Anyone could remove the accordion grate covering the tunnel."

"Did I tell you that in a drunken stupor, or what?" asked Johnson. "No, Chief."

"We do our homework," Evans explained. "That sort of information is available down at city hall."

"All right. I'm convinced. How can I help?" Johnson asked.

"First of all, keep quiet about our presence. We'll figure out every possible way of breaking into Building 15 without being seen. When we're through, we'll know everything, from door thicknesses to security codes. Then we'll provide you with a list of things you can do right away to make it more difficult for the likes of us to gain access. Important little things like camera angles, key and lock controls, badge and pass controls, hidden bolts, and sensors."

"We *have* badges and security codes. You know that," Johnson protested.

"Yes, you do," Evans agreed. "And that's an excellent example of what we're talking about. When you issue a badge, you should keep the person's ID until he returns the badge. Every time I've gone into Building 15, the guard has checked my ID and given it back with a security badge. I could have a half dozen passes by now for unauthorized entry. There are a lot of little things you can do to make it harder for the bad guys. Actually, Chief, it's the big things I'm most worried about."

"Like what?"

"Like the only thing between the Level Four lab and the street is one man with a wheel gun and a few puny doors that Pegleg could kick down."

"Don't go underratin' my metal appendage, Cap'n," Keith warned.

Three beers later, Chief Johnson was a believer.

At ten o'clock Evans left Clyde's and drove to Susan Dorn's house as he had promised. She was the kind of woman he respected and wanted to spend time with, and since their first romantic encounter they had spent several nights together. Each moment of passion seemed to get better.

As Evans turned up the street toward her condo, he felt a surge in his loins, followed immediately by anger that boiled his blood. He found himself driving around the block several times, searching for a motor home. Rage consumed him as he thought of the men laughing and joking at their expense.

Susan Dorn greeted him at the door. She pulled him inside and kissed him, hungry for affection he wasn't ready to give. Evans tried to still his anger. He returned the kiss and caressed her gently, but try as he might, he could not get the tape recording out of his mind.

Recognizing something was troubling him, she pulled away and asked, "What's wrong, Derek?"

"Nothing. Just a lot on my mind."

"Do you want to talk about it?"

"No. I don't want to bother you with it. It's nothing I can't handle."

She stroked his cheek and hair and ran her hand down his side. Slowly, ever so gently, she kissed him. For a few seconds Evans saw men laughing at them. Rage filled his mind and his body tensed. Susan felt the tension and pulled away again.

Looking into his eyes she said, "I'm sorry. I'm acting like a starved kitten."

Evans grinned sheepishly. He pulled her close. "I don't have a performance problem, if that's what you're thinking," he whispered, nibbling on her ear. "And it's nothing for you to worry about."

He stood up from the sofa and pulled her to her feet. Gathering her in his arms, he carried her to the bedroom and made passionate love to her for more than an hour, all the while seeing the image of the laughing men in a motor home.

The next morning, Evans followed Susan to work, scanning the side streets around her condo and the CDC for a motor home that fitted the description. He waited in the parking lot until she entered the building, then followed. At the entrance a panhandler with one leg accosted him.

"Hey, buddy. Spare a few bucks for a vet?" asked Ray Keith, holding out a tin cup.

He spat a gob of tobacco juice that landed with a splat at Evans's feet. Some of the saliva ran down his beard. Evans reached into his pocket and pulled out two dollars. Keith accepted the money with a crabby expression. "Is that all you can spare for a man who gave a good leg in the service of his country?"

"Get a job!" Evans snarled.

"I got one, you cheap asshole. But it don't pay for shit," Keith snapped back.

"Ray, don't give me any lip. I'm not in the mood for it."

"Two miserable friggin' dollars? While I was fightin' Saddam you were sellin' stocks and gettin' laid," Keith said, raising his voice. "Why, that fancy suit you're wearin' must have cost two G's. Come on, Mr. Fancy pants. Give to a real good cause," Keith persisted, shaking his cup in Evans's face. He smiled wryly. "I'm good, ain't I?" he whispered, too close for comfort.

Evans pulled back, assaulted by the reek of stale beer and tobacco on his breath. "What cause? Inebriation? You're carrying your cover a little too far, Ray," Evans muttered under his breath.

"Well, let's take this thing a giant step forward. How would you like to know where that white elephant is parked?" Keith leered.

"Where?" Evans snapped, glaring like a madman.

"Twenty bucks, Mr. Fancy pants."

"Rrraay," Evans rumbled. "One of these days I'm going to . . ."

"Gonna what, buck-o? Price just went up. Twenty-five bills."

"Rrraaaay!"

"Okay, okay. If you want to be like that, thirty bucks!" Keith grinned manically.

Evans exhaled and reached for his wallet. He handed Keith two twenties and waited for his change. Keith put the money in the cup and stared at him with a blank expression.

"Well?" said Evans.

"Well, what?"

"Where's my change?" Evans demanded.

"What change?" Keith asked. He gave Evans his best Charlie Manson face and shrugged.

"Where is that motor home, goddammit?" Evans hushed under his breath, his cheeks quivering with pent-up rage.

"You have to ask me nicely, Commander Donkey-dick, or I won't tell."

"I'm running out of patience. You're the only man in this world who can get away with this kind of insolence without an ass-kickin'!" Evans shouted.

People on the street turned to stare. Keith jumped at the intensity of the words. Evans took a deep breath.

"It's parked about two blocks over to the east. Here's the plate numbers," Keith said, pointing to the numbers written on his artificial leg.

"Thanks," said Evans, turning to leave.

"Don't mention it. You know," he added, "you used to have a sense a humor, once upon a time when you wore a uniform for a livin'."

Evans tried to calm down on his way to call on the men in the motor home. But nothing worked. With a glance he checked the plate numbers as he swept past in full stride. He stopped abruptly at the door and knocked like a salesman. When it opened, he coldcocked Rice with a right to the jaw, sending him to the floor unconscious. Barging through the doorway, he caught Verduchi by surprise. He grabbed him by the neck and violently swept him off his feet. With a crash that knocked the breath out of the technician, Evans pinned him to the table. With one hand squeezing Verduchi's Adam's apple, he glared at him like a madman. Verduchi's eyes bugged out in terror as he gasped and clawed at Evans's hands.

"Who do you work for?" Evans demanded.

"I . . . I . . . I . . . ," Verduchi choked out, "I don't know what you're talking about."

Evans squeezed down on the larynx so hard it was nearly crushed under his thumb. Verduchi gurgled and tore at Evans's fingers to no avail.

"If you don't tell me what I want to know, asshole, I'll snap your neck like a scrawny-assed chicken," he growled.

"FBI," Verduchi sniveled, barely audible.

"No you don't, worm! I do!" Evans bluffed.

With his left hand he smashed Verduchi in the solar plexus, sending him into a convulsion, gasping for breath. He released him just long enough to address Rice, who was regaining consciousness. With one quick right cross, Evans nailed him on the chin, sending him back into oblivion. Turning his attention back to Verduchi, he grasped him by the throat and threw him to the floor next to his partner. Evans deftly pulled the tape recorder from his own pocket with one hand while clutching Verduchi's larynx with the other. He waited for the snoop to get his breath before playing a few sound bites at full volume directly in his ear.

"Remember this, asshole? That's me! The FBI doesn't do that kind of shit. Last chance," he said, squeezing down on Verduchi's throat. "If you don't tell me what I want to know, I'll crush your throat and leave you here to die."

"S-Systems!" blurted Verduchi, eyes bulging.

"S-Systems? What the hell is S-Systems?" demanded Evans.

In all his years in special operations, Evans had never heard of S-Systems. *A CIA front company,* he thought.

"The Company?" he demanded, referring to the CIA.

"A private corporation," Verduchi gurgled, under the pressure of Evans's iron grip.

Evans was watching Verduchi's pupils. The man was lucky. He believed him.

"If you spy on me again, I'll kill you," he growled. "You got that?"

"Yeeesss, aaahhh," Verduchi gasped.

Evans pulled him up off the floor and in one lightning motion clipped the electronic sleuth on the point of his chin, knocking him out.

The infuriated SEAL took a deep breath and for a few seconds marveled at the equipment built into the motor home. Then he planted a front-thrusting kick into the console, shattering the main

computer monitor. He threw all the videotapes he could find into a
pillowcase and set them by the door. Still enraged, he yanked out the
wiring. Satisfied with his work, he grabbed the tapes and stormed
out, leaving the voyeurs unconscious in a pile of rubble.

Chapter 15

WITH FALSE PANAMANIAN papers, Aman Abruzzi Ayyad passed through
customs in Mexico City and traveled by bus up the spine of the Sierra
Madre Occidental. At the border, he crossed into Texas with a group
of wetbacks and made contact with Palestinian supporters in Laredo.
The next day, he traveled to the Texas coast and with the assistance
of the underground, rented several cars and hotel rooms. It was in
Kingsville that he made his next big mistake. He called Sala, his second in command, in port in Tampico, Mexico, and passed him the
coordinates for landfall.

Ayyad had selected the southern coast of Texas for infiltration
because it was not unusual for a ship sailing from Tampico to
Galveston, the *Nicosia's* next port of call, to pass by relatively close
to shore. His conduct in coordinating the mission, however, was in
direct violation of Ibrahim Nasrallah's explicit order not to use the
telephone. His short message was intercepted by S-Systems and translated into English in mere seconds. When David Shipler read the
telephone key report containing the coordinates, he immediately
called Rice and Verduchi and dispatched them to Padre Island. He
also called the Panama Canal Zone and put Lieutenant Alex Gomez
and his counterterrorist squad on a higher state of alert. As Ayyad
waited for the old freighter to pass by offshore, Shipler was closing in
on his rogue operation.

When Gomez received the call to launch the mission, Savarese
was in bed. Gomez hurried to the master chief's room and burst
through the door without knocking.

"Boomer! Let's rock and roll!" he yelled, turning on the light.

The master chief was astride a young Panamanian girl.

"Whoa, man! Sorry," Gomez apologized, mouth agape.

"Give me five, Boss. I'm as hard as a rock and I'm on a roll,"
Savarese groaned, without missing a stroke.

Gomez laughed as he stared at his pale butt pumping up and down. He flipped off the light and roared as he left the room. "You got three minutes, partner. Get your white ass in gear!"

Twenty hours later, Gomez, Savarese, and three men with Hispanic surnames were in the back of a C-130 Hercules in the darkling sky over the Gulf of Mexico. The *Prancer,* the CT squad's hydrofoil, was tied down inside on a special launching skid. There was so little clearance that crewmen at the back of the aircraft had to crawl over the boat to get to the front.

Savarese inspected the rigging and ripcords on the three parachutes that would convey the boat from air to sea, then he climbed aboard. He checked everything inside the craft twice, and when he was satisfied the vessel was ready for an airdrop, he leaned over the lieutenant's seat and spoke in his ear.

"We're good to go, sir," he said over the sound of the droning engines.

"Roger," acknowledged Gomez. "Buckle up."

The master chief checked each crewman's body harness, including the lieutenant's, before strapping himself into his seat. He pressed the button on the boat's internal communications system. "We're all buckled up, L. T.," he reported.

"Roger."

Their voices sounded distant and metallic even though they were only two feet apart. Gomez pushed his com-button and spoke to the pilot of the aircraft.

"Eagle one, this is Free Ranger, over."

"Roger, Free Ranger," answered the aviator.

"Ready for launch."

"Good copy," replied the pilot. "We're about ten minutes out."

Cool air swirled through the cargo bay as the ramp whined down to its lowest angle. The jumpmaster finished his final checks, released the rear tiedowns, and crawled up on the *Prancer.* As he worked his way forward over the boat, he passed Savarese.

"You fuckin' guys are crazy," he yelled.

"Hang on, lightweight. It's an 'E-ticket' ride," Savarese hollered back.

The jumpmaster shook his head with a toothy grin and crawled on to the front of the cargo bay.

From the cockpit of the *Prancer* Gomez had a clear view of the night sky behind the aircraft. He could see stars and clouds and, in the distance, the horizon. For several minutes the Hercules droned on toward an area of the gulf devoid of ships. With nothing to do but wait, the CT squad tried to relax. But they couldn't, knowing that the moment of greatest danger was near. There was a real possibility the parachute system would fail. If it did, the *Prancer* would smash into the sea and they would disappear to watery graves without a trace.

Savarese gave Gomez a thumbs-up and grinned. In the dim light of the cargo bay, all the lieutenant could see were the master chief's gleaming white teeth. As the moment for launch approached, their eyes fixated on the little red light on the right side of the ramp. When it turned green, they felt the boat shudder as the jumpmaster released the tiedowns at the front. The aircraft momentarily nosed up in a steep climb and they caught sight of the sea three thousand feet below. Gravity entered the equation to assist the launching skid and the *Prancer* rolled smoothly out of the cargo bay. The first drag chute deployed before the front of the boat cleared the ramp. It strung out a larger chute that in turn opened up the three main parachutes. The opening shock was mild compared to that of freefall parachuting. But the boat still pitched and yawed back and forth like a wild carnival ride. The five men in the *Prancer* held their breath while they waited for the mains to deploy fully and for the boat to settle down.

When it did, Savarese hit his com-button. "Cheated death again, L. T.," he croaked.

With chutes aloft, the men floated gently down to the sea like Apollo astronauts returning from the moon. Once on the water's surface the crew hauled in the silk and stored it. During parachute recovery, Savarese fired up and tested the powerful engines. When the *Prancer* was fully seaworthy, he signaled Gomez with a thumb's-up.

The lieutenant nodded in acknowledgment, then hit his com-button. "Baseplate, Baseplate, this is Free Ranger, Free Ranger, over?"

"Free Ranger, this is Baseplate. Roger, over," answered the radio operator in Texas.

"Baseplate, this is Free Ranger. Code green, over," Gomez reported, indicating his mission readiness.

"Roger, Free Ranger. Your course is two-two-zero degrees true. Speed fifteen knots. How copy, over?"

"Roger, Baseplate. I copy two hundred and twenty degrees, fifteen knots, over."

"That's a roger, Free Ranger. Baseplate out."

The radio went silent.

"Fifteen knots, my ass," Savarese complained. "I'll be lucky to keep this puppy down to fifteen knots at idle."

The *Prancer* was a marvel of stealth technology and electronic wizardry. Made of Kevlar and coated with reflective materials, she was invisible to radar. Powered by gas turbine engines and water jets, she could rise up out of the sea on hydrofoils for high-speed transit and turn about in less than her own length of sixty-five feet at moderate speeds. With a top speed reaching ninety knots, she could outmaneuver any vessel on the high seas.

Using high-tech radar, night-vision devices, and the Global Positioning System, the sleek stealth boat rumbled slowly toward the MV *Nicosia*. Scanning all directions for seaborne traffic, Gomez avoided other vessels by steering a course that kept them just over the horizon. At two o'clock in the morning he received orders to stop and hold his position. On his radarscope he watched two faint but separate signals depart the *Nicosia* on a westerly course toward Padre Island and directly toward him.

"Baseplate, two targets, heading west two-seven-zero degrees true," Gomez reported into his radio mike.

"Roger, Free Ranger. Good copy. Board and seize at your discretion. Baseplate out," replied the radio.

Gomez held his position and watched the blips on the radarscope. They merged and separated several times as the Palestinians slowly motored toward shore. At two thousand yards Gomez switched on a night-vision scope and focused on the terrorists.

"Wow," he exclaimed.

He could clearly see two rubber boats filled with men and equipment, riding low in the water.

"What is it?" Savarese asked.

"Two Z-birds, loaded to the max. I count ten men total."

"Piece of cake," replied his salty master chief.

At a thousand yards Gomez checked with his minigun operator to ensure that the weapon was in sync with the stabilizer. The heart of the system was a black globe the size of a large beach ball mounted on top of his mainmast. Inside were the marvels of the electronic age. Accurately aiming a gun from a boat bouncing along on the tops of waves was nearly impossible. But not for the *Prancer.* Gyros maintained the attitude of the sensors and the weaponry like the eye of a bird in flight.

Gomez let the rubber boats close to within seventy-five yards of his position, then, cautiously watching the terrorists in his nightscope, he hailed them over a loudspeaker.

"This is the U.S. Coast Guard," he lied. "Keep your hands where I can see them. Prepare to come alongside."

Sala was shocked and confused by the loud voice. It seemed to come from out of nowhere, like the voice of Satan out of the darkness. He reached for his AK and strained his eyes to see what lay ahead. That was all the provocation Gomez needed to justify action.

"Fire," he said calmly, as he pushed a button on his console.

The crewman responsible for the weapon didn't have to do anything, because the system automatically locked on target. His job was to ensure that it was locked on the correct target. He released the weapon and a stream of hot lead erupted from the whirling barrels, sending thousands of 7.62-caliber full-metal-jacket rounds at the exposed men in the rubber boats, pulverizing flesh and bone and equipment. In less than ten seconds, only greasy, boiling flotsam remained on the surface of the sea.

"Baseplate, this is Free Ranger. Targets destroyed," Gomez reported.

"Roger, Free Ranger. Sterilize the scene and make port. Ensure you make hangar in Galveston no later than zero four thirty."

"Roger, Baseplate. Good copy. Free Ranger out," responded Gomez.

"Sterilize the scene, shit!" Savarese growled. "You can tell that asshole has never been on a real-world op. There ain't nothin' left but a fuckin' hole in the ocean."

Gomez checked the scene before turning the boat toward shore and rocketing across the surface at sixty knots to a special hangar located in Galveston. Two days later he was drinking Cuba libres, gazing out over the Bay of Limón and daydreaming of killing Fidel Castro, while he waited for his waitress-lover to get off work.

From the beach on Padre Island, Aman Ayyad couldn't see what had happened out in the Gulf of Mexico. The action was too far offshore for the sound of the minigun to travel. But he knew something was wrong when he saw several official vehicles crossing the bridge from the mainland at high speed. Breaking radio silence, he tried to contact Sala's Zodiac. When he failed to raise him he panicked, abandoned his comrades, and ran to the road. Flagging down the first passing car, he escaped just minutes before the FBI cordoned off the area and detained everyone. At the barrel of a gun, the young fanatic forced the elderly couple in the car to give him a ride to their home at the far end of the island.

For several days he lay low, watching TV news and the vehicular traffic on the island. When it was safe to move, he manhandled his hosts until they were kneeling in front of him with their hands bound behind their backs. Then he spat out one word.

"Pray."

The old man knew what was coming. "Our Father, who art in heaven . . . ," he began.

Using a pillow to muffle the sound, Ayyad shot the old woman first because he didn't want to hear her screams in his sleep. She lurched forward on her face and quivered in a death spasm directly in front of her husband. The old man didn't beg for mercy. He just kept praying, knowing his time had come.

The crazed terrorist squeezed off another round, and there was silence. He torched the house to cover his tracks. Taking the couple's sedan, he headed northeast along the Texas coast. He knew it was only a matter of time before the police began to look for the vehicle, so he drove nonstop to Houston and then cut east into the bayou country of Louisiana.

Staying on the back roads, Ayyad looked for a place where he could dump the car. Near Lafayette he found it. It was an isolated house trailer sitting on a wooded lot near a swamp. A pickup truck and a nondescript midsize sedan were parked in the dirt drive. He drove by the trailer three times, checking the road for two miles in each direction before making his decision. Satisfied with the conditions, he pulled off the two-lane macadam into the yard of an abandoned house nearby and parked out of sight underneath a huge live oak tree.

Now is the time for waiting, he thought.

Patience, surveillance, and ruthlessness were the keys to success in Ayyad's world. He got out of the car and was assaulted by the smell of swamp gas seeping out of the bog. Early morning dew coated everything. Patches of fog drifting off the bayou clung to the tree line alongside the road. He cased the dilapidated house like a prospective buyer, checking it carefully to ensure that no one was living in it. When his reconnaissance was complete, he leaned against the side of an old oak tree, its enormous hulk covered in Spanish moss and epiphytes. Lighting a smoke, he drew deeply on the harsh tobacco.

As he enjoyed his cigarette and observed his next target, he reflected on his situation. Like his comrades, he was willing to give his life in the struggle against the Jew but not without a fair accounting. In his twisted mind, not even Operation Desert Decree could even the score. Too many of his people were dead. His father, his mother, his brothers, his sisters. All dead. Many of the *fida'i* chose a suicide bomb in the *jihad*. To Ayyad the *jihad* was a righteous cause that could earn him a special place in heaven.

The crowded refugee camps of Lebanon and Jordan were full of men like Ayyad. In the Sabras and Shatilas of the Middle East there was little to feed upon but hatred and militant Islam, espoused by religious leaders as demented as the masses. Filth, hunger, despair, and death warped the human soul. Radical religiosity eased the pain and justified outrageous acts of terrorism. Islamic leaders taught the *fida'i* that the United States was the incarnation of the devil—the Great Satan himself—and that all Americans were tools of Satan. A strike against any aspect of Satan had the full approval of Allah. And for a *fida'i* to lose his life in this righteous cause earned him instant access to heaven.

Ayyad knew that the death of ten or forty or however many Jews by a suicide bomb would not rid his father's land of them. Only Allah could do that. And Allah had chosen him, spoken to him in his dreams. In a hashish-induced trance he had heard the voice of God.

"Ayyad, my son."

"O Lord! O merciful Allah. How may I serve you?" he mumbled.

"I have chosen you to break the seventh seal."

"But I am not worthy, Allah!" he replied to the voice inside his head.

"You shall be the seventh angel. You will pour out your vial into the air, and there will come a great plague that will cleanse the earth of the blasphemous. I am the Lord God who judgeth all."

"Allah! Almighty Allah! It shall be as Ye command."

"Blessed are those who are persecuted for righteousness' sake. Those I shall spare the plague. You are the last of the righteous family of Ayyad."

And Allah granted him beautiful hashish dreams of heaven with golden-haired houris whose bellies were round and whose buttocks were large. They danced inside his head and beckoned him to their world.

The door to the trailer opened, breaking his drug-induced trance. A long-haired man dressed like a construction worker in jeans, t-shirt, and rawhide boots walked to the pickup, cigarette in hand. He fired up the truck and sped off down the road, baseball cap pulled back on his head. As he passed Ayyad's location, country music blared from the cab of the truck. It reminded Ayyed of a kanoon and drums. In his mind's eye he saw dancers whirling, their multicolored scarves floating around them. Ayyad took a deep breath and waited like a coiled viper.

Through the window of the trailer, he saw a woman moving back and forth, busy in the kitchen.

Perhaps there is a child, he thought.

He looked for signs in the early morning light. There was a swing in the yard and a bicycle propped up against the side of the trailer.

No reason to kill the child, he thought.

A half-hour and two cigarettes later, a yellow school bus rumbled down the road and stopped in front of the trailer, brakes screeching. A young girl about ten years of age burst through the door, turned back to kiss her mother good-bye, and ran to the bus. She looked back and waved before climbing on board.

Ayyad waited another half-hour before walking the hundred yards to the trailer. He rapped softly, and when the woman opened the door, he burst through like a storm trooper. Eyes wide with fear, the woman turned and ran toward the back of the trailer. He caught her by her hair in the middle of the living room and threw her to the floor. Screaming with terror, she clawed at him viciously. But she was no match for a trained killer. Unable to fight him off by pushing and kicking, she tried desperately to crawl to the back of the trailer. Using her long hair like a bridle, Ayyad pulled back her head and knocked her unconscious with a vicious punch behind the ear. Her face plowed into the floor and she lay motionless.

While she was out, Ayyad searched the trailer. He found the gun they kept hidden in the master bedroom. In one of the smaller bedrooms he discovered a small child, sleeping. The terrorist was eating

a sandwich and drinking coffee when the woman regained consciousness.

"Who are you? What do you want?" she abjectly pleaded, half-
conscious and fearful.

"Your car," he replied calmly.

"Take it! Take it! But please, don't hurt me. I have a baby." She
got up off the floor and collected her purse. "I have some money.
You can have it."

Pulling out her billfold, she opened it to find it empty. Her hands
were shaking so badly she dropped the purse. Blood was oozing from
her nose and lips where her face had hit the floor.

"I have the money, woman," Ayyad growled, with an evil expression in his deep dark eyes. He was road weary, exhausted, which
gave him a haggard and sinister appearance that was the very em-
bodiment of the woman's worst nightmare.

"My father will be here in a few minutes. You'd better go," she
warned. "Please. Take the money. Take my car. Whatever you want,"
she pleaded. "Just go."

No one was coming. Ayyad could tell by her demeanor.

"Quiet!" he yelled, staring at her with disgust.

Her faded cotton bathrobe had fallen open and he found himself staring at her. She had large breasts and big thighs. And golden
hair. She read his face, gathered her robe around her, and began to sob.

"Please don't rape me. Please. Please don't rape me," she begged.

"I do not rape women!" he yelled. "I am *fida'i!* I do not rape
women!"

He was insulted by the suggestion. Islam forbade rape. The sound
of his booming voice awoke the baby, who began to cry and a few
seconds later toddled out of the bedroom and into the kitchen. Seeing the little girl, the woman became even more agitated.

"Please don't hurt us," she begged, clutching the child in her arms.

"Let's go," he commanded.

"Please, mister. Just take the car. Take the money. I won't tell
nobody. Just let us go."

Ayyad put the barrel of the gun to the baby's head. "Let's go,"
he growled.

His black eyes were empty and cold, and his countenance con-
veyed the certainty of his demands. She stood up slowly and stumbled
for the door, child in her arms. Ayyad grabbed a towel from the
counter and wiped the blood off the floor. He tossed the woman her

purse and, with the towel covering his pistol, followed her out the door. He locked the trailer behind them and motioned her to the car.

"Get in," he commanded.

Comforting the baby, she cooed, "Shooooeee. It's okay, honey. Mommy's here. It's okay." She hesitated.

"My father will be here any minute. You'd better leave. He has a gun in his truck," she threatened, fear written all over her face.

Blood was oozing from her nose, and from time to time she wiped it with the back of her hand, mixing blood with the tears streaming down her cheeks.

"Get in," he snapped, holding the passenger door open.

"What are you going to do to us?" she asked, as she climbed into the car.

Ayyad dashed around the car and jumped into the driver's seat. He started the engine and sped the hundred yards to the abandoned house.

"Get in my car," he commanded, pointing the gun at the child.

"No! No!" she cried. "Please let us go."

Ayyad backhanded her with his fist, then placed the barrel of the pistol against the child's head. Crying and shaking with fear, the woman gathered up her baby and got out. As fast as he could move, he opened the back door of the old couple's sedan and held it for her, directing her with his pistol to get in.

"Please don't hurt us," she pleaded. "Please."

As soon as she was in the car, he slammed the door and jumped into the front seat. He shot the woman first at point-blank range. The back of her head exploded as the projectile ripped through her skull. Blood and brain matter splattered on the child. The sound of the 9-millimeter was contained inside the vehicle, causing the blast to numb the terrorist's ears to the sound of the screaming child. She clung to her dead mother, not knowing what had happened. With big puppy dog eyes, the baby looked up at him, tears streaming down her little face. For a moment Ayyad paused. He could take the child with him and abandon her up the road.

A moment of weakness could ruin years of planning, he thought. *Thousands of Palestinian children die every day and no one cares.*

"*Allah akbar!*" he screamed as he pulled the trigger.

Then there was only silence and the ringing in his ears. Ayyad quickly drove the old couple's car around the dilapidated house, gunned the engine, and pointed it toward the swamp. He jumped out at the very last second, just before it careened off the bank into the water. He did his best to cover up the scar on the ground where the bumper had scraped the bank, then faced Mecca and prayed. Finished with his awful trade, he climbed in the woman's car and continued his journey to Atlanta.

Chapter 16

DEREK EVANS DRUMMED his fingers on the heavy oak table as he listened to the academician testifying before Senator Carson's subcommittee on international terrorism. The Harvard poli-sci professor had been speaking nonstop for thirty minutes, and everyone in the room was bored to yawns.

"Terrorism is a political, ideological, and psychological phenomenon," Professor Lawrence Ginzburg stated. "Therefore, effective countermeasures must address each of these issues." The gray-haired educator cleared his throat and stopped his testimony long enough to pour himself a glass of water.

Criminals, crazies, crusaders. What's the difference? thought Evans. *It all boils down to the same thing. Assassinations, bombings, kidnappings.*

Evans studied the faces of the attendees. CIA, FBI, DIA, DEA, State Department. He was astonished at the number of so-called experts who had crawled out of the woodwork for the secret conference.

As soon as this guy is through testifying, these bastards are going to stampede each other for the senator's attention.

"The sociopolitical objective of terrorism in fomenting wars of national liberation follow a well-defined Marxist-Leninist formula," Ginzburg continued. "They begin with attacks against a hit list of prominent persons to demoralize and discredit the government. The psychological motive is to make the government appear inept and unable to protect its citizens. Repeated terrorist actions against the political, economic, and social order bring the final phase of this scenario to fruition, and that is to provoke the government into overreaction and repression of the society. This creates a climate for revolution. To break this algorithm requires action at all social, political, and economic pressure points. In summary, I believe nation-building policies are the most effective methods of countering terrorism."

"Thank you, Professor Ginzburg," said Senator Carson. "Gentle-men, let's take a short break. Please be seated again in fifteen minutes for a roundtable discussion."

With his gavel Carson dismissed the participants. They gathered in small groups as they headed to the restrooms and coffee dispens-ers. Intel spooks stuck together, as did the academicians and the military. CIA, DIA, NSA, and FBI men huddled like rugby players in a scrum. Evans was an outsider in Washington and no longer in uni-form, so he kept to himself, as did the bald-headed man seated across the table from him.

Evans pretended to scribble notes on his pad while listening to the jabber in the room. One man was arguing for media restrictions to prevent terrorists from achieving their publicity goals. Another was arguing for a larger reward program for turning in terrorists. When Carson returned from the restroom, he approached Evans di-rectly. Evans stood to meet him.

Speaking in soft, private tones, the senator asked. "What did you think of the professor's model?"

"It's too narrow."

"How so?"

"First, there are at least three distinct groups of terrorists—maybe five if you count Russian mafias and Asian triads. Each has its own tactics and perspective on human life. The professor accurately de-scribed the Latin American groups, who fight to overthrow oppressive regimes, but his model is a poor fit for the other groups."

"Go on," Carson ordered.

Evans couldn't help noticing Bullethead across the table. He was tuned in to their conversation like a parabolic mike.

"European terrorists are usually from the middle class, sort of yuppie terrorists. Very dangerous, though. They don't have well-de-fined causes. They're more antiestablishmentarian."

"Big word. I don't want these fellows rubbing off on you, Derek. You're here to increase the common sense quotient. Please continue."

"Middle Eastern terrorists have well-defined causes."

"Such as?"

"Such as a Palestinian homeland or Islamic fundamentalism. Unfortunately, they have a warped perspective on human life. Theirs and ours. The other groups are more or less criminal organizations. It all boils down to the same thing, though, whether it's a criminal, a crusader or a crazy."

"And what's that?"

"We have to protect ourselves, particularly our vitals," Evans asserted.

"I agree," said Carson. "So what's your preliminary assessment of our overall security around those vitals?" he asked as he glanced around the room.

Evans lowered his voice so Bullethead couldn't hear him.

"When it comes to AT, Senator, we are in big trouble. Any group of dedicated tangos could bust or sneak around our current defenses. All of the systems I've analyzed so far are static, reactive organizations. None of them have an exercise branch to drill and test their security force. They're all asleep on the job."

"I was afraid of that. That's why I asked you to check into the problem. I wanted a fresh look, but not acid indigestion," he said, brow furrowed.

Evans's Savannah River audit had graphically detailed the nuclear power plant's vulnerability.

"It's not in my nature to sugarcoat my reports, Senator. You're going to need something stronger than Tums. We could have caused a meltdown that would have rendered half of Georgia uninhabitable for the next fifty thousand years."

"Keep up the good work. I'll asked my doctor for a prescription," Carson replied with a tight smile. He gave Evans the once-over. "You have a lot of practical intelligence, a lot more than these slick-talkin' paper pushers. Speak up, and afterwards, stick around. There's someone I want you to meet." He glanced across the table at the chrome-domed bureaucrat who had been straining to hear their conversation. "Maybe things aren't as bad as you think."

"Yes, sir."

Carson returned to his seat and gaveled the room into session.

"Gentlemen, according to figures compiled by the State Department, assassinations are on the rise. The recent murder of embassy employees in Pakistan is very troubling. It was done in broad daylight on a busy street. Bombings also appear to be on the rise. What are your thoughts on the matter, Mr. Jackson?"

"Senator, the capture of those responsible for the World Trade Center bombing," replied Robert Jackson of the CIA, "was a great success and illustrative of the importance of cooperation among the FBI, CIA, and . . . uh . . . other agencies." He nodded at the bald-headed man.

Ronald Watson, the FBI's expert on terrorism, jumped in. "Senator, I most wholeheartedly concur. It is important to note that the major factor in breaking the Yousef case was the rewards programs. Regrettably, the murder of the two embassy employees in Pakistan was a result of the capture of Yousef in Islamabad."

Carson glanced at Evans. "For the benefit of all present, would you please explain the circumstances leading to Yousef's capture," Carson ordered.

"Yes, sir," the FBI man replied. "An individual close to Yousef, whom we now know to be the mastermind behind the World Trade Center bombing, a man known as Istok . . ."

Carson interrupted. "Yousef was the mastermind behind the Trade Center bombing."

"That is correct, Senator."

"For the record, Istok is the person who turned in Ramzi Yousef," stated Carson, clarifying the official record of the meeting.

"Yes, sir," verified the FBI agent. "Istok was involved in another Yousef plan to bomb a U.S. air carrier. He went so far as to take a bomb to Bangkok but was too afraid to carry out the plan. In fear for his life, he returned to Pakistan, where he provided us with information that led to the capture of Yousef. The rewards program was an important factor in Istok's decision." The FBI had been the lead agency in capturing Yousef, and Watson was pounding the point home.

"Do you think we should expand the rewards programs, Special Agent Watson?" Carson asked.

"Yes, Senator. I do."

"Gentlemen, " Evans interrupted, "if we rely on rewards to combat terrorism, we had better have a big checkbook handy."

Watson gave Evans a dirty look.

"I agree," Carson said loudly.

It was the first time Evans had spoken, and the men around the table eyed him.

"Was the success we enjoyed in the Yousef affair something we can look forward to in the future?" Carson asked, with a look of concern.

He was thinking of the Palestinian Freedom Council and intelligence reports that indicated the PFC was planning a major operation in the United States.

Watson piped up. "Yousef succeeded in bombing the World Trade
Center. The good news is, he failed to crash one tower into the other,
as was his plan. His men were rank amateurs. They didn't know how
to use explosives effectively. They made open telephone calls. One
man even went back to claim the deposit on the rental van they blew
up. The bad news is, the next wave of terrorists is not likely to repeat
those mistakes."

"Are you suggesting that we should prepare for a new wave of
better-trained terrorists?" Carson asked, more as a statement than a
question.

"Yes, Senator. I am. Those who are waiting in the wings in the
ranks of the PFC are."

"Strike that from the record," Carson interrupted.

Evans looked from eye to eye around the table. Some appeared
to know what PFC meant; others, like him, didn't.

"I don't think that we can discount Yousef as a serious player,"
interjected the DIA man. "You don't rack up the kind of frequent-
flyer miles Ramzi Yousef did using your personal MasterCard."

Jackson, the CIA expert, spoke up. "We are really talking about
two groups here. First, there are what I call state-supported groups.
We've learned a great deal about them in the last ten years. Our
capabilities to anticipate their missions have improved greatly, thanks
to David Shipler and the dedicated men in his organization."

The bald-headed man nodded graciously, accepting the acco-
lade. Little drops of perspiration appeared on his smooth pate.

"During the Gulf War, we successfully thwarted several hundred terrorist attempts," Jackson continued. "The other group of
terrorists is what one might call free-lancers. The term *free lance*
takes away the characterization of whether they're amateurs or professionals. Most of the free-lancers do make tradecraft mistakes."

Evans had found new respect for these so-called experts.

"There is a third group," the DIA man added. "The PFC is a
new breed of cat."

"Strike that from the record," Carson growled. "That concern
is secret, compartmented information."

After an hour of heated discussion, Carson tried to wrap it up.
"The reality, gentlemen, is that there will be more terrorist incidents
in the future, not just because of Islamic fundamentalism but because national and ethnic conflicts are growing at an alarming rate
around the world. Despite the fact that we have developed some

truly amazing capabilities and some remarkable cooperative arrange-
ments with a number of difficult governments, we are vulnerable to
attack. It would be a grave mistake to minimize terrorists' capabilities."

"Moreover, there are some targets we simply cannot afford not
to protect," Evans added emphatically. "Time is on the side of the
terrorist, who ultimately decides the where, the when and the how,
and that is one hell of a tactical advantage. Therefore, we must harden
our volatile industries, particularly those that are self-feeding, such
as nuclear, biological, and chemical. What I am suggesting is a bal-
anced approach of AT and CT, supported by an efficient intelligence
system."

Carson nodded his head in agreement. "Mr. Shipler," he said,
"I would be interested in your thoughts on cooperative intelligence,
particularly on the establishment of a worldwide terrorism center."

The pasty-faced bureaucrat hadn't spoken a word all day. He
wiped the perspiration from his shiny scalp with a handkerchief before speaking.

"Senator, hard intelligence does more to contain terrorism than
any other mechanism. We at S-Systems have developed several personality profiles that allow us to target key individuals."

The name S-Systems caused anger to course through Evans's
veins. He glared at Shipler like a raging bull.

"Our analysis reveals that more than 80 percent of terrorists are
males between the ages of twenty and thirty-five," Shipler continued. "They are single, of urban origin, and from the mainstream of
their societies. Once recruited, these young radicals advance by ap-
prenticeship with practical, hands-on education in boot camps in the
Middle East or elsewhere. They earn their way up the terrorist ladder
by means of bombings, kidnappings, and assassinations. Intelligence
is the key to intervention."

"What do you mean by boot camps?" asked the senator.

"There are terrorist camps that provide training in weaponry,
explosives, martial arts, kidnapping, and tradecraft. These training
centers are weak links that can be exploited for intelligence value."

Tradecraft was the term intelligence people used to describe
cloak-and-dagger affairs and clandestine communication methods.

"Mr. Shipler," said Evans, "terrorist organizations are compartmentalized pyramid structures in which the hardcore leaders at the
top communicate clandestinely with closed cells at the bottom. The
leadership rarely, if ever, takes part in actual operations."

"That is true, Mr. Evans," Shipler agreed.

"So the terrorists we apprehend are simply dumb-ass foot soldiers caught up in war."

"War? War, Mr. Evans? I think not. Criminals! Criminals conducting criminal acts against humanity," Shipler asserted.

"At the base of the pyramid, sympathizers provide money, safe havens, vehicles, and political and ideological support. Without that support, terrorist organizations couldn't exist. Are the Irishmen in Boston who sympathize with the IRA in Belfast guilty of murder because they give money to the cause?"

"Yes, Mr. Evans, they are partially responsible. What is your point?" Shipler asked impatiently.

Carson sat back and watched the interchange, puzzled why Evans had chosen to attack Shipler.

"If we know who these sympathizers are—these good American citizens who contribute to the IRA cause—should we strike them, Mr. Shipler?"

"Certainly not, and that's exactly my point," Shipler argued. "We must strike those intent upon attacking us."

He smiled thinly, thinking he had cornered Evans.

"Professor Ginzburg addressed root causes and proposed nation building as the solution to terrorism. You, Mr. Shipler, advocate direct action against the terrorist foot soldier."

"I advocate striking anyone intent upon striking us—the criminals who blow up airplanes and kidnap our citizens."

"Where do we draw the line, Mr. Shipler, between leader, attacker, supporter, and sympathizer if they are all partially responsible?" Evans asked.

"We neutralize those who intend to kill and maim."

"So we attack only the dumb foot soldier and leave the generals to plan another mission. What about the responsibility and accountability of all of those who make terrorism possible?" Evans demanded.

"I disagree with your analogy, Mr. Evans. We must surgically strike those who attack us. Leader or soldier. We can't challenge or champion every disenfranchised group in the world," Shipler argued.

"Mr. Shipler, contrary to what you might think, I concur. But one man's terrorist is often another man's hero. The righteousness of the conflict very much depends upon one's perspective. But any way you cut it, we have a moral right—and indeed an obligation—to prevent an attack on our nation. But how is it possible to judge men guilty of terrorism before an offensive operation takes place?" Evans asked.

"Absolute certainty is not always possible, Mr. Evans. However, modern methods of intelligence gathering may greatly exceed your expectations."

"I doubt that, Mr. Shipler," Evans replied.

There was a long pause before Watson brought up another subject. Later, after Senator Carson dismissed the committee, he asked Evans and Shipler to accompany him to his office for a private meeting. The short walk to his office was cloaked in silence. When the door closed behind them, the senator took the chair behind his desk and gestured for Evans and Shipler to have a seat in front of him.

"David, I've asked Commander Evans to evaluate the security of the nuclear facilities in the target area. His initial findings are very disturbing," Carson began.

Shipler nodded with a puzzled expression. "Sir, S-Systems is primarily an international intelligence-gathering organization. The majority of my assets are located outside the continental United States, so I'm afraid I have very little to offer Mr. Evans."

"I'm not asking you to allocate assets, David. There are lots of ways to skin a cat, and lots of people working toward the same purpose. Sometimes it's wise to collaborate," Carson admonished.

"Yes, sir. I understand. I assure you that we are doing our very best to cooperate with all concerned," said Shipler in a perfunctory manner.

"How is S-Systems contributing to the cause?" Evans asked.

"We are closely monitoring international criminal organizations, Mr. Evans."

"How, Mr. Shipler?" Evans pressed.

"I am not at liberty to answer questions concerning our modus operandi."

"Do the names Rice or Verduchi ring a bell?" Evans asked.

Shipler's eyes darted back and forth from Carson to Evans. His lips tightened and his eyes hardened.

"Let me be more specific. Do they work for you?" Evans demanded.

Shipler reluctantly answered. "Yes, Mr. Evans, they do." He had received a full report on the $75,000 of damage Evans had done to his motor home. He knew who the commander was, and he knew Evans had a number of his illegally acquired videotapes.

"What the hell is going here?" Carson barked. "I brought you two here to establish a productive relationship, not to referee a verbal boxing match."

"Senator, I think this will answer your questions."

Evans took the tape recorder out of his briefcase and placed it on Carson's desk. He pushed the play button and watched Shipler's face for reaction. Shipler shook his head and raised one eyebrow at the sounds emanating from the tape recorder. When Rice started joking about the size of the man's penis, the senator frowned.

"Well, you know how it is, Commander," said Shipler, in an ingratiating voice. "The boys got a little carried away in their idle time. No harm meant."

Evans's eyes blazed when Shipler used his military title, knowing that the spook had run a background check on him.

"Right. I see you recognize Rice and Verduchi. Do you know who the guy is that's getting laid?"

"No," Shipler lied, "but he sounds like he's enjoying himself," he said, trying to make light of the situation in front of the senator.

"He is. You know how I know, Shipler? It's me, asshole! Did you have a court order to bug me?"

"Just a minute here," Shipler snapped. "We were doing a favor for . . . for the FBI."

"Some favor. Senator, did you know these men play games like this?" Evans asked.

Carson's eyebrows lowered as he leveled his gaze on Shipler. "Is this how S-Systems conducts business, David?"

"Senator, I assure you it won't happen again."

"Have you fired the men in question?" Evans demanded.

"No."

Susan Dorn was reaching the height of climax. Evans stopped the tape and put the tiny recorder inside the breast pocket of his suit. "Do you intend to fire them?" he asked.

"Rice and Verduchi are experts in their field," Shipler replied.

"And what field might that be? Pornography?"

"We can't afford to lose their skills at this point in time," Shipler argued, with a sardonic expression on his face.

"They got something on you, Shipler?" Evans quipped. "Don't

answer that. Do you intend to obtain a court order before bugging another U.S. citizen?"

"Commander, we generally operate overseas, offshore, so we don't need a court order. We only looked into the Dorn matter as a favor to the senator, to the FBI," he corrected himself. "I reassigned the men to more pressing matters."

"So what's your professional assessment? Is there a threat to Dr. Dorn, the CDC, or to Georgia Power and Electric?"

"Not anymore," Shipler said with satisfaction.

"No threat to a major sporting event in the Atlanta area?"

"Not at the moment, Commander Evans," Shipler insisted, with a hint of indignation.

"None of this fits your neat little profile, does it?" Evans pressed.

"As we briefed Senator Carson, we intercepted several telephone calls between the southern exchange and the Middle East. We traced them to known members of the PFC."

"PFC?" asked Evans.

"The Palestinian Freedom Council. For your edification, Commander, that's a highly compartmented terrorist organization whose stated objective is to create a Palestinian homeland in Israel. We followed the development of their operation and neutralized it," said Shipler proudly, speaking to Carson as if Evans wasn't in the room.

"And just what sort of mission was the PFC planning to conduct?" Evans persisted.

"I'm not authorized to answer that question."

"We think they were preparing to attack the Naval Submarine Base at Kings Bay," Carson explained.

Evans's antenna went on high alert. Kings Bay was a nuclear submarine base on the Georgia coast just north of Jacksonville, Florida. Carson hadn't mentioned Kings Bay when he had hired him to do security assessments.

"Shipler, what am I thinking?" Evans asked.

"What?"

"What am I thinking? Right now."

"I don't understand, Commander Evans," Shipler replied, eyebrows raised.

"You don't know, do you? It's a good thing you can't read my mind, buddy, because you wouldn't like what I'm thinking. But then again, you can't read anyone's mind, can you?" he growled. "You don't know what you don't know, you dumb fuck!" growled Evans. "You can't read the mind of a terrorist. You only know what your eavesdroppers have heard. The information could be false. Everything in your neat little pile of dung could be a concerted effort to lead us astray."

"Evans!" Carson interrupted. "Do you remember Saddam Hussein's statement over Radio Baghdad during Desert Storm?"

"Senator, Saddam Insane made a lot of inane statements over Radio Baghdad."

"How about this one? 'Abdul, the table is set.' Remember that?"

"No," Evans admitted, not taking his eyes off Shipler.

"That was the signal to execute more than two hundred terrorist missions scattered around the world, the ones Bob Johnson alluded to today. None of them succeeded, Evans. Not one of them. Thanks to S-Systems. Thousands, perhaps tens of thousands, of lives were saved. We owe David and the other patriots of S-Systems a great deal."

"That may be true, sir. But I don't appreciate my privacy being violated by a couple of clowns and then their boss not doing anything about it," Evans replied forcefully.

"Commander, surely you ran across such exuberant transgressions during your time in the Navy," Shipler apologized, but the tone in his voice was derisive as if he looked down on military services. Evans grew even more enraged.

"You think you know a lot about me, don't you, Shipler?" he growled, staring at Shipler like an attack dog. "You're right. I did run headlong into some exuberant transgressions. And when I did, I kicked ass. Your boys, Shipler, know better than to use their sophisticated equipment to spy on innocent people. Do you remember me asking you about responsibility and accountability? About generals and foot soldiers?"

"Yes. I recall your inappropriate analogy," Shipler sniped.

"You're the general accountable for Rice and Verduchi. Right?"

"Yes."

"And you haven't fired them?" Evans continued.

"I assured you it wouldn't happen again," Shipler insisted with an edge of impatience.

"You better hope not, pal. Because I will hold you personally accountable," Evans said, shaking his finger in Shipler's face.

"Are you threatening me, Commander Evans?" Shipler demanded indignantly.

Evans bristled. He didn't nod his head yes or no. Shipler just sat in his chair, staring at Evans with a belligerent expression. Evans read the look and disliked what he saw.

"I can see you haven't gotten the message," Evans growled. With his left hand, Evans reached out as if to grab Shipler by the arm. When the bureaucrat went for the feint, he knocked him out of his chair with a right cross. Shipler was out cold, sprawled on the senator's plush carpet.

"Damn it, Evans! This is not the grinder at BUDS for Christ's sake," Carson shouted, referring to the SEAL training school in Coronado, California.

"Senator, are you planning on running for president some day? You ever get a little puntang on the side? Don't answer that question, sir. Someone may be recording this conversation. But do ask Shipler, when he wakes up. Ask him if he has a videotape of your last little peccadillo. Perhaps he can provide an edited copy, without Rice's blow-by-blow commentary on your performance. Better yet, he can probably get you a copy of your opponent in some seedy little motel or making a shady deal in the back room. Of course, it will come with a hefty price tag. I'll be in touch," said Evans, standing to leave.

"I got the message, hardass. Now sit back down!" Carson ordered. He exhaled with a gush and said, "Perhaps Big Brother is getting a little too big for his britches."

Evans stared at Carson for a few seconds before resuming his seat. The senator fumbled with his desk drawer and pulled out a bottle of Scotch and a couple of small glasses he had pocketed during a visit to the White House. He poured two stiff shots, all the while glancing back and forth at Shipler with a worried expression.

"This Scotch was gift from Margaret Thatcher," he said as he pushed a glass toward Evans. Then he glanced at Shipler again. "Should we call a doctor?"

"Nah. It wasn't a hard punch. Glass jaw."

"You know he'll probably sue you, not to mention the other nasty things he's capable of," Carson warned.

"Oh no he won't, not as long as I've got Rice's library of videotapes, and this," Evans said, patting the tape recorder under his suit coat. "You know, I put it on 'record' when I stuck it in my pocket. Would you like for me to turn it off now, senator?"

Carson chuckled. "Yes. Please. You've grown a lot since my days in the teams."

Evans nodded acknowledgment of the compliment and turned off the tape recorder.

"These people are not the kind of folks to fool around with, Derek. They are incredibly powerful."

"And I can understand why," Evans countered. "When a criminal does it, it's called blackmail."

Carson sipped his drink. "You're right, of course. I'll have to handle this very carefully," he said, studying the amber liquid in his glass. "This organization is doing some phenomenal things for the CIA, the DEA—shit, for the whole damn country. I had hoped to work you in with them." Carson glanced at Shipler, who was beginning to stir. "But that's out of the question now." He exhaled heavily and asked, "Have you calmed down?"

"Yes, sir," Evans replied, coolly.

"Good. Got your sense of humor back?"

Evans nodded.

"Excellent." Carson smiled. "You know, I assumed Susan Dorn was a feminazi. How about playing that tape for me again?" he chuckled.

Evans shook his head. "Not a chance, Senator. And if you recall, I never said who the lady was," he growled as he swirled his glass.

"Cheers," Carson toasted.

Evans drew hard on the harsh liquid and without blinking stared at Carson until the senator looked away.

Chapter 17

AMAN AYYAD PARKED the Louisiana car in the long-term lot of Atlanta's Hartsfield Airport and scanned the terminal before getting out. He had carefully wiped down every surface, emptied the ashtray, and driven through a car wash before going to the airport. Confident it was clean of any evidence that could tie him to the murders, he abandoned the vehicle. With any luck, it would be in the lot for months before anyone noticed it. By then Operation Desert Decree would be over and he would be back in Beirut. He took a small bag out of the trunk, being careful not to leave any fingerprints, and walked briskly to the terminal building.

Outside, he stopped on the sidewalk and pretended to check his pockets while using the glass as a mirror. He memorized the faces of everyone behind him before entering the terminal. Inside, he crossed the huge circular lobby, and purchased a Coke at a small sandwich shop on the rim. He selected a table where he could observe everyone coming and going through the atrium. Nearby at Houlihan's a piano man hammered away at the keys, entertaining a crowd gathered there.

For fifteen minutes Ayyad skulked like a snake, watching everyone in the atrium. Paranoia, a character trait useful to spies and terrorists, was an integral part of his nature. When he was satisfied no one had followed him, he purchased a newspaper, cleared the metal detector, and took the tram to Concourse C. He rode the escalator up and casually searched for the small restaurant where he was supposed to meet Walead Kasim. He passed it twice in both directions, carefully noting its layout. Then he selected a nearby coffee shop where he could observe planes taking off and landing. There he ordered a roll and coffee and began his vigil.

Watching and waiting were requisite skills for a terrorist. Years of training made him almost invisible. Certain mannerisms attract attention, and he had been schooled not to use them. His clothing was deliberately nondescript. With his head slightly bent forward, he read his paper while watching baggage handlers and service personnel working on the tarmac below. Fuel trucks came and went amid baggage trains and catering trucks. He studied the workmen, looking for weaknesses in security.

Outside the cafe, a hurried passenger grabbed a telephone. Ayyad's heart skipped a beat as he watched the man make a call.

The Great Satan is listening, he thought. *He hears everything, in every language.*

He lowered his eyes a little and raised his paper higher for fear the monstrous electronic spider might have its eye on him. A huge jumbo jet caught his attention as a tug pushed it back for departure. The sight of the big bird on the move temporarily quelled his nerves. Its giant wings shivered as it shuddered off under its own power for a rendezvous with the sky. He watched it taxi and wait in line and finally lift off in a thunderous roar, headed west into the sunset.

When it reached a thousand feet, he thought: *Now. Fire!*

In his mind's eye he saw the Stinger fly out of its tube and arc across the sky in a curved path, a vapor trail in its wake. He could almost see the flash of the explosion, igniting the fuel in one wing. As the plane winged its way into the sunset, an enormous ball of smoke and flame like the image of the space shuttle *Challenger* filled his mind. Then he thought of Omar Azed and his mission to acquire Stingers from the Pathan. His first impulse was to call to check on his progress. Then he thought of the Great Satan's huge electronic spider, watching, listening, waiting to entrap them. Ayyad had learned his lesson about the dangers of the telephone. The hard way.

All is the will of Allah, he silently prayed.

He watched airplanes explode in his mind's eye as he waited for his rendezvous with Walead Kasim.

Die, infidels! Die! In the name of the Prophet, you will all die!

He waited until ten minutes before the appointed hour then drifted back to a bookstore overlooking the escalator. When he spotted Kasim coming up, he studied the people around him. The man's professorial appearance was confirmed by his absentminded nature. He was so self-consumed, he ambled along without checking to see if anyone was trailing him. He failed to notice an attractive woman who was eyeing him like a lean cut of meat. She purposely bumped into him and dropped her bags.

"Excuse me," Fawcett muttered, caught off guard.

"Oh. It was my fault. I'm so sorry," said the woman.

Fawcett helped her collect her belongs and apologized again, but didn't pick up on her efforts to strike up a conversation. Ayyad observed a sinister-looking man nearby, waiting for an opportunity to grab the professor's laptop computer. But Fawcett never gave him a chance. He ignored the woman and ambled off, unaware he was so close to being a victim of crime. The woman shrugged her shoulders at her accomplice and headed in the opposite direction, looking for another victim.

Fawcett walked directly to the restaurant and selected a table. Ten minutes after rendezvous time, when Ayyad was satisfied Fawcett hadn't been followed, he made contact.

"Greetings. How are you, my friend?" asked Fawcett cordially, standing to shake hands.

With a smile and a handshake like a Westerner, Ayyad greeted the older man. Fawcett noticed that Ayyad's left hand, his unclean hand, was held close to his body. When they finished shaking hands, Ayyad's right hand touched his heart, in an Arab-style greeting. At times he forgot the Arab world and its customs.

"I am fine. And you, Uncle Kasim?" asked Ayyad pleasantly.

"Great. Coffee?"

"Yes, thank you," Ayyad answered politely.

Fawcett ordered, and while they waited for Ayyad to be served they chatted. After a decent interval of small talk, the young terrorist turned to the issues weighing heavily on his mind.

"Are the apartments and vehicles ready, Uncle?" He had men arriving on a set schedule, and he had to quarter them out of sight.

"Yes. But I must delay the operation for a few months," said Fawcett in his self-assured manner.

After a stunned silence, Ayyad, eyes ablaze, replied, "We cannot."

Fawcett studied the younger man's agitated face before responding.

"Why?" he asked.

"Desert Decree is composed of many cells, each operating independently. It must be accomplished according to the schedule. It would be most unwise to change any part of the plan at this late date."

"There is a man analyzing the security of the building where the material is stored. I think he is FBI or CIA."

"He must be eliminated, Uncle," Ayyad stated without emotion.

"No. No! That would not be wise," Fawcett exclaimed, taken aback.

"Uncle Kasim, I will see that he does not interfere with our plans," said Ayyad, confident of his abilities.

"He is a most unusual man. Very dangerous. He has the eyes of a hawk. Like yours. I saw him disarm a huge black man as easily as I could disarm a child," Fawcett muttered.

"I am not a huge black man, Uncle. I am *fida'i*," said Ayyad, too loudly.

They both looked around nervously to see if anyone had overheard the comment.

"I will blow him to Satan's door," Ayyad continued in a whisper. "This is a holy war, and Allah is on our side. One man is not a reason to delay Desert Decree."

Fawcett studied Ayyad's face carefully before speaking.

"It would not be wise to eliminate him. His death would draw attention to the laboratory. In a few days he will present his findings. The information should prove useful to our cause."

"Very well, if that is your judgment, Uncle Kasim. But we must proceed on schedule. The men will be arriving soon. Each group must remain isolated from the others in case the Great Satan has spotted anyone entering the country." Ayyad was spouting U.S. Special Forces doctrine verbatim from the books he had studied in terrorist training camps.

"Here are the keys to the apartments and the vehicles," said
Fawcett, handing Ayyad a heavy brown package. "The addresses are
inside."

"There is a stop sign on the corner near your apartment, Uncle
Kasim," said Ayyad, staring at Fawcett without blinking. "If I need
to talk with you, I will put a chalk mark across the letter O. Check it
every day. If you see the signal, meet me here at nine P.M."

"That is a bad time. Mondays and Wednesdays I teach from
seven to nine."

"Very well then. Make it ten-thirty."

"Okay."

Ayyad continued his briefing. "Never go to any of the safehouses,
Uncle. Once the men have infiltrated, it would not be prudent for
you to do so. If you need to speak with me, mark the sign, but do so
without drawing attention to yourself. If I see the signal, I will come
here at ten-thirty every night until we meet."

"I understand," Fawcett said.

"Find out where this specialist lives in case we have to neutralize
him before the mission," Ayyad persisted.

Fawcett nodded agreement.

"Uncle Kasim?"

"Yes?" Fawcett answered, staring into Ayyad's fiery eyes.

"Timing is critical. There are other missions which cannot be
delayed."

"What? I personally reviewed the plan with the senior members
of the Council," said Fawcett, shocked by the comment.

Realizing Fawcett wasn't privy to the nuclear submarine mission, Ayyad covered his tracks.

"Uncle Kasim, there are a few minor diversions you may not be
aware of. Compartmentation is the key to covert operations." He
studied Fawcett's face. "The future of our people is in your hands,
Uncle. In Lebanon and Jordan they are starving in refugee camps.
Jews stomp on their hands in Palestine. They kill our children for
throwing rocks to protest their oppression. We have no home," Ayyad
pleaded, playing on Fawcett's emotions.

"I understand the urgency. I just think it would be sensible to
determine what Evans is up to before we . . ."

"Evans? Ahhh, yes. The specialist," Ayyad mumbled, meeting
Fawcett's eyes. "It doesn't matter if he is FBI, CIA, or Mossad. Once
we have a biological weapon, we will control the Great Satan. Uncle

Kasim, this is your plan. Allah gave you special knowledge and the power to save our people."

Fawcett nodded agreement, but with great concern written on his face. He didn't know Allah the way Aman Ayyad knew Allah. He wasn't a Muslim. He didn't even believe in God.

"I must go now, Uncle," said Ayyad, getting up to leave. *"Assalam alaykum."*

"Take care," Fawcett replied.

He watched, frowning, as the young terrorist left the restaurant and merged with the crowd.

Chapter 18

BENEATH A BLACK and starless sky, an old pickup jounced down a dirt road in back country Louisiana. The two men and the boy inside the Ford were engaged in a traditional and noble Southern pursuit: the possum hunt. The lowly marsupial was easy to catch, provided meat and hides, and no one placed a limit on the number a man could kill.

"Pa?"

"Yeah, boy?" answered Charlie Kirkland, over the sound of grinding gears.

"Why does a possum dog hunt possums?" asked Jake, Kirkland's inquisitive twelve-year-old son.

In the back of the pickup rode two hound dogs, Little Red, barely more than a puppy, and Jefferson Davis III, a champion possum dog. Little Red was the boy's dog.

"A possum dog follers his instincts, Jake. He hates the smell of a possum, and if he catches one, he'll tear 'im to pieces. Once ol' Jeff Davis trees a critter, you gotta control him if you want to catch the possum alive."

Kirkland's farm provided ground-meat filler for numerous restaurants in the area. He wanted his prey alive so he could butcher them as demand required. Mixed with pork or beef, unsuspecting tourists couldn't tell their sausage was part marsupial.

"Some people think possums are stupid critters, Jake," said Eugene Widder, Charlie's best friend, "'cause they'll jump down out of a tree right smack dab into the middle of a pack of huntin' dogs. But they ain't stupid a-tall. Just skittish. They thrive around humans where other critters croak. So they gotta be smart."

"Yep. They're right witty," Kirkland agreed. "They'll eat just about anything. That's what gives 'em the advantage." He rounded a curve and downshifted the truck. "When your grandpappy was a boy, he used to sell possum hides for twenty cents apiece."

"That ain't much, Pa," Jake replied.

"It was during the Depression," Charlie explained. "The South has always been poor, Jake. And possums have always been here for the takin'. Meat's a bit greasy, but fillin'." He looked at his son's silhouette. "Why, when I was a boy we ate possum for breakfast, dinner, and supper," he joked, "and my mama made sheets out of fertilizer sacks. That's why I'm so tough. Eatin' possum and sleeping on sandpaper."

Charlie Kirkland actually made an excellent living. His freezer was full of fish, crab, oysters, squirrel, rabbit, deer, 'gator—all the bounty of the land but possum. Kirkland hated the taste of possum. As a boy, hunger had forced him to eat it for breakfast.

"You're joshin' me, Pa," Jake said.

"No I ain't. I guarantee. You didn't slide outta bed in a hurry in those days."

The truck took a nasty bounce in a chuckhole, nearly tossing Little Red out the back. Charlie jammed on the brakes and screeched to a halt in the middle of the road. They all piled out, leaving the engine running and the headlights on. No one in his right mind traveled the back roads of Louisiana at three in the morning. Charlie untied Jefferson Davis and walked down the edge of the road in front of the truck, taking advantage of the headlights. The dog sniffed and snorted through the grass.

Charlie urged him on. "Come on, Jeff. Find 'em, boy. Get 'em, boy. Get me a possum."

When Jefferson Davis failed to alert, Charlie tied him in the back of the pickup and drove to his second favorite spot. He pulled the truck off the macadam and parked underneath a huge live oak burdened with Spanish moss.

"Pa?"

"Yeah, boy?"

"Why do folks call this the hangin' tree?"

"'Cause folks used to hang nigras here in the old days."

"Aw, you're joshin' me again. They really hung nigras here?"

"Yep. Sure did. Lynched 'em right cheer," said Charlie, shining his flashlight through the windshield at a huge bough.

"I'm stayin' in the truck, Pa. There might be nigra ghosts around here," Jake declared.

"Suit yourself, boy. Ghosts do tend to stick around the places where they was kilt."

Jake's eyes got bigger. He shined his flashlight around underneath the enormous tree, looking for phantoms.

Kirkland and Widder got out and untied Jefferson Davis. The dog jumped down, stuck his nose to the ground, and immediately struck off on a possum trail.

"Get 'em, Jeff. Go get 'em, boy," yelled Charlie, urging the dog on.

As Jefferson Davis III trumpeted jubilantly along an invisible trail that led into the night, Jake sat in the pickup, watching his father's flashlight flicker between the trees. The sound of Jefferson Davis on the hunt was just too much for Little Red. He whined and begged and whimpered. When Jake's feeling for the puppy overcame his fear of ghosts, he got out and climbed up into the bed with him. Little Red was straining so hard on his leash he was choking. So Jake untied him. In a flash the pup bounded out like a coiled spring and immediately began sniffing the ground. But instead of following Jefferson Davis, he headed off toward the bayou behind the old house.

Jake followed cautiously as the dog ran back and forth along the terrorist's invisible trail. At the edge of the bayou Jake saw tire tracks and the ground scar on the bank. With his flashlight he followed the signs into the water. At low tide the car was floating rear end up, just below the surface. As he shined the light around, trying to make out the underwater image, the beam seemed to freeze in one spot, as if seized by the hand of a ghost. Jake's mouth dropped open and his face turned white. Through the murky water he saw the bloated face of a child floating underneath the rear window. He screamed like he had been bitten by a cottonmouth.

"Pa!"

Sheriff La Fay recognized the body as that of the missing child. Seeing the little girl inside the submerged vehicle, his experience told him he would find the mother in there too. As he stood on the bank waiting for the divers and the wrecker crew, his mind raced.

He must have been snot-suckin' drunk to kill his wife and his baby, he thought.

At first he had assumed the couple was having a marital squabble and that Lily Colton had taken off for a few days to clear the air. Then Jake Kirkland had discovered the car, and murder had entered the equation. His prime suspect was the spouse, Bill Colton, a known drinker and womanizer. Colton was locked up in his cruiser, parked underneath the old live oak.

La Fay was convinced he had his man until the wrecker pulled the car out of the water. When he saw the Texas plates, his primary theory evaporated. His report of a Texas vehicle found in a Louisiana bayou with two bodies inside hit Special Agent Thomas Durance's desk at FBI headquarters in D.C. the next day. Durance had been waiting for the car to show up since the Padre Island couple's charred remains were found and forensics had concluded that the old people had been shot. He'd run a standard vehicle check to determine the plate numbers and had put out an APB.

He called Senator Carson at home on a private line before leaving to investigate the crime scene.

"Carson here."

"Sir, the car just surfaced."

"Where?"

"Lafayette, Louisiana. Two bodies inside. A mother and a child."

"My God! This animal is leaving a trail of corpses. Tom, we've got to find out what this Desert Decree is all about. And we've got to stop this animal. Any eye witnesses? Do you know what this guy looks like?"

"Yes sir. We arrested four men on Padre Island who gave us the same description, for what little it's worth. Male, age twenty-eight to thirty-five, five foot ten, black hair, close-cropped beard."

"That's not much to go on," Carson said.

"That's why I called you, sir. Anything new in the world of secret, compartmented information I should know about?"

"No. Nothing new in SCI. What about the men you arrested?"

"They don't know anything. They're just mules. They thought they were helping to smuggle in Palestinian refugees. I've got them under surveillance."

"What are your plans?" the senator asked.

"I'm going to Lafayette this evening. Hopefully I can lift a print or find a witness."

"Good. Call me if you come up with anything."

"Yes, sir. I will. Out here."

The next day, Durance examined all the evidence Sheriff La Fay had compiled. When he visited the morgue and saw the shattered skull of the baby girl, he wanted to tear the killer limb from limb. The man he was after was twisted and deranged, and he was determined to catch him. Like Jefferson Davis III, the FBI agent was following an invisible trail. He sent a graphic report out on the wire that electrified and energized the law enforcement community throughout the country. Thousands of eyes began to search for Lily Colton's light blue Toyota Tercel.

The crime that led Special Agent Thomas Durance to Georgia, though, had little to do with Aman Abruzzi Ayyad. The engine's computer in the Colton's Tercel was relatively valuable and easy to steal, and it was a hot item for thieves in the Atlanta area. Less than forty-eight hours after Ayyad abandoned the Toyota in the long-term parking lot at Hartsfield, a gang of hoodlums conducted a smash-and-grab on several vehicles. By the time airport security arrived on the scene, the thieves were gone. It was the routine check of ownership that alerted Durance and drew him to Atlanta. Before leaving Louisiana, he called to check in with Senator Carson. Upon hearing that the FBI agent was going to Atlanta, the senator arranged a meeting between Evans and Durance.

The connection between the men was the U.S. Navy SEAL Teams. Thomas Durance had served with Derek Evans during the early days of SEAL Team Two. Carson had served in SEAL Team One. Both Carson and Durance had been badly mauled by war: Carson had lost a leg, Durance an eye. Both had won the Medal of Honor.

In Atlanta, Durance investigated the ransacked Toyota Tercel, and while he waited for forensics to complete their analysis, he met Evans in a coffee shop in downtown Atlanta. He spotted him instantly, even though decades had passed since they'd served together in the Teams. Evans was dressed in a business suit, Durance in blue jeans and polo shirt.

"Double Tap," he said, holding out his hand. "You look like a damn FBI agent." Durance called Evans by the nickname he had given him years before on a shooting range in back country Virginia. The term was slang for two rapid-fire shots.

"You look like a damn redneck, sir," Evans shot back, giving him a brisk handshake.

Durance had been a junior officer when he had won the Medal, in the days when the commander was still a junior enlisted man. He remembered Evans as a brash young petty officer hell bent for leather. After some small talk, Durance got down to business. He placed a composite drawing of the terrorist on the table between them.

"This is one bad dude, Double Tap. He left a trail of bodies from Texas to Louisiana." He recounted the crime scenes in some detail, from Padre Island to the bayou to Atlanta. "If I were going to ditch a car in a place to make John Law think I'd left the country, I'd choose an international airport," Durance concluded.

Evans's face grew serious. Deadly serious. "Tommy, do you remember Boomer Savarese?"

"Yeah. The kid who used to rent out a Vietnamese whorehouse and wear 'em all out?"

"That's the guy. But he's not a kid anymore. He's a master chief who's been everywhere and done everything twice. In a few months he's going to come to work for me."

"So?"

"So he stays in touch with my crew. He was off Padre Island about the same time your op went down."

Durance shrugged and raised an eyebrow, trying to fathom the significance. Evans studied the agent carefully.

"Close-hold information, Tommy," he said, holding up his hand like a Boy Scout swearing an oath of allegiance. His piercing gaze elicited the correct response.

"Okay, partner. Between you and me. It goes no farther," Durance swore.

"He took out a bunch of infiltrators who resisted boarding. A dozen or so heavily armed men went to the bottom just off Padre."

SEALs could never keep secrets from other SEALs, especially if women or combat action was involved. Savarese had told Swan, who had told Evans.

"Whoa," Durance groaned. "I haven't heard a thing about it," he said, eyeballing Evans with his one good eye.

"Do you have the big picture, Tom? Are you cut into the SCI program covering the PFC?"

"No. I wish I was," he said, shaking his head. "Are you?"

"Nah," Evans growled. "I only know what the senator felt comfortable about telling me. But he must have a good reason to worry. He's paying me out of his own pocket."

"That's interesting. Maintaining your cover, no doubt."

"Most likely," Evans agreed.

Durance breathed out heavily, as if ready to divulge a deep secret. "I have several HUMINT reports that indicate a Middle Eastern terrorist group is working the area," he said using the acronym for intelligence information collected by spies.

"The PFC?" Evans asked.

"Uh huh"

"What makes you think it's HUMINT?" Evans pressed.

"The nature of the information. Coordinates, times. The Padre Island op was ostensibly to bust a ring of immigrant-smugglers. But the senator suspected otherwise. That's why I'm involved."

"Could the source be COMINT?" Evans inquired, referring to information derived from telephone and radio intercepts.

"Maybe. I don't know." Durance studied Evans's face for reaction to his next statement. "It's nuclear-related."

"Makes sense. I attended one of Carson's subcommittee sessions," Evans volunteered, easing Durance's mind about divulging classified information. "He's got me evaluating the security of nuclear power plants throughout the South." Evans paused and focused on Durance's good eye. "Tom, I suspect the senator has information that the PFC is planning a major terrorist operation in the U.S. But after attending his closed session, I am concerned that we are relying too heavily upon COMINT."

"What makes you think that?" asked the agent.

"I crossed trails with an organization called S-Systems that uses a sophisticated setup to monitor enemies of the state. I think they are strictly off the books. To complicate matters, there is some sort of covert-action unit tied in to S-Systems that eliminates problems. Offshore."

"And you think Boomer Savarese is serving in this covert-action unit?"

"Yeah. I do. But I doubt that he knows the ramifications of his missions."

"If you're right, as soon as I catch this dude the problem is solved," Durance declared, gesturing at the drawing of his terrorist.

"Bullshit, partner. He's just a foot soldier. The generals have plenty of meat to throw in the meatgrinder."

Durance unconsciously reached up and touched his cheek. His glass eye was cosmetically perfect, but it was lifeless and unmoving. Evans tried not to stare at it, but he couldn't help himself. They had both been meat for the grinder of Vietnam. Evans had just been luckier than most. Being at the wrong place at the wrong time might win a man a Purple Heart or a Medal of Honor or a headstone. In war it was only a matter of inches.

Durance nodded. "I know what you mean. It ain't over till it's over?"

"My gut tells me it ain't over," Evans said.

"It's comforting to know we have a covert mechanism for dealing with the problem," said Durance. "Our judicial system is ineffective against terrorism."

"Tom," Evans said, shaking his head. "They're relying on COMINT, man. You know what that means? If anything major is going down, the tangos will leak false info as a diversion. I suspect S-Systems monitors all telephone calls regardless of the country of origin and winnows information that fits their neat little profiles."

Evans studied Durance's face for reaction. There was none but the agent's response disturbed the commander.

"What's wrong with that as long as there's plausible deniability?"

"It's illegal, Tom. Right to privacy, all that kind of shit. Remember?" Evans argued.

"Yeah, I remember. But don't forget the tangos leave a trail of bodies everywhere they go. Why do you care who stops them, as long as they're stopped?"

"They bugged my ass right here in the U.S. of A., buddy, without a court order," Evans snarled. "They claimed to be FBI when I busted them."

"Jesus Christ," Durance gasped. "Does Carson know this?"

"You bet he does. He set up a meeting in his office with a pasty-faced asshole named Shipler from S-Systems. It was Shipler's men who bugged me. I played them an audiotape of me in a compromising situation."

"What kind of situation?"

"Of me getting laid, man."

Durance grinned. "You're shittin' me."

"No, I'm not."

"What did this guy say?" Durance asked.

"Not much. Bureaucratic double-talk, so I knocked him on his ass right in the senator's office."

"Now I know you're shittin' me," Durance exclaimed.

"Nope. Knocked him out cold and had a drink with Carson while he drooled on the carpet."

Durance chuckled as he visualized the incident. "I can see you haven't changed much." He eyed Evans, then said, "Until the Padre Island incident, I was working the military angle. Remember the Navy Idiot Service?"

Evans nodded. The derisive nickname was commonly used within the ranks for the Naval Intelligence Service. "Situation FUBAR?" he asked.

"Yeah. NIS couldn't manage a wet dream without screwing it up," complained Durance. "Much less keep it secret." He held up his hand like a Boy Scout.

"Between you and me and a beat-up fence post," Evans swore as he held up his hand.

"We believe the tangos are planning a hit somewhere around Kings Bay," Durance confided.

"On what, or whom?"

"I don't know. The operation's got a code name."

"What's your source? COMINT?" Evans asked.

"There you go again. HUMINT, COMINT, FUCKINT, I don't give a shit who provides the info as long as I get this dude. He's a baby killer, man. The car at Hartsfield is a false trail. I'm bettin' he's headed for Kings Bay."

"Was the original information derived from eavesdropping or from a human source?" Evans persisted.

"COMINT, I think. Like I said, I'm not read into the SCI program covering the PFC."

"Do you know the sailor's identity?" Evans asked.

"No. NIS screw-up. There are a lot of angry bubbleheads down there, Double Tap," Durance replied. *Bubblehead* was a term submariners used to refer to themselves. "A number of boats have been decommissioned, causing unemployment in the ranks, and to make matters worse, there's the homosexual issue. The president opened up a can of worms, some crawled halfway out, and he slammed the lid on them. 'Don't ask, don't tell.' Remember?"

Evans nodded as his mind churned. "Tom, I need a deep background check. SBI type," he requested, referring to a special background investigation that required extensive research. "That's one of the reasons the senator set up this meeting."

"Do you know how much an SBI costs?" Durance grumbled.

"Yeah."

"Who?" the agent demanded.

"Nicholas B. Fawcett, a microbiologist who works at the CDC."

Durance nearly choked. "Why?"

"Just a hunch, man. A gut feeling. Something in this guy's eye raised the hair on the back of my neck," Evans answered.

"I can't justify an SBI based upon a hunch."

"Tie him to this tango," Evans suggested, glancing down at the composite.

"That's too big a stretch, Evans," Durance argued as he shook his head.

"I think the CDC is being surveiled. S-Systems was up to something when they bugged me. There is more going on than meets the eye."

"I'll buy that, but what's this Fawcett guy got to do with it?" Durance asked.

"I don't know. I've just got a bad feeling about the man."

Durance rubbed his chin as he studied Evans. "I'll tell you what. I'll call in a marker and check this guy out, but don't make a habit of it."

"Sure, Tommy, sure. Actually, here's a list of guys I need a simple BI on," Evans said, taking a sheet of paper out of his suit pocket. *BI* was short-talk for a background investigation.

Durance grabbed the list and glanced at it. "For the senator," he said, shaking his finger in Evans's face. He put the list in his pocket, threw a few bucks onto the table, and left.

Chapter 19

NICK FAWCETT CLIMBED the stairs to the fourth floor of Building 15 with a box of donuts in one hand and a medical journal in the other. He walked down the open breezeway past the locked metal doors that led to the Level Four laboratory and on down the hall to the small office shared by Lubeck and Dorn. He knocked lightly and entered.

"Greetings, ladies," he said warmly.

"Susan, beware of Greeks bearing gifts," warned Doris, spotting the box.

Fawcett placed the donuts on Lubeck's desk and took out an apple fritter. He waved it under her nose.

"Hot out of the oven," he teased.

"Nick. You dog. What do you want?" asked Doris, with a ravenous grin. She grabbed the pastry and took a big bite.

"Oh, nothing. Just a friendly visit from the lower levels of research," said Fawcett jovially.

If he had told her what he really wanted, Doris Lubeck would have choked on her fritter.

"Have a seat, if you can find one," Doris said.

"Susan?" Fawcett offered her a peek inside the box.

"Thanks," she said, selecting a glazed donut.

Fawcett moved a stack of books out of a rickety folding chair and placed them on the floor.

"Nick, I heard you guys just made some kind of breakthrough on HIV," Susan said, making polite conversation.

"Actually, there is a rather interesting study going on that just might portend good news," he said, cocking his head and raising one eyebrow. "It appears that shortly after infection, the viral count rises rapidly, then drops suddenly almost to zero. Apparently the virus retreats to the lymph nodes and other hiding places, chased by an angry horde of marauding t-cells."

"So the body initially overwhelms the virus?" Doris asked. She was all business when it came to science.

"Absolutely. And it takes several years for the nasty little buggers to mount a successful counteroffensive. But—and I stress the coordinating conjunction—when they do, the viral count soars and the battle devolves to internal trench warfare."

"Mutant strains," Susan offered. "Rapid viral replication followed by a strong immune response that initially overwhelms the infection. Not uncommon. The rebound is a resistant strain."

"That's our best guess," Fawcett replied. "So what's new in the hot zone?" *Hot zone* was CDC slang for the Level Four lab.

"How about a previously unknown virus from a common reservoir that spreads like influenza and kills with a 100 percent mortality rate," said Lubeck.

Fawcett pondered the statement before speaking. "The one Cal Poland and I brought back from Cameroon?"

"That's the one."

"Question. How long from initial exposure to expiration?"

Lubeck looked at Fawcett and then at Dorn. "See. I told you he was sharp. Handsome too." She looked back at Fawcett. "Less than four days. Here," she said, handing him the videotape of primates dying from the disease. "Take a look at this, but not while you're eating."

"Can I take this home with me?"

"Sure. But for your eyes only, darling," she said with a fake accent. "If the media got hold of that tape, they'd incite public hysteria."

"Four days? That's somewhat of a relief," he commented. "At least the disease is self-limiting."

"Not so fast. The infection may spread long before symptoms appear. Perhaps in as little as twenty-four hours after exposure," Doris explained.

"Are you suggesting that an asymptomatic person—say, a commuter on an airplane—could infect the other passengers?"

"Yes."

"Most disturbing," Fawcett replied. "Most disturbing. Question. How long does the virus survive outside the body?"

"That's the good news. No more than a few hours, thank God," Doris replied.

"It's very difficult to culture," Susan interjected. "If it fails to find a viable cell within a few hours, it breaks down."

"Does the virus survive in water or air?" Fawcett asked.

"No. They need a friendly suspension," Doris replied.

"I take it the virus survives well in your fridge?" he said, referring to the liquid nitrogen freeze.

"Yes."

"It's the rat, isn't it?" he continued, lost in thought. He had created a biological weapon using Ebola Zaire, but he hadn't been able to develop an effective vaccine. The new virus was much more virulent than Ebola and presented new possibilities as a biological weapon. While in Africa he had taken samples of the agent, but he hadn't been able to isolate and culture it in his makeshift lab in Panama City, Florida. He needed Lubeck's expertise and samples from the Level Four lab to accelerate the development.

"The rats are at it again, Nick," Lubeck answered.

"I suspected as much when I saw them running all over the affected villages. Do you still have the ones I brought back from Cameroon?" he asked.

"Yeah. And they're loaded with the virus," Lubeck said.

"I presume the next step is to discover the rats' secret for survival?"

"Right again. Want to help?" Lubeck smiled.

"Noooo! I'll leave the Lubeck virus to the experts." He smiled back. "Question. What are the prospects for developing a vaccine?"

"Good," Dorn replied, "now that we can culture the virus in the lab."

"Thank God for small favors," he said, thinking, *I'll have to press her for the culture process later.* "How many of these samples do you ladies have in your refrigerator?" he asked, brow furrowed.

"An even dozen," Lubeck replied. "Want some?" she kidded.

He grinned and shook his head thinking, *I wish it were that easy, Doris.* "No wonder you work such long hours," he muttered, almost to himself. "I never see you anymore."

"That's not my fault," Lubeck snapped.

Fawcett looked up, surprised, but he ignored the implications.

"Would it be possible for me to suit up and tour the hot zone? When you're not too busy, of course. I'm fascinated by your work."

"Is that *all* that fascinates you, Dr. Fawcett?" Lubeck demanded with a wanton smile.

Fawcett returned her knowing gaze and confidently shook his head. "Nooo," he replied.

"Then you can have a look in our pantry, but it'll cost you," she continued.

"What?" he asked, playing along.

"A bottle of wine and a thick juicy steak," Doris purred. "You've been working too hard and neglecting your friends on the fourth floor."

"You got it," Fawcett replied. "Anything else?"

Lubeck leered. "Oh, I'll think of *something*."

They both looked at Susan, who blushed.

"Susan, do we have a space suit big enough for Nick's butt?" Lubeck teased.

"Now you've gone and done it. No more apple fritters for me and, by extension, you," Fawcett countered.

He was trim for his age, and the gray in his black hair gave him an air of distinction. He stood up and looked over his shoulder, then shook his head and gestured to Dorn that he was satisfied with his findings. To Lubeck he said, "I guess I'll join a health club."

"Nick, you provide the wine. *I'll* provide the exercise." She giggled.

"Doris!" Susan gasped.

As Fawcett headed out the door, he glanced back at Lubeck. "*Arrivederci*, baby."

Chapter 20

OMAR AZED WALKED through Plaza de Santo Domingo in Cartagena and down the street to Paco's, a quiet establishment that served tropical drinks and seafood. He took a seat and watched the tourists strolling along the avenue of the old city. A large cruise ship was in port, and the town was teeming with Americans. He ordered and waited for his contact.

"All is the will of Allah," he mumbled to himself.

The waiter reminded him of the Panamanian he had killed in Colón. The mixture of Spanish, Indian, and African called mestizo was common in Central and South America but strange to the eyes of an Arab. To Azed, they all looked alike. The image that invaded his mind was the shock on the face of the mestizo forger when he realized he was going to die.

The sharp blade of memory rips up from my sternum, my throat, into the base of my brain, he thought. *Yes. Your tormented visage stares at me from beyond the grave.*

After the hit, Azed had walked immediately to the waterfront and boarded the *Crucero Express,* the ferry that linked Panama and Colombia with three weekly trips. Sixteen hours after killing the best forger the PFC had in the Americas, Omar Azed had debarked in the most popular tourist town in South America: Cartagena de Indias.

As he waited, the weight of his terrorist war against the Jews descended upon him.

All of us carry the past on our shoulders, he thought.

As a boy, the shock of death all around him had cracked away his brittle shell of self. He felt justified in killing Jews and Americans. But not a Panamanian. Not at close range. And for no apparent reason. The man's eyes had grown to an unnatural size just before Azed had pulled the trigger.

Mine is a heavy burden, O Allah. This sourness, which has welled up inside me, will last for a few days, and then it will be no more. Inshallah. There is no entertainment in seeing a man die from a bullet hole. No bright orange and crimson flames, not even a thunderous roar to remember. Just the fear of death in those strange eyes. There is no majesty in a body slumping to the ground, he thought, *unless it is a Jewish body. What would you do with your life, Omar, if not for the injustice of the Jews? You would be a completely different person.*

He convinced himself of the righteousness of his cause to justify his crimes against humanity. When he spotted an old couple of Middle Eastern descent entering the tavern, his internal turmoil evaporated like water in the desert. He made his presence known by calling the waiter over and requesting another drink. The old man eyed him but said nothing. He simply selected a nearby table and assisted his overweight wife. He took her shopping bag and placed it on the floor near the terrorist and in the same movement dropped a key. Without looking, Azed used his foot to scoot it under his table. Not even the old woman saw the brush pass.

Azed finished his meal, savoring the small langostino smothered in garlic before surreptitiously retrieving the key. At no time did he make eye contact with his benefactor. He just ate, paid his bill, and left. Walking slowly, observing the most common items bought by the American tourists on the streets, he made his way to the waterfront. This wasn't the first time he had infiltrated the U.S. via cruise ship. Thousands of passengers embarked and debarked daily all over Central and South America, spending their vacation dollars like play money. Near the ship, he chose a small tourist trap where he could watch the gangway of the huge vessel. The first thing he noticed was that no one was checking passports, coming or going. Azed knew that it was not uncommon for a passenger to make an entire tour of Central and South America aboard a cruise ship and never be asked for a passport.

It took him several minutes to spot the ship's security personnel among the passengers milling about the gangway, and when he did his heart sank. They looked Jewish. Anxiety gripped him like a vise. His breath stopped and his mouth went dry. He had heard that an Israeli company had won the contract to provide security for both the Carnival and the Princess lines. For several minutes he was in a complete state of indecision. Then he remembered his passport was good—fake but good. And he had a cabin key.

Allah be praised, he said to himself.

He bought several tourist items, put on a public face, and walked out of the store.

"Here we come, O Allah! Here we come!" he muttered to himself as he walked up the gangway with a large group returning from a package tour. His heart pounded as he neared the top of the gangway. Without looking at any of the security men, he helped an elderly couple step down off the gangway and onto the deck. He smiled at them as they thanked him, and he then walked directly to a hatch that led below decks. Heart pounding, he searched for his cabin in the labyrinth of passageways, afraid to look behind him for fear of seeing one of the security men. The elderly Middle Eastern couple had booked two rooms on the *Caribbean Queen*, and they had been using each part time to fool ship's services into believing both were occupied. They simply abandoned the use of the second room by turning the key over to Azed, allowing another poor illegal immigrant to enter the golden land.

Azed's pulse raced as he unlocked the door to his stateroom. He glanced up and down the passageway, then quickly entered and closed the door behind him. Dropping to the deck, he listened for footsteps and stared at the light coming through the crack under the door. When no one passed for several minutes, he relaxed his nervous vigil.

Later that evening he felt the *Caribbean Queen* get under way, but he was still too distressed to leave his room to watch the departure or the beautiful sunset on the turquoise water. In two days she would put into port in the Bahamas, and in four she would dock at her home port, Miami. On three previous trips no one had ever asked him for a passport. But still he couldn't relax. He prayed and fasted for twelve hours.

A day out of Cartagena, he calmed down enough to venture out of his room. He bought fresh clothes and toilet articles in the ship's stores and ate in a small restaurant. It was there that he saw a face that brought on a fit of paranoia. The man seemed to stare at him, and when he spoke to the waiter, Azed detected a thick Brooklyn accent, which to Azed meant Jew. He was just another passenger, but his curious eyes and confident voice drove Azed back to his cabin in panic, where he resumed his prayers, mentally preparing himself for the mother of all battles against the Great Satan.

Ayyad is a genius, he thought, as he sipped a cup of tea in the privacy of his room. Only the two of us know. *Only the two of us—and Allah—know that the first Zionist city to burn is New York.* He visualized a huge mushroom cloud rising up behind the Statue of Liberty and grinned maniacally. *Then Los Angeles.*

"Allah be praised," he mumbled.

Chapter 21

Tom Durance stared at the fingerprint as though it were a coded message. Forensics had found several prints in Lily Colton's car, but all of them belonged to the petty thieves who had stripped it. The absence of the owner's prints told him that the vehicle had been wiped clean. So he ordered the forensics crew back to the impound lot and personally supervised another search, which had turned up the single unidentified print he held in his hand. Out of habit he did a quick ridge count. It was a thumb loop on the left hand. As he stared at it, he wondered if it was the print of a man who could murder a mother and child at close range.

The FBI data bank was extensive, but it wasn't all inclusive. Durance had a gut feeling he wouldn't find a name and face to match the print in U.S. files. So he faxed a copy to his contacts in Europe. Their searches also turned up negative. Stuck to the trail like Jefferson Davis III, the champion Louisiana possum dog, he transmitted a copy of the print to a buddy in Tel Aviv, hoping he could provide a match. If anyone possessed an intelligence data bank on Middle Eastern terrorists, it was the Israelis. When the response came back negative, he slumped in his chair and called Senator Carson to discuss his lack of progress. With no name and no face, he was at an impasse.

Carson gave him a fax number and words of encouragement, and reminded him of their shared SEAL philosophy: Never give up. With little hope, Durance placed an enlarged photocopy of the single print on his fax machine and dialed the private number Carson had given him. Mission complete, he sat down at his desk and studied the features of the composite drawing, wondering if he was looking at the face of an international terrorist.

Two hours later Tom Durance was deeply engrossed in a case file when his fax machine began to whir. The first sheet to print out was a full-page, grayscale picture of an Arab man passing through customs at an airport he recognized as Cairo's. As his fax machine continued to hum, Durance compared the picture to the composite. Bile churned in his stomach as he realized he was looking at the face of the man who had murdered the young woman and her baby. For a brief instant he saw the man shoot the old couple in the back of the head. The composite was much better than he had expected. The artist had captured the eyes—hawklike, piercing, cold. Pulling the second page from the fax machine, he was amazed at the feast of detail in front of him. Name, aliases, place of birth, likes, dislikes, history of arrests, political affiliations, possible contacts in the United States and Europe.

"Hello, Aman Abruzzi Ayyad," he mumbled. "Terrorist. Baby killer. Now I'll get you, you son of a bitch," he growled like a junkyard dog.

Even as Tom Durance hounded his trail, Aman Ayyad pressed on with Operation Desert Decree. The shipment from Pakistan containing the Stingers had passed through the port of Atlanta less than twenty miles from the federal building where the FBI agent was working. Soon after landing, the cargo in the belly of the huge airplane was broken down into individual consignments and spot-checked by U.S. Customs. The volume of goods entering the port every day was staggering, overwhelming the agents assigned to Hartsfield. When a drug dog failed to alert on the cargo, Customs released the shipment, and the crates containing the missiles were dispatched to an independent freight forwarder located near the airport.

For several days, Ayyad kept watch on the small warehouse where the crates awaited pickup. When he was satisfied it was safe, he sent one man in to sign for them. The skinny wisp of a boy loaded the crates into a minivan and left the industrial district without incident. For two hours he doubled back and forth as he made the short trip south to Jonesboro.

Ayyad had planned a route that doubled back several times, allowing him to determine if anyone other than himself was following the minivan. Eventually they drove to an old farm that belonged to Al Fucra, a militant Islamic organization that maintained a number of isolated communities throughout the U.S. Men, women, and children lived and worked on the farm, and they provided excellent cover for his covert operation.

In one of the farm's outbuildings, Ayyad rendezvoused with several terrorist cells he had stationed in the Atlanta area. Six men quickly unloaded and stripped the shipping crates, carefully checking each item for hidden radio transmitters and other bugging devices. Then, while some buried the packing materials, the others examined the missiles and prepared them for travel. When preparations were complete, Ayyad uttered three words, "Allah be praised," and they all silently washed for prayer. They faced Mecca and thanked God for his blessings.

Ayyad bade each team good-bye as they climbed into their rental cars. He had been on missions with most of them inside Israel, and he trusted those to follow their orders precisely. Once in their safehouses, they wouldn't come out until he signaled them it was time for their part of the campaign to begin.

The cells left the Al Fucra farm in a caravan but split up when they reached the road connecting to the beltway. Ayyad decided to follow the youngest of the cell leaders, a man he didn't know very well. As instructed, he doubled back and forth over and over again, checking for a tail. He spotted Ayyad but ignored him. Finally, he took Interstate 285 around Atlanta and drove north on 85. Hours later, he parked in the driveway of a condo outside Charlotte, North Carolina. From a distance, Ayyad watched as the two-man cell carried the Stinger inside, hidden in a golf bag. As they locked the door behind them, a 737 flew low overhead, engines straining to gain altitude. Ayyad looked up through the windshield of his car to catch a glimpse of the bird as it roared overhead. His face twitched and his eyes sharpened like a hawk's.

Now, he said to himself. *Fire!*

In his mind's eye he watched the Stinger streak across the sky at supersonic speed.

Die, infidels! Die!

When the heat of emotion died, he drove southeast toward the Georgia coast.

Chapter 22

"DR. REINHARDT, I have three significant findings," Derek Evans announced. "First, I strongly recommend that you increase the budget for your security department. Chief Johnson needs ten more officers and sufficient funds to provide periodic training both to his personnel and to your staff."

The older man was deep in thought and wasn't focused on Evans's report. Troubled by the Lubeck virus and deeply concerned about his shrinking budget, he was in no mood to listen to a Beltway bandit. If the figures he had been given became law, he was facing cutbacks that would require him to lay off several world-renowned scientists. The last thing he wanted to hear was an appeal to increase the number of goons guarding the place.

"Secondly, I most strongly recommend that you relocate the security guard and monitoring station in the lobby of Building 15. The guard desk should be placed behind the security doors. People seeking access should do business through a small bank-teller-type window. As it is, a determined assailant could overpower the single guard in the lobby and open the door with the push of a button. In the meantime, I suggest you double the watch on duty in the lobby. Thirdly, I strongly recommend that you replace the security doors to the hot zone and . . ."

"Mr. Evans," Reinhardt bristled, suddenly snapping to attention. "That laboratory is on the fourth floor. To gain entry one must pass through steel security doors controlled by an armed guard."

"Sir, the viral material inside that lab could potentially be more dangerous than a thousand nuclear weapons."

"How, Mr. Evans?" Reinhardt demanded. "I fail to understand your reasoning."

"A terrorist," Evans explained.

"Absurd!"

"A fanatic. A crazy. A criminal. Some things are just so potentially destructive, they must be protected at all costs."

"Mr. Evans, I'll remind you that security issues are not the only problems we must deal with here at the CDC. There is an armed guard in the lobby and a sophisticated surveillance system inside this building. Moreover, the city of Atlanta has hundreds of policemen on duty," the old man pointed out testily.

"Dr. Reinhardt, the guard in the lobby is armed with a revolver. One man with an assault rifle could cut him to shreds in two seconds. A child could figure out that the button behind the counter opens the security doors."

"Then there are four flights of stairs, Mr. Evans, double steel doors controlled by a key card, and heavy-gauge steel inner doors controlled by a punch code," Reinhardt argued, displaying his command of the subject. "Those measures correspond to the exact specifications of the last expert who evaluated this facility." He said the word *expert* with a degree of derision. "Once inside, one must enter through a double air lock."

"Doctor, a fanatic will just keep shooting people until someone complies with his instructions."

"Preposterous. My people wouldn't open those doors for an armed assailant under any circumstances. And if a criminal were to gain access, what would such an ignorant person do inside a sophisticated lab, Mr. Evans? Make cocktails with frozen viral material?"

"Extortion, Doctor! Extortion."

"Ludicrous!"

"Doctor, I strongly recommend that you replace the inner doors with a vault door similar to a bank's, one with an external locking mechanism that cannot be overridden."

"Too costly, Mr. Evans," Reinhardt insisted.

"In the meantime, sir, I suggest you arm the technicians who maintain the control panel and place a monitor inside the control room so they can observe the hallway outside the lab."

"That is preposterous! I'll not have armed thugs patrolling my laboratories. I'll do no such thing!" Reinhardt shouted, standing to leave.

He strode out of the conference room shaking his head, leaving Evans and Chief Johnson alone at the long table.

"That didn't go down too well, did it, Chief?" said Evans, smiling sheepishly at Johnson.

"Now you see what I'm up against," replied the grizzled security chief. He took a deep breath and let out a sigh.

"It's the same everywhere I go, Chief. Denial. 'It can't happen to me.'" Evans locked eyes with Johnson. "Listen, we placed some glow powder in the access tunnel leading from the street."

"You what?"

"It's an invisible powder that glows under an ultraviolet light source."

"Oh, yeah," Johnson replied. "I knew that."

"Someone's been checking out the maintenance tunnel."

"Who?"

"We don't know. Maybe some wino looking for a place to sleep, or a city employee just doing his job chasing rats."

Evans pulled several nine-sixteenths bolts out of his pocket. They were designed with special heads requiring a star Allen wrench to install them.

"Here," he said, handing the bolts to Johnson. "Install a couple of these on each side of the metal grate. Do it yourself and don't tell anybody. Choose a dark place where the bolt heads are hard to see."

"I got it," said Johnson, looking at the bolts. "Pretty unusual head."

"Yep. Not likely you'll find a match in your toolbox, Chief."

Evans opened his briefcase and took out the special wrench required to turn the bolts.

"They're one-way, partner, so be careful with the installation," he said, handing him the wrench. "Once in, you'll need a cutting torch to get them out."

"Shrewd. Very cunning. You boys are just full of tricks," he said as Evans prepared to leave.

Johnson walked Evans to the lobby. Near the main security station he asked, "Do you think some nutcase might hit this place?"

"I don't know. I just know we need to do a better job protecting the stuff in the fourth floor lab."

"I wish they weren't cuttin' my budget. I'm gonna have to lay off some pretty good men," said Johnson.

Evans looked at him and smiled. "It ain't over till it's over, Chief. I spoke with Senator Carson about your situation. He can help influence the budget."

"Thanks."

As Evans left the lobby, Ray Keith went into his panhandling act.

"Hey, buddy, spare a few bucks for a homeless vet?"

Chief Johnson chuckled and ducked back inside the building.

"I've already donated to the cause a dozen times," Evans growled.

"Then how about a ride to the homeless shelter?" Keith said loudly, so anyone within earshot could hear.

Evans grimaced. "Sure," he said with a scowl, "but spit out that damn tobacco."

Evans waited for Keith to strap on his artificial leg and refused to carry his panhandling cup when Keith held it out. He walked slowly beside him to the parking lot but didn't open the car door for him. Keith was supposed to carry his own load in SOC Inc., and he knew it. He was just having fun jerking the commander's chain.

Once inside the car, Keith resumed the conversation in a different tone. "I took a few pictures today. Some Arabs. Pretty good ones, if I do say so myself."

"I'll be the judge of that," Evans replied.

"You think your lady friend can pick out her stalker?"

"Yeah." Evans backed out of his spot and drove through the parking lot to the street.

"I haven't seen that white elephant since you beat the shit out of those clowns, Commander Donkey-dick," Keith said, chuckling.

Evans cut him a vicious glare and checked the street in both directions. "You're pressing your luck again, buck-o," he said, as he headed for the apartment he had rented for Swan and Keith.

"Who were those perverts, anyway?"

"Low-level freaks from a private intelligence-gathering organization."

"How do we know they aren't selling info to the bad guys?"

"We don't have to worry about that, Ray. They see themselves as superpatriots, saving the nation. Hell, maybe they are. To hear some tell it, they busted Saddam's ass during the Gulf War."

"How?" asked Keith in disbelief.

"By providing the information that resulted in more than two hundred terrorist cells being wrapped."

"That's hot, Boss."

"I suspect they were the ones who planted the computer virus in the Iraqi defense system. It screwed up Saddam Insane's entire military machine."

"Couldn't have happened to a nicer guy."

"The virus sabotaged his communications network, radar control systems, targeting programs, the whole damn enchilada."

"Do you think the Iraqis are behind this shit?" Keith asked.

"Could be," said Evans, stopping for a red light.

As he glanced over at Keith, his eyes caught the face of the man in the car beside them at the light. They made eye contact for just an instant.

"Son of a bitch," Evans hissed as Ayyad looked away.

"What? What?" asked Keith, surprised by Evans's tone.

"Don't look now," he ordered, "but the guy next to us bears a damn strong resemblance to the composite drawing Tom Durance showed me."

For a brief instant, Evans made eye contact with the Arab again. Ayyad's hawklike expression and the quiver in his cheek told Evans this was more than a chance encounter. When the light changed, Ayyad sped ahead but slowed down before he hit the next block.

"Pull up beside him and I'll put a bullet in that baby-killin' bastard's head," Keith ranted.

"Goddammit, Ray. We don't know if it's the right guy. It might be a carpet salesman with a bad attitude."

"Let's follow 'im, Boss," said Keith, itching for action.

"Damn straight. But carefully," Evans responded, accelerating.

Ayyad slowed so Evans could pull up beside him. The Arab looked over at them with unmistakable hate, and then peeled out.

"That ain't no damn carpet salesman, Commander," Keith declared. "That man's got blood in his eye."

Evans changed lanes and followed cautiously. At the corner Ayyad turned right abruptly, as if to lose them. Evans jammed on the brakes, turned right, and followed warily.

"Ray, this guy is either the worst driver in Atlanta, or he's teasing us," he said as Ayyad slowed down so they could catch up again.

The terrorist turned right and headed into a low-rent district.

"Yep. He wants us to follow him, all right."

Keith pulled out his Colt .45 and checked the chamber and magazine. "Let me see your peashooter, Boss," he ordered.

Evans slipped the 9-millimeter out of his shoulder holster and handed it to Keith, who racked a round into the chamber and checked the safety before laying it on the seat between them.

"Boss, when are you gonna learn to carry your piece in condition one?" he chided.

"I don't trust the safety on that thing," Evans snapped.

Tires squealed as he turned into an alley and accelerated to thirty miles per hour.

"Well, then, carry a real gun, goddammit." Then Keith glanced up ahead and yelled, "Whoa, Boss, I don't like the looks of this shit."

Evans was speeding along, twenty-five yards behind Ayyad. The run-down neighborhood was perfect for an ambush.

"Me either," Evans exclaimed, looking for a place to cut out.

The alley spread out into a killing zone just as Evans spotted the blocker car. It pulled across his path as soon as Ayyad went by. Evans was doing thirty miles per hour when he yanked on the emergency brake. With the rear wheels locked up, the car rotated 180 degrees, knocking over several trash cans as it slid around. When the power turn was completed, Evans released the brakes and put the accelerator to the floor. He eased off when the tires broke loose, then hit it again just as the automatic weapons opened up behind them.

Glass and lead exploded through the interior of the car as the back window shattered. Bullets peppered the windshield. Evans scooted down so low he couldn't see over the steering wheel. He navigated by looking at the eaves of the buildings. Keith was bent over on the seat, holding both pistols, cursing when Evans reached speed.

"Turn this goddamn buggy around, Commander! No one shoots at my ass and gets away with it."

With an angry face, Evans jammed on the brakes and brought the car to a dead stop in a cloud of noise and smoke. He jammed the gearshift in reverse and accelerated backwards as fast as the rental car could go. When he hit thirty, he let off the accelerator, turned the wheels all the way to the left, and let momentum do the rest. The speed, combined with the abrupt turn, caused the front wheels to slide, pivoting around the rear tires. Halfway through the slide, Keith cut loose with his .45. His first two rounds caught a young Arab in the act of reloading a MAC-10, striking him in the chest. He squeezed to a surprise break on his second target, and his third round caught another terrorist in the middle of his forehead.

Evans jammed on the brakes and, before the car came to a complete stop, emptied a magazine in the direction of the third shooter on his side of the vehicle, pinning the man down behind a group of trash cans. Keith rolled out of the car and stumbled up on his one good leg. The third attacker was crouching behind a large plastic trash can, so he rested both hands on the roof of the car and took careful aim. He placed several rounds through the trash can, creating a deadly pattern that dispatched his target with his fourth shot.

"I hope this convinces you to pack a real gun, Commander Asshole," Keith snarled, doing a speed reload.

Evans gave him a dirty look and signaled with a nod of his head his intention to check the alley for more shooters. Keith covered Evans as he reloaded, and then they searched both sides of the alleyway, alternately covering each other's movements in a leapfrog tactic. Reconnaissance complete, they quickly searched the bodies for information. As Evans expected, there was none. Three minutes after the gun battle began, Ayyad's best hit team had been eliminated from the PFC's order of battle. Taking the Arabs' weapons, Evans and Keith sped from the scene. Even self-defense carries a heavy penalty in the United States.

Chapter 23

THE USS *GEORGIA,* SSBN 729, ascended from deep water off the Bahamas and eased slowly toward the continental shelf just below the surface at five knots. The attack center was dark and crowded with personnel, each with a specific function integral to the ship's fighting capability.

"Up scope," the officer of the deck ordered, as the vessel reached periscope depth. He flipped down the control arms before the scope reached terminal height. Grasping the handles, he stooped to place his face inside the rubber cowling. Squatting at first, and rising with the scope as it ascended to station, the tall, skinny officer scanned the horizon.

"Merchant, bearing two-two-zero degrees true, ten thousand yards," he said automatically.

"Merchant, bearing two-two-zero degrees true, ten thousand yards," repeated the contact coordinator of the watch, who then checked the ship's location on his chart. He had already plotted all the ships in the area from information provided by sonar. The dim light illuminating his small station was shielded from the OOD, Lieutenant Julius Kinney, by a curtain that surrounded the captain's chair and the periscopes located in the middle of the attack center.

With his face still in the cowling, Kinney turned a few degrees to his left, searching the horizon with the periscope. "Merchant, bearing one-eight-five degrees true, seven thousand yards."

The young petty officer repeated the information and marked the vessel type with his grease pencil.

"Merchant. Belay that. Cruise ship, bearing zero-six-five degrees true, six thousand yards."

Kinney focused the scope and read the ship's name on her prow: *Caribbean Queen*. For a few moments he wondered what it would be like to serve on such a luxurious vessel. Then he continued scanning the horizon for ships.

"Sonar, con?"

"Sonar, aye," replied the sonar supervisor.

"Zero-four-five degrees true, ten thousand yards?" interrogated Kinney.

"Trawler. No nets trailing," reported the sonar operator.

"Con, aye," Kinney responded.

"Captain on deck!" the petty officer of the watch suddenly shouted as the slim, red-haired commander peeled open the curtain and mounted the attack center platform.

The dim light from the quartermaster's table illuminated his face. He looked Kinney in the eye for just an instant, then stepped wide, as if trying not to touch him. Even in the dull red glow of the attack center, Kinney could read the look of disgust on his face. He had seen it before in the engine room.

"I have the con, Mr. Kinney," the captain said coldly.

"Aye-aye, sir," replied Kinney without emotion. He flipped up the arms on the periscope and stepped back.

The crew could feel the contempt in Captain Joe Fry's voice. It just seemed to ooze out from deep down inside. Kinney stepped aside as much as he could in the crowded confines of the attack center so Fry could assume his position behind the periscope. Soon after Fry put his face in the rubber cowling on the scope, Kinney slipped away without informing the chief of the watch that he was leaving.

Captain Fry was from Alabama and still a redneck at heart, even though he possessed a master's degree in nuclear physics. His Southern-fried conservatism permeated the warship, and it showed in every compartment. He smoked cigarettes, and so did most of his crew. To Lieutenant Kinney, a liberal from a wealthy New England family, it was a filthy habit, unbecoming the commanding officer of a ballistic missile submarine.

A careful man, Captain Fry was known to conduct unannounced inspections, personally checking and double-checking every aspect of his boat, every hidden corner. It was on one of his late-night inspection tours of the engine room that he had discovered Lieutenant Kinney's deepest secret.

The Ohio-class submarine was 560 feet long with a complement of 15 officers and 150 crewmen. But the crew lived only in the forward third of the ship, crowded into a space that by law would have constituted cruel and unusual punishment in a penitentiary. Most of that space was taken up by equipment used to control the vessel and by weapons systems. Enlisted bunks were squeezed along passageways stacked one on top of the other so close together a large man found them uncomfortable. Even officers lived in cramped and crowded conditions.

The aft two-thirds of the boat was spacious by comparison. It housed the nuclear reactor that powered the vessel. Few of the ship's crew ventured behind the thick doors that shielded the forward third of the ship from engineering. But Joe Fry checked everything at odd hours of the day and night. As the commanding officer, it was his duty. Engineering had been the watch station of Cary Radford, a fastidious young enlisted man who'd had a bright future in the Navy until Captain Fry's random inspection of engineering one night revealed Cary in Kinney's passionate embrace.

"Redneck son of a bitch," Kinney cursed quietly as he walked down the narrow passageway behind the attack center, remembering. He stopped for a few seconds and stared at the heavy hatch at the far end of the companionway, clenching his jaw and his fist in anger. At the ladderway descending to the berthing deck below, he met a young quartermaster with a cup of coffee in each hand. The sailor flattened himself against the bulkhead, allowing the lieutenant to pass. As he did, Kinney looked into his eyes for a brief instant.

Does he know? he thought. *Who did the bastard tell?*

The sailor seemed to avoid touching him in the narrow confines of the sub, as if he had a contagious disease. Kinney climbed down the ladder and walked aft to the officers' quarters, boiling with rage.

His room was not much bigger than a large closet. The walls were constructed of thin stainless steel—cold, unfeeling steel—and every inch of space was utilized with maximum efficiency. He slammed the door behind him and climbed into his bunk. Flipping on his reading light, he paused to look at a picture of Cary Radford that he had taped to the underside of the top bunk. Radford had been a teenager when the picture was taken. He beamed down at Kinney with happiness in his bright eyes. They had been on liberty together in Japan on his nineteenth birthday. Anger roiled in Kinney's guts. He knotted his fists and gave the top bunk a vicious kick.

For a few moments he contemplated suicide.

"Oh, God. What if Dad finds out?" he moaned to himself as he rocked back and forth in his bed.

The bunk was too short for his long body, but at least he could lie on his side and draw up his knees. The fetal position was a defensive posture. He heard the man in the bathroom next door grunt and then the sound of urine streaming into the bowl. A thin sheet of stainless steel was all that separated him from the commode and shower shared by the officers of the wardroom. Secrets were hard to keep on a nuclear submarine.

He ground his teeth. *Why? Why?* he asked himself as tears streamed down his cheeks. *Oh, Cary! I love you. I would have taken care of you.*

His mind focused as he gradually gained control of himself.

Don't ask, don't tell! he thought. *Pathetic.*

He wondered what kind of mental hell Cary Radford had gone

through before he had slipped the belt off his bathrobe, tied it around his neck, and kicked away the chair.

They probably put him on a lie detector, he thought, *and threatened to tell his family or to make the court-martial public.*

Then he remembered the boy's touch and the moments they had shared together during their first cruise. Six months at sea underwater without sunshine was bad enough, but it was torture for a homosexual cooped up with so many desirable men.

Captain Fry's face invaded Kinney's thoughts. That look. That sour, twisted look of disgust. *I dare him,* he thought. *He doesn't understand! What does he know about me? What gives him the right to judge me?*

Kinney knew his career was over. His life was over. It was just a matter of time. He prayed for an end to the torture. He prayed for God to sink the ship in deep water before it returned to port. He prayed for Fry to have a sudden coronary. He prayed for renegade Russians to launch a nuclear attack on the United States. This torment had gone on for more than a year, and the waiting was driving him mad. But it was Captain Fry's look of repugnance that most disturbed Kinney's dreams. He had stared at them in complete disbelief, then simply walked away, leaving the two of them to scramble and squirm like animals, not knowing what to do. For days Fry said nothing. Weeks passed, then months, with nothing but that look, that knowing look of contempt and loathing. That look had caused more fear than the specter of the brig. Radford had almost gone berserk waiting for the captain to act. Just before the *Georgia* pulled into port, Radford made his first suicide attempt. But the pills made him sick, and he threw them up before they could take effect. And still Fry said nothing of the incident.

I know why he waited. The bastard. He waited for his precious fitness report before he told NIS. He didn't want us to soil his spotless record.

But Captain Joe Fry had gone by the book. Soon after the *Georgia* was moored to the dock, he reported the incident to the commodore of the squadron. With all the media attention on the president's policy toward homosexuals in the military, the commodore personally reported the incident to the Naval Investigative Service.

After the suicide attempt, Radford was immediately transferred off the sub to a holding company for medical evaluation. He hadn't been arrested, but he was questioned and confined to the hospital.

For the NIS there were two issues: homosexuality in the Navy and fraternization between an officer and an enlisted man. The NIS was afraid the volatile issue of homosexuality in the military would explode in the media, so they delayed their inevitable discussion with Lieutenant Kinney. The fraternization they let go entirely.

During the sub's brief in-port visits, Kinney hadn't been able to contact Radford to tell him he was going to make a new life for them in Brazil. He never had a chance to tell him he had struck a deal that would give them enough money to live comfortably for the rest of their lives in Rio. Then came the shocking news that Radford had hung himself! The word had spread through the sub like wildfire, and several of the crew had gone out of their way to inform him. Consumed with grief and fear, Kinney had wondered if they were simply spreading the word or if they were telling him specifically because they knew about the two of them. Captain Fry had said nothing. The suicide and the political wrangle in Washington over homosexuals in the military paralyzed the NIS with indecision.

Captain black-heart-country-fried Fry enjoys torturing me with his silence and glares of contempt. Tears filled his eyes again, but resolve filled his body. *No one will ever find out,* he silently mused. *I'll disappear into the Amazon and you'll get what you deserve, you homophobic bastard. You'll all get what you deserve.*

Chapter 24

Doris Lubeck rushed out of the warm blue water of the Gulf of Mexico and up onto the snow-white beach, Nicholas Fawcett hot on her heels.

"Nick, you animal!" she cried, as she sprawled on the blanket.

Nick dropped down beside her, panting. When he recovered, he pulled himself to one elbow and looked down at her.

"Doris, there is something I've been wanting to ask you," he said seriously, still gasping for breath.

"Oh, Ah will, Nick! Ah will!" she drawled, pretending to simper like a Southern belle.

"Oh, no. No, no. Not that," he exclaimed, shaking his head. "I'm too old for that."

"Why, Nick, darlin', you did okay last night," she drawled.

"Doris, you are the most incorrigible woman I've ever known. You know that?"

He kissed her lightly on the lips and felt a surge in his loins. Doris was a good woman and a fantastic lover. She would do anything to please him. Anything.

Doris eyed him seriously. "Okay. Get it over with," she said. "I can tell when you have an academic issue weighing on your poor cluttered mind. What is it?"

"The medium you used to grow that virus?"

"Which virus?"

"The Lubeck virus, of course." He smiled.

"Oh, that one. What about it?"

"What's the secret?" he asked, curiously.

"Rat snot!" She giggled.

"Come on, Doris. I'm serious. I've been trying to culture a strain of Epstein-Barr virus without much success, and I thought perhaps your method would be of use," he lied.

He had been working for weeks to isolate and culture the new virus from his own secret hoard of samples he had brought back from Cameroon. But he hadn't had any success and quickly ran out of material to experiment with, forcing him to return to his original plan: Raid the hot zone for the impact it would have in the news media and use the material for extortion while claiming to possess a vaccine.

"I *am* serious. The mucus of the wharf rat stimulated the little buggers to grow like crazy. Simple deduction, Nick. Hosted by a rat. Spread by a rat. It had to be blood, urine, feces, or lymph. I tried a liberal dose of rat snot combined with a standard medium and voilà, the virus survived for weeks."

"Amazing. Why didn't I think of that?" Fawcett said, as if to himself.

"Why, Nick? *You* planning on brewing up a batch in the beach house?" she asked lightly. She knew he had a makeshift lab in his spare bedroom, but she had no idea he was working with dangerous materials.

Fawcett's face froze for an instant. She read the expression as profound thought. It wasn't.

"No, no. I was just hoping your medium would prove useful in my research. Unfortunately, your recipe may be virus-specific. It won't work for what I have in mind," he lied. "However, the logic is brilliant. In fact, *you* are brilliant."

"Is that *all,* Nick?"

She looked up at him with pleading eyes. He kissed her passionately, then drew back to look at her.

"Doris, I've been meaning to ask you. How's Susan these days?" he asked. His brow furrowed with a look of concern.

"She asked me to thank you for inviting her and Derek Evans down for the weekend, but you know how it is. One of us has to be there at all times during the critical part of the animal studies."

"She is very serious about Evans, isn't she?"

"Yeah. She sees him every chance she gets. I swear, she's like a schoolgirl some days. Makes me jealous."

"I don't understand the attraction. He seems so . . . physical, so unintellectual."

"Physical, Nick? Physical?" she said, placing her hand on his crotch and massaging him gently. "As for his intellect, I've had lunch with them a couple of times, and I think he's brilliant."

"But what's he up to? You know, a handsome guy like that could just be using her to get what he wants," Fawcett said, trying to draw her out.

"Maybe what he wants is what she needs," she purred.

His penis was beginning to respond, so she put her hand inside his swimming trunks.

"I heard he presented his findings to Dr. Reinhardt, and the old man tossed him out on his can. Did you know he recommended a vault door for the hot zone and guns for the technicians?"

"Yes."

"And you agree with that?" Fawcett asked with an expression of shock.

"Maybe it's the right thing to do. There are a lot of psychos out there. The World Trade Center bombing proves his case."

"And just what is that, Doris?"

"That sooner or later some nut will do something really crazy, like make a biological weapon to hold the world hostage."

Fawcett swallowed hard and said, "I heard that his recommendations were rejected."

"Wrong again, Nick. The CDC is going to receive special funding for security."

Fawcett's penis went flaccid. "When?"

"Next fiscal year." Doris looked at him with open desire. "Nick, we're down here for a break, honey. Put the CDC and its problems on the shelf for a while. Let's go up to the house and I'll feed you some oysters and a bottle of wine."

She pushed him down on his back and worked her tongue down his chest to his trunks. Placing her mouth over the returning bulge, she blew her hot breath through the material.

"Ah," he sighed. "Race you to the house."

"I got a better idea. Let's walk. Save your energy. You're gonna need it." She giggled.

As they walked toward the beach house hand in hand, Fawcett turned somber.

"Doris, do me a favor?"

"Sure, sugar," she said. "What?"

"Don't work nights next week."

"That's not fair to Susan," she replied.

"I'm planning something special, a late evening engagement."

"Oh, Ah will, Nick. Ah will," she said, turning on her Scarlett O'Hara voice again. Then she grew serious. "To hell with Susan Dorn. She got to go to Rome, didn't she? What are you planning, Nick?" she asked excitedly, like a little girl.

"Oh, a little surprise party."

"Oooh, I like surprises," she said, squeezing his hand.

Chapter 25

AYYAD DROVE ALONG a well-paved country road past fields bursting with tobacco, corn, cotton, soybeans, and peanuts. It was lined with smashed watermelons that had fallen off farm trucks. He turned off the crooked macadam highway that snaked into the foothills and headed down a red clay road deeply rutted by farm machinery. For half an hour he passed graying, abandoned sharecropper cabins shrouded in kudzu vines. Some of the shacks were still occupied by poor black families dressed in rags.

The Al Fucra farm he was searching for was in the middle of endless fields of corn and soybeans, pasture land and pine plantations. There several Black Muslim families, mostly old men and women, worked the soil for subsistence. The young, militant blacks were in Atlanta, Chicago, and New York working the streets.

Ayyad turned in to the dirt drive and pulled up under a pecan tree in front of the tin-roofed wooden shack that served as living quarters. Its weathered gray boards were buckled by time. Beans, tomatoes, okra, squash, and corn were planted all around the run-down buildings. Several women were shelling peas on the porch of the main house. They eyed him suspiciously. Finally an old woman with silver hair ambled off the porch and over to the car.

"You be lost, honey?" she asked.

"Allah be praised," said Ayyad.

"Praise be to the Almighty," said the old woman.

Ayyad held up a fifty-dollar bill.

"Honey, you be hungry?" she asked, taking the bill.

Ayyad nodded.

"Come up on the porch and sit a spell, and I'll fix you a plate of collard greens."

She didn't offer him a piece of the country ham she had stored in the smokehouse. She knew her visitor didn't eat pork. Muslim law forbade her to eat pork as well, but her tastes were purely Southern, and some laws were made to be broken.

Ayyad ate a big meal while the women shelled peas. They didn't ask him questions. They didn't want to know his business. They just chatted about the weather and the crops. After he had eaten, he parked his car inside an old barn and took out his prayer rug. Facing Mecca, he gave thanks to Allah for the food and the opportunity to serve his people. When night fell, he slept in the barn with blankets provided by the matriarch. The cot he slept on had provided comfort to others on the run.

When morning came, he picked up a hoe and went straight to the garden. For five hours he worked the soil like a demon, weeding around the old woman's vegetables. The sun felt good on his back, and the iced tea she provided him in unending quantities in quart Mason jars seemed to quench his inner thirst.

Omar Azed arrived late in the evening. Ayyad was watching when he pulled up under the pecan tree and gave the old woman a bill. She pointed in the direction of the barn and ambled back to her rocking chair on the porch

"Azed, the Great Satan is watching you," Ayyad joked from inside the barn.

"Then throw sand in his eyes," replied Azed with fire in his voice, "and cut out the demon's beating heart."

"*An-nasr!* Victory!" cried Ayyad.

"*Idbah al-adu!* Slaughter the enemy!" shouted Azed.

"*Allah akbar*. God is most great," Ayyad replied.

They embraced warmly, like brothers who had not seen each other for years. Ayyad offered him sweet tea from his Mason jar, taking care to wipe the rim with his shirt. For an hour they talked quietly of the battle to come. Then they faced Mecca. Kneeling on their rugs, they prayed.

"God is most great. God is magnificent and almighty. O Lord! Grant our land thy veneration. O Lord! Deliver us from the Jews. Deliver our land from oppression. O Lord! Grant peace and forgiveness to those in the struggle for freedom. O Lord! Thou art the peace. Peace is from Thee. So greet us on the Day of Judgment with the greeting of peace. Here we come, O Allah! Here we come! No partner have you! Praise and blessings are Yours. The Kingdom too! No partner have You!"

After finishing their prayers, they sat cross-legged on the ground in private reflection for a few minutes. Finally Ayyad got up and went to his car. He opened the trunk, removed a small nylon tote bag, and returned to sit with Azed on the ground. The twin warriors stared at each other with steadfast determination.

"This is the weapon Colonel Qaddafi promised," said Ayyad, glancing at the bag. "This is a gift of death for infidels. A gift of freedom for our people."

Azed nodded, his face showing the fire he felt inside. He knew what was in the satchel. He had trained for his part in Operation Desert Decree for years.

Ayyad unzipped the bag and carefully removed the soft cotton batting that swaddled the weapon. Azed anxiously helped him unfold the fabric. It surrounded a small wooden case the size of a cigar box. With great reverence Ayyad placed the case on the prayer rug between them and removed the fitted top, exposing a bottle of clear liquid lying on a bed of soft muslin. It was the size of a large bottle of cologne. A glass vial was affixed inside, sealed from the clear liquid that surrounded it. The vial contained a yellowish substance, the color of expensive olive oil.

Azed's eyes grew large as he stared at the weapon in awe. "*Allah akbar*," he mumbled.

"I have spoken with Prokaryotes. It is time to strike," said Ayyad.

Azed pitched forward, placing his forehead to the rug. He began to chant. "Greet us on the Day of Judgment with the greeting of peace, O Lord. Here we come, O Allah. Here we come!"

Ayyad joined in. "Here we come! No partner have You! Praise and blessings are Yours."

When Azed raised himself from prayer, his eyes fixed on the bottle as if in a trance. "*Idbah al-abu!*" he growled.

With great care, Azed repacked the weapon and placed it in the trunk of his car.

The next morning, the twin terrorists parted company, each on a suicide mission designed to change the map of the world.

Chapter 26

TOM DURANCE ATE dinner and then went back to his hotel outside the Naval Submarine Base at Kings Bay. His room was too small and it smelled of pine oil. Painted avocado green, it was depressing and confining. And his head ached terribly. But it always ached in the evening. The Vietcong bullet that had ripped out his left eye had left him with a permanent disability and constant pain.

His feet were tired too, so he sat down at the small table in front of the window and propped them up on a chair. For a few minutes he mused while waiting for the local TV news to start. His contact at NIS headquarters on the sub base was an agent named Duwillias, a tall, gangly man whose buffoonish appearance undermined his ability to acquire useful information. Durance had code-named him Ichabod Crane. Duwillias had bungled several operations designed to identify a navy man thought to be in contact with the PFC. The intelligence system was working backwards from communications intercepted between Lebanon, Jordan, and the U.S.

Desert Decree? What could that mean? It sounds like a Pentagon op plan; Desert Shield, Desert Storm, Desert Decree. I wish they would read me into the program so I could see the raw intel.

Durance picked up several files Duwillias had given him earlier that day. He selected one, but the light in his room was too yellow for him to see clearly, so he pulled back the curtain. The sunlight made his eye hurt. He opened a file marked *Sensitive*. Inside was the picture of a young sailor. He read the name, Second Class Petty

Officer Cary A. Radford, USN. He perused the file for a few minutes
and was shocked to read that Radford had hung himself six months
earlier over an alleged homosexual relationship with an officer.

*The don't ask, don't tell policy has certainly fucked up the mili-
tary, he mused. They don't know how to handle these kinds of cases
anymore.*

Then he remembered that the NIS was a hodgepodge of individuals: wannabe cops, rejects, and inexperienced beginners who
couldn't cut it in the law enforcement community. He finished reading the Radford file and for a while tried to make sense of the
information he had in his head, but he couldn't make the connections. The pieces just wouldn't fit. Infiltrators. Illegal immigrants.
Terrorists. A trail of bodies from Texas to Louisiana. Dead Arabs in
an alleyway in Atlanta. SCI intel to which he wasn't privy but which
according to Senator Carson, pointed to the sub base.

*What would an American sailor sell to Arab terrorists? Informa-
tion? And why? Greed? Would an angry bubblehead sell out his
country, and if he did, what type of information would he sell that
could be useful to terrorists? Maybe they're planning to hijack a nuke.
That's it. Now that the Cold War is over, we're downloading and
storing them out west. A shipment of nukes! Most terrorist attacks
occur while the victim is on the move. Why not nukes? Maybe they're
planning to hit a White Train.*

He made a note to check on future White Train shipments.

*What if Evans is right? What if we're depending too much on
COMINT and Desert Decree has nothing to do with Kings Bay?*

Durance thumbed another file labeled *Sensitive.* Inside was the
photo of a tall, lanky officer. Under the picture Duwillias had printed
the name, Lieutenant Julius B. Kinney, USN. Looking further, he
discovered that Kinney was Radford's alleged lover. He was surprised
to read that the incident that had embroiled the pair had happened
more than a year earlier. Then it hit him in the face like a glass of cold
beer: Ship assignment, USS *Georgia.*

"It's not the state, dummy! It's the ship!" he said out loud.
"The *Georgia's* the target." Then he thought. *But what on the Georgia? Evans is right. The bastards are relying on COMINT. They
overheard some dumb bastard say "Georgia" and they think it's the
state. The target could be anything from a nuke to the captain. Luck-
ily the ship is homeported here and not California. I'll question the
lieutenant tomorrow if the ship is in port.*

He studied Kinney's photo.

You were compromised, huh? And they left you hangin' in the breeze for more than a year. No wonder you're pissed. The question is, what did you sell to the PFC?

A few miles from Agent Durance's hotel, the USS *Georgia* came to an all-stop. From the top of the sail, Captain Fry issued maneuvering orders with a handheld radio to a tug that slowly warped his big, bullet-shaped boat alongside the pier. A whistle blew when a sailor with a monkeyfist threw over the first line.

"Ship's moored!" blasted the speakers.

Fry closely observed the line-handlers haul in the hawsers and secure the vessel to the pier. When he was satisfied that the *Georgia* was firmly moored, he released the tug and ordered the lines doubled up. He waited until the gangway was hoisted in place, then climbed down the ladder inside the sail and addressed his men. For an instant his eyes met Kinney's. Then he looked directly at the chief of the boat.

"Nice job, men," he said, speaking directly at the COB.

It was the way he said *men* that caused Kinney's jaw to clench.

Without a word to Lieutenant Kinney, who was the senior officer on the maneuvering watch, Fry left the attack center, barking out orders as he walked aft.

"Secure the sea and anchor detail. Set the regular port watch. Watch section two."

The quartermaster on duty repeated his orders over the ship's internal public address system. In the passageway behind the attack center, Fry paused near a line of sailors waiting at the bottom of the ladder leading topside. He turned back to face the quartermaster and yelled out the order they were waiting anxiously to hear.

"Pass liberty call!"

Speakers throughout the ship blared the words, "Now, liberty call. Liberty call. Liberty commences for sections one, three, and four. Liberty to expire on board oh-seven-thirty, Monday, October the nineteenth."

As the quartermaster piped the orders, the men in the queue cheered and Fry smiled benevolently. The sailors scrambled eagerly up the ladder and crossed the gangway to their wives and lovers waiting for them up on the pier. The *Georgia* had been out for only two weeks, but it had seemed like a lifetime to Lieutenant Kinney. He stoically watched the men climbing the ladder and bit his lip.

Cary's dead, he thought, *because of that homophobic bastard. The self-righteous son of a bitch. I'll bet NIS taps me on the shoulder as soon as I step ashore.*

He stared at the column of happy sailors pouring from the boat like rats deserting a sinking ship.

Better not come back tonight, boys, he said to himself, *or you won't live to regret it.*

When his duties were completed, Kinney left the attack center and walked by Fry's cabin on the way to his room. He stopped in the narrow passageway and listened at the door. He wanted to look the commander in the eye and tell him he was a murderer. The door was shut, but there was light seeping through the crack under the stateroom door. Then he heard the shower running. In panic he climbed down the ladder and walked quickly to his cabin.

The bastard is going ashore. The sorry bastard is going ashore.

He tried to think of an alternate plan, but he couldn't focus his thoughts.

It's too late. Maybe I should kill him now.

He was still trying to devise another plan when he heard the PA system announce Fry's departure.

Ding-ding, ding-ding, went the ship's bell. "USS *Georgia,* departing," blared the petty officer on watch.

The bastard's married to this boat, he thought to himself. *He's got to be on board tonight, or it's all for nothing.*

Kinney jumped from his bunk and hurried topside. He climbed up on deck and stared down the pier.

"Going ashore, Lieutenant Kinney?" asked Seaman Peters, one of the unlucky sailors in watch section two.

"Yes, but I'll be back later tonight," he replied with a stern, businesslike expression.

"Aye, sir."

"Did the captain say how long he'd be ashore?" asked Kinney, looking down the pier.

"Yes, sir. About two hours. He's supposed to return at nine, I mean, twenty-one hundred hours," the young sailor stammered, embarrassed for using civilian time when addressing an officer.

"Thanks," said Kinney, breathing a sigh of relief.

Kinney saluted aft and walked up the gangway. The *Georgia* was tied up at the end of the pier in a single berth reserved for ships with seniority. Junior ships often had to tie up abreast of other vessels,

forcing sailors to walk across the deck of a sister ship to get to the
pier. But the USS *Georgia* was stationed in Kings Bay, Georgia, and
accordingly always got prime berthing.

For a few minutes Kinney stood on the edge of the pier, survey-
ing the scene like a conscientious officer ensuring that his ship was
secure. The pier lights flickered on, illuminating the concrete structure in a pale yellow artificial glow. Two other submarines were tied
up abreast behind the *Georgia,* and another was moored on the opposite side at the base of the pier. The dock was full of sailors moving
up and down the two hundred yards to the shore, most of them
headed home for the night. Several vehicles were parked near the
other subs, offloading supplies.

Kinney walked to the base of the pier, smartly saluting sailors
along the way. At the small kiosk guarding the entrance, the petty
officer on duty was occupied with letting a vehicle through. He didn't
really check the vehicle. He just asked the sailor where he was going
and jotted the vehicle's plate numbers down in his logbook. He
snapped to attention and saluted when he noticed the tall, lanky lieutenant standing by his guard shack.

"Evening, Lieutenant," said the burly sailor. "May I help you,
sir?"

Kinney returned the salute.

"Yes. Please inform your relief that there will be a van arriving
for the USS *Georgia* at precisely oh four hundred hours."

"Aye-aye, sir."

Kinney watched him enter the information into his log before
speaking. "Pass it on verbally, if you would, please," he said, looking
the sailor in the eye. "I don't want any delays at four o'clock in the
morning."

"Certainly, sir."

The guard was from one of the other submarines. He had seen
Kinney around, but he didn't know if he was a nice guy or a hard
case, so he saluted again just to make sure he didn't receive a blast for
not noticing the lieutenant earlier. Kinney returned the salute, then
walked to his car. It was parked in the lot near the base of the pier.

As he unlocked the door, he searched the apron for NIS agents.
Seeing none, he got in and drove out of the lot. But as he left the pier
area he spotted a nondescript white sedan pull out behind him. It
wasn't an agent, but it caused his throat to close with fear. Checking
his rearview mirror every few seconds, he took a circuitous route off

base, then motored around town in aimless circles. An hour later he arrived at his health club, parked the car, and jogged to the entrance.

He went directly to the men's locker room and apprehensively dialed the combination to his locker. It was the dead drop between him and his Arab contact, a man he had never met face to face. With trembling hands he removed a gym bag and unzipped it just far enough to see inside. It was full of neatly stacked hundred-dollar bills. On top of the money he saw a passport and the identification papers he needed for his new life in Brazil. He searched for the keys to the rental van. When he found them, he memorized the license plate number on the tag and shoved them into his pants pocket.

Satchel in hand, he left the building and walked toward his car, all the while scanning the lot for the van. When he spotted it, he made no outward sign of recognition. He just continued walking and searching for a gangly NIS agent seated in an official government car.

Like a man with paranoid delusions, Lieutenant Julius Kinney drove in circles. Once his heart nearly stopped when he spotted a white midsize sedan that seemed to be following him. When he finally got a good look at the face behind the wheel, he calmed down. It was an old woman. He dared not go to the apartment he had once shared with Cary Radford. To kill time, he drove up and down Interstate 95. Near H-hour he stopped long enough to call American Airlines to make reservations for Rio in the name of John Albert Robbins.

Chapter 27

AYYAD DROVE TO three safehouses and picked up a vehicle with three men at each location. Leading the caravan on a circuitous route, he stopped at a small park on the Savannah River and conducted a mission inspection of the weapons he needed for the operation. In the trunk of each car he counted the B-40 rounds, launchers, and assault rifles. Then he gathered his men around a picnic table and did a time check to ensure everyone's watch was set to the same time.

"When I say 'Mark,' the time will be exactly twenty-one-thirty hours," he said.

He stared at the second hand on his watch, as did the men in his troop.

"Mark!" he snapped, when the second hand reached twelve.

He was meticulous about following the mission-planning procedures he had learned from U.S. Army field manuals. When everyone's watch was set perfectly, he led them in prayer.

"Almighty Allah, praise and blessings are Yours. Grant our land honor, liberation, and veneration, and grant those who venerate it peace and forgiveness. O Lord! Thou art the peace. Peace is from Thee. So greet us on the Day of Judgment with the greeting of peace."

His young terrorists joined in unison in a prayer they had memorized.

"God is most great. God is magnificent and almighty. O Lord! Grant our land veneration. O Lord! Deliver us from the Jews and deliver our land from oppression. O Lord! Grant peace and forgiveness to those in the struggle for freedom. O Lord! Peace is from Thee. So greet us on the Day of Judgment with the greeting of peace. Here we come, O Allah! Here we come!"

When Allah had received his due, Ayyad ordered them to station for the first skirmish of the mother of all battles. Each cell drove to a specific location, where they unloaded their weapons and walked a few hundred yards to a predetermined firing point. They loaded the first rounds in their B-40 rocket launchers and waited impatiently for H-hour.

At precisely three minutes to ten, Ayyad drove toward the main entrance to the Savannah River nuclear power plant and pulled to the side of the road twenty-five yards short of the gate. Big Bertha watched suspiciously as three men got out and walked to the trunk of the car as if to fix a flat tire. She strained her eyes to see their faces, but they were wearing baseball caps, and the streetlight above them cast shadows over them. She saw the muzzle flash of the AK assault rifle before it began to bark, but it was too late for her to take cover. Ayyad emptied a thirty-round magazine into her body. Jerking like a puppet on a string, Bertha fell back against the kiosk and slumped to the pavement, blood pumping out of her wounds in a torrent. The horrible sight was clearly visible on the closed-circuit TV monitor in security headquarters. Then B-40 rockets began pounding the plant.

Ayyad changed magazines and pumped thirty more rounds into the kiosk where Bertha's partner was hiding. At twenty yards, the

7.62-caliber projectiles ripped the building to shreds. Then one of the terrorists scored a direct hit with a rocket, and the guard shack exploded into splinters.

For two minutes rockets hammered the plant from all directions. Some exploded harmlessly against the massive walls of the cooling towers. Others hit electrical transformers and security lighting. Showers of sparks and debris rained down all over the campus. One rocket scored a direct hit on the security center. The dazed shift supervisor thought he was in a war zone and was being shelled by artillery. Windows exploded, sending shock waves through his body. Shrapnel flew through the room above his desk. Then came silence, an eerie stillness. For a few seconds he listened to his heart pounding in his chest. When he finally got the nerve to crawl out from underneath his desk, he discovered that all of the phones were dead.

Ayyad's men simply exhausted their ammunition, ran to their vehicles, and drove off. A few miles from the power plant, they stopped at predetermined locations just long enough to cache their weapons in case they were stopped on the way back to their safehouses. It was a simple mission designed to initiate a complicated battle plan. The senior members of the Palestinian Freedom Council knew that a thousand B-40 rockets wouldn't seriously damage the massive power plant. The attack was a diversion, a symbolic act designed to provoke a reaction. And it achieved the desired effect. Before Ayyad and his men reached their safehouses in the suburbs of Atlanta, the FBI and other law enforcement agencies had scrambled into action, focusing their efforts on Augusta, Georgia, and the Savannah River nuclear power plant.

Chapter 28

IN JACKSONVILLE, FLORIDA, 230 miles south of the Savannah River plant, Omar Azed stood up from the kitchen table where he had been drinking sweet tea and smoking tobacco from a communal waterpipe. With a nod of his head and quiver of his cheek, he indicated that it was time to go. His stomach was in knots, but he didn't let his apprehension show to the three young men in his cell. In silence, they gathered the equipment they had prepared for the mission.

They too were terrified, glancing at one another apprehensively with large and unblinking eyes.

Azed checked each man's gear, then his own. He carefully examined the packing around the nerve gas Ayyad had given him and placed it in his knapsack along with two gas masks. Wordlessly, the four terrorists loaded their packs into a minivan and drove north to the U.S. Naval Submarine Base at Kings Bay.

Outside the base, they motored along the fence line for several miles. A quarter mile beyond an all-night convenience store, Azed dropped his squad off in a wooded area and returned to the store. Without drawing attention to himself, he parked the minivan in the lot and, in keeping with his training, kept his head low, his face barely visible under a baseball cap as he pretended to make a call from a pay phone outside the store. He waited until the clerk was busy inside, then slipped off into the darkness, abandoning the vehicle. Keeping to the shadows, he jogged the short distance to the bushes where his men were hiding.

Still panting, Azed shouldered his backpack and led the way. Without speaking, they patrolled the fence until they located a vulnerable section. One after the other they inserted precut lengths of a broom handle into the fence, laying them across a corner to form steps. Four lengths of broomstick made a perfect ladder up the corner. One at time, the team helped each other climb over, avoiding the barbed wire at the top by covering it with a small blanket. When all four of them were over, they pulled out the sticks and threw them and the blanket into the palmetto undergrowth. Cautiously, as though moving through an Israeli minefield, they filed through the woods and maneuvered alongside a road to a small wooden bridge, which they ducked underneath. Removing their backpacks, they waited for Kinney.

At three-thirty A.M. Lieutenant Kinney returned to his health club, abandoned his car, and picked up the van the PFC agent had provided for him. He drove directly to the main gate, flashed his ID card, and received a temporary vehicle pass. His lieutenant's uniform even got a salute from the sleepy sailor on duty. Once inside the base, he drove directly to the bridge where the Palestinians were waiting and flashed his headlights. The terrorists scurried inside the van and hid their backpacks under the bench seats, expecting their accomplice to speed away from the rendezvous site.

But Kinney didn't move. "The money," he said, referring to the second installment of his fee. He stared at Azed until the Palestinian passed him a satchel full of cash.

"It is all there," said Azed as Kinney peeked inside the bag with a penlight.

"And the Swiss account?"

"On the paper," Azed replied, referring to the envelope lying on top of the neatly stacked blocks of bills.

"Very well," said Kinney brusquely. He checked the contents of the envelope, then slipped the heavy bag behind the driver's seat.

Azed removed the flask from its wooden box and held it up so Kinney could see it.

"How does it work?" Kinney asked.

"You break it; big bottle and little bottle."

The terrorist placed the weapon back in its protective crypt and passed it to Kinney, who immediately examined the glass vial inside the bottle more carefully with his penlight. He realized he was holding a binary chemical weapon that required the two liquids to be mixed to be lethal.

"What if some splashes on me?" he asked.

"You will die," Azed replied. The Arab held up a gas mask. "With this you can live."

"Very well. I understand." Kinney closed the lid and placed the box and the mask in his gym bag. Then he slipped the van into gear and drove directly to Pier 13.

"USS *Georgia*," he barked to the guard at the gate.

The sailor on watch was groggy at four in the morning. He had just arrived for duty and was still half asleep. Seeing Kinney's uniform, he waved him through without looking in the van.

Once on the pier, Kinney drove slowly out to the *Georgia* and parked just beyond her gangway. He got out and, with the driver's door still open, leveled his gaze at Azed. "If the mask doesn't work, you won't be able to get inside the submarine," he stated flatly, as he studied the terrorist's face for a reaction.

Azed's breath was coming in short puffs, but his nervousness didn't show on his face. "It will work," he insisted.

Kinney reached into the van and removed the keys. As he stuck them in his pocket he eyed the Arab. "Ten minutes," he said.

Azed nodded. Leaving the money in the van, Kinney turned and walked down the gangway with only his gym bag. The sailor on duty

was supposed to search everything that went onboard the vessel, but
Kinney was an officer and part of the ship's company, so he let him
pass without inspection. Even if he had inspected the officer's bag,
he wouldn't have recognized the cologne bottle as a weapon capable
of killing everyone on the ship.

Except for two streetlights, the wharf was dark, and it was deserted at that hour of the morning. Kinney had parked the van
twenty-five yards from the end of the pier, where a young sailor was
standing guard duty. The petty officer waited until the lieutenant
boarded the *Georgia,* then ambled toward the van. Azed saw him
coming and slipped into the driver's seat, where he could see the
submarine moored down below. The gangway leading to the sub was
lit up with a string of bulbs that descended at a steep angle. There
was only one man visible on deck. Armed with a pistol and dressed in
crackerjacks with a white Dixie cup hat, he was an easy target if they
had to rush the vessel.

Azed gripped his pistol as the guard walked up to the passenger-
side window. His stomach knotted up and adrenaline pumped through
his veins.

"Hey, dude. Got a smoke?" the sailor asked, looking up and
down the pier for an officer or a chief. He wasn't supposed to smoke
on duty. Then he glanced at the men in the back of the van. The
three Arabs were lounging back with their caps pulled down over
their eyes, apparently asleep.

Without speaking, for fear his accent would give him away, Azed
pulled out a pack of cigarettes and took out three smokes. He looked
over his shoulder at the *Georgia,* then back at the sailor before passing him the cigarettes and a lighter. Apprehensively, as if committing
a crime, the sailor lit one of the cigarettes.

As he passed the lighter back to Azed, he said, "Thanks, dude.
Night duty sucks, huh?"

Azed nodded without taking his eyes off the man.

"Later, man. I gotta guard the pier from crabs and shit." A hair's
breadth from death, the sailor turned and made his way back to the
end of the pier, hiding the lighted cigarette in his cupped hand.

Kinney stowed his gym bag in his stateroom and hurried to the wardroom. No one was there. In the galley the cook was busy, so he
slipped out of the wardroom and entered the mess deck. Only the
duty chief was awake, working over a stack of papers at one of the

galley tables. He looked at Kinney with sleepy eyes as he drew a cup of coffee.

"You're up early, Lieutenant. Skipper still riding your ass?" asked the salty chief.

Kinney glared at him, trying to fathom the intent of the words, wondering if he knew about his relationship with Radford. But the chief went back to work without a sidelong glance.

"You know how it is, Chief," Kinney replied.

"Yes, sir, I do. Hang in there, sir. Good thing about the Navy is, within two years either you'll transfer or your boss will. Never fails. Trust me." He smiled and went back to his paperwork.

"Is the captain on board, Chief?" he asked, in a businesslike manner.

"Yes, sir. He came back about twenty-two hundred."

Kinney breathed a sigh of relief. "Thanks, Chief."

He walked back to his room quaking with trepidation.

"Calm down. You have to do this for Cary," he mumbled under his breath. "For Cary."

He took Radford's picture from underneath the bunk and slipped it under his shirt next to his heart.

"For you, Cary," he whispered. "I'm doing this for you."

With new resolve, he retrieved his gym bag and left his stateroom for the last time. He climbed up a ladder and slipped into the attack center. It was deserted. He checked the indicator lights to see which hatches were open, then returned to the main hatchway.

The quarterdeck on a submarine is just a simple canvas awning covering the main hatch. The watch stood duty up on deck behind a small podium where access lists were maintained. He was supposed to check everyone's ID card and everything that was carried aboard the vessel, but as with all security jobs, vigilance was hard to maintain, especially at four in the morning. The sailor knew everyone stationed on the ship, and to him, checking ship's company constituted harassment.

Kinney stuck his head out of the sub far enough to speak to the young sailor. "Petty Officer Richmond," he called.

"Yes, sir," said the sailor, peering down at him.

"I'll be shutting the main hatch for a few minutes. We need to do some routine maintenance on the magnetic switch."

"Aye-aye, sir."

Every hatch that penetrated the hull of the submarine had a

magnetic switch that corresponded to an indicator light located in the attack center. A red minus sign or a circle indicated whether a hatch was open or closed, a visual reminder to prevent diving the ship with an open hatch. But the switches were notoriously unreliable and required frequent maintenance. Kinney's order was not out of the ordinary. When he closed the hatch, he sealed the vessel from the outside world. Even water under tremendous pressure couldn't breach the hull.

Inside the *Georgia,* air whispered through ducts past sensors that measured carbon dioxide and oxygen. But the system wasn't designed to monitor for nerve gas. Standing near the top of the ladder, Kinney removed the gas mask from his gym bag and put it on. Then he took out the bottle and stared at it for a few moments.

Losing his courage, he cried, "I can't. I can't do it."

Thoughts of Radford hanging by his neck invaded his mind. Then he felt the boy's picture underneath his shirt.

He's dead. He's cold and lifeless. And I am too.

In his mind's eye, Kinney saw Captain Fry's face that night in engineering. As anger boiled inside him, he gritted his teeth and hurled the glass bottle down onto a metal hatch cover. It shattered on the cold steel, mixing the two chemicals. A light white smoke briefly rose from the hatch, almost invisible, colorless, odorless. It slowly permeated the ship, pumped by the vessel's ventilation system.

When the smoke dissipated, Kinney climbed down the ladder and opened the hatch to engineering. On the way back forward, he ran into Commander Fry peeking out his stateroom door to see what had caused the sound of shattering glass. Fry was gasping for breath and his eyes were bulging out. Seeing Kinney in the gas mask, he realized the mortal danger his vessel was in, but it was too late. Fry fell to his knees in the passageway and crawled toward Kinney like a man possessed, saliva pouring from his nose and mouth. Gagging and gurgling, he cursed Kinney with incomprehensible sounds. Dressed only in his underwear, he slumped to the cold deck. Kinney gaped at Fry as he convulsed at his feet, mesmerized and exhilarated by the sight of such a powerful man reduced to a quivering mass of white flesh.

You caused this, he thought, looking down at the corpse. *You had the power to destroy the world with this ship, and that made you a big man, a god to judge me and Cary, to destroy our lives. Rot in hell, you bastard.*

The sound of the ventilators circulating the poisonous gas

brought him back to reality. Massive filters were simultaneously scrubbing the air clean. But he dared not take off his mask. Pockets of the gas might linger for hours. Kinney hoped it would linger long enough to kill the Palestinians too. He quickly checked the ship for survivors and, seeing there were none, opened the main hatch.

"Petty Officer Richmond," he yelled through the gas mask.

The sleepy sailor walked over and peered down at him with a bewildered expression. He didn't recognize the strange gas mask.

"Give me a hand, please," Kinney shouted, reaching up.

When Richmond clasped Kinney's hand, he found himself yanked off balance. He careened headfirst down the hatchway and landed with a thump not five feet from his dead captain.

From the van, Azed saw the sailor fall. When Kinney climbed up out of the submarine, he grabbed his backpack and said, "Here we come, O Allah! Here we come!" Before abandoning the van, he reached back and flipped a switch concealed inside the satchel containing the lieutenant's blood money.

Azed led his men down the gangway at a trot. As the Palestinians scrambled down into the *Georgia* like rats scurrying into a hole, Kinney climbed in the van. The guard at the end of the pier heard a vehicle door slam, but he was too busy watching crabs playing around the cement pilings to pay much attention. He looked up when Kinney started the engine and stood up, for fear he would receive a reprimand for not doing his duty. Guarding the end of the pier was a meaningless assignment he had received for shirking his watch responsibilities earlier in the day. He saluted the lieutenant as he turned the van around and watched as he drove up the pier. He was lighting his last cigarette with a butt when the explosion shook the pier.

BOOM!

The shock wave nearly knocked him into the water.

"Shit, man!" the sailor shrieked, eyes bugged out.

Then money began raining down around him.

"What the fuck!" he howled.

The force of the explosion obliterated the van and showered the length of the pier with debris and thousands of twenty-dollar bills. When the guard at the kiosk ran down to investigate, he saw part of a human torso. It was bloody, burnt, and smoking, and entangled on what was left of the steering post. Then he saw the head and most of the chest lying on the pier, with the arms splayed on a flaked hawser. Nausea overwhelmed him and he began to heave. Hand over his mouth, he ran up the pier to his telephone.

Chapter 29

WHEN OMAR AZED closed the main hatch of the USS *Georgia,* he sealed out the world. Nothing short of a cutting torch could open it from the outside. Still wearing his gas mask, he opened his backpack and removed a clear plastic bag full of a white substance with the consistency of powdered sugar. He sprinkled it liberally over the area where Kinney had shattered the bottle and ordered one of his men to sweep up the mess.

When the toxin was neutralized, he removed a wicker basket from his backpack. It contained several canaries. Two of them were sealed in large Ziploc bags.

From a book, Aman Ayyad had learned of the use of canaries to test for poisonous gases in coal mines. He realized it would be a simple but effective means of testing a ship for nerve gas as well. He and Azed had experimented for days to determine how large a plastic bag was needed to sustain a bird for a couple of hours. The birds in the basket were still alive, indicating that the ship's ventilators had cleaned the air of nerve gas in the area directly beneath the main hatch. Azed opened the lid to the basket and captured one of the tiny creatures.

"Sami, check the forward part of the ship," he ordered. The gas mask distorted his voice. As he handed the bird to Sami, he said, "If it dies, come back immediately."

"Okay," Sami replied, as he gently grasped the bird's feet. It fluttered and tried to get away.

Azed removed another canary and sent Nazir aft on the same mission. When both men returned with living birds, the troop descended a deck and repeated the inspection. Feeling more confident, Azed unsealed a plastic bag and removed a third bird. He sent Nabil, Sami, and Nazir in different directions with orders to meet in the captain's stateroom in ten minutes.

The last bird he saved for himself. Canary in hand, he walked aft to the mess deck. The duty chief was slumped over a table, dead. In the galley, the cook was sprawled on the deck, eggs burning on the grill. Azed turned off the grill and continued his reconnaissance. Using the bird as a living sensor, he climbed down a ladder and searched a berthing space. Several crewmen were curled up in the passageway. With his boot he moved the bodies out of his way. Most of the sailors were still in their bunks. He stopped and checked a body for a pulse, and then another, reassuring himself that no one had survived the attack. Suddenly, the canary began to struggle to free itself. In seconds it too was dead.

Azed ran from the compartment as if the Great Satan himself were chasing him. He scrambled up several ladders to Fry's stateroom and rendezvoused with Nabil, Sami, and Nazir. Their birds were still alive. Sami had removed his mask. When he saw the dead bird in Azed's hand, his eyes grew large with fear. As quickly as he could, he donned his gas mask.

Lying in bed, half asleep, Tom Durance had felt the concussion of the explosion in his hotel room. He jumped up, threw on his clothes, and ran outdoors. It was still too dark to see the column of smoke rising from Pier 13, but the nature of the blast and its timing demanded investigation. Using a portable light and siren, he raced to the scene.

The van was still smoking when he arrived. Flashing his badge at the kiosk, he ran to investigate. Money was scattered up and down the length of the pier. Twenty-dollar bills floated like flotsam around the submarines. Near the smoldering van he saw part of a body lying on the side of the pier and caught a glimpse of a lieutenant's bar on a shredded khaki collar. He walked closer to investigate. A bloody photograph was partially visible under the shredded shirt. He slipped it out far enough to make out Cary Radford's face.

"Lieutenant Kinney, I presume," Durance said to himself.

Omar Azed waited ten minutes before sending his troops on another inspection. He kept his gas mask on until they returned from their scouting missions. Seeing the birds were still alive, he took off his mask and called the FBI.

A woman answered. "Federal Bureau of Investigation. How may I direct your call?" she asked pleasantly.

"This is Commander Two from the Palestinian Freedom Council. I want to speak to the man in authority. Immediately!" he demanded.

A few seconds later, a man picked up. "This is Special Agent Dukowski. How may I help you?"

"Can you record this telephone call?" Azed asked gruffly.

There was an awkward moment of silence.

"Yes, I can."

"Then do so," Azed commanded.

"Please be advised that this telephone conversation is now being recorded. It is a violation of federal law to . . ."

"Shut up, Dumbkowski!" Azed yelled. "I am Commander Two of the Palestinian Freedom Council, and I am in command of the submarine *Georgia*. I have the following demands: The president of the United States will release the men he put in jail for the World Trade Center attack. If they are not released within four hours, I will kill the men on this ship. I will begin by launching the commanding officer from the torpedo tube."

"Uh, sir . . . uh, I need to ask you some questions. We receive a lot of prank calls here, and uh . . ."

"Dumbkowski, shut the fuck up! Clinton will release Yousef, Abouhalima, Ajaj, and Salameh within four hours, or I will kill the captain."

"What is your name, sir?"

"I told you my name, idiot. I am Commander Two of the Palestinian Freedom Council."

"Sir, what is your address?" the rookie continued, working his way down a checklist.

"I told you, the submarine *Georgia!*"

"And where exactly is that, sir?" Dukowski asked.

"Georgia!" Azed screamed.

"I'm not familiar with submarines, sir," said Dukowski, trying to keep Azed on the phone for a trace.

"The submarine is in Kings Bay. To prove I speak the truth I will launch the captain from the torpedo tube as soon as I can force him into the chamber."

Azed was stalling until his men could figure out how to operate the launch system. Fry's body had already been crammed into the outboard torpedo tube.

"Sir? Sir?"

"Do not worry, asshole. I will leave the phone off the hook so you can trace the call." Azed paused. "If anyone attacks this vessel, I will fire torpedoes and launch nuclear missiles. You tell Clinton that!"

Dukowski got his trace. He grabbed the recording and ran upstairs.

"I got a strange one, sir," he said, bursting into his superior's office.

Special Agent Strickland looked up with a nasty expression. He didn't like the night watch, and he didn't like people barging into his office, especially a new guy like Dukowski. He completely let loose when he heard Azed's demands.

"Is this a hoax or what?" he asked.

"I don't know, sir. We just deployed the SIT to Augusta. Do you want me to recall them?"

"Dukowski."

"Yes, sir."

"Call the Pentagon and find out if this is a hoax," he ordered in a mock-patient voice. He picked up his telephone but stopped short of dialing. "Give HRT a heads-up. Special Agent Watson may need them." The FBI's Hostage Rescue Team was a fifty-man SWAT crew trained in explosive entry techniques.

"Sir, HRT deployed to Augusta with the SIT two hours ago."

"Shit." Then he thought out loud, "Where's Durance?"

"He's at Kings Bay," answered Dukowski. "He's following up on that Texas infiltrator case."

The Kings Bay military police were not trained for a major incident. Their experience amounted to little more than handling the occasional drunken sailor and a few domestic disputes. Durance pulled out his badge and flashed it at the closest MP.

"Get everyone off this pier," he ordered. "Cordon it off."

"Yes, sir," replied the young sailor, eager to oblige. His eyes were big and his face was white with shock.

Durance walked down the pier to the gangway of the *Georgia*. The hatches were all closed. He glanced at the other subs and noticed theirs were too.

Must be SOP to batten down the hatches in case of trouble, he thought.

"Hey you," shouted Durance, noticing an older military policeman near by. "FBI," he said, flashing his badge.

Just then the *Georgia* shuddered, and a huge gas bubble erupted at her bow. A naked body appeared on the surface amid the roiling water and ejected air.

"Oh, Jesus," Durance exclaimed. He stared at the body.

"That's Captain Fry!" exclaimed the overweight policeman, pointing at the horrible scene.

"How do you know?" Durance snapped.

"The red hair!"

"Get everybody off this goddamn pier. Right now! Set up a perimeter, and don't let anyone out here! Quickly! Quickly!" Durance yelled.

The man rushed off, shouting orders, to no avail. Everyone was in a state of confusion.

Durance walked back to the kiosk, where a group of people had gathered trying to get a look.

"Get the base CO on the phone, please," he ordered.

"Sir, I called the CO. He's on his way over here," stammered the guard.

Durance scanned the road and spotted the captain's sedan speeding up behind a group of onlookers. He rushed over to the car window.

"FBI," he said, flashing his badge.

"What's going on here?" asked the older man.

"Sir, I need to clear this entire area. Can we get those submarines under way?"

"What the hell is going on here?" the irate officer demanded.

He got out and surveyed the scene. Then he eyed Durance with suspicion.

"I'm not sure, Captain," Durance replied. "We've got part of a body, perhaps a lieutenant off the *Georgia,* lying on the pier," he said, pointing down the wharf. "The other part is hung up on the steering post of that van. And there's money scattered all over the place. And just a few minutes ago the *Georgia* launched a body out of her forward torpedo tube."

The older officer almost choked. "Captain Fry did what?"

"Sir, I think Captain Fry is the torpedo," Durance said somberly.

"Oh, my God," muttered the senior officer, as he strained his eyes to see down the pier. "George," he growled at his executive officer.

"Yes, sir."

"Get everyone under way. Use the tugs to help ease these boats out beyond the quay. And call JSOC. Get a team of SEALs down here right away."

"Yes, sir."

"Captain, is it possible to set up a communications center in one of those buildings?" Durance asked. "If my instincts are correct, we're going to need a lot of secure phone lines."

"And just exactly what do your instincts tell you, Agent?"

"Durance. Tom Durance."

"What do you think is going on here, Agent Durance?" the captain demanded.

"I think Arab terrorists have seized the USS *Georgia.*"

The naval officer stared down the pier like a soldier with battle fatigue. "Dear God," he mumbled, "help us." He gave Durance a blank look and said, "The *Georgia* is loaded with nuclear missiles."

Chapter 30

DEREK EVANS LISTENED intently to the news bulletins on his car radio as he highballed down the highway at eighty miles per hour. All the stations were reporting the same thing. Terrorists were executing the crew of the USS *Georgia* and launching them out the ship's torpedo tubes. When the president came on and made a strong statement vowing not to give in to terrorist demands, Evans cringed. *Ill advised,* he thought. *There are times to hunker down behind the dike and observe what the enemy is throwing at you before sticking your neck out.*

Twenty hours after the sub had been seized, Evans drove up to the main gate of the Naval Submarine Base at Kings Bay, where a line of cars and media vans was waiting. The traffic was hopelessly snarled even though the smart people in the area had hightailed it long ago.

What am I doing here? he thought. *If those fanatics light off a nuke, these vultures will become crispy critters,* he thought. *And me too.*

He waited patiently for his turn to speak to the gate guards. They were turning almost everyone away. When he got to the head of the line, a muscular sailor in camouflage fatigues approached his car window.

"Sir, the base is under a total lockdown. Are you on official business?"

Evans handed him his Navy ID card. "I'm working on a special project that deals with international terrorism. I may be able to help, son."

"Sir, I'm sorry, but I can't allow anyone access to the base unless they're on this list. Are you on the list, sir?"

"No."

"Sir, I'm under strict orders from my CO," the petty officer insisted. "No one gets inside this base except on official business."

"Listen, sailor, I may be the only man with the keys to that submarine. Please let me in," Evans urged with a deadly serious expression.

"Commander," said the sailor with a curious expression, "you look familiar. Are you a SEAL?"

"I was. I retired after my CO tour."

"I thought I recognized you, sir. You were my XO at BUD/S."

Evans looked for a trident, the SEAL breast insignia, or the tattoo that one had once been worn over his left breast pocket. The sailor caught his roving eye.

"I . . . I quit during Hell Week, sir," the young petty officer stammered, embarrassed by the revelation. "You tried to talk me out of it, but I wouldn't listen. I been kicking myself in the ass ever since."

Evans didn't remember the sailor from the hundreds of others he had put through Basic Underwater Demolitions/SEAL training. "Sorry to hear that. I'm sure you would have made a good SEAL," he said, not meaning it.

"Sir, I'm going to let you through. But please don't tell anyone my name if you get in trouble."

"Don't worry, buck-o. Just hope the stupid bastards in charge of this Mexican standoff will listen to me, or we'll all turn into powder in a blinding white flash," Evans warned.

Fear crossed the sailor's face, and he swallowed hard as he glanced back at the base. Leveling his gaze back on the commander, he said, "Yes, sir. I catch your drift. As soon as my watch is over I'm getting as far away from this place as I can."

He waved Evans through. Once Evans was inside the base, it was easy to locate the target. The *Georgia* was the only ship in port. Moreover, armed men surrounded the base of the pier. By the shape of the antenna farm, Evans knew exactly where to find the tactical operations center. He parked his car out of the way and walked to the building. The entrance was guarded by base policemen, but so many men were coming and going he easily slipped past security with a group of FBI agents. Inside he located Tom Durance.

"Double Tap, how the hell did you get in here?" asked Durance, surprised by the visit.

"Jumped the fence."

"Yeah, I'll bet," Durance said, eyeing Evans's suit and tie. "I got a better question. Why the hell would anyone want to get in here? Would you believe I finally cornered my tango and he's armed with nuclear missiles?"

Evans raised his eyebrows. "How do you know it's the same guy?"

"The pier watch ID'ed him from a photo. He bummed a ciga-rette from him just before he hit the sub. So I say again, what the hell are you doing here?"

"I can help."

"Shit. If you got a way to get in that sub, you're in the wrong business, good buddy. You should've been a magician."

"I didn't say I had a way to get in. But I know how to kill the bastards inside without much of a fuss, quietly, without setting off a nuke. Interested?"

"You bet!" Durance blurted. His eye came into sharper focus. He knew Evans wasn't joking. "Come with me, partner," he ordered. "I'll get you in to see Watson right away."

They walked down the hall to what had been the conference room of the squadron's commodore the day before. Durance knocked, and the two men entered without waiting for a reply. A number of officers were seated around the conference table. Evans recognized several of them. One was the CO of SEAL Team Six, the East Coast counterterrorist team.

"Sorry to interrupt, sir, but this is Commander Derek Evans, former CO of SEAL Team Five. He knows how to take down the sub without a lot of fuss."

All eyes focused on Evans.

Watson studied his face. "We've met," he said brusquely, "at Senator Carson's conference on international terrorism. Looks like the bastards beat us to the punch, Evans. Have a seat. I'll get to you in a just minute."

Watson and the other officers and agents finished a discussion on the Arabs' ability to launch a missile without the authorization codes and were considering the ramifications of a meltdown of the reactor core when a messenger entered.

"Sir, they just launched another man."

Watson slumped back in his chair exhausted. "That makes twenty-one dead. Goddammit!" he yelled. "The bastards are killing a man every fucking hour! We gotta do something and fast."

"Sir," said the messenger, trying to get his attention.

"Yes," Watson snapped.

"The president just publicly refused to release any of the prison-ers from the Trade Center bombing."

"Has anyone checked the core temperature of the men who have been ejected from the sub?" Evans interrupted.

Everyone stared coldly at him.

"Look, Evans," said Watson with a vicious expression. "You may have a heavyweight for a boss on Capitol Hill, but around here you're just another lightweight asshole! *Capisce?* I said I'd get to you."

Evans controlled his anger and turned to the CO of SEAL Team Six. Ignoring Watson, he asked calmly, "Jim, how many men could you rush aboard that sub before the crew figured out what was going down?"

"Not very many, Derek," the man in uniform responded.

"You think the crew is already dead, don't you?" asked Durance.

"Give me a fucking break, goddammit!" Watson yelled.

"Listen to the man!" Durance yelled back. "I know what he's thinking. The officer who was blown up on the pier sold out. That's why there's twenty-dollar bills scattered all over hell. The crew is dead, Ron. A core temperature will establish the time of death."

The CO of the SEAL team spoke up. "A few tangos couldn't control the crew."

"Who says there are just a few?" Watson demanded.

"The *Georgia* is on the end of a pier, Ron, on a Navy base full of people. How many men do you think they could get on board without someone seeing them?" Durance asked civilly. "I'll tell you how many. The queer officer got them on board. The pier watch said he saw four, five men tops inside that van. For his efforts, Lieutenant Kinney got a bomb up his ass."

"So where is this conversation leading, Durance?" Watson barked, running out of patience.

"Elementary, my dear, Watson," said Evans, with an angry scowl. He got out of his chair and walked over to the exhausted FBI boss. "The entire crew is dead! *Capisce?* Otherwise they would have rushed the bastards by now. Check the core temperatures. I'll bet you they're all the same. Have the coroner check for nerve gas. And," he said, shaking his finger in Watson's face, "if you want to confirm how many bad guys are onboard that boat, call your friend David Shipler. He can have a team here in a few hours. They have a factory just up the road in Carolina."

Watson eyed Evans without blinking. "Okay, Evans," he growled, "assuming you're right and the crew is already dead, what the fuck difference does that make? The tangos are still inside that sub, locked up with a shitload of nukes."

"Elementary, Watson. We kill the bastards with nerve gas, the same way they did the crew of the USS *Georgia*."

"And just how the hell do we do that?" Watson snapped. "Drill a hole through four inches of HY-120 steel before they pop off a nuke?"

"We could punch a hole through the hull with explosives and flood the vessel with gas before they could react," said the uniformed SEAL captain.

"Just a minute here. Just a minute," Watson interrupted. A light bulb had gone off inside his head. "Strickland," he said to his number two man, "get Shipler on the phone right away. Ask him if he can help us out. And get the coroner in here. Tell him we need an estimated time of death for the first few and the last few bodies we recovered from the bay. And have him check for nerve agents. Right away."

"As you were saying, Captain?" he said, focusing on the SEAL Team commander.

"We could blow a hole in the hull with a shape charge and flood the boat with nerve gas before they could respond."

"Evans, you agree? What if they've rigged one of the missiles or the reactor? Could they detonate the device before the gas took effect?"

Evans sat down next to Watson with a troubled face. "Explosives might work, but there's another way that's quieter. Some years ago, I replaced an electrical instrument on the bottom of an SSN. Don't ask me what it was, 'cause I don't know. It was just a large instrument attached to the bottom of the sub with a huge one-inch rubberlike cable running out of it. This cable ran through the outer hull, up through the ballast tanks, and through the pressure hull into the sub. At the pressure hull there was a large locking nut that compressed this incredible rubber grommet where the cable passed through the steel. In fact, there were several electrical cables passing through the hull. We could use a wrench to back off on the nut and drill a hole through the rubber with ease."

"And you're suggesting we covertly flood the sub with nerve gas through this hole?" Watson asked.

"Yes. A couple of SEALs could scuba out and enter the outer hull through the seawater intake. The ballast tanks are high and dry next to the hull. That's how a sub works. It rides on a bubble of air. They could remove the nut, slowly drill through the rubber grommet with a battery-powered drill, insert the nozzle from a gas bottle inside the boat, and then quietly release the gas. No noise. No fuss."

"But they could still put on their gas masks," Watson argued.

"Colorless and odorless. Got the picture?"

"Yes, I do. Go on."

"With the right kind of equipment, we can communicate with the operators every step of the way. I suspect Shipler's boys could keep us informed of what the tangos are up to inside the boat while the operation is in progress. They might even be able to tell us when the bastards croak."

"Evans?" said Watson.

"Yeah?"

"Do me a favor?"

"Sure."

"Stay on the right side of the law, man. I don't ever want a shifty-thinking son of a bitch like you on the other side." He paused. "And if I've pissed you off in any way, I apologize five times over."

Watson extended his hand and Evans shook it.

"Okay," said Watson. "I can get TSD to build some kind of needlelike nozzle and provide the gas. Who does the mission?" he asked, looking at the commando leaders. TSD was the technical support division of the CIA. They were known for their ingenuity in producing James Bond–type equipment.

"HRT," snapped the unit's commander. "The boat is inside territorial waters."

"We have more experience at underwater operations," the SEAL captain cut in.

"Master Chief Boomer Savarese," Evans thundered, "and the swim buddy of his choice. He helped me change out that whatchamacallit on the USS *Aspro* a few years ago, and he's a steady hand under pressure. And Watson?"

"Yeah?"

"Don't fool around with TSD too long. They've had almost a day to figure out how things work inside that boat. Get the gas and we'll make it work with tools from the country store. Not a big problem. Just make sure the gas is colorless and odorless."

"And very, very deadly," Watson finished. "Okay. You get this Master Chief Savarese character here, and I'll call the director and give him a heads-up so he can brief the president."

"Sir," protested the HRT commander. "This is my area of responsibility."

"This is a presidential decision, gentlemen. Make no mistake about that. No one goes rogueing off on his own," Watson said, staring hard at Durance and then at the unit commanders. "My recommendation will be to support Evans's plan all the way. Is that clear? He's been there, and he knows the mission and the men."

Watson turned his attention to an alternate plan. "Captain," he said, speaking to the Team Six commander, "if you would please put together several explosive charges to penetrate the hull in case we have to take her down in extremis. Work with HRT on methods of entry. You guys try and get along, okay? Think big. A fucking laser torch or something."

"Sir," Watson continued, addressing the CO of the base, "please contact your maintenance people and get me the exact specifications of the hull penetrations Evans is talking about. Ask them if they've got one of those grommet things so we can determine the thickness and hardness of the rubber. Now if you will excuse me, I need to discuss this with the director."

As the group filed out of the room, Watson called to Evans, "Evans. Stick around. I want to talk to you."

When they were alone, Watson looked Evans squarely in the eye. "You may as well know we're planning to plant explosives under the sub," said the agent. "Enough to blow her out of the water and kill the men inside, but not enough to rupture the hull. What are your thoughts?"

"Two concerns," Evans replied, holding up two fingers. "First, if one of the tangos has his finger on a dead-man switch, this part of the country will be uninhabitable for the next fifty thousand years."

"And the second?" asked the agent impatiently.

"The explosion may not kill all the tangos. That vessel was designed to handle incredible pressure. A big boom might just be an E-ticket ride for a man lying down in a bunk."

"Those are the same objections expressed by your Team Six buddy. Thanks, Evans. While we're waiting for TSD to come up with your nerve gas, explore all the options with the men. Okay?"

"Sure thing."

Chapter 31

WHEN THE SECURE call came in to Lieutenant Gomez, Boomer Savarese was busy with an Army corporal from the administrative department at Fort Sherman. She was only twenty-two, and she had never met

anyone with a line like the master chief's. If she had known he was an
E-9 under cover, she wouldn't have consumed all the rum that had
obliterated her inhibitions.

Gomez listened at the door for a few seconds and, not hearing
any sound, opened it without knocking. "Boomer, time to rock and
roll," he said, turning on the light. "Whoa! Sorry, man."

Savarese's tan body was straddling the milk-white blond. She
tried to hide her face in the pillow. Gomez quickly switched off the
light. "Boomer, we've got to work out some sort of signal, man," he
said, talking to the dark.

"Why, Boss?" asked Savarese. "You want some?"

"Jesus, Boomer. Cut the crap." But Gomez chuckled.

"Give me half an hour, Boss. As soon as I finish up here I'll be
ready to hose down any son of a bitch you want."

"We've got ten minutes to be on the runway with our swim gear
or we'll miss our plane."

"What's up?"

"I don't know. They want you and the swim buddy of your choice
in Kings Bay, Georgia, in three hours," said Gomez.

"In-fuckin'-possible!" Savarese grunted.

"Not in an FA-18, it's not."

"Then you'd better get another bird, sir, 'cause I ain't sittin' on
your lap all the way to the U.S. of A." roared Savarese.

"Well, I'm certainly not sittin' on yours, tripod."

"Jealous."

As Gomez walked out of the room, Savarese yelled, "Hey, Boss,
sure you don't want some?"

He heard a smack as the girl slapped Savarese on the butt.

With CNN blaring in the background, Evans and Durance reviewed
the tactical situations. The CNN anchor paused for a special report
showing an airplane on the tarmac in Tehran. The prisoners from the
World Trade Center bombing were climbing down the steps like returning POWs.

"Give 'em an inch and they'll ask for a mile," Durance commented.

No sooner had he spoken the words than one of the FBI nego-
tiators walked into the tactical operations center, complaining, "Now
Commander Two wants Sheik Omar Abder Rahman released."

"And it won't stop there," added Durance.

"Do we know who this Commander Two guy is?" asked Evans.

"I'd bet a paycheck it's Aman Abruzzi Ayyad," said Durance. "The pier watch got a pretty good look at him. He picked his photo out of a stack of pictures."

"Do you have a bio on him?"

"Here. See for yourself," said Durance, passing Evans a file.

Evans opened it and took a hard look at Ayyad's photo. "This is the dude who tried to whack me."

"Somehow I'm not surprised. You must have been too close for comfort when you were working the Savannah River plant," Durance suggested.

"Any significance to his nom de guerre?"

"Not that we know of," answered the FBI negotiator.

"What are you gettin' at, Double Tap?" Durance asked.

"Remember the Sandinistas?"

"Vaguely."

"Well, there was a Commandante Zero, Uno, Dos, Tres, et cetera. Get the picture? You've got to admit the title 'Commander Two' implies that there is at least a Commander One."

"Maybe Commander One was the guy who hit the Savannah River plant. A diversion op," the HRT commander mused.

"You'd better hope so," Evans declared. "If this is the diversion, I don't want to think about the primary objective."

"Don't even talk that kind of shit, man," said Durance, glaring at Evans. "What could be worse than a bunch of Arab fanatics barricaded inside a submarine loaded with nukes?"

"A hit on the White House?" offered an agent.

"Shit, that'd be a favor," another growled.

Evans stared at Durance blankly and shook his head. He knew what would be a worse target: the viral material on the fourth floor of the CDC. It had the potential to ravage the entire planet.

When David Shipler arrived, he eyed Evans with disdain and kept his distance. Watson explained the situation and asked Shipler if his equipment could help. Shipler smiled knowingly at the FBI agent. Pulling Watson aside, he spoke to him privately.

"Ron, we can help, but our participation must be completely confidential. We must operate in such a manner that S-Systems is not identified in the news media." Shipler's bald head shone like a bowling ball under the room's bright lights. Little beads of perspiration were popping up on his polished dome.

"That won't be a problem, David."

"And I can't allow Mr. Evans anywhere near my equipment," Shipler continued.

"Sure, David. Sure." Watson looked at him curiously.

Shipler picked up a phone and dialed a number. He spoke curtly and hung up. A few minutes later Rice and Verduchi came marching through the door. Rice took one look at Evans, made momentary eye contact, and grabbed his partner's arm. They both did an about-face like two of the Three Stooges.

Shipler yelled at them from across the room. "Rice! Verduchi! Over here!"

Rice stopped in his tracks and turned around reluctantly. Evans knew they were sweating bullets, so he pretended to read at the conference table. All through their briefing, which Watson conducted in the corner, Rice kept sneaking glances at Evans. When the voyeurs trooped out, Evans chuckled out loud.

A half hour later Shipler received a preliminary assessment from the snoops, which he relayed to Watson in private. "Ron, our equipment is capable of audio surveillance only. I want to stress that. Our initial analysis is based on such sounds as speech, coughs, snorts, sneezes, flatulence, and so on. As far as we can determine, there are only four men inside the submarine."

"Only four? Are you sure, David?"

"We are fairly confident of that figure. They speak Arabic to each other. So far not a word of English has been spoken, except on the phone between your negotiator and Commander Two. He's the apparent leader. Incidentally, his name is Omar Azed, or at least that's what his men call him. I sent off a query to see if we have any information filed under that name."

"Azed, huh? Not Ayyad?"

Shipler raised his eyebrows and shook his head slightly.

"Thanks, David," said Watson.

"Gents," said Watson to the group gathered around the conference table, "here's the situation. As soon as CNN reported that Sheik Rahman was on the ground in Tehran, Commander Two demanded that we wire-transfer a billion dollars to a numbered account in Lichtenstein. He stated that if the money isn't delivered within twelve hours, he will fire a torpedo. Admiral, could you give us a damage assessment?" he asked the senior officer seated at the far end of the conference table.

"If they are successful in arming the torpedo," the admiral replied.

"They're capable of it," Shipler interjected.

The admiral looked at Shipler, then back at Watson. "Given the firing angle, a torpedo launched from the forward outboard tube would hit the breakwater. I don't think the explosion would cause much damage. It would take out part of the seawall, of course, and shower the area with water, and in the confines of the harbor it would create a surge, but it wouldn't destroy any buildings or piers."

"The torpedoes aren't nuclear?" Watson asked.

"No. Actually, there are no nuclear torpedoes on that vessel," the admiral declared.

"Well, thank God for small favors," Watson muttered.

"We should evacuate Kings Bay, however," the admiral continued grimly. "The sub is fully loaded with missiles, each with multiple nuclear warheads. I suggest we move the TOC to an underground bunker."

"The town is empty, except for the media jackals camped out around the gates. We're staying right here until this thing is resolved, one way or the other," Watson growled. "Anyone wants out, hit the door now."

He looked somberly at the faces around the conference table.

"Okay, gents. Here's the deal. The president has authorized the Evans mission, if and only if we can assure him that all the crew are dead. David, are you sure?"

"With a 99 percent confidence factor, we believe there are only four men aboard that vessel, and they're all speaking Arabic. When your negotiator demanded to talk to the senior crewman, Commander Two slammed down the phone and made a joke intimating that we were demanding to speak with a dead man. He told his colleagues that President Clinton wanted to buy the crew out on an installment plan. They all laughed, and one of the men commented—I translate the Arabic loosely—'Tell them we'll give discounts for corpses.'"

"Can they fire a torpedo?"

"Yes. Three of them served as crewmen on a Russian submarine."

"What?" Watson blurted.

"The Iranian Navy?" Evans asked.

"Yes," Shipler answered, looking at Watson.

"The Iranians bought two subs from the Russians a few years ago," Evans explained.

Watson nodded.

"I recently received the results of an international background check on Nabil, Sami, and Nazir," Shipler continued. "You're not dealing with amateurs here. They are very bright young men who are well trained."

"Can they launch a missile?" Watson wanted to know.

"No. Not yet. But they're working on it. If there is an assault on the ship, they plan to martyr themselves by detonating one of the missiles inside its launch tube. They have already gained access to a silo and are studying the firing mechanism."

"How long do we have before they figure it out?"

"Impossible to predict. Days. Hours. Azed ordered them to target the first missile at New York City, the second at Los Angeles. They've been working steadily at it for hours."

"Can they get the sub under way?"

"They think so," answered Shipler. "But they're afraid to open the hatches to cut the mooring lines."

"Religiously devout?"

"Yes. They pray five times a day. It's the only time there's not a watch on the periscope."

"Excellent intel," the HRT commander interrupted. "If we have to take her down by force, we should hit them while they're praying."

"Agreed," said Watson. Then he changed the subject. "I think it's obvious they've been studying the *Negotiator's Handbook*. Get us to talk. Get us to give a little, and then, just keep upping the ante. The last demand will be for all Jews to move out of Palestine. Since that's not going to happen we have to take the offensive."

Watson turned his attention to Evans. "Are you confident in the ability of those two characters we flew up from Panama?"

"Yes."

"I thought you said they were military?" Watson asked.

"They are," Evans replied flatly.

"Since when did the SEALs start sporting ponytails and handlebar mustaches? They look more like Hell's Angels than sailors," said Watson.

"Don't let their appearance fool you. Master Chief Savarese has nearly thirty years in the SEALs."

Watson gave Evans a hard look. "You're the expert," he said.

One of Watson's assistants passed out small handheld radios.

"David," said Watson, "that brick has a special crystal in it that scrambles the signal. Keep me informed of everything that goes on inside that sub." He looked at the hostage rescue team commander. "HRT on standby! I want to make it perfectly clear that we don't have authorization for an explosive entry. Is that clear?" He glared at the warriors. They nodded acknowledgment as he eyed each man individually.

"Okay, cowboy," he said to Evans. "Saddle 'em up."

Chapter 32

"COMMANDER, YOU KNOW I hate this fuckin' AUGA mask," Savarese complained.

"It's the only way we can communicate, Boomer," Evans said.

"Once you launch my ass, I don't want to communicate," the master chief argued. "I ain't wearin' the goddamn thing. The L. T. can keep you informed. I'll just kill the bastards and get back to my horny little señoritas in the Zone."

The AUGA was a full face mask that covered the eyes, nose, and mouth, allowing the diver to hear and talk inside it. The only reason they were using it was to communicate with Evans. Savarese had no idea what kind of equipment was onboard the submarine or whether it was capable of intercepting underwater communications. But years of experience had taught him to keep his mouth shut in enemy territory. Communications was a double-edged sword. As a radioman in Vietnam, he had learned the hard way to turn off his radio until needed. The simple sound of a radio breaking squelch in a quiet jungle was enough to get a man killed.

"Savarese, the president himself approved this mission, and he may cancel it any time for any number of reasons," Evans growled.

"C'mon, Loco. Quick! Get in the water before the bastard chicken-shits out," Savarese said to Gomez.

Evans glared at Savarese. "Would you get serious, goddammit?"

"I am serious."

"If you're gonna be such a damn prima donna, I'll do the op myself," Evans snapped.

"Nah. No way! Two officers without an enlisted man for guidance?" He shook his head. "Bound to fuck it up."

Gomez looked at Evans and grinned. Both of them had risen out of the enlisted ranks.

"Give me the damn thing," Savarese croaked. "I'll use it, but it's against my better judgment. But I ain't talkin' on it. It violates every principle of OPSEC I ever taught you two cake-eaters."

OPSEC (operational security) was an absolute necessity for men who worked in small groups behind enemy lines. Savarese sat down at the edge of the water, slipped his fins on, snorted heavily, and spat a large gob of saliva into the full-face mask. Using a finger and a little bay water, he carefully rubbed the inside of the mask, making sure the saliva covered the entire surface. Spit was the magic ingredient that prevented fogging. He dipped the mask in the bay and rinsed it out lightly.

"These goddamn things leak like a sieve, Loco. Probably drown our sorry asses, and if the booger-eaters hear you talkin', they'll launch a friggin' torpedo. That'll give you one hell of headache, sir. You think them damn Cuba libres are bad. Try a torpedo upside your rock head," Savarese grumbled as he put on the last of his gear.

"Boomer, we ain't gonna talk on the damn radio unless we *have* to," Gomez insisted.

"It's the unless-we-have-to part that bothers me, sir," he declared.

In the light of a streetlamp at the foot of the pier, Evans checked their swim gear, a simple air bottle plus fins and lifejacket, like a diving supervisor on a training mission. He gave them an okay-sign when he finished.

"Come down on her from the bow, but not too far. Don't get under the reactor, or you'll fry your balls," Evans warned. "There's not much shielding under the reactor core."

Savarese's eyes turned wild inside the mask. "I'm sure glad I got laid before I left the Zone."

Evans chuckled. Savarese knew the ship was hot underneath the reactor core. He had done thousands of diving operations in his twenty-nine years of service as a frogman.

"That's about all he does down there, Commander, pole vault from one sperm dump to another," said Gomez through his face mask.

"You know what I always say, Commander?" asked Savarese.

"No. What's that?"

"There's only two things that make life worth livin', and that's true love and homegrown tomaters." He chuckled and squatted down in the bay. "You thought I was gonna say fuckin' and fightin', didn't you?"

"Well, it wouldn't be the first time I've heard it," Evans replied, handing Savarese his gear bag.

"A man's gotta be more careful how he launches his purple-helmeted, deep-heat-seeking love missile nowadays," Savarese continued.

"What? AIDS slowing you down?"

"No. Child support."

Gomez and Evans laughed, knowing Boomer's entire paycheck went to his scattered spawn.

SEALs are a strange breed. In times of danger they joke and cut up to cover their inner disquiet. Savarese knew the gravity of the situation. He knew that he could be instantly vaporized if they screwed up the mission. Verbal grousing was his way of being macho.

The divers waded into the water chest deep. Dipping their heads under the surface, they checked each other's gear for leaks, then looked back at Evans for the signal to commence the dive. The commander had his ear stuck to the brick talking to Watson. When he was through, he gave them a thumbs-down, the divers' signal to descend.

For several minutes they swam on the surface on their backs, using Evans as a range marker. Standing on the shore, he was a comforting sight they had seen many times before. But he grew smaller and smaller as they kicked their way out to the end of the pier on the opposite side from the USS *Georgia*.

Gomez stopped at the last piling and faced his partner. The sun had long since set and it was pitch dark in the brooding waters of Kings Bay. There was no light except for the lamps illuminating the pier above.

"Ready, Boomer?" he whispered.

"Yep."

Gomez switched on his radio. "Commander, we're at I.P.," he reported, meaning the initial point of reference they had agreed on to commence the underwater part of the mission.

Evans had concurred that underwater communication was unwise in case the terrorists were using the ship's electronic equipment to monitor the bay. The plan was for their last transmission to be from the surface, above the water. If Evans had to speak to them underwater, it would be to abort the dive.

"Loco." Evans's voice had a note of urgency. "I just received a call from HQ. The tangos are talking about getting the sub under way. Hustle up."

"Roger," replied Gomez. "Boomer! Let's haul ass!"

"I heard the man, L. T.," said Savarese in a steady voice. "And he's wrong about this one. Now is the time for calm, deliberate action, sir. Follow me."

Gomez gave Savarese a squeeze on the arm, and they both sank beneath the water, holding on to the pier piling with gloved hands. As they descended, it grew colder and darker until the visibility was zero. They maintained physical contact with each other and watched their depth gauges glowing phosphorescent in the dark.

Gomez stopped at thirty feet and turned on a low-powered flashlight. Barnacles and crabs covered the pilings, and small fish darted in and out of his beam. The water was still turbid from all the ships leaving the harbor, so they edged their way around the pier, using the pilings as navigation aids. On the *Georgia* side they swam back toward shore, counting the pilings as they went. They heard the ship and felt its presence long before they came to its sleek black hull. Descending silently underneath the bullet-shaped hull, they followed its curve to the bottom, searching for the seawater intake.

Savarese turned on his low-powered flashlight as they worked their way aft. A hundred feet from the bow, they came to a large hole in the bottom of the vessel covered by a metal grate. Through it passed the water used to flood and empty the ballast tanks, which caused the sub to rise and to sink. It was just large enough for one man to slip inside without his scuba. Savarese shined his light on his hand and signaled Gomez with an okay sign. With a ratchet, he carefully removed the bolts securing the grate and let it fall to the bottom. Then he took off his scuba, placed it between his legs, and silently slipped inside the sub.

Gomez watched as his partner slithered into the hull like an eel. He carefully fed out the tether line, keeping slight pressure on it to keep it from tangling.

Savarese inched his way through the intake housing, being careful not to let his rubber-coated scuba bottle, which he held tightly between his legs, bang against the wall of the intake pipe. With his shoulders almost touching the sides, he slowly worked his way to the ballast tank. Ten feet inside the vessel, he broke the surface underneath the pressure hull.

The ballast tank was full of sea growth and matter that looked like dissolved toilet paper. He flipped on a more powerful beam and was glad Evans had insisted on a full face mask. Everything from oil to feces floated on the surface. Directly above him, not two feet away, was the object of his mission. With two strong tugs on the line, he signaled Gomez to send up the equipment bag, and with the lieutenant keeping the line taut at the bottom, he pulled it up.

Underneath the sub, Gomez heard the screw turn over before he felt the rush of water against his body. He grabbed onto the seawater intake and held on with all his strength. The current gradually increased until it was so strong he had to pull himself up inside the intake to prevent it from ripping off his face mask. With his legs dangling out of the bottom of the hull, he held on to the equipment line, knowing that if he lost his grip the screw would chop him up like a chicken bone in a garbage disposal.

Inside the TOC, chaos reigned. Watching the *Georgia* strain at her mooring lines on a closed-circuit TV monitor, Watson agonized over the decision to order an explosive entry. He called Evans in a panic. "Evans! Evans! This sub's under way!" he shouted into the radio.

The experienced commander's voice shot back at him. "No, it's not, Watson. I'm on the pier. The lines are doubled up, and they're holding. If the tangos want to get this vessel under way, they'll have to come out and cut the mooring lines."

"If they open up a hatch, I'm going to order an assault!"

"Hang on now. Buy me some time," Evans said calmly.

Watson could hear water churning in the background.

"If they pop the hatch, turn on the spotlights," Evans ordered. "That will keep the rats in their holes for a few minutes so we can kill them."

"What if one of them walks out with an ax, Evans?"

"Shoot him in the leg. Get Commander Two on the phone. Stall. Negotiate. Buy a little time so we can kill the bastards," Evans growled.

"I roger, Evans, but I can't let that ship get under way. Watson out."

Keeping an eye on the periscope, Evans scurried across the pier and hid in the shadows. He searched the bay behind the *Georgia* for body parts. Seeing no human flotsam, he breathed a sigh of relief.

Underneath the pressure hull, Savarese felt the sub strain at its moorings. He calmly opened his waterproof bag and took out a snake light, being careful not to let seawater get inside the bag. Twisting the light around a cable, he set up a workstation. Using a large wrench, he tested a few cap nuts. It took him several tries to break one free. When he did, he unscrewed it by hand and slid it down the cable, exposing the rubber grommet seated around the electrical cable.

Being careful not to drop his drill, he pushed the bit through the plastic bag protecting the tool from seawater and placed it against the grommet. It cut through the rubber easily. When he neared the electrician's tape that technicians had placed on the bit as a depth gauge, he eased off the pressure and let it work its way through to the inside of the submarine without force. When he was sure it was inside the vessel, he removed the bit and stuck an ungloved finger over the hole to feel for a vacuum. Air from the ballast tank tried to rush through the quarter-inch hole, so he placed a wooden peg in it to temporarily seal it off. To prepare the nerve gas, he first taped the bottle securely to one of the electrical cables leading into the sub. He left enough slack in the hose so he could easily work with the nozzle. Carefully and quickly, to prevent air from rushing into the sub with a hiss, he removed the wooden peg and inserted a needlelike device deep into the hole. Twisting it back and forth, he worked it up inside the ship. Then he waited.

When the sub stopped shuddering, he signaled Gomez that he was through. When he felt the line pay out, he worked his body down the pipe until just his head was above the water and slowly cracked open the valve on the nerve gas. He watched the grommet for a few seconds to make certain that the nozzle was secure inside the sub, then placed his ear next to the valve to listen for the sound of gas escaping through it. Hearing a distinctive hiss, he signaled Gomez to pull him out of the sub. The lieutenant pulled the tether line with steady pressure until Boomer's legs appeared at the entrance of the seawater intake. Then he grabbed one ankle and hauled him out in one smooth motion. Once clear of the intake, they hugged the bottom of the hull, sprinted around the pier, and headed for the shore as fast as they could swim.

Evans and Durance were waiting for them at the base of the pier. They helped them out of the water and stripped off their gear. Evans looked at Savarese with a knowing eye as the old salt pulled off his face mask.

"Piece of cake, Commander," Savarese bragged.

Evans frowned. "Roger that. Let's go see how you did."

They worked their way around a building and walked quickly to the TOC. Still dripping, they listened for Shipler's report on the radio. Watson was waiting with a telephone in one ear connected to the director. The director had two telephones: One for Watson and one for the president of the United States.

Shipler's voice cut through the silence of the TOC. "Ron, this is David."

"This is Watson. Go."

"There are no signs of life on the *Georgia*."

"Thank God," he said, as a cheer went up. "I'll have the negotiator ring Commander Two to check for a response."

Several minutes later Shipler reported back.

"Ron, the phone is ringing. We have tuned and refocused our equipment over and over to pick up any sounds of life. There are none. We believe the terrorists are dead."

While Watson reported the information to the FBI director, Evans drew a cup of coffee and plopped down in a chair, exhausted.

"Let's get a beer," said Savarese. "I know some good ol' girls up in Charleston who just might drive down for a party, if they know I'm here. Better yet, I know some gals down in Jacksonville who just love purple-helmeted, deep-heat-seeking love missiles."

Everyone stared at him, bewildered by the suggestion.

Chapter 33

WHILE LIEUTENANT GOMEZ and Master Chief Savarese were swimming in the waters of Kings Bay, two delivery trucks drove down an alley near Building 15. The drivers stopped and parked their vehicles so they concealed a manhole cover from view. In the pale yellow light of a streetlamp, they got out and walked up and down the lane as if looking for an address. A cat shrieked at the sound of a boot heel, causing them to jump.

After a thorough reconnaissance to ensure that no one was watching, they pulled the cover off the manhole and slid open the side door on one of the vans. Ayyad and five heavily armed comrades scrambled out and scurried down inside the sewer system. Quickly and quietly, with efficiency born of practice, the drivers covered the manhole and sped away. The insertion took less than a minute.

A few blocks away, Nick Fawcett climbed the stairs from Level Three to Level Four and walked down the breezeway. At the far end of the passageway, where the stairs descended to the basement, he saw his own reflection in one of the doors. His stomach surged with fear and his hands began to tremble. In a few minutes, Ayyad's team would storm through those doors, and his life as Nick Fawcett would end. His knees buckled, and he had to steady himself against the banister to regain his composure.

It's time, he said to himself. *It's time to change the course of history.*

He leaned over the cement balustrade and stared down into the atrium between the wings of the building. To calm his nerves he recited his mantra.

> Jerusalem's stone is the only stone that can feel pain,
> It has a network of nerves.
> Write down that I am an Arab.
> Write down on the bloody stone of Jerusalem that I am an Arab,
> And that the number on my identity card is 50,000.
> I have eight children and the ninth is due this summer.
> Are you angry?
> Are you angry?
> Blue shadows among the olive trees of the valley,
> Where once my village stood,
> Now gone to a hard Jewish plow.
> No monument, no flowers,
> No blood-soaked rag worn by my parents!
> Their ghosts ever wander the ruins of Deir Yassin!
> My village!
> My village!

In control of his emotions now, he took a deep breath and walked with resolution to the steel doors leading to the Level Four laboratory. He inserted one of Doris Lubeck's key cards, and the lock released with a loud click.

Inside the tunnel, Ayyad turned on a flashlight and led his raiding party down the shaft for a hundred yards to a larger culvert under the street. Thousands of telephone and television cables ran along overhead, above water pipes and gas lines. Turning ninety degrees, the Palestinians patrolled down the tunnel past access shafts that led to the large buildings lining the street above. Ayyad stopped at the one leading to the basement of Building 15 and checked his watch. With his flashlight, he motioned for his men to take a break and sat down on a large water pipe for a smoke.

Here we come, O Allah. Here we come, he silently prayed. *I will break the seventh seal, O Lord, and pour out the plague that kills the infidels. All is the will of Allah.*

At precisely five minutes to ten, he waved his flashlight again and headed up the concrete access shaft. When he reached the expanded metal grate blocking his way, two of his men stepped up and hastily began removing the bolts that secured it to the walls of the tunnel.

"Commander," whispered one of the men. "I can't remove the bolt."

"What?" Ayyad, annoyed, shined his light on the bolt and gritted his teeth when he saw the special head. It was hopeless and he knew it. Using their hands, several men tried to rip the grate out of its wall anchors, but it wouldn't budge. Then they tried kicking a corner loose, without success. All the while, Ayyad kept looking from his watch to the metal grate blocking his path.

May a camel urinate on your grave, Kasim, if you chicken out, he thought, afraid Fawcett would flee if he were late.

He considered using a grenade, but the sound of the explosion, even underground, might give away the element of surprise. With precious minutes passing, he gave up.

"Let's go," he snapped.

At a trot, they backtracked to the main tunnel under the street. There they took a left and ran to the first shaft leading in the same direction as Building 15. Ayyad led the way into the unexplored tunnel. Seventy yards down the culvert, he came upon a manhole and climbed up to street level. Using his shoulder, he moved the cover to the side just far enough to peek out. When he saw that the area was dark and secluded, he pushed the cover off and scurried to the shadow of the nearest building. The last man out closed the cover. Moving fast, weapons in hand, they headed for the lobby of Building 15. Hiding in a clump of azaleas, they waited until the lobby was clear before scurrying inside, weapons at the ready.

From the coffee shop across the street, Keith glimpsed a movement in the shadow of Building 15 and hobbled over to the window for a closer look. It was dark outside, and the bright lights inside the café created a mirror effect on the glass. By the time he was in position for a better look, Ayyad and his men were already inside.

"Hey, Sam. You see that?" he asked, rubbing his eyes.

Decker was sweet-talking the counter girl. "See what?"

In the reflection Keith watched Decker grin, take a bite of Keith's donut, and put it back on the plate.

"I thought I saw some guys running toward the lobby of the germ factory," he explained, still peering out the window.

"You probably did, knucklehead. Nightshift. It was probably a carpool of lab techs late for work," Decker suggested. He broke off another chunk of Ray's donut and gobbled it down.

"Maybe. But I think I'll check it out. I'm gettin' tired of watching you feed on my donut," he said, looking at Decker's reflection in the window.

When Decker saw Keith glaring at him in the window, he grinned and gave him an amphibious salute.

"Pretty soon you're gonna look like a cop," said Keith as he hobbled back to the table.

Decker furrowed his brow, waiting for the punch line. "Yeah?"

"Yeah. Like a fat fart on a power trip. That's what excessive quantities of donuts do to cops."

"Not me, man. I'm into seafood. I see food and I eat it," Decker joked.

A sour expression crossed Keith's face. He shook his head in exasperation. "You also got a pacemaker stuck in your heart, shit-for-brains. You should be eatin' celery and carrots. Let's go check it out," Keith dared him. He reached down to feel the comfort of the .45 hidden inside his artificial leg.

"Wait till I finish my latte," said Decker.

"How can you drink that milky shit?"

"It's gooood, man," replied Decker. He smiled at the girl licentiously.

"Yuck! I like my coffee hot and black."

"Like your women, I suppose?"

"Why not? If'n it's free, I take," said Keith.

"I'll bet you like them big ol' chunky-butt girls too?" Decker joked, chuckling with the counter girl, who was as skinny as spaghetti.

"Hell yeah, man. More to love," grinned Keith. "'sides, a man in my condition can't afford to be choosy."

He limped out the door, leaving Decker to choke down the rest of his donut.

The security guard behind the reception desk had to look twice. Six armed men wearing ski masks were running into the lobby pointing weapons at him. He reached down for his revolver but thought better of it and slowly put both hands in the air as far as he could reach.

"Open the door!" Ayyad yelled, a twisted expression on his face.

He was high on adrenaline, sweating, nerves raw. The change in plans had thrown him into a state of near panic. The frightened guard complied, and when the metal security door clicked open, two tense sappers rushed inside.

"Lock the door!" Ayyad shouted to the two men stationed at the lobby entrance.

While they were bolting the entry doors, Ayyad jumped over the reception desk and relieved the guard of his pistol. Then he scanned the security monitors. A young woman was walking down a flight of the stairs on one of the screens. The others were clear.

"Let's go! Let's go!" he yelled.

He motioned with his pistol for the guard to move back. "Come with me," he commanded.

"Anything you say, man. You got it," said the guard, holding both arms up as high as he could. Manning a desk at the CDC was just a part-time job. He didn't want to get shot for minimum wage.

Once all his men were inside, Ayyad pushed the security door closed and pointed his silenced pistol at the guard's forehead. The man's eyes expanded as he realized what was about to happen. Then the weapon exploded in his face. Brain matter and blood splattered the cinderblock wall behind his head. The body slumped to the floor, a pile of lifeless flesh.

In a sprint, the six Palestinians ran to the stairway and scrambled up the steps. At the second-floor landing, Ayyad grabbed the young woman he had seen on the monitor. Before she had time to scream, he shot her at point-blank range. Three of Ayyad's men were halfway to the third-floor landing before the body hit the linoleum.

The assailants sprinted all the way up to the fourth floor and down the breezeway to the stainless steel security doors that led to the hot zone. Using the butt of his pistol, Ayyad pounded on the doors. Fawcett opened it from inside and stared aghast as the six young Arabs rushed inside. He was already a bundle of exposed nerves, and the look on Ayyad's face threw him into a state of total panic.

"You're late! What happened?"

Ayyad motioned for two of the men to go down the hall to cover the entrance to the lab. "Someone changed the bolts in the tunnel. We had to come through the lobby," he said, high on adrenaline.

"What?" shrieked Fawcett. "You fool! Security will be all over us before we can get the material out of the lab!"

Fawcett wanted the world to know the hot zone had been plundered. To be successful, Operation Desert Decree required media attention. But he didn't want a shootout with the cops in the middle of the street. His knees buckled again. Ayyad reached out and pinned him to the wall just as the door clicked loudly behind them. Doris Lubeck walked through, deep in thought, and looked up to see half a dozen armed men wearing ski masks. Her mouth opened wide. Then she saw Fawcett.

"Nick!" she gasped.

One of raiders pinned her against the door. Ayyad read Fawcett's eyes and pushed him harder against the wall. Putting the pistol in his face, he growled through clenched teeth, "Let's go."

He shoved Fawcett down the hall and motioned for his men to follow with Lubeck. Like a single organism with weapons pointed in every direction, the terrorists trooped toward the hot zone.

"Who *are* these people, Nick? What do they want?" Lubeck asked in a quavering voice.

One of the terrorists shoved her so hard she fell to her knees. Another grabbed her by the hair and began dragging her down the hall. Looking over his shoulder, Fawcett saw the brutality and shoved Ayyad aside. He grabbed the young Arab and pushed him away, then helped Doris to her feet, draping a protective arm around her.

"Nick, who are these people?" she repeated urgently.

"I don't know, Doris," he lied. "Just . . . just do what they say."

Ayyad pushed Fawcett and Lubeck toward the lab. At the entrance he ordered Fawcett to open the door.

"I can't. I don't work in this lab. I . . . I don't know the combination," he pleaded, staring down the barrel of Ayyad's pistol.

Ayyad turned the weapon on Lubeck, "You. Open the door."

"She doesn't work in this lab either," Fawcett lied.

Bewildered, Ayyad glared at Lubeck and then at Fawcett. Then he shoved the barrel of his pistol into Lubeck's cheek.

"Open the door, or I will kill you," he growled.

Doris looked into his eyes. "No. Go ahead. Shoot. Get it over with! Because I'm not . . . going . . . to open . . . that door," she enunciated.

"If you don't, I'll shoot him, then you!" Ayyad threatened. He pointed the gun at Fawcett while staring into Lubeck's eyes.

Fear and a dozen other emotions crossed her face simultaneously. For a moment she wavered, but when she focused on the hate in Ayyad's eyes, she made up her mind.

"Doris, do what the man says, for Christ's sake!" Fawcett pleaded.

"Nick, I'm sorry. I . . . I can't," she cried.

Suddenly Ayyad pounded on the door with the butt of the pistol. He shoved Lubeck's face in front of the small window for a few seconds, then jerked her down out of sight. Just as he expected, one of the technicians opened the door to see if she needed help. The six Arabs stormed inside the control room and quickly overpowered the two technicians on duty.

Ayyad knew he was in control. He eyed Susan Dorn, who was working inside the laboratory, completely unaware the CDC was under siege, then turned to Fawcett. "Get the virus," he commanded.

"What?" gasped Lubeck. "Nick! No!" she pleaded.

Ignoring her, Fawcett picked up the intercom and spoke.

"Susan. This is Nick Fawcett," he said pleasantly.

Dorn looked out through the plastic face mask of her protective suit and the portholes in the lab. She waved at him, unaware of the crisis outside her hermetic world.

"What are you doing up here, Nick?" she asked cheerfully. "Is Doris with you?"

Her voice was distant, distorted by the intercom.

"Yes, Susan, she is. Listen, Susan. This is an emergency. I'm going to place a go-box in the air lock. I want you to put a sample of each of the viral agents in your freezer inside it and seal it for transport."

"What? No way, Nick. You know I can't do that," Dorn objected, straining to see who was in the control room. She walked over to the porthole and stared out. Ayyad grabbed the intercom from Fawcett and screamed into the microphone.

"Do it! Immediately!"

Susan jumped at the sound of the shrill words.

"Don't do it, Susan!" Lubeck yelled as loudly as she could.

Ayyad raised his pistol and fired two quick shots into Lubeck's chest and face. The concussion from the bullet smashing into her skull was louder than the slide action on the silenced pistol. Susan watched in horror as Doris flew against the wall and slumped to the floor, leaving a smear of blood and brain matter. The horror seemed to take place in slow motion, as if time had dilated to encapsulate it. Both Fawcett and Dorn screamed at the same time when the realization of what had happened registered.

"Ayyaaaaaad!" Fawcett screamed, as he rushed toward Lubeck. The crazed terrorist stood directly in front of the porthole not two feet from Dorn, separated only by the thick glass of the window.

"He dies next!" Ayyad bellowed, pointing the pistol at one of the control technicians.

"I can't!" Dorn cried, in anguish.

Ayyad fired two shots into the man's chest. He gasped for breath, groaned, and slid to the floor, ripping at his shirt, as if trying to remove stinging bees. He stopped suddenly as blood frothed from his lips.

One of Ayyad's gunmen placed a metal container the size of a picnic cooler inside the air lock and slammed the hatch shut.

"Fill the box now, or he dies!" Ayyad ordered, pointing the pistol at the other technician.

"Please, please," Thomas begged. "Dr. Dorn, I have children at home. Please."

As Susan hesitated, Ayyad leveled the pistol at Thomas, sighting down the barrel.

"Wait!" Dorn's assistant yelled. "I'll do it."

The lab tech hurried to the freezer and removed several metallic bottles the size of a thermos jug. Holding them in his arms like cordwood, he hurried to the air lock.

"Stop! *You* bring them out," Ayyad ordered, pointing at Dorn with a bony finger.

She entered the air lock and helped the technician load and vacuum seal the shipping container.

"You bring them out," Ayyad repeated. "And you," he shook his pistol at the male technician, "back inside."

The lab tech stepped back into the lab and closed the inner door. As soon as it was sealed, Dorn started the decontamination shower.

After only a few seconds, Ayyad began screaming over the intercom.

"Enough! Enough! Get out here! Now!"

Dorn protested that everyone could be infected, but Ayyad

continued to yell until she turned off the disinfectant. When she opened the outer door, her protective suit was dripping with hot liquid. One of the Arabs yanked her and the shipping container out of the lock, while another shoved Thomas inside. A third man tied the door shut with a phone cord he had ripped off the wall.

"Let's go! Let's go!" Ayyad shouted.

He pulled Fawcett away from Lubeck's body. In shock, Fawcett kept repeating the same words over and over. "Doris, I told you not to work nights. I told you not to work nights."

Ayyad yanked him to his feet and shoved him toward the door. One of the Arabs half-dragged Susan out into the hallway by the hood of her space suit. Moving as fast as Fawcett and Dorn could travel, the raiding party burst through the security door and out onto the breezeway. They turned toward the lobby stairs and met fate head on.

Ray Keith and Sam Decker knew something was up when they found the lobby empty and the doors locked. Building 15 was supposed to be open twenty-four hours a day. Anticipating the worst, they had worked their way around the front of the building and picked the lock on a maintenance door used by workers who cared for the potted plants in the atrium. Once inside, the two ex-SEALs made their way toward the fourth-floor lab. When they saw the woman's body on the second-floor landing, they had unholstered their pistols and advanced with caution, leapfrog fashion, toward the hot zone. They had just entered the fourth-floor breezeway when Ayyad and his men burst through the security doors two hundred feet in front of them.

For an instant, time stood still as the two sides faced each other like gunfighters on the street of an old Western town. The SEALs recognized Fawcett, and they saw a person dressed in a space suit. But the scene in front of them didn't make sense. Several armed men wearing balaclavas were moving rapidly, assault rifles in hand. The two images didn't fit. When the gunmen began to raise their AKs to shoulder-ready, Ray Keith brought his pistol to bear. He had done it ten thousand times. Slow is smooth, smooth is accurate, accurate is fast. Aiming to avoid the scientists, he placed his first round between the eyes of the first commando. The man went to the deck like a head-shot deer on the run. A split second later, Decker double-tapped two rounds in the center of the next man's chest. Then the assault rifles opened up, spraying bullets down the corridor. They careened along the walls, the deck, and the ceiling, bouncing and skidding toward their targets. A shower of metal and concrete fragments hit Decker and Keith before they could duck behind the corner.

"Goddammit, I'm hit!" Keith yelled, "And it's my good leg," he groaned.

"It wouldn't have hurt your peg leg, dumbass," Decker returned, breathing out a huge gush of air.

"You hit?"

"Yeah," Decker whispered.

Blood was streaming down his arm, his head, and his leg. Keith rolled on the floor and peeked out around the corner. Bullets were ricocheting all around as another burst of rifle fire exploded along the breezeway. He dropped another terrorist who was in the act of tossing a grenade. It bounced off the corner and rolled back up the breezeway a few feet.

Boom!

Fragments cracked into the walls and ceiling all around, peppering them with flakes of cement and hot metal. With blood streaming down his face, Decker scooted on the floor until he was lying on top of Keith. Using the corner as cover, they squeezed off a few rounds as the Arabs fell back behind the double doors. Keith and Decker lay back on the cold cement bleeding from fifty tiny wounds. While they waited for help to arrive, they groused and griped like two old women.

"I hate grenades," Keith grumbled.

"Me too. You hit bad?"

"Hell, I don't know. I'm bleedin' all over. How 'bout you?"

"I'll see you and raise you one bullet hole. I just hope nothing hit my pacemaker," Decker said.

"Is that all you're worried about, dipstick?" Keith snarled. "The first thing I checked was my dick."

"'Cause that's where your brains are, dickhead." Decker picked a metal fragment out of his leg. "I think they're all flesh wounds."

"You got a chaw?"

"Yeah. Course I do," said Decker. He searched his pocket and pulled out a pouch of tobacco.

"Man, I sure hope you don't have AIDS," said Keith, taking the blood-soaked pouch from Decker's dripping hand.

Susan Dorn looked out from her space suit as if in a dream. The terrorists were scrambling like madmen, dragging her and shoving Fawcett around the pipes and equipment in the basement, moving like rats being chased by a broom. She still had the hood of her suit zipped closed, and as she depleted the oxygen inside she began to breathe faster and faster. In a daze, she grew faint and passed out.

Ayyad dragged her the rest of the way to the access shaft and tossed her against the wall like a soiled rag. He turned on Fawcett, almost hysterical, and shook him violently by the shoulders. "Uncle Kasim! Uncle Kasim! Take care of her. We might need her to escape," he yelled.

Still in shock, Fawcett unzipped Dorn's plastic hood. The fresh air soon brought her back to consciousness.

While Fawcett attended Dorn, Ayyad ripped open the door to the maintenance shaft and dashed inside. A few seconds later he reappeared and jumped to one side, just before his grenade exploded inside the tunnel.

Through the smoke and cordite, he shoved Fawcett and dragged Susan to the expanded metal grate blocking their path. The two young Arabs carrying the medical container put it down long enough to bend back the mesh, then dragged the scientists and the container through the hole. Ayyad shoved Dorn and Fawcett down the tunnel and guided the troop to a rendezvous with his waiting trucks.

Chapter 34

As RAY KEITH and Sam Decker shot it out with terrorists at the CDC, a team of experts was busy sweeping the USS *Georgia*. No one at Kings Bay had slept during the standoff, and no one was going to until the entry team had cut through the hatch and checked the interior of the vessel for nuclear booby traps, a process that took hours. When word finally came that the *Georgia* was clear, a cheer went up through the TOC. It was over.

Evans slumped into a conference room chair and listened to the special bulletin blaring on the television. CNN was reporting that the FBI had successfully taken control of the *Georgia*. "Man, those guys have sources everywhere," he said.

"No shit," said Durance. "That info had to come from someone inside this building."

"Maybe they saw torches at work on the hull," suggested Evans.

"And maybe money talks," Durance observed. He handed Evans a large manila envelope.

"What's this?"

Durance smirked. "The wheels of justice turn slowly."

Evans looked at him with a puzzled expression.

"The background checks you asked for."

"Oh," Evans grunted.

"Let's go grab a beer, Commander," Savarese yelled from the open doorway. "You too, you worthless fan belt inspector," he added with a wry smile. "The CO is opening up the chief's club just for me. If you two cake-eaters have the gumption, I'll stand you a round or two . . . or three or four."

"I'll be over in a bit, Boomer," Evans answered, "as soon as I wind down."

"Me too," Durance added.

"Wind down? Hell. I did all the work," Savarese grumbled. "I'll be expecting you two." He did an about-face and headed down the hall like a bull in rut.

Evans opened the envelope absentmindedly and thumbed through the reports until he got to the one marked *Nicholas B. Fawcett*. He scanned it for a few moments until his eyes froze on the words *adopted from Palestine*. A surge of adrenaline coursed through his body. He read the sentence out loud for Durance.

"Adopted from Palestine in 1949 by a prominent California surgeon named Nicholas B. Fawcett."

He turned the file around and pointed at it.

"So what?" said Durance. "A lot of people are adopted."

Evans jumped up from the table. "Not from Palestine." He hurried for the door.

"Hey, where are you going?"

Evans ignored the question as he rushed down the hall. His blood ran cold as he crossed the parking lot. Durance's words came back to him: *What could be worse than a bunch of Arab fanatics barricaded inside a submarine loaded with nukes?*

"How about the most dangerous substance on earth in the hands of a brilliant Palestinian scientist?" he said out loud.

He jumped in his car and headed for Atlanta with a deep feeling of foreboding. Every few minutes, he tried to call Fred Swan on his cell phone.

Evans was only an hour outside Atlanta when he finally made contact with Swan, who apprised him of the incident at the CDC but for security reasons didn't elaborate. He told Evans the name and location of the hospital where Keith and Decker were being treated and that he would fill him in on the details as soon as he arrived. By the time Evans pulled into Atlanta General, the broken SEALs were out of surgery and in the recovery room.

"Hi, Boss," said Swan, upon meeting him in the waiting room. "You look like shit."

"Hey," Evans grumbled, "I resemble that."

"No sleep?" asked Jennings.

"Not in the last three days." Evans yawned. "How are they doing?"

"Pretty good, considerin' they're chock-full of holes," Swan reported. "Mostly frag from the grenade spalding off the cinderblock walls."

"They had to put Ray under, though, to work on him," Jennings volunteered.

"Oh?" Evans replied.

"Yeah. He wouldn't stop bitchin', so the docs gassed him just to shut him up." Jennings chucked.

"CNN is saying the FBI took down the sub without losin' a man. That true?" Swan asked.

"Sort of," Evans growled. "What happened at the CDC?"

"The bad guys got the bugs out of the hot zone," said Swan, studying Evans's face, "and they nabbed two of the scientists. I didn't want to tell you on the phone, but one of 'em is your lady friend."

Evans felt hollow in the pit of his stomach. He swallowed hard as he visualized Susan Dorn in the hands of crazed fanatics. Fear and rage flooded his veins at the same time.

"Was Lubeck the other scientist?"

"No, Boss. They killed her. Shot her in the face. The other one was that Fawcett guy you had us watchin'."

"Damn," Evans exclaimed. "That's too bad. She was one hell of a woman." He thought for a second, then asked, "How do you know Fawcett was a hostage and not a player?"

Swan raised his eyebrows and looked at Jennings before answering. "I don't know. I just assumed. Sam said the bad guys came bustin' out of the lab shovin' the scientists in front of 'em," explained Swan.

"Ray said he could have dropped 'em all if your woman hadn't been in the way," Jennings added.

"How many were there?"

"Six to start with," Swan answered.

"Sam and Ray took out three of 'em before they threw the grenade that fragged 'em all up," Jennings grinned proudly. "Three to zero, pistols against assault rifles and grenades, is a fairly good score in a gunfight, I'd say."

"So the FBI actually took down the sub?" asked Swan, not believing the news reports. "How'd they do it?"

"They had a secret weapon," Evans replied.

"What kind of weapon?" asked Jennings.

"Loco Gomez and Boomer Savarese."

"Well, *that* explains their unusual success," Swan observed. "They come at it underwater?"

Evans nodded. "You broke the code."

"Gassed 'em, huh?" Jennings guessed.

"It's amazing how great minds think alike," Evans replied with a big yawn.

"Boss, you gotta get some rest. You look like a trainee right out of Hell Week," said Swan. "Let's bust in and visit Bionicman and Pegleg and then you can hit the rack. J. R. and I will stick around here."

"Nope. I got a key to Dorn's condo. I want to go over it before the FBI tramples through it. Maybe there's something there that might help us find Fawcett. Let's meet at your place in about four hours," Evans continued. "I got some things I want you guys to do right away."

"Sure, Boss," they answered in unison.

Evans didn't want to incriminate Swan and Jennings by telling them he intended to break into Lubeck's condo and Fawcett's house. It was better they didn't know, in case he was arrested. He wanted to look over everything slowly before the police sealed the residences. He figured Durance would eventually let him see the forensic reports, but eventually was too late, and a report was far from the real thing. The trail was hot, and he wanted to get on it.

As they walked down the hall toward the recovery room, two aides wheeled the wounded SEALs out through the double doors of the recovery room and headed toward them.

Keith was bitching at Sam. "I got two of 'em, goddammit. I told you that. And if the doc hadn't been in the way, I'd a got 'em all."

"No. That's not the way I remember it. I got two of 'em and you got one. You missed with your second shot."

"I never miss, and you know it, dick breath!" Keith yelled. He raised his head up off the gurney to look at Decker wheeling down the hall in front of him and spotted Evans and the boys coming toward them. "You were scared!" he shouted at Decker.

"Not on your life, buckaroo!" Decker sang out.

Evans stopped Decker's gurney in the hall.

"Excuse me, sir. No visiting in the hall," said the orderly.

"I'll just be a minute, son." He yawned. His eyes were bloodshot and he needed a shave.

"Sir, we have to take these men to their room. You can visit them during visiting hours."

Evans didn't move.

"Sir, I'll have to call security if you don't get out of the way," the young man insisted.

"Ray!" Decker shouted in an excited voice. "Aren't those the guys that shot us up?"

The orderly looked at Evans and swallowed hard.

"Yeah. It's them all right!" Keith yelled.

The two aides abandoned their gurneys and ran up the hallway, scared out of their wits.

"Great, guys. Just great," said Swan. "Now you're gonna get us shot up by a bunch of rent-a-cops."

"Misery loves company," Keith laughed.

"You guys all right?" Evans asked seriously.

"Hell no," Keith snarled. "We're shot plumb full of holes. I don't remember this being part of my job description."

Evans smiled. "I can tell nothing hit your larynx. You haven't stopped bitchin' since you woke up."

"Hell, he was bitchin' while he was under," Jennings added.

"You look like shit, Commander Asshole, sir, I mean Commander Donkey-dick. Sir!" Keith chuckled and then stuck his tongue against the side of his cheek, making it stick out. "Been worried about us, huh?"

"You bet. Haven't slept a wink."

"It shows. You look like shit, and if you don't get outta here before that rent-a-cop shows up, you're gonna look a whole lot worse. It's a big chunky-butt woman who loves pinto beans." Keith laughed out loud.

"You guys take care of each other, okay? We've got to go finish your light work, seeing as how you let three of 'em get away with my girlfriend," said Evans.

"I hope your shootin' is better 'n Sam's," said Keith. "He's losin' his touch."

"*Me?* I got two and you got one, dammit. I ain't losin' my touch."

"Oh, no. You got it back-assards, as usual," Keith growled.

"Me, losin' my touch? That's ridiculous. You wouldn't be here if I hadn't dropped the clown with the AK," Decker insisted.

Jennings and Swan pushed the gurneys down the hall toward the elevator with Decker and Keith bickering every step of the way. They stopped in front of the elevator doors, and Swan pushed the down button. It opened with a ding.

"We're outta here, guys," said Evans.

As his visitors stepped inside the elevator, Keith shouted, "I want a Purple Heart and a bonus."

Swan stopped the door with his foot.

"Bonus? I let you keep the proceeds from your panhandling. That's bonus enough," Evans returned through the crack between the doors.

"Ah, no." Jennings laughed. "That's not near enough. He was saving that for a big SOC Inc. party until he saw how big your tab was at Clyde's Bar and Grill."

"What tab?"

"Let loose of the door, Popeye," Keith yelled.

"Why, Pegleg?" asked Evans.

"Let loose of the door, dammit."

"Don't want him to know you ran up a two-thousand-dollar bill in his name, huh?" Swan chuckled. He let the door go. Evans was boring holes in Keith's head with his glaring eyes as the elevator doors closed.

Chapter 35

AFTER THE RAID on the CDC, law enforcement officials throughout the world were placed on the highest state of alert in the search for Susan Dorn, Nicholas Fawcett, and the terrorists. Photographs of Dorn and Fawcett and images of armed figures dressed in black, taken from CDC videotapes, were plastered in all the newspapers, as well as the faces of the terrorists who had been killed. Television news shows filled the airways with pundits and talking heads endlessly discussing the potential for biological disaster. People throughout the world were alarmed to a state of near panic.

Six days after the attack, when Tom Durance invited Evans and his crew to view a videotape at the federal building in downtown Atlanta, Evans accepted, expecting to see his broken SEALs in action on the CDC's security cameras. And he was also hoping Durance would fill them in on the latest information. But the agent surprised him.

"Guys, what I'm about to show you is close-hold information," he said, raising his hand like a Boy Scout taking an oath.

Evans, Swan, and Jennings gave him a quizzical look.

"Really close-hold for the moment. No decision has been made with regard to the initial demand, but I'm sure that in the wake of the USS *Georgia* incident, the president will acquiesce."

"The White House, the secretary general of the UN, the FBI, the CIA, and the major news networks all received a copy of this videotape on the same day. For the moment, there's an executive gag order in place. The bottom line is, well, you guys take a look at the tape and then we can gab about it."

Durance pushed the play button on the VCR and slumped into a chair. The video began with the words *Palestinian Freedom Council* superimposed on a waving Palestinian flag. The amateur filmmaker opened up by panning a homemade laboratory as patriotic Arabic music played on the sound track. Evans noted that there were no windows or doors visible, and no details to indicate where the video had been shot. The pan stopped momentarily on a rack of vials on a makeshift lab bench, then moved to center on a familiar face. The music stopped.

"My name is Dr. Nicholas Bernard Fawcett, M.D., Ph. D., and professor of prokaryotic studies at the Centers for Disease Control in Atlanta, Georgia. My given name is Walead Kasim, and I am a senior member of the Palestinian Freedom Council."

His face was drawn and weary, as if he hadn't slept in days. He paused long enough to pick up a vial of liquid from the rack.

"In this small vial there are more than a trillion viruses, a sufficient number to kill every man, woman, and child on this planet. I will henceforth refer to this agent as the Lubeck virus, in honor of my recently deceased colleague, Dr. Doris Lubeck."

For a few seconds Fawcett appeared to struggle with his emotions. He took a deep breath and held the small bottle between his thumb and forefinger, staring at it with a blank expression. Then he placed it directly in front of the camera lens and continued to speak in a professorial tone.

"This is the most deadly virus known to science. It has the capacity to kill a human being in less than four days, and it has a mortality rate of nearly 100 percent. The method of transmission is similar to that of the common flu, and it can survive in an aerosol form for several days, depending on humidity and air temperature."

Fawcett placed the vial back in the rack with more than a dozen similar vials and picked up a spray can.

"This looks like a common household insect fogger. However, as you can see," he continued, turning the can so the bottom was toward the camera, "it is specially designed to receive a vial."

With a pen he pointed out the cavity in the bottom of the can and a needle that protruded down from the center of the cavity. It was obvious the can had been modified to receive and penetrate the rubber seal in the top of a virus vial.

"With these weapons, Palestinian soldiers can destroy cities."

He paused as the cameraman panned back to frame his face. The gravity of the moment overshadowed the amateurish nature of the camera work.

"The following are graphic examples of what will happen to individuals infected with the Lubeck virus."

The film cut to various scenes of the primates in the Level Four lab succumbing to the disease. The label on one of the cages was clearly readable: Mussorgski. There were several scenes leading up to the animals' demise and necropsy, followed by selective footage of an African village. Dissolved human forms lay scattered around native huts. The images stopped abruptly, and the camera jerked up, focusing on Fawcett again.

"Now that I have your undivided attention, there are several points I wish to make before I present our demands."

Fawcett's eyes were determined, ablaze. He held his head high, like a vizier.

"The war between Arab and Jew goes back more than five thousand years. We, the children of Abraham, are bitter enemies fighting over the same patch of parched desert soil. I will endeavor to explain our cause before I present our demands, which you must meet or die."

He paused long enough to pick up a note card from the lab bench.

"A mere century ago there were almost no Jews in the land now known as Israel. I will henceforth refer to that land as Palestine. Now there are millions, and the number grows daily. In 1917, the time of the First World War, Palestine was a British Protectorate, as a result of the breakup of the Ottoman Empire. In an effort to pacify powerful Jewish interests, the British government issued the Balfour Declaration. I quote." Fawcett read from his note card:

"His Majesty's government views with favour the establishment in Palestine of a national home for the Jewish people, and will use their best endeavours to facilitate the achievement of this object, it being clearly understood that nothing shall be done which may prejudice the civil and religious rights of existing non-Jewish communities in Palestine, or the rights and political status enjoyed by Jews in any other country."

He put down the card. "For this, Your Majesty, England must pay," he said as an aside, then continued his lecture.

"In 1917, Palestine was still Palestine, Arab and Jew eyeing each other like two hungry dogs over a scrap of meat. And then came Hitler. Like the American Indian, a flood of illegal immigration drowned my people and my culture. In 1947, after World War II, when the United Nations voted to partition Palestine into two states, one Arab and one Jew, they voted for the death of Palestine, and the Palestinian people. In May 1948, when David Ben-Gurion announced the birth of the state of Israel, he announced the death of the country of Palestine, and the world did nothing. Seven hundred thousand Palestinians were forced to flee their land so that an artificial religious state called Israel could be created. I was one of those people. As a child I watched the Zionists kill my mother and my father in the village of Deir Yassin. They were slaughtered like sheep on an altar to consecrate the creation of the Jewish state."

Fawcett became visibly emotional but quickly regained his composure. He continued in an angrier tone.

"In 1900, we didn't exist. In 1917, we were transformed into subhuman beings. In 1948, we were turned into refugees. In 1967, you turned us into terrorists," he railed, pointing an accusatory finger at the camera.

"The Jews continue to seize Arab land and subjugate Palestinian peoples. Oppression is the highest form of terrorism!" he asserted loudly. "Israel is not a secular state caring for its inhabitants. It is a religious state oppressing those who are not of the Jewish faith. The Jews have lost their uniqueness in history. They have lost their sense of values. They have become the Nazis of the Middle East! The Israeli army is an army of occupation that oppresses and tortures the true owners of the land. Daily, Palestinians die horrible, violent deaths, at the hands of jackbooted torturers no better than the Nazis from whom they fled."

He paused, his eyes glittering with fervor.

"Yesssss! When will Dachau and Auschwitz appear in Judea and Samaria?" he railed, head held high.

"They have stolen their cousin's land, and now they kill him for protesting the theft. We are Semite. They are Semite. Yet they oppress us and violate our dignity as a people. And you make this possible." He glared, pointing a finger at the camera. "For this you will pay!"

He paused. When he resumed, his tone was calmer.

"We have protested, we have bargained, and we have warred for our inalienable rights—the right to life, liberty, and the pursuit of happiness in our own land. And the world has turned a deaf ear. From guerrilla warfare to the intifada, we have sought redress, while the United States funded the building of a superpower. While you support the Jewish state with billions in aid, they steal Palestinian land and torture Palestinian people for protesting the theft. For this you will pay!" His voice rose again to a crescendo. "These are our demands, and they will be fulfilled, or you will suffer the scourge of the Black Death."

A hand off-camera placed a large poster board beside Fawcett. On it were neatly printed in block letters the names of the world's major countries in one column, beginning with Israel and the United States at the top. Beside each country was a dollar amount in billions and a numbered bank account in one of several countries ranging from Switzerland to Lichtenstein to Libya. The largest amounts were levied on Israel, the United States, the United Kingdom, France, Germany, Russia, Saudi Arabia, and Kuwait.

"Money is power. But it is not the only power the Western world understands," Fawcett continued, picking up a vial from the rack.

"If these funds are not deposited within one week, Palestinian soldiers will release the virus in the capital of each country that has not paid its debt. This concludes the explanation of our grievances and our demands. You will comply, or you will die."

Fawcett stared into the camera with determined, unblinking eyes until it faded to black.

Swan broke the stunned silence. "Damn! Are we in a world of shit, or what?"

Durance looked at Evans. The commander's face was blank except for a hint of sadness. His eyes were empty and far away, as if in a trance. Durance spoke, but Evans didn't hear him.

"The PFC is demanding that the videotape be shown nationwide on all the major networks within the week, or they will shoot down a passenger aircraft with a Stinger."

"They got Stingers?" Swan asked, alarmed.

"Probably," Jennings commented. "We gave a bunch of 'em to those Afghan freedom fighters. That's how they kicked the shit out of the Russians. Rumor has it several leftovers are floatin' around on the black market."

"That's correct," Durance confirmed. "They used nerve gas on the *Georgia,* so there is no reason to believe this is a bluff. Besides, it doesn't matter. They have the Lubeck virus."

Durance leveled his gaze on Evans. "We've got less than five days before airplanes start falling out of the sky. I know you have photos and perhaps video of a number of people associated with the CDC. I suspect they include Fawcett. Your methods of collection are not at issue here. I'll keep that confidential. But I have to evaluate your material."

Evans was staring at the blank television screen.

"Double Tap? Did you hear a word I said?" Durance demanded.

"Yeah, yeah, sure. Fred will get the stuff over to you right away." Evans changed the subject. "Where was that video shot?"

"Hell, we don't know. Could be anywhere. Europe, the United States, Lebanon."

"No. Not Lebanon and not Europe. The construction of the room is consistent only with the United States," Evans insisted.

"The boss is right," said Jennings. "The plywood over the window was Georgia-Pacific. Your experts must have some idea where the tape was shot."

"I don't see what difference it makes. They have the Lubeck virus, and they obviously have the capacity to employ it. They may even have a vaccine for their people," Durance said. Then, capitulating to their skeptical expressions, he threw up his hands. "Okay, okay. There's a big argument going on at headquarters over the construction materials seen in the video. One camp thinks the lab is here in the South. The other thinks it's out west somewhere. That plywood is sold all over the damned country. And I repeat, it really doesn't matter. By now clandestine cells could have smuggled that virus into every city on that list.

"Can I have a copy of the tape?" Evans asked.

"Hell, no!" Durance exploded. "Not until after the gag order is lifted."

"Then you don't get any of my shit. And we got a bunch," Evans countered.

"I'll just get a court order," the FBI agent said with a sour expression. "And then you'll have to explain how you collected it."

"Go ahead. Get your damn court order." Evans stood to leave.

"Sit down, asshole. You know I can't let you have a copy of that tape," Durance pleaded.

"Too bad."

Durance gave Evans a dirty look. "I'll have to edit it," he finally conceded.

"No. There's something there. I just don't know what it is," Evans shot back.

Durance stared at him in disbelief. "You know I can't give you that goddamn tape, Derek."

"Tell you what. Just leave me here with it for a while. I want to watch it a few times."

"Okay by me," said Durance, relieved.

"Fred. J. R. Go get everything we've got," Evans ordered.

"Roger, Boss," said Swan.

Both SEALs jumped up and headed for the door, eager to leave the room.

"Let me see everything *you* have on Fawcett," Evans demanded.

"I don't have much more than that FBI report you saw at Kings Bay," Durance replied.

"What about his houses, cars, all that sort of stuff?"

"You show me yours and I'll show you mine," Durance agreed, somewhat flustered.

Evans watched the videotape ten times and read the FBI's Fawcett file six times. Durance finally had to ask him to leave. They were closing the federal building for the night and he didn't want to be locked inside with a hardheaded zombie.

On the way to the parking lot he pressed Evans for his thoughts. "What the hell is up with you, Double Tap?"

"I'm thinking of going fishing in the mountains of Idaho," Evans answered.

"Idaho? Come on. Give. What's on your mind?"

"You wouldn't believe me if I told you."

"Try me."

"You know how sometimes you know something, but you don't really know it?" Evans said with a far-off expression in his eyes.

"No, I don't," Durance snapped. "You're babbling."

"One time I looked out my window just as this teenage kid was approaching my house. I watched his eyes case the place, and I knew he was coming back. He did." Evans smiled cunningly. "But he didn't get what he wanted."

"Will you get to the point?"

"I don't know *how* I knew it. I just knew it. Body language, eye movement, some unexplainable clue that jumped into my head. I think the word is *ineffable*."

"What the hell does that mean?" Durance grumbled.

"It means you can't put it into words. I just knew he was coming back to rob me."

"Would you please tell me what all that has to do with a bunch of fuckin' tangos?"

"There's something I know that's not in the FBI report," Evans replied. "It's inside my head, and it's on that videotape. It's something Fawcett said or something I saw."

Evans was talking almost in a trance, trying hard to tease a small clue out of the recesses of his brain.

"All I know is, when I saw the videotape something inside my head went click. I can't dig it out of my subconscious yet, but I will!" he said almost to himself.

Derek Evans knew where to go to think, to search his soul. The beach. From Atlanta, he had his choice of the Atlantic or the Gulf of Mexico. He had grown up in Panama City, Florida, on the Gulf, and he had a love for the sea that ran as deep as the sea itself. It was this love that had motivated him to pursue a career in the Navy, and it was that feeling and an image deeply imbedded in the Fawcett video that called him.

He left his apartment and drove around the beltway twice, letting his mind wander. Then something compelled him to head southwest from Atlanta on Interstate 85. At State Route 231 in Montgomery, Alabama, he got off the expressway and headed due south to the Gulf. For a while, he drove aimlessly along Highway 98 near Panama City listening to the radio. The highway ran along the Gulf

Coast, sometimes within sight of the water. When he could smell the sea and feel the sea breeze, he began to relax. As he neared Long Beach, a song by Chris De Burgh came on.

> The lady in red
> Is dancing with me,
> Cheek to cheek.
> There's nobody here,
> It's just you and me,
> It's where I wanna be.
> But I hardly know this beauty by my side.
> I'll never forget the way you look tonight.

Evans switched off the radio as images of Susan Dorn flooded his mind. She was wearing a simple off-the-shoulder red silk dress that clung to her slim body. In her ears were tiny, heart-shaped jade earrings, and around her throat was a single jade pendant suspended from a golden chain. A Chinese art treasure. With her hair cascading over her bare shoulders in gentle waves, she smiled at him, and he felt the smoothness of her touch, the sweetness of her kiss, the fragrance of her hair. For a moment he felt she was near. Very near.

Chapter 36

HAVING GROWN UP on the Gulf of Mexico, Derek Evans convinced himself that it was his roots that were calling him home. When he reached Long Beach, a resort community west of Panama City, Florida, he rented a room in an inexpensive motel and took a walk along the seashore. Memories of his youth flooded his mind as the sand squeaked beneath his feet. He had forgotten how extraordinary the sand was along the panhandle. It was finer than granulated sugar and as white as drifting snow, so white that tourists often passed off their beach pictures as snow bathing. The afternoon sun was blazing in the west, and even through his Oakleys the reflection off the sand was intense. He thought about heading the other direction, but something drew him west. The sea breeze in his face seemed to open his mind, so he started jogging down the beach. Images of Susan Dorn invaded his thoughts, so he ran harder to escape them.

She's a beautiful woman, he thought. *She deserves more out of life than to become a statistic in a war against terrorism.*

He didn't know how he could help the FBI find her. All he could do was follow his instincts. With helplessness eating at his guts, he tried to clear his mind, but no matter how hard he ran, he couldn't escape the image of Susan held captive by Arab fanatics. So he ran faster and faster, until he was sprinting. He kept up the pace for as long as he could. Finally, panting and exhausted, he bent over at the waist and placed his hands on his thighs for a breather. The Fawcett tape popped into his mind as he stared down at the sand. The camera jerked from the floor of the lab to the scientist's face. Evans let his thoughts run free, like water cascading down a hill in streams. As the surf murmured and seagulls squawked, it hit him like a bucket of cold water. He was staring at it. Sand. Snow-white, powdered-sugar sand. Not the coarse brown sand of the Atlantic or the Pacific but the snow-white powder of the panhandle. That's what he'd seen on the videotape. It was on the floor of Fawcett's makeshift lab.

A beach house, he thought.

When the camera jerked around to reframe, it had flashed an image and a subliminal message that had burned into his brain. Then another image flashed across his mind. It was of himself and Susan Dorn at lunch with Doris Lubeck.

Why lunch? It was something Doris said, he thought. *She was going off with Fawcett for the weekend. To the beach. But where?* he thought. *Where?*

"She never said where," he mumbled.

He sat down to rest.

"Where? Where was she going?"

Evans lay on his back and stared up at the sky.

"Where was she going?"

Closing his eyes, he let his mind roam. An image of Dorn's condo popped into focus.

Don't force it, he commanded himself. *Let it flow. It's a puzzle, but you know the answer.*

For several more minutes he lay on his back, taking in deep breaths of salt air, meditating, letting memories surface like bubbles. Then a bubble burst.

Her dresser.

He zeroed in on an image of Susan's dresser, as if focusing a set of binoculars.

Something on her dresser. Yes. A picture. A picture of Doris, buried in snow up to her neck. But it wasn't snow. It was sand. And in the background was a high white snowdrift, a sand drift.

Evans sat up bolt straight.

There are only two places like that. Destin Beach and Greyton Beach, he thought.

"Destin Beach is too crowded for Fawcett. He has a house on Greyton Beach," he said out loud. "And it's not in his name."

He sprinted back to his hotel and called Tom Durance. When the agent's answering machine kicked in, he hung up, deciding not to leave a message. It was only a hunch, so he quickly changed clothes and drove west down Highway 98 to the turnoff that led to the Gulf.

Greyton Beach lay halfway between Long Beach and Destin, buried in the middle of a papermill crop of loblolly pine. It was just a sandy road that ran parallel to the Gulf for a couple of miles in each direction. When Evans was a boy, there had been nothing out there but sand and surf. He drove down the narrow road expecting to see a few cottages and was surprised to find a large number of luxurious houses lining the coast in both directions. It was almost sundown when he arrived, so he drove to the end of the sandy road in each direction, searching the tourist houses for clues, for Fawcett's silver Caddy, anything that would indicate he was in the area. But nothing struck him. He drove back to the intersection and parked his car on the side of the road. Out of the corner of his eye, he noticed an elderly couple watching him as he walked through a vacant lot to the berm overlooking the beach. But he didn't wave or look at them. He let the sun dip below the Gulf before going to their door for help. The old man answered with a cautious expression.

"What can I do for you?" he said, standing behind a locked screen door.

"Is there anywhere around here I can rent a room for the night?" Evans asked.

"I'm afraid not. You'll have to go over to Long Beach or Destin to find a motel."

"I was looking for a bed-and-breakfast around here. You see, I have an associate who owns one of these houses, and I don't know which one. I thought maybe I could locate him tomorrow."

"What's his name?" asked the woman.

"Fawcett. Dr. Nicholas B. Fawcett," Evans answered, watching the old man's eyes for clues.

His pupils constricted slightly as he studied Evans.

"That name rings a bell, but I don't recall anybody with that name owning a house around these parts. Come on in and sit a spell. We'll try and help you if we can."

He unlocked the screen door and motioned for Evans to enter.

"I'm Curtis McCoy, and this here is my wife Juanita."

"Pleased to meet you, Mrs. McCoy, Mr. McCoy. I'm Derek Evans."

"Would you like a glass of sun tea?" Juanita asked sweetly.

"Yes, ma'am, I would. It's been quite a while since I've had a glass of sun tea."

She shuffled off and reappeared in less then a minute with three glasses.

These people are lonely, Evans thought, accepting the huge glass. *I'll bet not much gets past them.*

The McCoy house was small and unpretentious compared to the expensive beach houses lining the shore. But it had a commanding view of the Gulf and of the only road into Greyton Beach.

"We don't get many visitors," said McCoy. "Most of the houses along here are owned by rich Yankees who don't come down here very much. I keep an eye on a fair share of them. You from around here?"

"Actually, I grew up in Long Beach. But I've been away in the Navy for a long time," Evans explained.

"Curtis was in the Navy," Juanita volunteered excitedly. "He was a Seabee."

"I know those units well, ma'am," Evans replied. "I spent most of my time in special operations. Frogmen and Seabees share the same bases."

"So you were in the UDT?" Curtis asked, with a doubtful expression. UDT stood for Underwater Demolition Team.

"Yes, sir. You know, the Navy decommissioned the UDTs. They're all called SEAL Teams nowadays," Evans explained.

Curtis McCoy gave Evans a hard look, as if he didn't believe him.

"I didn't know that," he said. "I was a chief when I got out, but that was some time ago. You look a bit too young to be retired, mister."

Evans smiled and pulled out his wallet. "A lot of people take me for a younger man. Probably all the mandatory exercise."

When he showed Curtis McCoy his blue ID card, the tone of the conversation changed. McCoy sat up a little straighter.

"I guess I ought to be calling you 'sir,' seeing as how you out-rank me by a bushel and a peck."

"I defer to your age and wisdom, sir." Evans smiled. "You know, when I was a boy there wasn't anything out here," he said, changing the subject. "How many houses on Greyton Beach?" He took a big pull on the iced tea and watched the old man closely for his answer.

"Oh, about a hundred waiting for the next hurricane to blow 'em down so the Yankees can collect on their big insurance policies. Just a matter of time. The government pays for it, you know. Tax money." He eyed Evans. "Not many people live out here. This feller you're looking for. You say he's a doctor?"

"Yeah. Out of Atlanta. Sometimes he comes down here with his lady friend. Doris Lubeck. She's a doctor too."

"What does he look like?"

"Five-eleven. Slight build. Early fifties. Black hair streaked with gray. Deep-set eyes. Drives a silver Cadillac and talks like a professor."

"Curtis, that sounds like that feller with the big house down near the end of the Long Beach road," said Juanita. "You know, the big one that's always boarded up."

"Might just as well be the feller down the Destin road too, Ni-ter," Curtis protested.

"Would you show the house to me?" Evans asked.

"Sure. But it's getting dark. How about you come back tomor-row, and I'll show you the both of 'em," McCoy suggested.

"There's something I want to talk to you about, Chief. Maybe we could walk a spell, and you could point one of them out from a distance," Evans said.

The tone of his voice made Curtis McCoy snap to. Evans sounded like a commander. It had been a long time since anyone had called him chief, and he liked it.

"Aye-aye, Commander. Let's go. I'll show 'em to you," he said briskly, heading for the door. "The walk will do me good."

As they ambled slowly down the sandy road, Curtis McCoy pointed out the few permanent residents. Most of the houses were weekend getaways, several of which were boarded up. Halfway to the end of the road, McCoy stopped and faced Evans in the waning light.

"This Fawcett feller you're looking for, he wouldn't be the one they've been showing on the news lately, would he?"

Evans stared at the old man, not knowing what to say.

"I watch the news all the time. That's about all I've got to do anymore. Watch the world go by on TV and up and down the Greyton road."

"Chief, take this card," said Evans, handing him a business card. "That's the number of an FBI friend of mine in Atlanta. His name is Thomas Durance. He won the Medal of Honor in Vietnam, so you can trust him. He'll vouch for me."

"I believe you are who you say you are, Commander Evans," McCoy protested. "I just asked you a simple question. All I was looking for was a simple answer. Are you hunting for those terrorists?"

"Yes, Chief, I am. But I'm not the FBI or any kind of law enforcement official. And I don't have much to go on but a gut feeling. The scientist they abducted was my lady friend," he explained.

"Well, son, my eyes aren't so good, but not much gets past me down here on Greyton Beach. Hell, I live right at the intersection, so no one comes out here that I don't see or hear. Back at the house, all those questions you were asking set me to thinking. Putting two and two together, I think you just might be on the right track. That feller who owns the house Niter was talking about looks a lot like that feller who's been on TV. And about ten days ago some folks drove in early in the morning, before first light. I haven't seen hide nor hair of them since. There's lights on at night, mind you, but no one's been on the beach. I'd say that's a mite peculiar, wouldn't you?"

"Yes, indeed," Evans answered. "Chief, let's watch these folks for awhile, and if your suspicions are correct, we'll call the FBI. Then you take Juanita and leave until this thing is over."

"Can't."

"Why?"

"I don't have a car. And the bus only runs out here once a week."

"Here. Take my keys. And here's the key to a room I rented over in Long Beach. It's the Seabreeze. Right on the beach."

"Thank you, sir," said McCoy, accepting the keys. "I'd like to stay and help you, but I don't want Juanita to get hurt."

"Thank you for trusting me, Chief."

"Well, I'll do you one better, Commander. I'm the caretaker of the house next door to this feller. I'll let you in and we can watch his place for a spell from inside. If someone sees us, they'll just think it's me caretaking or the owners come for a stay. Come on. I've got the key hid under the porch."

Chapter 37

THE TWO YOUNG Arabs in the Charlotte safehouse had smoked ten cartons of cigarettes and consumed all the food in the house while waiting for the call that would signal the commencement of their mission. They weren't privy to the details of the battle plan, but they knew that Operation Desert Decree was huge because they had deployed with two dozen other Palestinians on the same oceangoing freighter. At the Al Fucra rendezvous near Atlanta, they had prayed with others who hadn't made the trip with them by sea.

During the early part of their isolation in Charlotte, they had jumped each time the telephone rang. But on every occasion the voice on the other end of the line had tried to sell them something. Then came news of the USS *Georgia*. They had cheered when the newscaster reported that Palestinian terrorists had seized the nuclear submarine. Praying and rejoicing all during the standoff, their emotions had turned to absolute despair when the special bulletin reported that the FBI had retaken the submarine. For several days thereafter, they had argued about what they should do. Should they stay or should they run? Ayyad had ordered them to wait for a call. So they waited. They waited and waited, agreeing to stay until the food was gone. Then their hopes soared again when they saw the news reporting the CDC raid. With renewed fervor, they prayed to Allah and dedicated themselves to their small part in the war against the Jews.

They were playing cards at the kitchen table and drinking sweet tea when the telephone rang. Expecting another sales pitch, the younger of the two men picked up the phone.

"Hello," he said in his best American accent.

"Allah be praised," said the man on the other end of the line.

The young man recognized Ayyad's voice, and his eyes widened.

"Allah is most great," he replied nervously.

"Here we come, O Allah. No partner have You. Here we come," Ayyad said.

Then the line went dead. The young *fida'i* stared at his companion in shock.

"Here we come, O Allah," he said solemnly.

They went into the living room and dropped to their knees, facing Mecca.

"God is most great. God is most magnificent and almighty. O Lord! Grant our land veneration. O Lord! Deliver us from the Jews . . . ."

When Allah had received his due, they placed the Stinger on the sofa like a holy relic and packed up everything they had brought with them. Then they sterilized every room as they had been taught to do in tradecraft school. To remove fingerprints, they wiped down every surface with ammonia, from the handle on the toilet to the door-knob. They even bagged the trash and set it by the door for disposal far away from their hideout.

After completely sterilizing the house, they carefully soaked the floor with lamp oil and set the timer on an incendiary device Ayyad had given them at the Al Fucra rendezvous. In one trip they loaded the car with their clothes, their trash, and Allah's revenge and eased down the road, being careful not to speed. The short leg of their journey was to their firing point in the approach corridor of the airport. The long leg was a circuitous, around-the-world trip back to a refugee camp in Jordan.

At a deserted location in the flight path of Charlotte/Douglas International, they stopped, opened the trunk, and waited for a big passenger plane to enter the approach pattern. They didn't have long to wait. The shooter selected an incoming plane and let it pass over-head. He scanned the area one last time to ensure no one was watching and, with his accomplice standing lookout, he pulled the Stinger from the trunk and hoisted it to his shoulder. He quickly fixed the airplane in his sights and tracked it until it was at sixty degrees on final ap-proach to the runway.

He squeezed gently on the trigger, and the rocket exited from its tube with a swoosh of thunder, blasting off after the Boeing 747 at supersonic speed. Seeking the heat of the aircraft's engines, it caught up to its target in seconds like a falcon striking a dove. The initial explosion occurred under the left wing inside the inboard engine, ripping the wing to shreds and rupturing the fuel tank. Without lift, the big bird rolled to the left, and the fuel ignited in a secondary explosion. It plummeted the remaining five hundred feet to earth in a huge, roiling ball of flame, scattering debris over a wide swath just short of the runway.

Their mission complete, the two *fida'i* got back in their car and drove north nonstop to the Canadian border. Their part in Operation Desert Decree was finished.

Chapter 38

NICK FAWCETT UNLOCKED the door and carried a tray of food in to Susan Dorn. The window in the bedroom was boarded over with a sheet of three-quarter-inch plywood, and only a dim lamp and a small TV illuminated the gloom. Without the television it would have been difficult for Susan to tell night from day. She had it tuned to CNN to follow events as they developed.

Fawcett knew Dorn was glaring at him, so he avoided eye contact. But he needed companionship, someone to understand him, to understand his motives. Susan was the only person in the house with the intellectual capacity to discuss the issues that tortured his soul. But she attacked him again as she had done the last time he had visited her.

"How could you do this, Nick? Doris trusted you. She loved you, you bastard!" she lashed out. Even after almost two weeks of captivity, her rage and contempt were still fresh.

He placed the tray on the dresser and turned to face her. When he saw the loathing written on her face, overwhelming sorrow filled his heart. He swallowed hard and his eyes watered slightly. He couldn't get Doris out of his mind. He hadn't been able to sleep, and every time he entered the bedroom they had shared on their weekend getaways, he could smell her, taste her, feel her presence.

"Susan, I loved Doris. I didn't want to see her hurt. She was a casualty of war."

"War? War? Doris was murdered, Nick!"

"I am an Arab, and the number on my identity card is fifty thousand. Are you angry?"

"What? You're talking nonsense."

"Blue shadows among the olive trees of the valley, where once

my village stood. Now gone to a hard Jewish plow. No monument,
no flowers. No blood-soaked rag worn by my parents. Their ghosts
ever wander the ruins of Deir Yassin!"

Dorn stared at him, puzzled.

"Susan, I was born in Palestine. The Jews killed my mother and
my father."

"Nothing justifies killing more innocent people, Nick."

"What if I gave you a choice, Susan? What if you never say another word for the rest of your life, and the result is that ten thousand
people die? But if you utter one word—just one word—only one
thousand people die. Your choice, Susan? Ten thousand or one thousand? Do nothing or do something? Either way a lot of innocent
people die."

"That's not a choice. You're talking nonsense again."

"That's my dilemma, Susan. If I do nothing, thousands of my
people continue to live in a state of abject slavery, dying a slow death
under the jackboot oppression of the Israeli army. If I act, perhaps I
can change the balance of power, the course of history."

"Terrorism is not the answer, Fawcett!" Dorn exclaimed.

"My name is Walead Kasim. I am a Palestinian, and we are at
war. The United Nations created Israel at the expense of Palestinians. I am simply presenting the bill for our losses."

"Murdering millions will not solve the problem."

"No one else has to die, Susan. Don't you see? What I am doing
is forcing a bully to pay for a crime he's committed. They'll pay the
money. No one is going to release a plague. I promise."

Dorn hadn't seen the videotape presenting his demands, but he
had told her about it during their last heated discussion.

"I saw that maniac of yours murder two people like stepping on
insects. One of them was my best friend. She loved you, you son of a
bitch!" Dorn shrieked. She was near hysterics.

Fawcett was close to breaking down as well. The weight of Susan Dorn's words was almost unbearable.

"I'm doing this for my people, Susan. My oppressed, dispos-
sessed people," he said solemnly.

"You'll get your blood money, Nick, but they won't let you keep it.
They'll get it back. And if that psychopath spreads the virus, you and
your people won't have any use for money. There will be no safe place."

His eyes locked on to hers as he thought of the brilliance of his
plan.

"When the money reaches a certain amount, Susan, it will hit an electronic trigger and fracture like glass into millions of tiny accounts scattered throughout the world. I developed a computer program that will make the money virtually impossible to trace. Money is power, Susan, and I mean to gain power for my powerless people. The world took away their land, their homes, their lives, and I'm going to give them back. I deeply regret the loss of life. I . . . I . . . I regret it with all my heart and soul."

"Your trained killer doesn't have any regrets. He has no soul. He's an animal that will kill you, if you get in his way."

"As a boy, Susan, the Jews beat him until they thought he was dead. They buried him alive. It was a miracle that he survived. He is a dedicated freedom fighter," Fawcett argued, trying to justify his unconventional war.

"He's a murderer, and by association, Nick Fawcett—*Walead Kasim*—you're a murderer too!"

A tear rolled down Fawcett's cheek. But when he looked back at Susan, determination took over his emotions.

"I have the knowledge, and knowledge is power. I am in control of this military operation," he said solemnly.

"If you're in control, Nick, destroy the virus before that maniac causes a pandemic," she pleaded.

"No. Not until my people have been paid for their losses."

"Then let me go."

"I can't do that, Susan. Not yet."

"Why not? I don't know where we are. I can't tell the police anything they don't already know. Put a blindfold on my face and dump me somewhere along the beltway."

"I can't, Susan. Not yet."

"I'll tell you why you can't. He won't let you. You're not in charge of this savagery. He is, and he's a pathological killer. He's going to kill me when he no longer has a use for me. I'm your backup, Nick."

"I won't let him hurt you, Susan. I promise."

Susan almost laughed. "Won't, Nick? You couldn't prevent him from killing Doris. The only reason I'm alive is for insurance, in case anything happens to you, Walead Kasim." She spoke his Arab name with such derision that it angered him.

"I'm in control, Susan. He knows that," Fawcett argued.

"If that virus infects anyone, even by accident, and the disease spreads to the general population, there won't be any place on earth to hide, not for Jews or Palestinians or anybody."

"Susan, I have a boat in the marina. We'll be leaving soon. I want you to know that I'll make sure you can get out of this room in a reasonable amount of time. I'll destroy the virus as soon as the money is paid. I'm not a monster. You'll see."

The CNN anchorman interrupted their conversation. "This is a special report. This just in from our CNN news affiliate in Charlotte, North Carolina: A Boeing 747 on final approach to Charlotte/Douglas International Airport has just crashed, scattering debris over a wide area. Eyewitnesses reported seeing a rocket hit the plane just short of the runway. We go now to . . . ."

Fawcett switched off the television set. The small lamp on the nightstand illuminated half his face, shadowing the anguish and guilt he felt.

"Only a monster could do that, Nick. A monster!" Susan screamed.

Fawcett rushed out of the room, locking the door behind him.

Distraught, and seething with pent up anger and fear, Susan jabbed the remote control several times before the TV came back on. Then she spotted the butter knife Fawcett had left on the food tray. *The hinges!* she thought. She cranked up the volume on the TV, grabbed the knife, and went to work on the hinge pins.

Chapter 39

THE TWO ISLAMIC militants were playing cards and watching Monday night football in a safehouse near Atlanta when the telephone rang. They didn't understand the game, but it helped pass the time. The senior of the two men answered the call.

"Allah be praised," said the voice on the other end of the line.

The young radical swallowed hard and replied with the counter-sign. "Allah is most great."

"Here we come, O Allah! No partner have You! Here we come," said the voice.

"Here we come, O Allah!" replied the young radical, his eyes wide in disbelief.

When the line went dead, he jumped up from the table and shouted, "*Idbah al-adu*! Slaughter the enemy!"

"Not so loud!" his teammate remonstrated.

In silence they sterilized the house and spread the fuel that would render most evidence useless. After prayers, the team leader retrieved a tiny vial from his shaving kit and a canister from the kitchen cabinet. Federal Express had delivered the items to him in separate shipments just the day before. Inside the packages, marked as documents, were books with hollowed-out centers containing the two weapon components. For a few seconds he stared at the vial, unable to make sense of his mission. It was too easy.

How could such a tiny bottle kill all the infidels in the world? he wondered.

Conceptually he could not comprehend germ warfare or the consequences of releasing trillions of lethal viruses into a stadium filled with people. But he had his orders, and he was determined to carry them out in exact detail. He put the vial in his shirt pocket and the can in his baggy pants, then nodded to his partner that he was ready to go. His comrade set the timer on the incendiary device and they left the condo with everything they had brought with them.

At the stadium, the assassin left his subordinate in the car, tossed their trash in a barrel, and walked inside to join the cheering crowd. The Falcons were hosting the Redskins, and the noise was deafening. For a few minutes he scanned the stands as if searching for someone, then he walked to the windward side of the field. Taking one last look at the crowd, he walked briskly down the exit tunnel. Still on the move, with the breeze in his face, he removed the vial and the actuator can from his pockets. At the mouth of the tunnel he stopped and waited until he was alone. Then, in one swift movement, he inserted the vial into the can, placed it on the cement, and pressed down hard on the red button. Standing upwind, he watched the weapon long enough to see a thin mist issue forth and drift up the tunnel. He dashed to his waiting accomplice, and they sped away. Their part of Operation Desert Decree was over.

Evans and McCoy watched the glow of a cigarette as a man on the beach side of the house inhaled. He was sitting on a wooden porch overlooking the sea less than fifty yards away. In silence they waited for a clue that would definitively prove to Evans that he was on Fawcett's trail. Several minutes after taking up surveillance they saw the flare of a match illuminate a curtain at the front of the house.

"You see that, Commander?" McCoy whispered.

"Yeah," Evans replied. "Smoking is a terrible habit."

"You think those terrorists are holed up over there?"

"Sure looks like it."

The house, built high up on pilings, had a small porch in front and a larger one on the beach side. Two nondescript cars were parked underneath on each side of a maintenance room that housed the hot water heater and an electric meter.

Evans watched the guard on the back porch smoke one cigarette after another. An hour into his vigil, a third man appeared. Evans strained his ears and caught the faint sound of an unfamiliar language floating on the breeze.

"Curtis, I think it's them. They're speaking Arabic."

"What are you going to do?" McCoy asked.

"I'm going to watch the place. Gather more intel. Go on back to your place and wait for me."

"Aye-aye, sir."

Evans walked to the front door with the old sailor and helped him quietly down the steps.

"Chief," he whispered.

"Yeah?"

"Thanks."

"You're mighty welcome, Commander," McCoy replied, excited by the adventure.

As the old gent shuffled down the road, Evans slinked over to Fawcett's house like a cat on the prowl. Once underneath it, he sneaked from piling to piling until he could make out voices up above.

"Did you give the order to shoot down that plane?" Fawcett roared.

"What plane, Uncle Kasim?" Ayyad asked.

"The one that just crashed in North Carolina!"

"Uncle, you must calm yourself. This is war, and in war there will be casualties," Ayyad said coolly.

"I gave them a deadline!" Fawcett shouted. "Now nothing we say will have any credibility."

Underneath the house, Evans could hear the shouting, but he couldn't clearly make out the words.

"Uncle, I had to show the devil we have power," Ayyad argued in a more forceful tone. "Otherwise the Great Satan will do something devilish like he did to Azed."

"Hundreds of innocent people just died so you could make a point?

They would have aired the tape, and they would have transferred the money without further violence. There was no reason to kill all those people," Fawcett moaned. "Now every man, woman, and child on this planet will curse us. They will hunt us down and tear us to pieces like wild dogs."

"Uncle, we have the viral weapon. They cannot do anything as long as we have the virus." Ayyad smiled. "Allah has given us this power over the infidels."

"You don't understand because you are an ignorant imbecile!" Fawcett bellowed, shaking his finger in Ayyad's face.

"No! I am *fida'i!* And I will bring the Great Satan to his knees," Ayyad shouted back. "See," he pointed at Fawcett's computer, "we have the money."

Seeing numbers scrolling by on his monitor, Fawcett rushed to his keyboard and typed a few strokes. A spreadsheet filled the screen.

Ayyad grinned. "The Great Satan knows we have the power."

Fawcett was astonished. Billions of dollars were being deposited by the second in the numbered accounts he had established.

"Operation Desert Decree is a success," he mumbled. "Time for this madness to end."

"Time for us to go, Uncle Kasim. Get the weapon," Ayyad ordered.

"No!" Fawcett shouted. "We have achieved our objective. We have no further use for the virus. It must be destroyed."

"No," Ayyad grunted. "We need it to make more weapons. I used them all on the Jews and the Great Satan."

"You what?" Fawcett shrieked. "You went into my lab without my permission? You idiot! You could be infected! You could be spreading the disease right now!"

"Oh no, Uncle. Allah spoke to me. He told me to break the seventh seal, to let loose a great plague on the infidels. This I have done by using the Great Satan's electronic spider." He smiled maniacally. Reading the fear on Fawcett's face, he continued, "Don't be afraid, Uncle Kasim. Allah will protect us. We are the righteous. He will spare the Palestinian people."

"You don't understand," Fawcett mumbled.

"Get the virus. Now!" Ayyad commanded.

"No!"

"You will do as I say, or I will kill the woman," Ayyad growled.

Fawcett stared at him in disbelief. Seeing the determination in his eyes, he relented. "Okay. But I will take this up with the Council," he boomed as he marched off toward his makeshift lab.

"As you wish, Uncle Kasim. But hurry. We must meet our ship in four hours."

Something in the way Fawcett had relented struck a chord in Ayyad's twisted mind. He stared at him suspiciously as he headed down the hall to suit up.

Susan had made efficient use of the butter knife. She was busy in Fawcett's lab injecting vials with a solution of alcohol and formaldehyde when he entered his lab in a space suit. His face filled with apprehension when he saw her unprotected, with only a sheet wrapped around her mouth and nose. He closed the door and walked to the lab bench.

"Susan, get out of here," he said from inside his protective hood.

"No. I'm going to sterilize this room if I have to burn it down."

"There is no virus in those vials. Just a sterile solution."

Dorn stared at him, not knowing what to believe.

"You were right about Ayyad. He ordered the release of the virus," he said.

"Oh, my God! No!"

"He doesn't know it's only sterile water. The Lubeck virus is still in the freezer," said Fawcett in a defeated voice.

Dorn looked into his eyes through the protective hood. They were troubled and weary. "I want to believe you, Nick," she said softly. "But I can't. I'll help you sterilize the lab," she insisted.

"No, Susan. I tried to create a vaccine in this lab. It could be contaminated. I'll help you out my bedroom window. Then I'll sterilize the virus and decontaminate the lab. I promise."

She studied his eyes for a few seconds.

"Okay, Nick. But I'm going to call the police as soon as I get to a telephone," she warned. "And the CDC. This whole area will have to be quarantined."

"Yes, of course," he agreed.

Fawcett crossed the room and cautiously opened the lab door to peek out. Ayyad kicked it in and stood in the doorway.

"Get the virus. Now! Or I'll do it myself," he yelled.

"No!" Fawcett shouted back.

"Get the virus, Uncle!" he yelled. "We must go now!"

But Fawcett stood his ground, arms folded in defiance. In a fit of anger, Ayyad dashed into the lab, shoved Susan Dorn out of the way and grabbed the vials on the lab bench. When his pockets were full, he rushed to the freezer for the biohazard container.

As the young radical rifled the shelves, Fawcett shouted, "No, Ayyad! No! We don't need the thermos. One vial is enough!"

Ayyad looked up at him suspiciously, then grabbed the biohazard container. As he stood to leave, Fawcett blocked his path. At first Ayyad tried to manhandle the scientist toward the door. But Fawcett resisted with all his strength. Since Ayyad was packing a weapon, his strong hand was occupied. The scientist wrenched the thermos from Ayyad's arm and backed away. In a fit of rage the crazed terrorist opened up with a long burst from his MAC-10. The machine gun chewed into the scientist's protective suit, and for a moment, Fawcett appeared to dance like a puppet as the slugs ripped through his body and slammed him back into the lab bench. Susan screamed as the weapon chopped from left to right, rising as it spat out its lethal load. She fell next to Fawcett, oozing blood from her chest and stomach.

Evans heard the machine gun cut loose above his head and knew he had to act. He ran to the beach side of the house and up the steps two at a time. The guard, startled by the sound of the weapon, was looking inside. Evans caught him with a front-thrusting kick just as he turned around to see who was behind him. The young Arab flew against the wall with such force the whole house shook on its stilts. Evans grabbed the machine pistol from the guard with one hand and jammed a palm up into his face. Cartilage and bone crunched under the force of the blow. Taking the weapon, Evans slipped through the doorway and stepped immediately to the side. He dropped to one knee and engaged an Arab who came running into the room from the hall. With a three-round burst, he blasted the man in the chest, then rolled to take cover at the base of a bar as 9-millimeter bullets ripped into the counter and shelves above him. Splinters of wood peppered his arm. Glass and whiskey showered down on him. He scrambled to cover and fired back with a short burst.

Ayyad heard the exchange of gunfire on the beach side of the house and panicked. He grabbed the biohazard container and dashed for the front door. With the Great Satan breathing down his neck, he ran down the beach toward the marina.

For a few minutes Evans was pinned down behind the bar. He exchanged several quick bursts, then fired into the wall in the direction of his adversary. An Arab groaned and appeared momentarily, struck by one of the bullets passing through the plasterboard. As the man crawled down the hall, Evans maneuvered to the corner. He took a quick peek, then blasted the man before he could take cover. Hearing noise beyond his victim, he cautiously inched his way down the hall until he came to the open lab door. Through the doorway he saw a person in a protective suit lying in a pool of blood and a female figure curled up in a fetal position nearby. Not sure who the people were, he entered cautiously, eyes scanning like radar. His heart sank when he recognized Susan's slender form. He rushed to her.

"Susan! Susan!" he shouted, eyes glancing back and forth between her and the open door.

Her eyes rolled around in their sockets, half focused, glazed.

"Stay with me, Susan!" Evans pleaded.

"Derek," she gurgled, blood frothing at her lips. "Contaminated. Get . . . out," she moaned.

Evans used the sheet wrapped around her nose and mouth to dress her wounds. Weapon in hand, he ran to the nearest bedroom and ripped more sheets off a bed. With thick layers of cloth, he bound her up as best he could. She came to several times while he was working on her.

"Derek, he took the virus. He's insane. You've got to stop him," she begged.

"Take it easy, Susan. I'll get him."

"He's going to leave the country. Nick's boat. It's in the marina. You've got to stop him," she repeated.

"I'll get him, Susan. As soon as an ambulance arrives."

"No, Derek! No! This place is contaminated. You may be infected too. Everything and everyone must be quarantined."

"You need medical attention, Susan. Right away."

"Derek, please. Please," she begged, staring into his eyes. "Set this house on fire, and stop him before he kills everyone."

Then she passed out from pain and loss of blood.

"I'll call the CDC. They'll quarantine the area."

Evans was on fast-forward. He pulled out his cell phone and called Tom Durance in Atlanta. When the agent answered, he filled him in and told him to get a crew from the CDC to Greyton Beach as soon as possible. Susan was still unconscious when he terminated the call, but alive. He knew there was nothing more he could do for her. Adrenaline pumping, he sprinted from the house and down the road to the McCoys'.

"Mr. McCoy!" he shouted from the street.

When the old man appeared at the door, Evans yelled at him. "Quarantine Fawcett's house. Don't let anyone go inside it until Agent Durance arrives. Now throw me the keys to the car."

"Yes, sir," said McCoy. He tossed Evans the keys, saluted, and watched him speed away down the Long Beach road.

The only marina was several miles down the coast toward Long Beach. It was twenty miles around, or five miles straight down the beach. Evans floored the accelerator and drove to the end of the road and down the beach as far as momentum would carry him. With the car buried to the wheelwells in the sand, he jumped out and ran, pacing himself for the chase.

Chapter 40

EVANS'S YEARS OF SEAL conditioning were put to the test. Stressing his body to the limit, he ran as fast as he could, spurred by images of Susan Dorn, bloody and struggling for life. He arrived at the marina just in time to see a sailboat clear the harbor under engine power. In bright moonlight he saw Ayyad on the stern, tiller in hand. Exhausted and out of breath, he ran out on the dock and began pounding on boats until a man appeared in a disagreeable mood. He was a salty Southerner in his forties, and he had a pistol in his hand.

"Buddy, I just called the cops, so you'd better get the hell out of here," he threatened.

"Good. We need the police. See that boat?" said Evans, pointing at the mouth of the marina.

"Yeah."

"Who does it belong to?" he demanded.

"I don't know. Do you know what time it is?" the angry sailor growled.

"Listen. You know those terrorists who've been on the news lately?"

"Yeah. So what?"

"I have reason to believe one of them is on that boat. I have to catch him, and I need your help," Evans insisted.

"You got a badge?"

"No. I'm not a cop."

"Then have another drink and go back to bed, asshole!" shouted the man, losing his cool. He ducked back into his boat.

"Hey, you!" yelled Evans, pounding on the cabin.

"I warned you," roared the sailor, coming out the hatch with his pistol at the ready.

He was surprised when Evans deftly twisted it out of his hand and put him on his knees with an aikido wristlock.

"I haven't got time to argue with you, pal," said Evans, releasing the sailor's hand. "I need your help. The man on that boat," he said, pointing to sea with the pistol, "is in possession of the deadliest virus known to mankind. I have to stop him. I need the fastest boat in the harbor. Now!" Evans said, handing the pistol back to the sailor.

The sincerity in Evans's voice and the gesture of giving back the pistol got through to him.

"Why didn't you say so?" The man declined the pistol. "You keep it. If what you say is true, you'll need it."

"Thanks."

"You know, the Navy and the Coast Guard have some fast boats down in Saint Andrews Bay," he volunteered.

"Too far," Evans shook his head. "He'll be out of sight in half an hour. The bastards slip in and out of the country from big ocean-going freighters passing up and down the coast. By the time the Coast Guard arrives, that sailboat will be on the bottom."

The windjammer was slipping away into the darkness.

"Okay. Just a sec."

The sailor climbed down into his cabin and quickly reappeared, zipping up his jeans.

"Let's go," he shouted, jumping up on the dock.

In his bare feet he led Evans to a sleek thirty-footer and jumped on board. He fished around for the keys under a seat cushion and scrambled to the helm.

"Cast off," he yelled.

He turned a key and the motors rumbled to life. With each revolution the boat shook like a dragster at the starting line.

"You'd better stay here," Evans warned, holding a mooring line.

"That'd be just fine with me, buddy," he hollered over the sound of the powerful engines. "But you know I'm gonna call the cops."

"You do that," yelled Evans. "Call the Coast Guard too, and the FBI. Ask for Tom Durance."

"Durance?"

"Yeah. Tom Durance. Tell him I'm chasing the guy who killed the kid in Louisiana. He'll understand."

"Durance. Got it."

Evans held the line until the sailor climbed up on the quay, then threw it into the boat and jumped down into the cockpit. He pushed against the pier with all his strength to move the boat, turned the wheel in the direction of the dock, and bumped the throttle forward to kick the stern out. When she was clear, he backed down hard, spun the wheel in the other direction, and slammed the throttle down. Engines thundering, he cruised through the marina fast, causing boats and buoys to bob and chafe at their moorings. When the speedboat cleared the marina and entered the Gulf, the ride got rough. Evans looked ahead in the moonlight, searching the night horizon like a hawk. He spotted the sailboat a couple of miles to his southwest.

There he is, he thought. *And there is nothing he can do to out-run me in that windjammer. He was packing a 9-millimeter when he left Greyton Beach. So he can't have very many rounds.* Then he thought, *Maybe he had weapons and ammo stashed aboard the boat. One thing is for sure; he'll start shooting at me as soon as I'm in range. I'll buzz him to see what he's packin', then keep him in range till the Coast Guard arrives.*

Evans scanned the horizon fore and aft. When he saw the fire on the shoreline in the area of Greyton Beach, he lost his stomach. His inner voice told him Susan Dorn had started it. The thought that pounded his brain was, *Is she in the house?* Something in his gut told him that she was. She had made the ultimate sacrifice, like her dad. Now it was his turn.

"I'm gonna rip out your tonsils, you fucking animal," he roared as he sped toward the sailboat.

I'll buzz him and then come down on his bow, he calculated, as he closed with the sailboat.

Evans had a lot of experience skippering small boats. He had seen rough weather bringing boats alongside ships that were under way and alongside offshore oil rigs during the course of training men to board and seize. As a young SEAL he had even done the climbing and, at times, the driving. Confident in his abilities, he closed the distance to the windjammer at full speed, passing within three feet of her stern. His wake tossed the sailboat like a cork in a storm. Ayyad emptied an entire magazine in his direction and was reloading when Evans came down on his bow at full speed and backed down at full power. The engines in the powerboat nearly exploded. Just after the vessels made contact, Evans ran forward and leaped onto the bow of the sailboat.

The collision knocked the Arab to the deck. He jumped up and emptied half a magazine at the drifting speedboat. Then he saw Evans and emptied the other half in his direction. He was reloading when the SEAL peeked around the cabin. Caught off guard by the boarder, the terrorist's eyes grew in size, and his body coursed with adrenaline. He clicked home a fresh magazine and cut loose with the full thirty rounds. Evans dropped to the foredeck as hot lead ripped into the cabin, sending a shower of wooden splinters and glass all around him. One of the bullets hit a gas lantern. Fed by gushing propane, fire quickly spread through the cabin.

Evans seized the moment. In a charge, he closed the distance to the stern, trying to reach his adversary before he could reload. Ayyad saw him coming and swung the machine gun wildly, using it as a club. But he was no match for the battle-hardened SEAL. The MAC-10 sliced the air harmlessly past Evans's side, and then Ayyad swung up at his chin, but missed again. At apex, the burly SEAL caught the Arab with a front-thrusting kick to his exposed rib cage. A short rib snapped under Evans's heel. Off balance and with the boat rocking violently, both men went to the deck. As soon as Evans regained his balance, he charged again. Grabbing a gaff, Ayyad swung wildly, but Evans parried and ducked. Like a baseball player swinging with full force, the motion twisted Ayyad's body against his broken rib. The searing pain caused him to let go of the gaff, and it flew overboard.

Evans followed the parry with a circle sweep of his right leg that knocked Ayyad's feet out from underneath him. He crashed to the deck with a thump. On their knees, they traded blows, gouges, rips, and tears until Evans hammered a right cross into Ayyad's face that knocked him senseless. He snared one of Ayyad's hands and twisted counter to the joint and the pitch of the boat. Twisting with both hands, he snapped the wrist bones and took Ayyad to the deck. A gush of air exploded from the terrorist's mouth as he crashed against the gunwale, pinned by Evans's shoulder.

In war, every general knows when a decisive battle has been won. Evans knew it was over. He grabbed Ayyad by the throat and planted a knee in his stomach. Their eyes met, as the terrorist gasped for air, clawing at the SEAL's fingers with his unbroken hand. Evans stared at him as he slowly increased the pressure on the Adam's apple until it crushed under his thumb, collapsing the throat. Gurgling and writhing on the pitching deck, Ayyad struggled for breath. With their gazes locked in a death stare, Evans watched the life force leave the terrorist's eyes.

When his mind could focus on matters other than fighting for his life, Evans realized that the boat was completely engulfed in flames. In vain, he searched for the biohazard container. With fire singeing his hair, he jumped overboard seconds before the propane tank in the forward bilge exploded.

Evans swam to the powerboat and waited until the windjammer burned to the waterline and sank. He searched the flotsam for the biohazard container and, when he failed to find it, tossed over a buoy to mark the spot. At full speed, he roared back to Greyton Beach and ran the boat up on shore just as Durance arrived by helicopter with specialists from the CDC. Evans was immediately placed in quarantine. Through the plastic shell of his gurney, he pleaded with Durance for information about Susan Dorn, but in the confusion and conflagration, the agent was not able to answer his questions. Evans was in the slammer at the CDC when Swan confirmed what he already knew in his heart. Susan had been consumed in the fire.

For weeks the Coast Guard and experts from the Navy's Experimental Diving Unit in Panama City searched the sunken sailboat for the stainless steel thermos containing the virus. Fishermen were still searching with nets when Evans was released from quarantine two weeks later.

Epilogue

VICTOR FERNANDEZ AWOKE to the sound of a rooster crowing in his neighbor's yard. He rolled out of bed and padded barefoot across the dirt floor to the rickety wooden chair where he had hung his trousers. He quietly slipped them on and walked outside. The early morning air was chilly. A shiver ran down his spine as he urinated against the royal palm wall of the hootch. It was a small hut made of *guano,* the Cuban word for palm fronds. It was all that his family owned. He walked back through the open door for his shirt, still hanging on the back of the chair. His mother had patched it so many

times it was nothing but patches held together by thread. As he slipped
it on, he looked at her face sticking out from underneath the blanket.

She is always tired and sad these days, thought the boy.

There was never enough to eat, and what there was she gave to
the children. He was the man of the house now, and it was time to
check the beach before others cleaned it of every edible form of life.
She stirred in her sleep, moaning, her ebony skin so black it shone in
the dim early morning light coming through the open window. His
little sister and brother slept beside her on the makeshift bed. The
little boy was out of the cover, and his ribs showed through his bare
skin like a starved dog's.

Maybe I can find a conch, he thought, *if I get to the beach
before the others. Or a langostino.*

There was nothing to eat in the house. No chickens in the yard.
No fruit on the trees. No rice in the cardboard box that served as the
cupboard. Nothing left in the pot over the charcoal fire in the middle
of the dirt floor. Since his father had taken the raft to Florida, everything was up to him now. They hadn't heard from him in more than
a year. The distance from Cuba to Florida was only ninety miles, but
it might as well have been a thousand. They all feared he was dead,
but no one dared talk about it. Victor sighed and headed for the beach.

The sun rose from the sea, and he could see others beachcomb-
ing along the shore. The harbor of Cardenas sat like a giant open
mouth catching the flotsam of the Straits of Florida. Wearing his
straw hat, Victor walked along the shore picking up whatever valuables or food he could find and placed them in a large plastic bucket.
A mussel, a small crab, and a small fish cornered in the shallows were
all they needed to survive another day. He walked deeper into the
water, looking for urchins.

When the sun was two hours high, the visibility in the clear Gulf
waters was excellent. Jellyfish pumped along, trying to escape the
suction of the shore. Victor spotted a Portuguese man-of-war sailing
offshore in deeper waters, free from the troubles of land. A man-of-
war bird circled the sky above, then slanted back its long black wings,
and plunged into the sea. Shortly it emerged, took flight, and circled
the area again.

He sees something, the boy thought.

He waded deeper into the water. Along the bottom in front of
him scurried a langostino. With excitement Victor pursued the creature, using his feet to herd it. In three feet of water he trapped the

animal in a patch of broken coral heads. He ducked his head under-water and, using his bare hands, grabbed the spiny animal. It kicked its large rear fin trying to escape and dug its spines into the boy's hands, but with no success. Hunger drove Victor. He pulled the lob-ster from its crevice and twisted the body to sever its spine. With a huge grin he put it in his bucket and waded toward shore with his prize catch of the day.

Twenty yards from the beach he spotted something shiny, wash-ing back and forth in a pocket of coral. He eagerly retrieved his new find and, in the bright morning sunlight, examined the strange ob-ject. It was a stainless steel container not much larger than a wine bottle. One end was sealed with a stainless steel cap. He tried to read the sticker on the side, but it was in English. Victor only spoke Span-ish, and even if he could have read the words, he wouldn't have understood them. Biohazard Level Four. He unscrewed the cap and looked inside.